Emma Blair was born and lives in Devon.
She is the author of many novels including
Scarlet Ribbons and *Flower of Scotland*, both of which were
shortlisted for the Romantic Novel of the Year Award.

For more information about the author, visit
www.emma-blair.co.uk

FORGET-ME-NOT

Emma Blair

SPHERE

First published in Great Britain in 2001 by Little, Brown and Company
This paperback edition published in 2011 by Sphere

A CIP catalogue record for this book
is available from the British Library.

ISBN 978-0-7515-4742-9

Printed and bound in Great Britain by
Clays Ltd, St Ives plc

Sphere
An imprint of
Little, Brown Book Group
100 Victoria Embankment
London EC4Y 0DY

An Hachette UK Company
www.hachette.co.uk

www.littlebrown.co.uk

FORGET-ME-NOT

Chapter 1

1912

'An actress!'

Minna Wilson smiled at the horrified expression on her son's face. He was outraged. 'She's quite a respectable woman, Tim, even if she is in the theatre. She comes highly recommended.'

'By whom?' he queried harshly.

'Do you remember the Goodchilds, who were here several years ago? Well, she's a relative of theirs.'

Tim could remember the Goodchilds very well. A pleasant enough couple, as he recalled. Certainly no trouble of any kind.

'Besides which,' Minna went on, 'I have a vacant room needing filling, actress or no.'

Despite his initial reaction, Tim was beginning to warm to the idea. An actress at The Berkeley – how exotic! Certainly different from the usual clientele who stayed at the small boarding house, which was their main source of income since his father died, the other being his salary from the *Torquay Times*, where he worked as a junior reporter. 'What's her name then?'

'Mrs Davenport.'

He wondered what she was like. Young, old? Good-looking, plain, downright ugly? He doubted it was the latter. 'It'll certainly make a change,' he conceded.

Minna's eyes twinkled with amusement. It would that all right. Their regular guests, those in residence all year round, were all elderly, living out the remainder of their days in a climate far more favourable than wherever they'd come from.

'She's arriving tomorrow,' Minna declared, 'and is apparently engaged to be playing the season at the Pavilion.' The Pavilion was a brand-new theatre that had only recently opened.

'Is she indeed,' Tim mused.

'I've to expect her in the afternoon off the London train.'

At that moment their conversation was interrupted by the appearance of Major Sillitoe *en route* for his daily stroll, during which he would undoubtedly be calling into several of the many pubs that the town boasted. The major, now retired, had fought with great distinction in the Boer War, and could be something of a bore himself when he got started on the subject. He was someone Tim tended to avoid if possible.

'Ah, good morning, Major,' Minna beamed.

Sillitoe, a small man with a very large moustache and a florid complexion, doffed his hat. 'Good morning to you too, Mrs Wilson. And a lovely one it is.'

'Off for your walk, I take it?'

'Quite so. I shall head in the direction of Torre Abbey Sands, I think. I haven't been that way for some while now.'

'Well, enjoy yourself, Major.'

He gave a small, courteous bow. 'Thank you very much. And how are you, young Tim?'

Tim loathed being called young. Twenty years old, he didn't consider himself that at all. Why, he was the male head of the household and a wage earner in a highly respectable profession. Young indeed! He forced a smile to his face. Paying guests were paying guests after all. 'Fine thank you, Major. It's kind of you to ask.'

'Now don't you be late for supper,' Minna declared after the major had taken his leave. 'That's happened too often of late.'

'Can't help it, Ma. Blame the job, not me. I can only get away when I'm finished. You know that.'

Minna sniffed her disapproval. 'Your editor, Mr Ricketts, is a slave-driver and no mistake. I don't suppose it matters what hours he keeps, being a bachelor with no family obligations or responsibilities.'

'That's how it is, Ma, and there's nothing I can do about it. Anyway, I love my job. Surely that's all that counts. The hours are irrelevant.'

'Not when your meal is spoilt, they're not.'

He laughed. 'My meals are never spoilt, and you know it. Cook always sees to that.'

'If anything it's you who's spoilt, and that's the truth of it. Now I'd better be getting on, I've lots to do.'

Tim was at the door when an idea struck him. The forth-coming repertory season at the Pavilion had been mentioned in the paper of course, but only in general. Perhaps Ricketts might be interested in a feature on one of the cast – Mrs Davenport, for example: what she'd previously done, who she'd worked with, and so on. The more he thought about it, the more he was convinced that Ricketts would fall for the idea.

He decided to mention it at the next day's morning meeting where suggestions were put forward and discussed.

It was later that afternoon when Tim stopped to stare admiringly at the motorbike parked by the kerb. What a beauty, he thought. An absolute cracker. He noted the machine was a Royal Enfield operated by a chain drive, the latest thing. A small inscription on the green-coloured petrol tank informed him it had a 325cc capacity.

'Do you like it?'

'Oh, yes,' Tim breathed, eyes gleaming. 'Very much so.'

'Sit on it, if you care to.'

'May I!'

The man standing alongside made a gesture with his hand. 'Go ahead.'

Tim swung himself onto the leather seat and then let his weight settle. 'I suppose it goes fast?'

'Like the wind.'

That was music to Tim's ears. He could just imagine himself roaring along the country lanes. What a glorious sensation that must be.

'Can you ride a bike?'

Tim reluctantly shook his head. 'I've never had the opportunity, I'm afraid. But it wouldn't take me long to learn. I know how everything works and what to do.' Reaching down, he lovingly caressed the chassis.

'Sadly, I'm going to have to sell it,' the man stated softly.

'Sell?'

'Have to. My wife, bless her, thinks it's far too dangerous.

Stuff and nonsense of course, but that's what she believes. She's been nagging me for months now and I don't suppose I'll get any peace till it's gone.' He heaved a sigh of resignation.

'How . . . how much are you asking?' Tim hesitatingly inquired, dreading the answer, which was bound to be far more than he could afford.

'Why, are you interested?'

Tim nodded.

The man's brow furrowed. 'I haven't really thought of a price yet. I'd have to give that some consideration.'

Tim fumbled for his wallet, from which he produced a business card. 'Would you telephone me there when you've decided. Give me first refusal?'

The man studied Tim's card. 'The *Times*, eh?'

'That's correct, Mr . . . ?'

'Oh, Coates, Jeremiah Coates. Well, Mr Wilson, telephone you I shall, when I've made up my mind.'

'If I'm not there, leave a message. I can either telephone back or call round and see you.'

'Fine then. I'll be in touch. You have my word.'

Tim reluctantly dismounted from the bike. Although he'd been astride it for only a few minutes, getting off again was like losing a limb. He just had to have that machine. He *had* to. He coveted it more than anything he'd ever coveted in his life before.

Coates slipped on a pair of goggles and sat where Tim had just been. How Tim envied him. He envied Coates with every fibre of his being.

'Goodbye then.'

'Goodbye, Mr Coates.'

And Tim watched the bike and its rider disappear into the distance.

'Have you got the account of the Women's Institute meeting?' Ricketts snapped as Tim entered the office.

'Yes, sir.'

'Anything of note?'

Tim shook his head. 'Just the usual stuff.'

Ricketts grunted. 'Get it written up all the same. And be quick about it.'

'Yes, sir.'

Ricketts glared at Tim. 'Are you being impertinent? I don't think I like your tone.'

Tim feigned innocence. 'Not at all, sir. I didn't mean anything by my tone. I wasn't aware it was different from usual.'

Ricketts regarded Tim dyspeptically. Cheeky whelp, he thought. There was no respect nowadays. The lad was far too much of a smart aleck for his own good. He'd better watch it. 'Get on with it then.'

Tim hurried over to the long desk that he shared with the other reporters and hastily busied himself.

'He's in a right old mood today,' Harry Nutbeam, their sports reporter, who was sitting alongside Tim, whispered a few minutes later when Ricketts' attention was elsewhere.

'You can say that again.'

'He was fine to start off with, and then suddenly, bam! His ulcer must be playing up again.'

'I just wish he wouldn't take it out on us, that's all.'

Harry nodded his agreement. 'Fancy a pint later?'

'If I've got time.'

Their conversation ceased abruptly when they realised that Ricketts was staring at them. Tim's fingers flew over the keys of the battered Imperial typewriter, one of a number they all shared, as he recounted what had occurred at the WI meeting. He did his best to make something that had been tedious in the extreme sound at least vaguely interesting.

The train swung round a bend and Elyse Davenport glimpsed what she presumed must be Torquay. Thank God the journey was almost over. She'd never been one to enjoy travelling. Arriving and departing, yes, but not the actual journey.

She lit a cigarette, her umpteenth since leaving Paddington, and wondered what Torquay was going to be like. At least it would be a change from London, and the doctor had assured her that the mild climate, combined with the sea air, could only do her persistent cough the world of good.

She should give up cigarettes of course, that was the sensible thing to do, but then she'd never been exactly the most sensible of people. She smiled. Sensible people didn't become actors – sense was the last thing they required.

Her smile vanished as she thought of her husband Benny, currently playing a small part in the West End. What a mistake she'd made in marrying him, taken in completely by his dashing good looks and boundless charm. She'd fallen hook, line and sinker. More fool her!

Where had their dreams gone, their plans? She was damned if she knew. They'd somehow dissipated – not overnight, but a little at a time, until one day they'd all vanished, leaving nothing but emptiness in their place.

How she'd ached with love for Benny, idolised the man. And now? They barely tolerated one another. When he wasn't onstage it was an endless round of pubs and late-night supper clubs, spending what money they had, and often money they didn't. It was a relief to be away from him for a while. Another good reason to accept the job in Torquay.

She coughed and reached for her handkerchief. Amazingly she never coughed when performing. But perhaps that was not so unusual when you thought about it. Any actor would tell you that onstage all ills and pains simply disappeared. As did the need for all bodily functions.

When she'd finished her cigarette she ground it out in the ashtray. Not long now, she told herself. She couldn't wait to stretch her legs.

Minna came bustling through when Daisy, the maid, informed her that Mrs Davenport had arrived. She found the actress standing just inside the doorway.

'Mrs Davenport, welcome to The Berkeley,' she beamed.

'Why, thank you.'

Elyse gazed about her. It was hardly The Savoy, but then what had she expected?

'How was your journey down?' Minna inquired politely.

'Long.'

Minna gave a low laugh, immediately warming to Elyse. 'I'm sure that's an apt description. Went to London myself once and it seemed to take for ever and a day. There and back.'

What an elegant woman, Minna was thinking. And beautifully dressed, in what she took to be the height of fashion.

The suit that Elyse had on was in a shepherd check and the skirt ankle-length. It boasted a fancy overcollar, with silk braid trimming on the sleeves. Round the waist was a matching belt and deep side-pockets below were also trimmed with silk. The wide-brimmed hat was of straw and boasted a posy of artificial pansies at the front.

'I imagine you could use a cup of tea before you go on up,' Minna said. 'I thought we might share a pot and some cake in the dining room.'

'That's a wonderful suggestion,' Elyse replied. 'I'm quite parched and, dare I say it, just a trifle hungry.'

'Then let me show you the way,' Minna declared and instructed Daisy to take Elyse's cases up to her room.

'You should see that Mrs Davenport who arrived earlier. She's quite a bobby-dazzler,' Daisy confided to Tim when he arrived home.

'Really?' He had to admit he was curious about the lady, whom he now hoped to interview, as Ricketts had approved his idea.

'Major Sillitoe just gaped when he saw her.' Daisy giggled. 'I swear he was like a fish on a slab. All poppy eyes and mouth wide open.'

That vision made Tim smile. 'Where's Ma?'

'I don't know, Master Tim. Around somewheres. And 'ee's late again. You've missed the staff supper.' It was the custom for Minna and Tim to eat with the staff, the evening meal taking place in the kitchen after the guests had finished in the dining room.

Daisy suddenly pressed closer to him. 'Here, have you been drinking? I swears I can smell beer.'

He placed a finger across his lips. 'Don't tell on me, but that's why I'm late. I stopped off for a few with my colleague Harry.' A few was what he'd intended, but it had ended up being considerably more than that. The time had somehow flown and now he wasn't at all hungry, but he knew he'd have to have something or there'd be hell to pay. From Cook as well as his mother.

'Here,' said Daisy, digging in her apron pocket. 'Have a peppermint. That'll disguise the pong.'

He gratefully accepted the offered sweet, deciding that if Minna did accuse him of drinking, he'd say he'd only had one in the line of duty, which did occasionally happen. 'Is Mrs Davenport about? I want to meet her and have a word.'

Daisy shook her head. 'She went straight up to her room after dinner, saying she was having an early night. She's no doubt worn out by the journey here from London.'

Tim swore under his breath at having missed her. His own fault really for having stayed out so long. It had never crossed his mind that she might want an early night. Oh well, he'd just have to collar her in the morning. There was nothing else for it.

Cook wasn't best pleased when he turned up in the kitchen, but it didn't take him long to get back in her good books again. Since he was a tiny lad he'd always been able to wind her round his little finger. Cook adored him.

The peppermint had done the trick, for neither Cook nor Minna detected alcohol on his breath.

Tim pulled a face when the clock in the hallway bonged the hour. Mrs Davenport still hadn't put in an appearance and now he'd have to leave, as he had to report to the office before going out on a story that had already been set up.

He'd return later, he decided, and hope to catch her then.

Elyse stared at the Pavilion theatre, which she found pleasing to the eye. She'd never played a brand-new theatre before so the prospect was exciting.

She sucked in a deep breath of sea air, thinking how wonderful it was. Already she felt better for being by the seaside. Such a contrast to the noise and smell of London, where the air at this time of year hung like a thick, damp blanket.

She toyed with the idea of going inside and introducing herself, then decided against it. She'd turn up for rehearsals on Monday morning as instructed and all the introductions could be made then. It wouldn't do to appear overeager. She was an older, established actress after all, and it was best to be seen in that light.

She recalled the Café Addison, which she'd passed a few minutes earlier. Time for a coffee, she decided, after which she'd find her way back to The Berkeley, where she'd study the script of the first play they were doing, *Trelawny of the 'Wells'* by Sir Arthur Wing Pinero. She had the part of Imogen Parrott, an experienced and rather flamboyant actress. Rather like herself, really. So she didn't anticipate having any trouble with that. All she'd really have to do was learn the lines and moves. The rest would come naturally.

'There's a telephone call for you, Tim,' Harry Nutbeam declared, hurrying by on some errand or other.

'Who is it?'

'Don't know. Didn't say,' Harry called back over his shoulder.

Tim rose from the desk and made his way down the office to the pair of wooden telephone booths at the rear. He went into the one with the receiver off the hook.

'Hello? Tim Wilson speaking.'

'Ah, Mr Wilson, it's Jeremiah Coates here. I promised to ring.'

Instantly a vision of the Royal Enfield flashed before Tim's eyes and his heart started to race at the thought of owning it. 'Have you decided on a price then?'

'I have.'

Tim found himself holding his breath as he waited to hear.

'I think thirty pounds would be about right. That's five less than I paid for her.'

Tim's spirits slumped. Just as he'd expected. Way beyond his pocket. He'd been stupid to dare hope.

'Mr Wilson, are you still there?'

'I am sorry. I'm afraid that's too much for me, Mr Coates. You'll have to find another buyer.'

'I see.'

'I wish . . . well, I truly wish I did have that kind of money, but I simply don't. Nor is there any way I can get it. I apologise for wasting your time.'

Coates understood, having watched Tim's face when he'd been astride the bike. 'I'm sorry too. I'm sure the bike would have given you a great deal of pleasure.'

'I know it would have, but there we are. Unfortunately it's not to be.' Pie in the sky, Tim thought bitterly.

There was a pause, then Coates said, 'Can you come anywhere near the figure?'

'No, sir, I'm afraid I can't. It's well beyond me. Again, I apologise. I should have known better.'

Coates smiled wryly to himself. He'd been young once too. 'Well, if you do come up with it, let me know. I'll give you my number.'

Tim hastily scribbled down the telephone number on the top sheaf of the pad and ripped it off. In his mind's eye he was still seeing the bike, and himself on it riding through the lanes around Torquay.

When he emerged from the booth he carefully folded the paper and placed it into his pocket. A useless gesture really, as he was well aware, but he just couldn't bring himself to throw the number away.

'Here, you should see the clothes that Mrs Davenport has hanging in her wardrobe,' Daisy enthused to Euphemia, the other maid of the household. 'I just been up there doing out her room.'

Euphemia's eyes opened wide. 'Nice, is thae?'

'A lot more than nice. They's as grand as I's seen. Fit for a queen to wear, they be.'

'Oh!' Euphemia breathed. 'That so?'

'As true as I'm standing here. All colours of the rainbow too. Pink, cream, blue – you name it. Suits, dresses, everything you can think of, and all the very best quality. Bought in Bond Street every last item, I should imagine.'

'Can I go look?'

Daisy quickly shook her head. 'We don't knows when she'll be back. And Mrs Wilson would have a fit if she thought you'd gone in there to pry. No, you'll just have to wait till it's your turn to do her room and then you can have a peek.'

Euphemia sighed. 'Imagine having clothes like that. You'd be able to turn any man's head.'

'Well, that's something you and I will never know about. Neither of us is ever likely to own a dress like one of thae. God knows what they cost each. An absolute fortune, I'll be bound.'

'It must be a wonderful thing to be an actress,' Euphemia mused. 'Though I couldn't stand up in front of others as they do, meself. I'd be far too embarrassed.'

'Me too,' Daisy agreed. 'All thae folk gawping and staring at you. And how do you remember all thae words? 'Tis beyond me.'

Daisy glanced around to ensure Minna wasn't about. They'd have been told off if they were discovered gossiping. Minna might be a fair employer but there were limits. Time-wasting was most definitely frowned upon.

'That ain't all,' Daisy went on, dropping her voice to a conspiratorial whisper. 'She's got a box crammed full of jewellery.'

Euphemia's eyes went wide again. 'Is that a fact?'

'Emeralds, rubies, diamonds – they was all there. A box full of treasure and no mistake.'

'Crikey!' Euphemia exclaimed softly, thoroughly impressed.

'The top of the box was lying open so I could hardly miss what was inside. Fair took my breath away, it did. 'Twas like gazing into Aladdin's cave.'

'She must be really rich.'

'Stinking, I'd say. Though what baffles me is – if she's so wealthy, what's she doing here instead of staying at The Imperial?' The latter was Torquay's foremost and most exclusive hotel.

Euphemia shook her head in bewilderment. She couldn't understand that, either. The Berkeley was only a run-of-the-mill boarding house after all. Hardly the place for nobs to come.

'There was a diamond bracelet, which I just couldn't stop meself trying on. It was gorgeous, Euphemia. Absolutely gorgeous. All sparkly and shiny-like. It must have cost hundreds.'

'I'd like to try that on too.'

Daisy winked. 'Take your chance when you does her room. Make sure you put everything back as it was, mind. We don't want her complaining to Mrs Wilson. That would mean the sack.'

'Oh, I'd be careful. She'd never know.'

'A box full of treasure,' Daisy repeated. 'Life just ain't fair sometimes. It could make you spit.'

Euphemia heard the sound of approaching feet and recognised the tread. 'Mrs Wilson, get on,' she warned.

They both hurried about their business.

Tim glanced up from the article he was writing as the presses started to roll. As always, the floor began to shake. The latest edition of the *Torquay Times*, a weekly paper, would hit the streets the following morning.

Tim loved to hear the presses. There was something immensely satisfying about listening to the sound – din, more like – that they made. It never failed to give him a thrill.

'Fancy a drink again tonight?' Harry asked, coming over and sitting on the desk. 'Patsy's coming.' Patsy was John Pattrick, by far the oldest of the reporters and an imbiber of legend. No-one knew how old Patsy was, not even the management, it was claimed.

'I can't, Harry. I've got someone to see.'

'A girl?' Harry teased, his eyes twinkling.

'No, a lady. It's about a story I intend doing. I want to interview her.'

'Oh?'

'She's an actress who's come to stay with us for a while. She'll be appearing at the Pavilion.'

Harry was intrigued. 'An actress! Sounds *interesting*.' The latter full of innuendo. 'What's she like?'

'Haven't a clue. I've still to meet her.'

'Is she famous?'

'I shouldn't think so, but I'll find out.'

'Lucky old you,' Harry teased. 'I wouldn't mind interviewing an actress. Is she from London?'

Tim nodded.

'Better still.'

Tim laughed at his friend's lustful expression. Harry was well known as something of a womaniser, although Tim suspected that a lot of it was sheer blarney made up by Harry himself.

'Why don't you bring her to the pub after the interview, then I can meet her too?' Harry suggested hopefully.

'Don't be daft. A woman like her doesn't go into a pub, you should know that.'

'She's an actress – they do all sorts, I'm told. Break the rules. They are Bohemians, don't forget.'

'Well, I shan't be asking her and that's that. Besides, she might be old enough to be my mother.'

Harry's eyes twinkled again. 'But you do have an awfully attractive mother, Tim. I've always said that.'

Tim blushed bright red. He simply couldn't envisage anyone seeing Minna in a sexual context. The whole idea was disgusting.

'Well, she is,' Harry protested.

'If you're not careful you'll get a smack.'

Harry hastily removed himself from where he was sitting. 'Don't be so touchy. It was a compliment.'

Tim had had enough of this conversation. The reference to his mother had annoyed him. 'Go away. I've work to do.'

'All right, all right. Keep your hair on.'

Tim couldn't resist the jibe. 'Which is more than you'll be able to do in a few years.'

That infuriated Harry, who was extremely sensitive about his receding hairline. 'Bastard!' he muttered so that only Tim could hear.

Tim laughed and resumed typing. After Harry had gone he thought of Mrs Davenport. He'd nipped home earlier hoping to catch her, but she'd been out. He hoped she was going to be easy to interview and that her story would make good copy.

Chapter 2

E lyse glanced around the dining room as she sipped her coffee. What a motley collection, she mused. Why, the average age must be in the seventies. And there was that dreadful Major Sillitoe smiling at her again, the old goat. She'd thought earlier that he was going to suggest she share a table with him, but thankfully had been spared having to make a polite refusal.

The Misses Ward seemed quite sweet, she thought after having had a brief chat with them on the way in when they'd introduced themselves. Originally from Exeter, they'd said. Thin-faced and beaky-nosed, they were like a couple of birds nattering away to one another.

She wondered about Benny and what he was doing. Another hour till his curtain up, so he could be anywhere. She'd drop him a line over the weekend, she decided. Just to let him know she'd arrived safely and that everything was going well. A common courtesy, that was all.

'Mrs Davenport?' a male voice inquired a few minutes later as she was heading back to her room.

The speaker was a pleasant-faced young man. 'That's right.'

'I'm Tim Wilson. My mother's the owner.'

He'd make a good juvenile lead, she thought. He had the right sort of looks. 'I see.'

'I also work for the *Torquay Times*, one of the local rags.' Other guests were coming out of the dining room now. 'Would you care to step into our private parlour so that I can have a word with you? I'd be terribly obliged.'

She guessed what this was about. 'Are you a reporter?'

'I'm afraid so.'

Ah, she was right. 'You want an interview, I presume?'

'If you'd be so kind. I intend doing a feature.'

Elyse was quite used to this kind of thing. She'd been interviewed on countless occasions in the past. 'Perhaps you'd lead the way,' she consented.

The parlour that Tim led her into was a rather gloomy room with a large aspidistra by the window. She'd always loathed aspidistras. She noted that the wallpaper and furnishings had seen better days, although the genteel shabbiness did have a comfortable feel about it.

'Perhaps you'd care to sit.' He gestured towards the biggest and best of the armchairs.

'Thank you.'

Not a beautiful woman, Tim was thinking, but definitely handsome, if somewhat past her prime. She also had an air about her, a sort of charisma that he found a little disturbing. In a crowd she would have stood out. A prerequisite for an actor, he supposed, knowing nothing about the breed.

'Are you enjoying Torquay so far?' he inquired politely, settling himself into an armchair facing hers.

'Very much so.'

'Have you been here before?'

She shook her head. 'This is my first visit.'

He flipped open the notebook he'd brought along and quickly glanced at the questions he'd prepared. For some reason he found himself quite nervous.

Elyse picked up on this and it amused her. 'If you don't mind me saying so, you seem a trifle young to be a reporter,' she teased.

Tim coloured.

'Oh dear, I hope I haven't embarrassed you.' She was rather enjoying this.

'Not at all,' he lied.

'Did you go straight into the job from school?'

Young! School! Did the wretched woman have to bring these things up? 'Yes,' he mumbled, squirming inwardly. 'I did.'

'Really.'

Now what did she mean by that? He wished now that he hadn't thought of interviewing her.

'Do you mind if I smoke?'

He blinked, caught offguard. 'Please, go ahead.' He leapt to his feet. 'I'll find you an ashtray.'

She lit up while watching him through slitted eyes. Good figure, she thought and wondered if he had any experience at all with women. Probably not, she decided. Nothing more than hand-holding and the occasional kiss. She'd have bet a week's wage he was a virgin.

'Lovely,' she said, accepting the ashtray and placing it on the arm of her chair.

'Would you care for a drink?'

'That would be nice,' she smiled. 'Do you have any Scotch?'

Again he was thrown. 'Do you mean whisky?'

'I believe that's what Scotch is.'

He cursed himself for being such a gauche fool. 'I think there's some in the kitchen. I'll fetch it.'

'I hope you'll be joining me.'

'Of course.' That was only good manners.

She smiled again as he hurried from the room. Behave yourself, Elyse, you're being quite naughty. The poor lad doesn't know whether he's coming or going. Still, it was amusing.

Tim returned with a tray on which there was a half-empty bottle of whisky, two glasses and a jug of water, which he set on a table covered with a heavy, green embroidered cloth. 'Shall I pour?'

She nodded.

He wasn't at all sure how much to give her. 'How's that?' he queried, holding up a glass.

'Fine. The same again of water.' She preferred soda but doubted whether that was available. She continued to watch him through ribbons of smoke curling their way ceiling-wards. 'Thank you,' she said when he handed her the glass.

She noted that he poured himself a particularly small measure, and couldn't decide whether he wasn't used to alcohol or was simply making sure he didn't get befuddled.

'Bottoms up!' she toasted when he'd seated himself again.

He mumbled something in reply and they both drank.

She's smoking and drinking whisky, Tim was thinking. Harry was right about actors breaking the rules. He'd never come across a woman who drank whisky before. Gin, yes, but never whisky.

'So, what would you like to know?' she asked huskily.

'Excuse my ignorance about theatrical matters, but are you famous?'

It was like a cat playing with a mouse, she reflected. Delicious. 'Not really. Although I have to say I'm well known in West End circles. I have acted with some of the best, you know. Gerald du Maurier for a start.'

Tim scribbled that down.

'And Miss Irene Vanbrugh for another.'

Tim had never heard of her, but duly noted the name all the same.

They followed that line of questioning for a few minutes, then Tim decided to change tack. 'And why Torquay?'

'You mean why did I accept an invitation to come here?'

'That's right.'

She leant back in her chair and studied him. She could see a lot of his mother in his face and wondered where Mr Wilson was and what he was like. She'd tell Tim what he wanted to hear, she decided. Always the best policy in these situations.

'For years I've had a yearning to come to Torquay, having heard so much about it,' she replied smoothly. 'And this was my chance. It's also a pleasant break from London, which can be so dreadfully dreary at this time of year.' What she didn't say was that it was the only offer she'd had and the West End was fully cast for at least the next six months.

He wrote that down in his notebook. 'I see.'

'I shall be doing Lady Macbeth later in the season, which I've never played before. The chance to do that was an inducement in itself.'

'And who's playing Macbeth?'

'I have absolutely no idea, not having met the cast yet.

That will happen on Monday morning when we begin rehearsals.'

Tim was becoming more and more aware of the perfume she was wearing, which had started to pervade the room. It was strong and musky, heady in the extreme. He found it, like the woman, unsettling.

'Are you coming to our opening night?' she asked, gazing directly into his eyes.

He suddenly felt as though he'd been pinioned to the wall. 'Of which play?'

'Why, *Trelawny* of course.'

'To be honest, I hadn't thought about it.' She glanced away and he was released as suddenly as he'd been held.

'Well, I insist that you do. And your mother. I shall see that complimentary tickets are provided.'

'Then we'll be there,' he croaked. Christ, she was forceful! 'At least I shall. I can't speak for my mother. She may have other plans for that night.'

'Afterwards you must come backstage to my dressing room for a drink and tell me how wonderful I was. And if you didn't think so, you will lie and still tell me how wonderful I was.'

He laughed. 'I'm sure you will be.'

Elyse sipped her whisky, which was now almost finished. He'd hardly touched his.

'Where are you from?' he asked, suddenly serious again.

'London.'

'Whereabouts in London?'

Her smile was enigmatic. 'Kensington. Have you ever been to London?'

'I'm afraid not.'

'Then you must one day. There's no other city like it in the entire world. It's the most exciting place, especially if you're in the theatre.'

'Well, I only hope Torquay won't be too dull for you.'

She didn't answer that.

'Now, what about Mr Davenport?'

The last thing she wanted to do was talk about Benny. 'I thought this interview was about *me*, darling,' she gently chided him but with an underlying steel in her voice.

'It is, but . . .' He broke off in confusion, flustered and unused to being called darling by anyone other than Minna.

'Let's leave my husband out of it, shall we?' Her tone was now as sweet as could be.

'If you wish.'

'What I wish is a spot more whisky. Is that possible?'

He was instantly apologetic. 'Sorry, I'm being a poor host. I hadn't noticed your glass was empty.'

It wasn't, so she drained it there and then. 'You should be able to get this on expenses, you know. Entertaining a client, or subject, if you prefer.'

That was true enough, he reflected, heading back to the bottle. If Ricketts passed it, that was. Ricketts was notoriously stingy where expenses were concerned, demanding a receipt for everything. Well, if a receipt was required then one would be produced. He'd simply buy another bottle to replace this one.

Elyse fumbled for her handkerchief and coughed discreetly into it. Damn this cough – would it never be gone? It had become a trial of late.

'Are you all right?'

'Too many cigarettes, I'm afraid. I've become a slave to

them over the years. And please don't mention giving them up. I know I should, I just haven't got round to it yet.'

She wouldn't smoke so much if it wasn't for Benny, she thought darkly. That was what anxiety did to you. Tobacco had become her pacifier, her consolation, her constant companion.

Elyse briefly closed her eyes. She was tired and had been since arriving in Torquay. All that sea air, she presumed. Hopefully she'd acclimatise before long.

Tim hadn't missed the look of profound sadness that had flitted across her face. Now what had that been all about? He hoped it had nothing to do with him.

'Now where were we?' he smiled when he sat down again.

They continued from where they'd left off.

What a woman, Tim thought after Elyse had left. She'd polished off the entire contents of the whisky bottle and smoked goodness knows how many cigarettes. Yes, Harry had certainly been right when he'd said that actors were different. Very much so. Mrs Davenport had stunned him.

At least she'd given him enough material for a decent feature, which he was looking forward to getting started on. And she'd agreed that a photographer could call at the theatre next week and take her picture. He'd go along as well, Tim decided.

All in all he didn't know what to make of Mrs Davenport. She was a whole new experience for him. Fascinating, yes – that was the word that suited her. Fascinating.

And a little scary, if he was honest.

It was Minna's weekly visit to the grave, always bringing

fresh flowers whenever possible. She bent and began removing the old ones from the vase in front of the stone.

For the first few years she'd cried every time she came, but eventually that had stopped. You couldn't cry for ever. At least she couldn't.

It had been a sudden death: one moment he'd been there, the next gone. He wouldn't have felt anything, the doctor had assured her. The heart attack had been massive, claiming her husband's life in a flash.

She glanced up at the dates chiselled into the stone. How young he'd been, no age at all. A man who should have had decades ahead of him.

And what a mess he'd left behind – a terrible financial mess. They'd lost everything. Her beautiful house, gardens, carriage and pair, the lot. All swallowed up by the debts he'd left outstanding.

Thank God she'd had some money of her own. Who knows what would have become of them if she hadn't had that to fall back on. She'd used it to buy The Berkeley and give Tim a decent education. The school she'd sent him to hadn't been quite top-drawer, but good enough.

What a shock it had been having to work for her living, but she'd coped, turning from a life of pampered leisure to running a boarding house catering mainly for the elderly and retired. Now, if she was honest, she rather enjoyed it, even if their standard of living was nothing like it had been previously.

She shook her head sadly. Redvers had been a lovely, adorable man, but, as it turned out, no businessman. Then she rebuked herself, because that wasn't entirely fair. He hadn't been that bad a businessman – successful for a long time, till his judgement failed and he'd made a string of disastrous investments.

Well, he'd paid for that with his life, the stress having proved too much, overcoming him on that fateful day when his heart had seized up.

There was a part of her that said it would have been awful if he'd lived, for the shame and ignominy of being poor, of having let her and Tim down, would have been agony for him. She could just imagine how he'd have become eaten up by bitterness and self-pity. A parody of his former self.

But as a woman and wife, who'd loved him desperately, she'd have wanted him to live, no matter what. Their being together was all that would have mattered. Wealth was lovely, but love and ongoing companionship were everything. Except that Redvers wouldn't have seen it that way.

She began rearranging the new flowers in the vase.

Elyse lit a cigarette as she watched the rehearsal in progress. They were currently involved in a scene that didn't include her. As companies went, it wasn't a bad bunch, everyone being friendly, with 'darling this' and 'darling that'. She wondered how long it would be before the bitching and back-biting started, as it always did.

James Erskine, the leading man, made his exit and smiled at her: she smiled quickly in return. She wondered if he'd come across, but he didn't, sitting down instead beside Polly Emery, the main female juvenile.

The stage director conducting the rehearsal was a grossly fat man called Mellon. A nasty piece of work and no mistake. One of those vicious men who hate women, while pretending otherwise, with a tongue as sharp as any knife. His boyfriend was Paul Arthur, who'd been engaged to play small parts and, as far as she could see, couldn't act for toffee.

The scene came to an end and Mellon announced in a loud, fruity voice that they could take a coffee break. He immediately left the room, heading off somewhere.

'Mrs Davenport.'

It was Ronnie, one of the assistant stage managers, or ASMs as they were known. A lad of about fourteen, Ronnie was hoping one day to be an actor himself.

'There's a reporter and photographer from the *Torquay Times* to see you. They've asked if you'd meet them on "the green".'

'Right, Ronnie, thank you. Inform Mr Mellon when he gets back where I am.'

She'd already cleared this with Mellon, publicity being in the play's interests after all. As she gathered her belongings several envious glances were shot in her direction, as the onlookers wished it was their picture about to be taken.

The auditorium was dark, but the stage lights were on and the set for *Trelawny* was already half-completed. She swept imperiously down the centre aisle and mounted the side-stairs that took her onto the stage itself, where Tim and his colleague were waiting.

'Good morning, Mrs Davenport,' Tim greeted her, giving her a slight bow.

She smiled at this. 'We can't take long over this, so I hope you can be quick about it. I am in the middle of a rehearsal.'

'We understand perfectly,' Tim acknowledged. 'We're just thankful you've been able to spare us the time.'

She noted that the photographer had already set up his tripod and camera. 'Now, how would you like me?'

'I thought I'd take you against this part of the scenery,' the photographer suggested, gesturing to a flat depicting part of a sitting room.

'That suit you?' she asked Tim.

'Oh, perfectly.'

'My left side is the better one,' she informed the photographer, who bridled slightly at being told what he considered to be his business.

'Of course.'

Elyse knew that he could photograph whichever side he liked, but he'd end up choosing a left profile. They always did.

'How are rehearsals going?' Tim asked politely as she positioned herself.

'Slowly. But we have blocked the play now and are moving on.'

Tim had no idea what blocking a play meant, but decided not to show his ignorance by asking. He found it rather daunting being on the stage and could only wonder what it must be like when the audience was there. Not a profession for him, that was certain.

'How do I look, by the way?' The dress she'd picked to appear in was of taupe silk Charmeuse made with a one-sided drapery on the skirt forming a graduated tunic at the back. The button-trimmed front section of the waist gave it a basque effect. Like all her clothes, she'd had it run up by a seamstress she knew in Clerkenwell who was a sheer genius at turning out currently fashionable items for cut-rate prices. The dress cost a fraction of what it would have done if she'd bought it in the West End.

'Absolutely charming,' Tim responded graciously.

The photographer disappeared under the black cloth at the rear of his camera. 'Could you move just a little bit forward, please,' he called out.

Elyse did so.

'A trifle more.'

She did so again.

There was a small explosion as the picture was taken.

'Just keep holding it there, please,' the photographer called out, hurriedly changing plates.

Tim was looking beyond the set to where there was an assortment of objects. Ropes tied off in cleats disappeared into the high space above the stage, this area being known as the flies. To one side of the proscenium arch was what he took to be the electricians' box from where the stage lights were controlled, with a bank of levers sticking out from the console itself. But it was the smell that intrigued him most, a smell that any actor would instantly recognise as being peculiar to backstage, its main ingredient being that of the size or glue used on the canvas covering the flats. The flats were so called because that was exactly what they were: a wooden frame covered by canvas on which was painted whatever scene was required – a wall in a room, a distant view, and so on. He found it all highly exciting.

There was another small explosion as a second picture was taken. The photographer took six in all, from various angles, before pronouncing himself satisfied.

'Thank you for your cooperation, Mrs Davenport,' Tim said to her when it was over.

'My pleasure. Where are you off to now?'

'Back to the office and then out on another story. One not nearly as interesting as this.' He pulled a face. 'A council meeting actually. It's bound to be deadly dull. They all are.'

She laughed. 'Poor you.' She noticed then that Ronnie, the ASM, was hovering nearby. 'Ronnie, will you show these gentlemen out. I must get back to rehearsal.'

'Yes, Mrs Davenport.'

The photographer muttered his thanks, still miffed at being told his job, and began gathering up his equipment.

'No doubt I'll see you later.' Tim smiled.

'No doubt.'

And with that she left them, sweeping away as imperiously as she'd arrived.

'It'll do,' Ricketts pronounced grudgingly, having just read Tim's feature article on Mrs Davenport. Actually it was excellent, but he wasn't going to tell his young reporter that, believing in being sparse with his praise. 'Let's see the pics.'

Tim placed the six in front of him, and Ricketts slowly went through them. 'She *is* a looker,' Ricketts breathed with a gleam in his eye. 'She'll pull them in. Well, the men anyway.'

'She was very cooperative.'

Ricketts suddenly threw down the photographs. 'Actresses! Tarts each and every one. Believe me, lad, I know.'

Tim bit back an angry reply. He couldn't see how Mrs Davenport could possibly be called a tart. Different, yes, but that didn't make her a whore.

'And she's staying at your mother's boarding house, is that right?'

Tim nodded.

'I'm surprised at your mother allowing her to. She'll lower the tone.'

Tim wanted to retort to that, to defend his mother and Mrs Davenport, but he knew better than to challenge Ricketts in any way. So he said nothing.

Ricketts tapped a photo. 'That's the one we'll print. It's the best by far.'

'Yes, sir.'

'Send it through with your article then.'

'Yes, sir.'

Tim went to pick up the photographs, but Ricketts stopped him. 'Just the one I indicated. I'll keep the rest for a bit, then they can go into the library.'

Now why would he want to keep them? Tim wondered. Then it dawned on him. Ricketts was taken with Mrs Davenport. Fancied her, as Harry would have put it.

The editor leant back in his chair. 'I haven't been to the theatre in a long time. I think I'll go on opening night as critic and write the review myself.' He nodded his head. 'Yes, that's what I'll do.'

Tim didn't mention that he would also be there as a guest of Mrs Davenport, thinking it best not to. He just hoped Ricketts didn't pester him afterwards to be introduced.

The old lecher.

'What's wrong with you then, Daisy?' Minna demanded. 'You've got a face like fizz.'

Daisy hadn't realised it showed. 'I'm sorry. It's nothing.'

'Of course it's something. Now, out with it.'

Daisy signed. 'It's that Mrs Davenport. Every time I goes

to clean her room there's always cigarette ash everywhere. It doubles me work.'

'You mean, on the carpet and suchlike?'

The maid nodded. 'Absolutely everywhere. I've never known a messier smoker.'

Minna didn't like the sound of this at all. The mess was bad enough, but what about the risk of fire? Even a small blaze could lead to the whole place going up in flames. This was very worrying indeed. She was going to have to speak to Mrs Davenport.

Cook, who was making batter for a cake, glanced up. 'And you'd better say about the jewellery as well.'

Minna frowned. 'Jewellery? What jewellery?'

'She and Euphemia have been talking about it. I's overheard them several times,' Cook explained.

Daisy shot her a furious glance.

'Go on, Daisy,' Minna urged.

'I wasn't prying, Mrs Wilson. Honest I wasn't. But she leaves the box open a lot and you can't help but notice what's inside.' She gulped. 'You wouldn't believe it. Diamonds, Mrs Wilson, thae and all sorts. Rubies, emeralds, gold bracelets. A king's ransom.'

Minna considered this revelation. 'And she just leaves the jewellery box open?'

'That's right. It's on top of the dresser in plain view. If 'twere mine I'd hide it and no mistake. Lucky for her both Euphemia and I are honest as the day is long, as you well know.'

'Just as well,' Minna muttered grimly. If either girl had been caught thieving, Mrs Davenport would undoubtedly have brought charges and what a scandal that would mean.

As for Mrs Davenport, it was wrong of her to put temptation in their way. Had the woman no sense!

'Like Aladdin's cave, I said to Euphemia, and she agrees with me. A fortune in treasure just lying there.'

Something would have to be done about this, Minna decided. She'd speak to Mrs Davenport, and as soon as possible. Directly the woman returned from rehearsal, she decided.

In the meantime she'd have a look herself to make sure the girls weren't exaggerating.

Now what was this all about? a frowning Tim wondered, having just finished reading the letter that had come to him at work.

Jeremiah Coates was requesting Tim to call round one night for a drink and was asking him to telephone and say when would be convenient. It must be about the motorbike, but why get in touch when the man knew he couldn't afford the machine?

It just didn't make sense.

Chapter 3

'Ah, Mrs Davenport, there you are. Can I have a word?' Minna had been keeping an eye out for Elyse's return from rehearsal and had now caught her just coming through the door.

Elyse took in Minna's expression. 'Yes, of course.' She was extremely tired and looking forward to a long soak in the bath before dinner. She was also irritable, for the rehearsals weren't going well. Mellon, the stage director, was a complete idiot in her opinion, and nasty with it. He was succeeding in making life difficult when there was absolutely no need.

'I thought we might go into my private parlour.'

'Oh dear,' Elyse smiled. 'This sounds serious.'

Minna didn't reply to that, instead ushering Elyse through to the room that she remembered well from her previous visit.

'Shall we sit down, Mrs Davenport?'

Elyse occupied the same chair as before. 'Have I done something wrong?'

Minna was finding this difficult. She hated confronting guests about misdemeanours. It was very unsettling. 'There *are* several things, Mrs Davenport.'

'Oh?'

Minna cleared her throat. She had the beginnings of a headache, which wasn't helping matters. She knew what that meant – it happened every month at around this date. 'It's your smoking, Mrs Davenport. The girls have been complaining of the mess.'

Elyse had been about to ask if she could light up, but now she thought better of it. 'I see.'

'You get ash everywhere apparently and they're complaining that it doubles their work when doing your room.'

Elyse was instantly contrite. 'I must apologise, truly I must. And hold my hand up as guilty. I've always been the same, I'm afraid. I just don't know how I do it. I try to use the ashtray, but . . . more often that not I don't. I simply drop ash without realising it.'

Minna's expression became slightly less grim. At least the woman wasn't trying to deny it. 'You must understand the anxiety that causes me, Mrs Davenport. What if there was a fire and the house went up? What then? Not only might there be loss of life, but I would be deprived of my livelihood.'

'Yes, I can see that.'

'So, what's to be done? The obvious thing is for me to ban smoking in the room. But that wouldn't be fair as I allow several of the gentlemen guests the use of their pipes. I can hardly permit that while barring you.'

'It has been very careless of me,' Elyse admitted. The possibility of a fire had never crossed her mind, although it should have done. She felt quite ashamed at the thought of endangering others.

'Well?' Minna prompted.

'I can only give you my solemn promise that I'll be more careful from here on. And I mean that.'

Minna nodded.

'I would hate anything untoward to happen. Truly I would.'

'It's your own life you're putting in danger as well, don't forget.'

'Yes, I appreciate that.'

'If it happens again, Mrs Davenport, I shall have to ask you to leave.'

Elyse didn't reply to that.

'So, you will be more careful in future?'

'You have my word.'

'Then that's good enough for me.'

Elyse had no doubt that Minna meant what she said. The threat of asking her to leave wasn't an empty one. And she liked it at The Berkeley. It suited her. In a funny way she felt right at home.

'That's settled then,' Minna declared somewhat brusquely. 'Now we come to the other matter.'

Elyse groaned inwardly, while racking her brains trying to think what else she'd been up to.

'It's the jewellery in your room.'

Elyse stared blankly at her. 'I beg your pardon?'

'The jewellery. Daisy mentioned it and I took the liberty of going up to your room and seeing for myself. Surely they can't be real?'

Elyse burst out laughing at the absurdity of it. 'Heavens, no! It's stage jewellery. Tat. You could buy the entire contents of my box for under a fiver.'

Minna smiled. 'I thought as much. It's the mountings

that give the game away. They're not very good, are they?'

'They don't have to be. From out front, in the auditorium, they look all right. And Daisy thought they were the genuine article?'

'Both she and Euphemia. They've been quite excited about it apparently. Thought the equivalent of the Queen of Sheba had come to stay.'

'Well, tell them from me that . . .' Elyse broke off. 'Better still, if you send them up to me before dinner I'll soon sort the matter out. Agreed?'

'Agreed.'

Elyse laughed again. 'Genuine indeed! I only wish they were.'

Daisy and Euphemia came rushing into the kitchen where Minna and Cook were. 'Look what Mrs Davenport gave me!' Euphemia squealed, flashing a diamond ring.

'And me!' Daisy was brandishing a gold bracelet.

Minna smiled. 'I take it she explained.'

'Oh yes, and we all had a good laugh. I'd never heard of stage jewellery before. But I suppose it makes sense, when you think about it.'

Euphemia clasped the hand with the ring on it to her bosom. 'I shan't be telling anyone 'tis a fake. Let them think what they will. I won't be letting on otherwise.'

'Mrs Davenport says she can easily replace these when she gets back to London,' Daisy went on. 'And she insisted we take them. Ain't that so, Euphemia?'

'That's so, Mrs Wilson. She insisted. Said she'd be right upset if we didn't.'

Euphemia beamed, her face ablaze with excitement.

'I feel like a proper toff, I do. A real lady.'

'Well, you're not,' Minna reminded them sternly, bringing them both back down to earth. 'And I think it's time you got back about your duties.'

'Yes, Mrs Wilson,' they both chorused and left the kitchen as quickly as they'd entered it.

'Stage jewellery,' muttered Cook, shaking her head. 'Whatever next, I ask you!'

It was still light when Tim found Oaklands. He couldn't remember how many times he'd been up and down the Cockington road but he had never noticed the house before, or even suspected its existence. It lay up a lane and was screened from the road by trees.

Tim thought the house, stone-built with a slate roof, rather splendid. In fact it reminded him of the house they'd lost when Pa died. That too had been large and splendid. He was surprised when Jeremiah Coates himself answered his knock.

'Tim, come in! Pleased to see you.'

Again Tim was surprised, this time by the use of his Christian name. Oh well, he didn't mind that at all. 'And it's nice to see you, sir.'

'Jeremiah, please. We can forgo the formalities.'

Tim followed Jeremiah into a wood-panelled study dominated by a large desk covered in papers.

'My inner sanctum. The holy of holies,' Jeremiah explained with a chuckle. 'Now, what would you care to drink? I have some rather excellent claret if you wish.'

'That sounds wonderful.'

Jeremiah poured Tim a glass from a decanter, then indicated

that he should sit. 'You must be wondering what this is all about?'

'Yes, si . . . Jeremiah. I can only think the motorbike.'

Jeremiah had also sat. 'True enough.'

'My circumstances haven't changed. I still can't afford it.'

Jeremiah's eyes twinkled. 'We'll discuss that in a moment. I happened to mention you to my wife and it was she who made the connection.'

Tim was puzzled. 'Connection?'

'You're the son of Redvers Wilson.'

Tim nodded. 'That's right.'

Jeremiah's expression became thoughtful. 'A sad loss. I was at the funeral, but you probably don't remember me. You were very young then, I recall.'

'You knew my father?'

'Indeed I did. I can't say we were friends – business acquaintances more like. But I admired and respected him.'

Tim dropped his gaze, his emotions mixed as they always were when the subject of his father came up. That was a wound that had never properly healed. And, he suspected, never would. 'Thank you,' he whispered.

'Now that I realise who you are I can see your father in you.'

'Most folk think I take after my mother.'

'Maybe so,' Jeremiah mused, 'but I can still see your father. A good man, if I may say so. A kind one.'

Tim drank some of the claret, which was indeed first-class. 'People have always spoken well of him.'

'And so they should. When I say "kind", I have personal experience of that. Redvers did me a favour once which, because of his death, I never got to repay.'

'Favour?' Tim frowned.

'To do with business. I badly needed an introduction and he was able to provide it for me, for which I was terribly grateful. Thanks to that introduction I managed to secure a lucrative contract.'

Tim nodded that he understood.

'We had mutual friends, that's how we knew one another. And once we travelled up together on the same train to London. A most agreeable journey.'

Tim couldn't quite see where this was leading. 'So what has all this to do with the motorbike, Jeremiah?'

The older man regarded him steadily. 'As I said, I owed your father a favour that I never repaid. Now perhaps I can. Or at least make a token gesture. I want you to have the bike, lad. A gift from me to you.'

Tim was completely taken aback. 'But I couldn't possibly . . .'

'Oh yes, you can,' Jeremiah interrupted.

'But it's worth thirty pounds!'

Jeremiah made a gesture of dismissal. 'That's nothing to me. Nothing at all, I assure you.'

Tim's mind was reeling. The motorbike was to be his after all. That beautiful machine! Oh glory be.

'It's the least I can do to try and clear my debt,' Jeremiah continued. 'Please don't say no.'

Tim took a deep breath, then another.

'Put my conscience at ease, lad.'

He had another swig of claret. It was his lucky day right enough. He couldn't have been more delighted, or elated. Nor could he wait to get on the bike and try her out. His! He just couldn't believe it.

'So?' Jeremiah prompted.

'I can only thank you. I'm . . . lost for words, I suppose. Overwhelmed.'

Jeremiah laughed. 'Here, let me top up that glass for you.'

Tim ran a hand over his face, stunned by this turn of events. He wanted to jump to his feet and shout 'Hurrah!' But of course he didn't.

'How's your mother faring, by the way?' Jeremiah queried. 'I never met her, I'm afraid. A handsome woman, I thought at the funeral. Though that was hardly the place to see someone at their best, she being the widow after all.'

Tim accepted the refill and then went on to explain about Minna buying and running the boarding house. 'She rather enjoys it actually. Though it's a far cry from what we were used to.'

Jeremiah's face was wrinkled with concern. 'I never knew that your father was in financial trouble when he died. I just never heard. I assumed . . . Well, I assumed your mother would have been provided for.'

'We've managed so far. Though I have to admit there have been occasions when things have been tight. But that was mainly in the early days when we were getting established and finding our feet.'

Jeremiah nodded solemnly. 'A resourceful woman, enterprising too. I admire that. Awful for a woman to have been left in those circumstances. Part of my problem is that I'm abroad a great deal. Travelling here, there and everywhere. I'm only in Torquay for about three or four months out of the year.' His face darkened. 'That's something I'm going to have to change. My wife hasn't been well of late and has taken to spending quite a bit of time in bed. I shall have to be around more to be with her.'

'I'm sorry to hear that,' Tim sympathised.

Jeremiah shrugged. 'It's just one of those things sent to try us.'

They were interrupted at that point by a pretty young lady appearing in the doorway. 'There you are, Papa.' Then she noticed Tim. 'Oh, I am sorry. I didn't realise you had someone with you.'

Both men came to their feet.

'Let me introduce you, my dear. Katherine, this is Tim Wilson. Tim, this is my daughter Katherine.'

'How do you do.' Tim smiled.

'I'm delighted to meet you, Mr Wilson.'

'And I you.'

Tim took in the pale blonde hair and deep blue eyes. How old? he wondered. Roughly the same age as himself, he guessed. She certainly was pretty, with a good figure too.

'Tim's here about the motorbike,' Jeremiah explained. 'As from about ten minutes ago it belongs to him.'

'Thank goodness for that,' Katherine exclaimed. 'You know what a worry it's been to Mama. Ridiculous really, a man your age owning such a contraption.'

Jeremiah chuckled. 'I haven't exactly got one foot in the grave yet.'

'Still,' she quickly retorted, 'it was ridiculous.' She eyed Tim speculatively. 'Are you local, Mr Wilson?'

'Tim, please. Yes, I am.'

'Tim is the son of a business acquaintance of mine who's now sadly dead. Tim himself is a reporter on the *Times*.'

Her eyes opened wide. 'In London?'

'No, no,' Tim hastily corrected her. 'The *Torquay Times*. One of our local rags.'

'How jolly for you. It must be very interesting.'

'It can be,' Tim assured her.

'Katherine is only recently home from Switzerland, where she's been attending school,' Jeremiah stated.

'Really,' Tim murmured, not knowing what else to say.

'I was there for three years,' Katherine declared. 'It seemed like a lifetime.'

'You didn't enjoy it then?'

'On the contrary, I loved every moment. Switzerland is a wonderful country. Have you travelled much, Tim?'

He shook his head. 'I'm afraid not. That opportunity has never come my way.'

'But you'd like to?'

'Very much so.'

She turned again to Jeremiah. 'Mama is asking for you.'

'Tell her I'll be right up just as soon as I've seen Tim out.'

Katherine smiled at Tim. 'I hope we'll meet again.'

'I'm sure we will. Torquay is quite a small place, after all. We're bound to run into one another.'

After she'd gone Tim commented to Jeremiah, 'Absolutely charming.'

The older man nodded. 'It's good to have her back. He took a deep breath. 'Now, I have a suggestion to make.' He hooked an arm round Tim, who laid his drink aside. 'You did say that day in the street that you couldn't yet ride a motorbike. Am I correct?'

Tim nodded.

'Then why don't you return here this Sunday after luncheon and I'll teach you the rudimentaries. There's plenty of ground for you to practise on before you take it away. Is that a good idea?'

'Oh yes, rather.'

'That's settled then. I shall be expecting you.'

At the door Tim said, 'I can't thank you enough, Jeremiah. Truly I can't.'

'Don't mention it, lad. Now I'd better get on up to Ruth.'

'Till Sunday then.'

'Till Sunday.'

As he retraced his steps along the lane Tim wondered if Katherine would be there when he next called.

He certainly hoped so.

'Coward,' Tim muttered to himself, sinking wearily onto his bed. He'd fully intended telling Minna about the motorbike on arriving home, but just hadn't found the courage to do so. One thing was certain, she wasn't going to be best pleased. In fact, there might be all hell to pay if Minna took the same attitude as Mrs Coates, which she probably would.

He'd put the deed off until the bike was safely installed behind The Berkeley in the small shed where he intended keeping her. That way it was a *fait accompli*.

He yawned. God, he was tired. It had been a long day, during which he'd stayed out of the office as much as he could, Ricketts being in one of his particularly foul moods. Poor Harry had come in for a blast at one stage, which had been totally undeserved. Afterwards Harry had whispered to him that it was his dream to smack Ricketts good and hard sometime. But of course it would never happen. Harry valued his job too much.

The motorbike was his! Excitement bubbled anew in Tim.

He still hadn't really taken in this stroke of good fortune. Not only his, but a gift into the bargain. He shook his head in disbelief and amazement.

He stood and was about to strip off when he realised that he needed to relieve himself. He yawned again, then smiled, thinking he'd probably dream of the bike that night.

Outside in the corridor he paused as a familiar smell enveloped him. Familiar from his interview with Mrs Davenport, it was the unmistakable odour of her perfume. That plus something else. And then it dawned on him; it was perfume and cigarette smoke combined. For some reason he found it highly erotic.

He stood for a few moments savouring it, thinking that she must have passed along the corridor within the past few minutes for the odour still to be there. Erotic in the extreme, he thought, and blushed.

He hurried on his way.

'I wondered if I might buy you lunch?'

Elyse glanced up at James Erskine, who'd just spoken. 'Why, that would be lovely. Thank you.'

'As we don't have too long, I thought perhaps the Café Addison just over the way. The food there is served relatively quickly.' It was also cheap, but he didn't mention that.

'Fine.'

He helped her on with her light summer coat. 'You're going to be very good in this, you know.'

Truth or flattery? She searched his face and couldn't make up her mind. 'It's nice of you to say so.'

'I wouldn't unless it was true.'

She wondered about that. He was an actor after all. It

was a way of life with many of them – the profession being as precarious as it was – to ingratiate themselves continually. 'You're not bad, either.'

He gave her a small bow. 'I'll take that as a compliment.'

'It's meant as one.' Nor was he. He was proving a better actor than she'd first thought, bringing a depth to his character where many would have failed to do so. His comic timing was also extremely good – with that something that couldn't be taught or learnt. At least not in her opinion. You either had it or you didn't.

'So what do you think of our intrepid stage director?' he asked her as they crossed the street.

She glanced sideways at him. 'To be honest, not a great deal.'

Erskine laughed. 'That's putting it mildly. When it comes to directing, the man doesn't know his backside from a stage weight.'

'You're not a fan either, I take it?'

'Hardly. We'd all get on a great deal better if the fat idiot just stayed away.'

Elyse couldn't have agreed more.

The Café Addison was only about half-full, so they had no trouble securing a table. 'I'm ravenous,' Erskine declared, picking up the menu.

Elyse wasn't particularly hungry and often went without a midday meal, preferring a stroll along the promenade instead. She glanced at what was on offer and decided to have the herb flan. That would be more than sufficient.

After they'd ordered, with Erskine plumping for the steak-and-kidney pie followed by something called Devonshire junket and Elyse saying that she wouldn't have a pudding, he gazed across the table at her. 'I'm looking forward to doing the Scots piece. I shall be playing the thane, if you didn't already know.'

'I didn't, but had guessed that to be the case.'

He reached over and placed a hand on hers. 'I hope that, between us, we'll be able to give Torquay something to remember.'

She removed her hand onto her lap. 'Have you done the part before?'

He shook his head.

'Me neither. So it'll be a first for both of us.'

'I have played Hamlet though,' he murmured coyly.

'Really. Where?'

'Bridlington.'

She forced back a smile. 'I can't say I know either the place or the theatre there.'

'A passable rep. No more. But the company was terribly good when I did my stint with them. I thoroughly enjoyed the experience. Of course, I've never played the West End as you have.'

Now she did smile. 'How did you know that?'

'Mellon had a proof programme lying on his chair. I sneaked a glance while he was on the floor and read your biography. Most impressive, I have to say.'

She didn't reply.

'It's always been my ambition to appear in the West End. I have been up for things on a number of occasions, but so far no luck.' He shrugged. 'Just don't have the right contacts, I suppose.'

'That does help,' she replied softly. Was that what lunch was about, her contacts? He wasn't being very subtle if it was.

'So why have you come to Torquay?' he queried, changing the subject.

She gave him the same reasons she'd given Tim. The last thing she would have admitted was that it was the only work available at the time. Or that she needed the money.

The conversation was interrupted by the arrival of their main course, as the black-and-white-clad waitress fussed over them. From the looks she gave Erskine it was plain that she was an admirer.

'Where do you live?' Elyse inquired.

'Do you mean in Torquay?'

'No, I mean your home.'

He shrugged. 'Don't have one. I move from rep to rep and that's it. Everything I own is in my trunk and goes with me.'

'Do you have an agent?'

He shook his head. 'I do it all myself. I've made something of a reputation in the provinces, so it isn't as difficult as it might sound. A few letters and I'm usually fixed up.'

'I take it there isn't a Mrs Erskine?'

He laughed, obviously highly amused at the idea. 'Darling, I hardly earn enough to keep myself, far less a wife.' His expression changed to one of melancholia. 'Though I have to admit there are times when I would love to be married and have children. However, so far that's been impossible. Perhaps one day.'

'I don't have children either,' she murmured, thinking the herb flan delicious.

'Intentionally?'

'Yes and no.'

He stared at her in puzzlement, but she didn't elaborate,

considering it not a fit subject on such a short acquaintance. He didn't pursue the matter.

They ate for a while in silence, but every so often his eyes keenly probed hers.

'Is your husband in the business?' he asked eventually.

'Yes, he is. Benedict Davenport. Have you heard of him?'

Erskine thought about it. 'Can't say I have. Sorry.'

'He's in the West End right now, at The Duchess. Not a large part unfortunately, but a showy one. He was mentioned in all the reviews.'

'I'm envious,' Erskine admitted. 'I'd give my eyeteeth for a chance like that.'

'Your day will come,' she sympathised.

'Will it? I sometimes wonder.'

It was on the tip of her tongue to offer to mention his name to a few people when she got back to town, then she decided against it. At least for now. She'd wait till she'd seen him in a variety of roles so that she could be sure of his talent.

A handsome beast, she mused. And oodles of charm – at times he positively oozed it. She couldn't help but wonder if he was any good in bed.

That made her think of Benny. Now there was another charmer who knew a trick or two about how to please a woman. When he was in the mood, that is. In the mood and sober. It was a long time now since they'd last made love, and on that occasion it had been a bit of a flop. It had never been said between them, but she suspected – no more than that – that he'd completely lost interest in her sexually. And, she had to admit, it was the same for her. Their marriage had become a sham, a pale shadow of what had once been.

She'd sometimes wondered if he had other women, but if he had he'd been damned careful about disguising the fact. She hadn't yet been able to catch him out. Perhaps it wasn't just her, but he'd lost interest in sex altogether. It did happen.

As for her, sex had simply become something in the past. It didn't unduly bother her that that side of her life had ceased to exist, or at least she didn't think it did. On the other hand, if the opportunity arose with the right person . . . who knows?

'A penny for them?' Erskine queried.

She laughed and shook her head. 'Nothing really.'

'You were looking very serious just now.'

'Was I?' she replied, feigning innocence.

'Very.'

She pushed her plate away. What little appetite she'd had was gone. Sitting back, she watched him tuck into the remainder of his meal.

He became aware of her studying him and realised how heartily he'd been eating. 'I always enjoy my food,' he smiled. 'There have been many times when I, like most actors, have gone without. Especially when I was younger and just starting out.'

She knew exactly what he meant. She'd gone through lean times herself. Suddenly she found herself warming to James Erskine. He was good company.

Chapter 4

T im placed the latest edition of the *Times* back on the desk and smiled. His article on Mrs Davenport had taken up nearly an entire page and wasn't bad at all, if he said so himself. He was more than pleased with it. The photograph was excellent too.

'You look like the cat who just ate the cream.' He glanced round to find Harry Nutbeam standing alongside. 'Going in for a bit of self-congratulation, are we?' Harry teased.

'And why not?'

Harry plumped himself onto the desk. 'Don't let Ricketts see you looking so smug. You know what he's like.'

Tim nodded. 'Only too well.'

'It is quite good, though,' Harry admitted. 'Well done.'

'Thank you.'

'Now, let's get down to important matters. How about a drink tonight? I for one could sink a bucketload.'

Tim considered that. 'All right. Round the corner?'

'As soon as you can get away.'

'I'll be there.'

'Good.' Harry jumped to his feet.

When he had gone Tim reopened the paper and reread

his article. He'd even been given a by-line, which delighted him. What was it Katherine Coates had said: did he work for the London *Times*?

One day maybe. Now that would be something.

'You're late again,' Cook accused, waving a wooden spoon at Tim.

'Sorry.'

'And you're stinking of booze. I can smell it from here.'

'Well, it is Friday night after all. And I did have something to celebrate.'

'Hmmh!' Cook snorted, eyeing him up and down. 'You'd better tidy yourself up a little before your ma catches sight of you. Your tie is all to the side and your hair looks like a bird's nest.'

He grinned. 'We had a smashing time.'

'Evidently,' she retorted sarcastically.

'What's to eat?'

She sniffed disdainfully. 'Salmon fishcakes with cucumber mayonnaise.'

'Sounds wonderful.'

'Well, they might not taste it, as they should've been eaten hours ago. Serve 'ee right if they's spoilt.'

'What's to go with them?'

'Sauté potatoes, caramelised carrots and some other veg.'

He rubbed his hands together. 'Yum yum.'

'Yum yum indeed,' she replied, voice dripping with sarcasm. 'Now you gets yourself sorted while I dishes up.'

Tim was just finishing his meal when his mother came into the kitchen. She stopped to stare disapprovingly at him.

'I had to work late on a story,' he lied.

She came closer and sniffed.

'Yes, I have had a couple of pints, Ma. Only that.' Another lie, as he'd had five.

'There's no need to tell him off for being late. I's already done so,' Cook declared.

'You get worse. I swear you really do get worse. Where is it all going to end? I ask myself,' Minna scolded.

'He'll be smoking and going out with dirty women next,' Cook jibed.

Minna threw up her hands in horror. 'Heaven forbid!'

'I don't even know any dirty women,' Tim muttered. Thinking that he wished he did. Fat chance!

'I take it you're in for the evening?' Minna queried.

He nodded.

'Well, at least that's something. And talking of smoking, Mrs Davenport wants to see you. She said to go up and knock on her door.'

'It must be about the article I did on her, Ma. Have you read it?'

'Haven't had time to pick up the paper.'

He was disappointed. 'Well, I hope you do.'

She softened a little to hear the hurt in his voice. 'Of course I'll read it, son. When I get the chance.'

'Just don't forget. You too, Cook.'

Minna knew, but Tim didn't, that Cook couldn't read. Minna would have to do that for her.

'Now where's thae girls? There's still lots to do in here,' Cook complained.

'They'll be back shortly. They're in the dining room laying up for breakfast at the moment.'

Tim came to his feet. 'Thanks, Cook. That was terrific.'

'You're lucky you gets anything at all,' she answered waspishly.

He went quickly to her and pecked her on the cheek. 'I do appreciate it.'

'Get away with you!' a flustered Cook replied, beaming her pleasure at the kiss. She'd never been married, having spent her entire life in service.

Tim chuckled to himself as he left the kitchen and headed upstairs.

'Come in!'

He halted abruptly, taken aback to find Mrs Davenport clad only in a nightdress and frilly négligé, both cream-coloured. 'I'm sorry,' he stuttered. 'I didn't realise.'

She laughed at his expression. 'Don't worry, I'm quite respectable.'

He'd never seen a woman, other than Minna, in night attire. He found it most disturbing. Particularly as Mrs Davenport had a far fuller figure than he'd imagined. Quite voluptuous really. He now noticed a corset draped casually over the back of a chair.

Elyse smiled at him. 'I'm just about to have a glass of gin. Care to join me?'

'If you think it's all right?' In her room? Just the two of them? He wasn't sure about this at all.

'Of course it's all right. There's only water to go with it, I'm afraid.'

'That's fine.'

He watched as she produced a bottle and two glasses. The bottle was already opened and about one-third of its contents had gone. The measures she poured were huge.

She handed him a glass and indicated the jug and basin. 'Help yourself.'

He poured himself an equal amount of water. 'You?'

'Please.'

'Cheers!' he said, raising his glass to her.

'Down the hatch.'

He shuddered as the fiery liquid burnt its way down his throat. Gin and water, ugh!

Elyse laid her drink aside and lit up. 'I wanted to say how good I thought your article was today.'

'Thank you.'

'You've got talent.'

He blushed and looked down at the rug he was standing on. He mustn't stare at the swell of her bosoms, he told himself, though it was hard not to. He drew in a deep breath, filled with the headiness of her now unmistakable perfume. He'd have recognised it anywhere.

'I was amused to notice that the picture chosen was of my left profile. I said that's what would happen.'

'That was the one the editor picked.'

She regarded him steadily, thinking again what a good juvenile lead he would make. Nor was she unaware of his being uncomfortable in her presence.

'I like to be relaxed when I come in at night. I hope you don't mind?' she smiled.

Tim knew she was referring to the nightdress and négligé. 'Not at all.'

She had a swallow of gin, all the while continuing to regard him steadily. 'I've just been rehearsing my lines.'

'Oh?'

'You know, for the play.'

He nodded. 'I understand.'

'But I'm having trouble with act four. There's a section I just can't get to stick.'

He wasn't sure what to reply to that so he said nothing.

'Now that you're here . . .' She broke off and frowned quizzically at him. 'If you don't have to rush off to anything would you go over them with me? It would be a tremendous help.'

He gulped. 'I, er . . . I wouldn't know how.'

'It's easy. You say all the lines other than mine.'

'I'm . . . not sure.' He felt completely at a loss.

'I really would be obliged.'

The sexiness in her voice was making him tremble slightly and go cold all over. No, warm all over. No, both at once.

'Do you need to rush off?'

He shook his head.

'It wouldn't take long.'

He downed the rest of his drink and blinked. God, that was strong. Especially on top of the beer he'd had earlier.

'That's settled then,' Elyse purred. 'Now let me refill that glass for you and we'll get started.'

What had he let himself in for! He couldn't take his eyes off her backside as she swayed towards the bottle . . . There were beads of sweat gathering underneath his collar.

'I'm playing Imogen Parrott,' she called back over her shoulder. 'You'll be reading a character called O'Dwyer. Don't try to act, just say the words that will give me my cues. Are you with me?'

'Yes,' he croaked.

She returned his glass and gave him some sheets of

handwritten paper. 'We'll start here,' she declared, pointing. 'You say, "I can't hear myself speak for all the riot and confusion," and then I carry on till we get to the end of the scene.'

It seemed simple enough, but it was going to be embarrassing to do.

'Ready, Tim?'

He swallowed hard. 'As I'll ever be.'

'Good chap. So on you go.'

He stuttered and stumbled over the first page and then gradually got the hang of it. Elyse meanwhile moved about the room, only 'drying' twice, as she called it, during the scene.

'Can we do that again?' she asked anxiously when they'd finished.

'Of course.'

'It is a big help, Tim. Honestly.'

He was beginning to rather enjoy himself now, assurance taking hold of him. Wisely he did as instructed and did not try to act, though he did attempt to put feeling into the words.

They went through the scene six times in all before Elyse pronounced herself satisfied. 'I've got it now,' she declared.

He grinned at her. 'There was no hesitation that last time. You had everything off pat.'

'As you have to. Or should do, anyway.' With a flourish she lit another cigarette. 'You have a rather good voice actually.'

That surprised him. 'Really?'

'Completely untrained of course, but the basics are there. Perhaps the theatre could be another career for you, should you ever tire of journalism.'

He laughed, bemused by that idea. 'I don't think so. I'd be scared half to death every time I went onstage.'

'Oh, you get used to it,' she replied airily. 'It can be, and should be, enormously exciting. I just adore it.'

'Well, rather you than me.'

She came over and took the pages away from him. 'I can't thank you enough. My husband Benny usually does this for me when I'm in town. I've always found it easier learning the lines and cues by hearing them than by reading from the page.'

He cleared his throat. 'If we're done, I really should be going.'

'Not before you have another gin.' When she saw he was about to protest she held up a hand. 'You wouldn't leave a lady to drink on her own, would you? That would be most ungentlemanly and discourteous.'

He shrugged. 'If you put it that way.'

'I most certainly do.'

Again he was fascinated by her bottom weaving its way towards the bottle. It was as though he was hypnotised by it.

'Now sit down and tell me more about yourself,' Elyse said to him when she returned from pouring their drinks. 'I want to hear.'

It was another hour before Tim managed to leave and go to his own room. If he'd been drunk on arriving home, then he was a lot more so now. He was going to have a terrible hangover in the morning, that was certain.

What a woman Mrs Davenport was – he'd never met her like before. She'd almost overwhelmed him with her femininity. Not that he was complaining; on the contrary, he'd thoroughly enjoyed the experience. As for that bottom and those breasts!

He hoped she asked him to help her out with her lines again.

'That's it, Tim, you're doing fine!' Jeremiah Coates called out encouragingly.

It was Sunday and Tim had come to Oaklands as agreed. For the past twenty minutes Jeremiah had been instructing him, explaining everything patiently and in detail.

Tim took the motorbike into a wide arc, wobbling a little as he went but otherwise in control. It wasn't nearly as difficult as he'd imagined.

'And again!' Jeremiah urged, indicating Tim to do another arc by waving him on.

It was the most glorious sensation, one that Tim would have been hard put to describe. He prayed he didn't make a fool of himself either by crashing or by falling off.

Katherine was standing in a window watching his progress. When the lesson was over she'd go out and suggest tea. In the meantime she'd stay indoors, not wanting to put Tim off by her presence.

Tim opened the throttle a little further and the bike surged forward. Don't get overconfident, he warned himself. Just take it easy and remember all that Jeremiah has taught you.

He started laughing to himself. This was fun with a capital F. Thrilling too: oh yes, definitely that. The feeling of power at his disposal was incredible, and the steady throb between his legs was music to his ears. He couldn't wait to ride the Royal Enfield through Torquay. Harry Nutbeam would be jealous as hell!

He broke out of the arc and headed for some trees, his intention being to circle them before deciding what he'd do next. With every passing second his confidence was growing, as was his expertise. Already he felt familiar and at ease with the machine.

Eventually, for he could have ridden the bike for the rest of the day, he turned in the direction of Jeremiah, his face glowing with exhilaration.

'Well done,' Jeremiah said as Tim pulled up alongside and killed the engine.

Tim beamed. 'Wonderful. Simply wonderful.'

Jeremiah laughed, delighted to see that Tim had enjoyed himself so much. He helped Tim pull the bike onto its stand, then clapped him on the shoulders.

'I was beginning to think you weren't coming back.'

'I certainly didn't want to.' He took a deep breath. 'Jeremiah, I really can't thank you enough.'

'Forget it, lad. Say no more.'

Katherine came strolling across, her golden hair shining in the sunlight. 'Congratulations, you didn't fall off once. Not like someone I could mention.'

Jeremiah looked embarrassed. 'Trust you to bring that up.'

'Well, you did fall off the first time you rode it. I was there, remember?'

Tim found that highly amusing, though he did his best not to show it. That would have been rude.

'I thought we might have some tea and have ordered it to be brought outside,' Katherine declared. 'We may as well make the best of this weather as autumn is just around the corner.'

'What a splendid idea,' Jeremiah replied, rubbing his hands together. 'Tim?'

'Oh, I'd love a cup, thank you very much.'

'Then shall we make our way over to the verandah?' Katherine suggested.

Jeremiah and Katherine, walking side by side, led the way while Tim, pushing the bike, brought up the rear. He couldn't wait to get on again and drive it home.

They were just sitting down round a table with an umbrella over it when they were joined by a white-haired woman who emerged from the French windows.

'Ruth, darling!' Jeremiah exclaimed.

Tim was immediately on his feet, realising this was Mrs Coates whom he hadn't yet met. What he saw was a frail, terribly thin woman whose face was sunken to the point of almost being cadaverous. Her skin was sallow – yellow you might say – but her eyes remained bright and piercing.

'So you're the young man who's relieved my anxiety,' Ruth said, extending a hand.

Tim shook it carefully, her hand feeling skeletal in his. 'I take it you're referring to the bike, Mrs Coates?'

'I most certainly am. I never had a moment's peace every time Jeremiah went out on it. Dangerous things, if you ask me. All right perhaps for young people, but not for someone his age.'

'I'm not that old,' Jeremiah muttered good-naturedly.

'You are for motorbikes,' Ruth rebuked him. 'Of all the daft notions.'

'Well, Jeremiah's loss is my gain,' Tim declared.

'Did you watch Tim, Mama? Wasn't he ever so good?' Tim blushed.

'No, I didn't watch.'

'I did. From an upstairs window.' Katherine smiled at him. 'You're awfully clever to pick it up so very quickly.'

'A natural, I'd say,' Jeremiah boomed. 'Clearly has an affinity with machines.'

Ruth sat and the two men followed suit. 'I understand you're a journalist, Tim?'

'That's right.'

She leant forward a little. 'Tell me, have you ever reported on a murder?'

Tim shook his head. 'I'm afraid not.'

'What a pity,' she sighed. 'I'm an avid reader of crime fiction, you know. I find it ever so enthralling.'

'The gorier, the better,' Jeremiah smiled.

'Oh, absolutely. Lots of blood and mystery. Right up my street.'

They were interrupted at that point by a maid arriving with a large tray of tea things. 'Ah, scones, jam and clotted cream. My favourite!' Jeremiah enthused.

Tim couldn't help but think how pretty Katherine was looking. She was wearing a pale-green dress made of silk georgette crêpe. It had a long roll-collar hanging loosely from each side of the neck to fall over a ribbon girdle of the same material as the dress. The sleeves were three-quarter-length ending in silk trim. She was the very epitome of an English rose.

'Next year Katherine will be going up to London for the Season, won't you, my dear?' Ruth said to her daughter. 'It'll be her coming-out.'

Tim knew all about the Season. 'You'll be presented to the King, then?'

'Hopefully,' Katherine smiled.

'I only wish I could accompany her, but that's impossible sadly,' Ruth sighed, 'although Jeremiah will be going with her as chaperon.'

'Are you looking forward to it?' Tim asked Katherine.

She nodded. 'Especially being presented at Court.'

'I remember when I was. A long time ago now. All those handsome young men and gay parties! I've never enjoyed myself so much in my life.'

'Is that where you met Jeremiah?'

Ruth gazed lovingly at her husband. 'Indirectly. He was a friend of one of those who showed an interest. But once we'd met, that was that.'

Jeremiah reached across and clasped Ruth's hand. 'And I've never regretted a single moment of it.'

'Nor I, darling. A marriage made in heaven.'

Katherine broke the spell by saying quietly, 'I hope you'll be visiting us again, Tim?'

'Don't be so forward,' Ruth scolded. 'Not the done thing at all.'

'Sorry, Mama. I didn't mean to be.' She looked down at her lap in confusion.

'But of course he'll visit us again. Won't you, Tim?' Jeremiah declared. 'Anyway, I shall be wanting progress reports on how you're getting on with the Enfield.'

'I'd love to visit if I may,' Tim replied. He glanced sideways at Katherine, who'd now regained her composure. Yes, he certainly would.

Elyse slammed her dressing-room door shut behind her. God, she was angry! Absolutely fuming.

'Elyse?' came James Erskine's voice from out in the corridor.

'Yes?'

He poked his head in. 'Are you all right?'

'That man, that bloody man! He's quite impossible.'

James closed the door again. 'I quite agree. He couldn't direct traffic, far less a play.'

She lit a cigarette, drawing the smoke deep into her lungs.

'You must try and not let him get to you,' James advised softly. 'Mellon is a prize ass and we just have to put up with it.'

Elyse had another name for the stage director, one a lot more down-to-earth. 'If only he'd shut up and let us get on with it. But he won't, he keeps interfering with the most ridiculous moves and instructions.'

'I know, I know,' James consoled her. 'But we'll get it right despite him. Just wait and see. I promise you.'

Suddenly she smiled. 'You're a sweetheart, James. Thank you.'

'There's nothing to thank.'

'Oh yes there is. I appreciate your support.'

'Think nothing of it.'

She went to the large mirror facing her make-up table and studied her reflection. Picking up a brush, she swiftly and expertly pushed several stray strands of hair back in place.

'I've had an idea,' James murmured.

'What?'

'Why don't you and I go out to dinner tonight? My treat. We can enjoy ourselves by tearing Mellon apart over a good meal.'

That appealed to her.

'I thought we might try The Imperial. They have a French chef there apparently.'

She laid the brush down and turned to face him. She was becoming quite fond of James Erskine. 'What time?'

'Shall I pick you up at . . . say, seven-thirty? How would that do?'

'Fine.'

'That's agreed then.' He took a deep breath. 'Now, we'd better get back to the fray.'

Elyse ground out the remains of her cigarette.

'Feeling better now?'

'Lots.'

She hooked an arm through his as they walked along the corridor.

'Ma, I want to show you something.'

Minna glanced up from the following week's menus that she was making out. 'Not now, Tim. I'm busy.'

'It's rather important, Ma.' He was nervous as anything, having been steeling himself all day for this moment. He just wanted to get it over and done with.

Minna laid down her pen. What now? This was the third time she'd been interrupted. 'Can't it wait a bit?'

He shook his head.

'All right then,' she conceded reluctantly.

His heart was hammering as he led her to the rear of the house and out to the back, while Minna wondered what this was all about. It was still daylight, so he didn't have to worry about a lamp as he opened the shed door.

'What do you think, Ma? Isn't she a beauty?'

Minna stared at the motorbike in horror. 'Whose is it?'

'Mine.'

'*Yours!*'

Tim winced at the near-shriek in her voice.

'Where . . . where did you get it?'

He explained about Jeremiah Coates and how Jeremiah had owed his father a favour, repaying it by giving him the bike for free.

Minna was aghast, not knowing what to say. Tim on a motorbike! Her little boy owning one of these dangerous contraptions.

'You must return it,' she croaked.

'No, Ma, that would be insulting.' He stuck out his jaw defiantly. 'I'm grown up, Ma, and this is something I want. I'll be careful, I promise you.'

'But . . . but . . .' She trailed off, lost for words.

'Ever so careful, Ma,' he repeated. 'You have my word on that.'

She saw the defiance on his face. He *was* grown up, she reminded herself. A man now, able to make his own decisions. And what was she going to do – order him from the house? That would be ridiculous.

'I don't like it, Tim,' she stated grimly. 'I don't like it at all.'

He put an arm round her and squeezed. 'You'll soon get used to the idea, Ma.'

She wasn't at all certain about that. What would Redvers have said? She had a sneaking suspicion he'd have approved. Probably would have wanted to ride the bike himself. She felt her resistance crumbling. If Redvers would have approved, then so should she.

'You swear you'll be careful, Tim?'

'My word of honour, Ma.'

She had to admit the bike did have a certain beauty about it. Rather elegant in a way. If such a contraption could be called elegant.

'It'll be expensive to run,' she argued.

'No, it won't. And I can easily afford the petrol. You get a lot of miles to the gallon. Jeremiah assured me of that.'

'Did he indeed!' She wanted to hear more about this Jeremiah, whom she vaguely remembered from the past. Perhaps Redvers had mentioned him at some point.

'I'll be going to work on her in the morning,' Tim declared, shutting the shed door.

Minna retreated inside, desperately needing a cup of good strong tea and a sit down.

Tim grinned. That had been easier than he'd anticipated. He'd been certain she'd raise the roof.

Wait till he showed it off to Harry! The bugger's face would be as green as grass.

Chapter 5

S he hadn't had so much fun in ages, Elyse thought, sinking onto the single chair provided in her bedroom. How
extraordinarily funny James could be, his wit devastating.

She smiled at the memory of their meal together. He
hadn't been joking when he'd said they'd tear Mellon apart.
The stage director's ears, wherever he was, should have been
red-hot.

James wasn't only good company, but easy to be with.
The conversation between them had simply flowed, with
hardly a let-up. As nights out went it had been first-class.

They'd discussed so many things – plays they'd been in,
parts they'd played, the inevitable actors' anecdotes, of which
James had far more than she. On top of everything else, he
was a superb story-teller.

The food had been excellent too. She had a prawn concoction to start with, followed by beef Wellington and then
the most gorgeous chocolate roulade to finish. The wine had
been Merlot, with brandy afterwards.

She closed her eyes, thinking how very full she was, having
eaten far more than she would normally. She'd have to cut
back for the next couple of days to compensate.

James . . . a lovely name. Far nicer than Benny, which she'd always considered rather common. Benedict was fine, but too much of a mouthful to use all the time, so Benny he was called.

James had told her he'd been born in Wolverhampton of a Scots father and Irish mother, neither of whom had anything to do with the theatre. He'd run away from home at the age of thirteen and, after a number of years doing this and that, had finally ended up playing small parts in a local rep. He'd enjoyed it so much that he'd pursued the 'business' as a career.

She'd noticed his hands in particular: long and delicate fingers with beautifully manicured nails. She shivered, thinking of those hands on her body, a flush of desire creeping into her belly.

He'd made it plain that he wanted a relationship with her, not actually coming out and saying so, but it had been there. So what was she going to do about it? She didn't know. Not yet.

It wasn't exactly uncommon for actors on tour or playing the provinces to have affairs while away from home. There was companionship in it after all, and comfort. There was also the great satisfaction of sex. Harsh fact that it was, there were those – male and female – who just couldn't do without it.

He'd surprised her by not trying to kiss her at the door. All the way back in the motor taxicab she'd wondered if she'd allow him to or not, and she still hadn't made up her mind when they arrived. In the event she hadn't had to make a decision where that was concerned.

In a way she was disappointed, wondering what it would

be like to be kissed by James. Some men were terrible kissers, but she didn't think he would be. At kissing, or anything else. She'd got the impression, she didn't know how, that he was more than competent in that department.

Elyse sighed with contentment, feeling totally replete. She'd offered to pay half the bill but he'd refused, remind-ing her – insisting – that it was his treat. Well, she would return the gesture by taking him out one evening. That was only fair after all. Other women might never think of such a thing, but she was an actress and that was how actors behaved. They'd go to The Imperial again, of course. Unless he came up with a better idea.

She'd leave it for a couple of weeks, she decided. Yes, that was what she'd do. In the meantime, well, she'd just see how things developed.

But she wasn't completely against the idea of a romance. Not at all. She just hadn't realised how much she'd missed the intimacy.

Or perhaps it wasn't simply that. It was the notion of intimacy with James that attracted her.

'I don't believe you, you're lying!'

Tim grinned at Harry, having just told him about the Royal Enfield. 'If you doubt me, go over to that window and look down at the pavement. It's parked right outside.'

A still disbelieving Harry strode across the room and peered out.

'Convinced?' Tim queried, joining him.

'That isn't yours.'

'It is.'

'Nonsense.'

'You'll see when I drive off on it.'

Harry turned to stare at his colleague. 'Honest?'

Tim made the sign of the cross over his heart. 'Honest.'

'Bloody Nora!'

'I thought you'd be impressed.'

'Impressed! I'm downright jealous. How did you afford it?'

Tim tapped his nose. 'That's for me to know and you to wonder about.'

Harry took another look at the bike. 'I'd give my eyeteeth for one of those. Can I drive it sometime?'

'Nope. Nobody's driving it but me.'

'I'll buy you a drink?'

'It's still no.'

'Several drinks?'

Tim laughed and walked away. Harry's reaction was even better than he'd anticipated. God, but he'd enjoyed that!

'Have you two nothing better to do than stare out of windows?' Ricketts bellowed at them.

Tim wondered where the editor had sprung from, since he hadn't been there moments ago, having been downstairs with the printers.

'Sorry, Mr Ricketts,' Harry apologised and hurried back to the desk, where he'd been in the middle of writing a football report when Tim had told him about the motorbike.

'Wilson, come here,' Ricketts barked. 'I want you to go to the magistrates' court this morning,' he stated when Tim was standing before him. 'Patsy was supposed to be doing it, but he's sent a note round saying he's ill.' Ricketts shook his head. 'Ill, my arse. Of the self-induced kind, no doubt.

I'd bet a week's pay he's got another of his bloody hangovers.'

'I'll leave right away, sir.'

'Do that. You know the drill there?'

'Yes, sir.'

'Then hop to it.'

Ricketts ran a hand over his face as Tim hastened away. Sometimes he thought Patsy was more trouble than he was worth. But he daren't sack him, for there would be a public outcry in Torquay if he did. Patsy had for years been writing a column that was adored by their readership. When the paper hit the streets the first thing many people did was turn to that sod's column. He'd also been in the job so long he'd become practically invaluable. If there was anything happening in Torquay or the surrounding area, then Patsy was bound to know about it. The man was a jewel. A drunk, yes, but also a jewel.

Ricketts glared at Harry, who was now pounding away on a typewriter for all he was worth.

No wonder he had an ulcer.

'Fifteen minutes, Mrs Davenport!' the call boy informed her, rapping on the dressing-room door.

'Thank you.'

Elyse went back to staring in her mirror. Her make-up was perfect. All she could do now was wait to go on.

This time it was a tap instead of a rap. 'May I come in? Are you decent?'

'I'm decent, James.'

He was carrying a neatly wrapped bunch of flowers. 'For you,' he smiled.

'Oh, James, they're lovely!'

'Not nearly as lovely as you. If I may say so, you look quite stunning, Imogen,' he replied smoothly.

She too smiled at the reference to her character name. 'I'll put these in water straight away,' she declared. There were several vases by the sink for just that purpose.

'So how do you feel?' he queried as she ran some water into one of them.

'A little apprehensive. But then I always am on opening nights. You?'

'The same, I suppose. But I'll be fine once I'm on. That's the norm with me.'

'I hope you won't forget to come round afterwards and have a drink?'

'Wild horses wouldn't keep me away.'

She placed the vase beside her table. 'I think they'll look best there. I just wish I'd bought you something now.'

'I had your card. That was more than enough.'

Elyse sighed. 'Almost time.'

'I'll leave you to it then. See you "on the green".'

'James!'

He halted and turned again to her.

She went swiftly across and pecked him on the cheek. 'Thanks again. You're a real sweetheart.'

He didn't reply to that.

Then he was gone, leaving Elyse staring after him, her emotions mixed. But all thoughts of James were immediately banished when the five minutes were called.

She was standing in the wings listening when the curtain went up and applause swept the auditorium in appreciation of the set.

It was a good start.

* * *

'What do you think so far?' Tim asked Minna as they headed out of the auditorium during the interval.

'I'm thoroughly enjoying myself.'

'And Mrs Davenport?'

'She's very good indeed.'

Tim considered her performance far more than that. The woman positively shone onstage, and he hadn't been able to take his eyes off her. She was completely charismatic, spellbinding.

'It's awfully hot in here,' Minna complained quietly to him. 'I could use a cool drink.'

'Then I'll get you one, Ma. What would you like?'

'Lemonade would be nice.'

'Nothing stronger?' he teased.

'No, lemonade or some squash would be perfect.'

They went into the bar, which was already crowded. Tim instructed his mother to wait while he fetched their drinks, and he was pushing through the throng when he spied Jeremiah and Katherine at the other end. She spotted him at the same time. He waved and she waved back.

When it was his turn to be served he ordered the lemonade, plus a large gin and tonic for himself. He was damned if he was going to have something soft.

'Hello, Wilson.'

Tim's heart sank on hearing that voice. He turned to find Ricketts alongside. 'Are you enjoying it, sir?'

'Oh, yes. I shall give it a good review.'

Tim smiled to himself. The *Times* always gave plays a good review, that was their policy. Then again, there were good reviews and *good* reviews.

'I'd like to meet Mrs Davenport afterwards and tell her how delightful her performance is,' Ricketts said, a gleam in his eye.

Oh, hell! Tim thought as Ricketts stared expectantly at him. 'I can't help you there, I'm afraid, Mr Ricketts.'

Ricketts frowned. 'Are you sure?'

The last thing Tim wanted was to land Mrs Davenport with his editor. That would be ghastly for her. He recalled now Ricketts keeping back some of her photographs. 'I'm sorry. I just can't help. I would if I could,' he lied.

Tim picked up his drinks and left the editor gazing after him. That had been a chance to get into Ricketts' good books, but not one he was taking up.

'I saw Mr Coates and his daughter Katherine,' Tim informed his mother on rejoining her.

'Oh?'

Tim looked back to where they'd been standing, but they'd disappeared, probably hidden by the crowd. He'd have liked to speak to them and introduce Minna, but the crush was too great.

Then suddenly they were chatting to a couple who were old friends of Minna's, remaining with them until the bell rang warning that the play was about to restart.

The bar instantly began to empty, everyone being keen to view the next act. The hubbub was one of expectation.

'It's going well, don't you agree?' James said to Elyse. The pair of them were sitting in the green room, where tea and coffee were available and where the actors could rest when not onstage.

Elyse nodded.

'An appreciative audience. They've picked up every one of my laugh-lines.'

Elyse was seized by a fit of coughing. Clutching her chest, she bent over.

'Are you all right?' James asked anxiously.

It took her a moment or two to catch her breath. 'I'm fine,' she wheezed. 'I shouldn't smoke so many damned cigarettes. They'll be the death of me.'

'Don't say that!' James exclaimed in alarm. 'It's tempting fate.' Like all actors he was highly superstitious.

She laughed at his expression. 'Don't worry. It was only a joke.'

'All the same,' he murmured darkly.

Elyse sucked in a deep breath, then another. 'Right as rain now,' she declared, promising herself not to have another fag till the play was over. If she could last out, that was.

Other members of the cast were milling about, chatting quietly among themselves, laughing occasionally. There was no sign of Mellon, who'd be out front taking notes. The actress playing Miss Trafalgar Gower, an older character part, was sitting coolly doing a crossword, her way of passing time between appearances.

'Here we go again,' James said when it was announced that the curtain was about to rise.

He squeezed Elyse's wrist before leaving her, being due onstage several scenes before her next entrance.

Trelawny ended to rapturous applause, the cast being given a standing ovation. Tim had been one of the first on his feet, quite bowled over by what he'd seen. He clapped especially hard when Elyse stepped forward, at James' invitation, to take an individual bow. He'd thought her magnificent.

'Do we have to go backstage?' Minna queried as they made their way up the aisle.

'Of course, Ma. We've been invited.'

Outside on the pavement, to Tim's delight, they ran into Jeremiah and Katherine.

Tim hastily made the introductions, thinking how exquisite Katherine looked. They exchanged pleasantries, with Minna thanking Jeremiah for his gift to Tim, then chiding him slightly for having made it.

'I have my motorcar parked nearby. Can we give you a lift home?' Jeremiah offered gallantly.

'We're going backstage at the invitation of Mrs Davenport,' Tim replied.

'Ah!'

'She's a guest of ours at the boarding house,' Minna explained.

'I see.'

'Don't forget your promise to visit us again,' Katherine whispered to Tim as they were parting.

'I won't.'

'Charming people,' Minna commented when Jeremiah and Katherine were out of range.

'I like them.'

Minna glanced sideways at her son, having heard a special note of warmth in his voice. Now that was interesting! She'd have to find out more about the Coates family. Torquay being the size it was, that wouldn't be too difficult. She'd also thought it pleasant to meet someone who'd been a friend of her husband's.

Fred was the stage doorkeeper, who ruled his small domain with a rod of iron. He was small and gnomelike, with terrible teeth and a head that was almost bald. He was quite grotesque in appearance with the reputation of being something of a bully. He stared belligerently at them when Tim explained that they were there at the invitation of Mrs Davenport.

'She didn't say nothing about it to me,' Fred replied, folding his arms across his chest.

'Then please go and ask her. You'll find out it's all right.'

'Can't desert me post. Who knows who'd sneak by.'

'Damn,' Tim muttered to himself. He'd been so looking forward to this.

He tried arguing with the doorkeeper, but Fred was immovable. Unless he was informed, Tim and Minna couldn't go any further. Minna began to shift her feet in embarrassment.

She was just about to tell Tim that they should leave when Ronnie, the ASM, came hurrying up with a note, which he gave to Fred. Fred slowly read the note and scowled.

'It seems you're expected after all,' he growled, without a hint of apology in his voice. 'On you go then.'

'If you're the Wilsons, then I'll show you the way,' Ronnie declared brightly.

'Thank you,' Tim replied somewhat stiffly. He was furious with Fred. The man had been so unnecessarily rude.

'I presume the note was from Mrs Davenport?' Minna queried as they were led into a labyrinth of corridors.

'That's right. She meant to have a word with Fred when she arrived at the theatre, but clean forgot.'

'Well, no harm's done,' Minna replied, still slightly miffed. She wasn't used to being refused entry anywhere.

'People do try and get in, you know,' Ronnie explained. 'And that can lead to trouble. I appreciate that he's a bit of a monster, but Fred was only doing his duty.'

'A few manners and pleasantness wouldn't have gone amiss, though,' Minna muttered.

'Here we are,' Ronnie announced when they arrived at Elyse's dressing room, its door wide open and the sound of merriment coming from within.

Tim came up short in astonishment when he saw Elyse's face, this being the first time he'd ever come across full stage make-up. Everything was so thick and exaggerated that it positively screamed at you. She might have been a tart.

Elyse excused herself from the person she was talking to and came straight over. 'Welcome, both of you,' she gushed. 'I hope you didn't have any trouble with the dreadful Fred. My fault, but when I arrived earlier my mind was just full of other things.'

'We understand,' Minna answered courteously, glancing curiously around.

'We thought you were simply wonderful,' Tim smiled, still taken aback by the make-up.

'Why, thank you.'

'No, I mean it. Truly, truly wonderful. You were a revelation out there.'

'What a darling, sweet boy to say such things.'

Tim winced at being called a boy. How he hated that. But his mood changed instantly when Elyse kissed him on the cheek. 'Thank you.'

James Erskine, his face also heavily made up, joined them.

'Can I get you good folk something to drink?' he inquired. 'There's gin, whisky and wine. Take your pick.'

Elyse introduced them and Minna said she'd thought the play had gone terribly well, which clearly pleased James.

'Ma, what'll you have?' Tim asked.

'A glass of red wine, please.'

'And you, Tim?'

'A G and T, I think.' He ignored his mother's disapproving look. It was a party, after all.

'Come and meet everyone,' Elyse declared, hooking an arm round Minna's.

It was certainly a jolly occasion, Tim thought, as more introductions were made. He was fascinated by the woman who'd played Miss Trafalgar Gower – she'd looked so regal and grand onstage, and here she was standing with what smelt like a neat tumblerful of gin in her hand and a cigarette dangling from the corner of her mouth.

A few minutes later Mellon arrived positively bursting with *bonhomie*, his gestures being expansive in the extreme. His boyfriend Paul Arthur was with him.

'Congratulations! Congratulations, everyone!' he shouted, beaming round the company.

Tim would have been surprised to learn that the actors, without exception, disliked Mellon intensely. But then they were actors. Hands were shaken, backs slapped, with everyone thanking Mellon for his excellent directing. Even Elyse was effusive in her praise, though she couldn't stand the man.

Tim noticed the cards pinned above Elyse's dressing table and had a look at them, noting that they were from individual members of the cast, plus other names that meant nothing to him. He counted seventeen cards in all.

'And who are you, dear boy, if I may ask?'

Tim turned to discover that he was being addressed by a slightly drunk Mellon. He explained who he was and why he was there. He felt discomfited by the way Mellon was staring at him. It gave him the creeps.

Elyse suddenly materialised beside them. 'Don't waste your time, my darling,' she crooned to Mellon. 'The lad isn't trade.'

Trade? Tim wondered. What was she talking about?

'Pity,' a disappointed Mellon murmured, eyeing Tim up and down.

Elyse took Tim by the arm and whisked him away, declaring loudly that he must meet Percy Moxton, who'd played O'Dwyer, the part of the low comedian in the play and the character Tim had read while helping Elyse learn her lines.

'Did you understand what that was all about?' she whispered to Tim, who shook his head. 'Just as well perhaps.'

He was baffled. 'Come on, tell me.'

An amused Elyse gazed at him. 'Our friend Mellon prefers young men to the opposite sex.'

Tim went cold all over. Dear God, he thought, immediately glancing back at Mellon.

'Do you understand now?'

'Yes, of course,' he choked. 'What does "trade" mean?'

'It was my way of letting him know you're not of that disposition. That you aren't available.'

He swallowed hard. 'Thanks, Elyse.'

'It is the theatre, darling. There are lots of his kind in it. You get quite used to it after a while.'

He was suddenly aware of her perfume, which somehow seemed even more overpowering than usual. 'You must think me a naïve idiot.'

'Not at all. Now, why don't we have another drink? My glass is empty.'

'I'll get one for you,' Tim volunteered and made his way over to the temporary bar where anyone could help themselves.

On his return he saw a laughing James Erskine deep in conversation with Elyse. He prayed she hadn't been telling Erskine about him.

'Well,' sighed Tim as he and Minna left the theatre. 'What did you make of all that?'

'Not exactly my cup of tea, son. Those people were quite . . . bizarre. Though entertaining, I have to admit.'

Tim hadn't wanted to leave so soon, but Minna had insisted, reminding him that she had an early start in the morning. Enough was enough as far as she was concerned.

'What about you?' Minna queried.

He considered that. 'It was certainly different. Exciting in a way. Rather fun, really.'

'It was certainly different all right,' she agreed. 'I can't even begin to imagine what your father would have thought of them. He was quite conventional you know.'

'You mean prudish?'

'Not in the least, but definitely conventional. A gentleman through and through.'

Tim couldn't quite see what being a gentleman had to do with it. Though obviously it meant something to Minna.

'Let's stroll over to the esplanade railing for a minute,' Minna suggested.

'If you wish.'

When they reached the railing Minna stood staring out over the water, where the moon was reflected. 'How peaceful the bay is tonight,' she commented. 'So tranquil.'

Tim didn't answer that.

'I really should try and get out more often. It's just that the boarding house takes up so much time. There's always something else to do. Yet another task to be tackled.'

There was a wistfulness in her voice that disturbed Tim. With a shock he realised that she was still a relatively young woman, and good-looking too. Perhaps for the first time in his life he was seeing her as a woman and not merely as his mother.

'Can I ask you a question?' he inquired softly.

'Of course.'

'Have you ever considered remarrying?'

She turned to him in surprise, then brought her attention back to the bay.

'Ma?'

'Your father and I were too close for that to happen,' she answered finally, with a catch in her voice.

'He did die a long time ago.'

'That's got nothing to do with it.'

Tim drew in a deep breath. 'I'm sorry if I've upset you.'

She shot him a smile. 'You haven't. Not in the least. But it's one of those things that's difficult to explain.'

'Particularly to your son?' he teased.

She took his arm and pulled herself close to him. 'I suppose so.' She hesitated, then went on. 'What Redvers and I had together was very special. We were made for one another. It broke my heart when he died.'

'But would Pa have wanted you to be lonely for the

rest of your life? I don't believe so, from what you've told me about him and what I remember.'

What would Redvers have said, Minna wondered, he being a practical man after all? And she had to admit that she was lonely. Oh, not in the sense that she didn't have people around her – that certainly wasn't the case. She was surrounded by them, morning, noon and night.

Not at night, she corrected herself. Morning, noon and evening. The nights, when she closed her bedroom door, were something else. But another man? She just couldn't envisage it. Out of the question. Yes, most definitely out of the question.

'Ma?'

'Let's go home. I'm getting cold,' she declared, with finality in her tone.

Tim realised the subject was closed. When they next spoke it was of a different matter entirely.

Chapter 6

They were the first submarines Tim had ever seen and he thought them incredibly sinister. Black and sleek, three of them were in the Inner Harbour, where they'd docked late the previous night. Now it seemed that all Torquay had turned out to gape and marvel at them.

Tim had been despatched by Ricketts to get the story and had brought along a photographer. They'd do the photos first and then he'd try and interview someone connected with the subs. A captain would be best of all: otherwise one of the officers.

'Nasty-looking buggers, aren't they?' commented Ironmonger, the photographer. Tim enjoyed working with Ironmonger, for the pair of them got on well together.

'You can say that again.'

'Almost evil.'

Tim nodded. That was an appropriate word to describe them – evil. But not one that he could use in his report. They were British vessels after all, part of the Royal Navy.

Once the photographs had been taken, Tim sent Ironmonger back to the office to develop them while he went hunting for a suitable candidate to interview.

'Any chance of speaking to the captain?' Tim asked a lieutenant who'd just come ashore.

The lieutenant stared at him as though he was mad.

'Press,' Tim explained. 'The *Torquay Times*.'

The lieutenant brushed past him without answering and strode on his way.

'Charming,' Tim muttered.

There was a group of ratings unloading boxes from a lorry, to whom he posed the same question. The only reply he got was to be laughed at and told to sod off.

He began to realise this wasn't going to be easy. Normally the navy was cooperative, but not this lot, it would seem. He spotted another officer and hurried over.

'No interviews with anyone, old boy,' the officer informed him. 'Those are the orders. And quite specific they are, too.'

Tim's heart sank. 'I'm not trying to find out any official secrets. Just the usual: what you're doing in Torquay, how long you'll be here, any local chaps aboard. That sort of thing.'

The officer shook his head. 'Sorry.'

'Can you at least tell me the name of these ships?'

'Boats,' the officer corrected him. 'Submarines are boats. And I can't give you their names, which is why they've been painted out. Hush-hush.'

Well, their names might have been painted out, but they still had their numbers showing. Forty-five, forty-six and seventy-one. That shouldn't be too difficult to check. So at least he had that.

An hour later found Tim in a back-street pub where he'd located a group of off-duty ratings having a drink at the bar. He chose a spot close to them and ordered a pint.

Their accents were mixed, the hat bands blank, other

than the letters HM, so there were no clues there as to the names of the subs.

'How long are you lads in port for?' He smiled at a rating standing beside him.

The rating turned and studied Tim. 'Who wants to know?'

Tim held up a hand. 'Just being curious, that's all. Submarines are a bit of a novelty here.'

'Are they indeed,' the rating growled.

Not very friendly, Tim thought. 'Been to Torquay before?'

'Maybe.'

'Sailors usually like it here. I've heard many a one say how much he's enjoyed himself.'

The rating grunted and turned his back on Tim.

Ricketts would kill him if he didn't come back with a story, Tim thought despondently. It should have been straightforward, after all.

He waited a few minutes before trying to strike up a conversation with another of the ratings. He had no luck there either, this one being as tight-lipped as the first.

Then the group moved away to another part of the pub, giving him the distinct impression he was the reason they'd moved. He didn't fancy pursuing the subject any further with them.

He drank up and left, with the intention of trying to find other off-duty ratings who might be a bit more talkative.

He was passing the Café Addison's window when he spotted Katherine Coates inside, sitting with another young woman. She saw him too, smiled and beckoned him inside.

'Hello,' he said when he reached their table.

'We're just having coffee. Care to join us?'

'Yes, please,' he replied enthusiastically. This was an unexpected treat.

'Tim, this is Louise Youthed, a good and dear friend of mine. Louise, Tim Wilson, who works for the *Torquay Times*.'

Tim shook hands before sitting down. A plain girl, he thought of Louise, and rather plump. 'So what brings you into town?' he asked Katherine.

'The submarines of course. We came to look at them.'

Louise giggled. 'Tell him the truth, Ka – that was only an excuse to go shopping.'

Ka? Tim didn't like that. He much preferred Katherine.

'Well, I suppose that is the truth,' Katherine confessed with an impish grin that Tim found totally captivating. 'Not that we really need an excuse. We'd have come shopping anyway.'

A waitress came over and Tim ordered another pot of coffee. 'What have you bought so far?' he inquired of Katherine when the waitress had left them.

'Nothing so far.'

Louise giggled again. 'I've bought some underthings, but I can't say what.'

Tim regarded her with amusement. 'I see.'

'And what about you, Tim? Are you on a story?' Katherine queried.

He sighed and pulled a face. 'I am, but so far not doing very well.' He explained about trying to interview someone off the subs.

'I wonder why the secrecy?' she mused.

Tim shook his head. 'Search me. You'd think we were at war the way they're carrying on.'

Katherine's expression clouded. 'Papa was talking about that only the other day. He believes war isn't far off.'

Suddenly the mood round the table was sombre. 'Does he indeed,' Tim replied quietly.

'He's certain it has to come.'

'Between us and Germany?'

'Papa says everything's building up that way. When he was last on the Continent he was selling his interest in various companies over there. A prudent move, he called it. Taking his money out while he still can.'

'War would be horrendous,' Louise commented and shuddered.

'It doesn't bear thinking about,' Tim agreed, musing that a war between Britain and Germany would be a virtual clash of Titans. Which Britain would win, of course.

'It's a terrifying prospect,' Katherine said as Tim's coffee arrived.

'Shall I pour for you?' Louise offered.

'Please. That's kind.' He turned again to Katherine. 'It'll all probably come to nothing, mind you. There have been scares before, which have just fizzled out.'

'This time it's different, according to Papa. He's quite worried. And knowing him, he'd have to be to sell off well-paying investments. Don't forget, Papa has been over on the Continent a great deal in recent years so he knows the mood there.'

Christ, Tim thought, a combination of fear and excitement fluttering through him.

'Anyway, enough of that!' Katherine declared brightly. 'Let's talk about more cheery things. How are you getting on with your motorbike?'

Tim waxed lyrical about it.

* * *

Tim slumped onto a chair in front of a typewriter to write a story he didn't have. He'd tried, tried and tried again, but he hadn't been able to come up with anything, finally arriving at the bitter conclusion that it wasn't even worthwhile finding out the names of the submarines. Three unknown subs was how he'd describe them. At least that might add a bit of mystery.

'I've got a message for you,' Harry Nutbeam declared, strolling over.

'Oh?'

'Someone called Louise Youthed rang and said you've to contact Katherine as soon as possible. It's urgent.'

Tim frowned. What could this be about? He'd only spoken to her a few hours ago.

'She's at home waiting for you to get in touch,' Harry added.

Tim came to his feet. 'Thanks, Harry.'

'Sounds interesting,' Harry teased. 'Is she nice?'

'Ravishing.'

'Really?'

'A complete knockout.'

Harry gave a low whistle. 'You sly dog, you. Do I get to meet her?'

Tim laughed. 'Don't be stupid.'

'I thought as much.'

Tim made his way to the telephone boxes, remembering the number, so he didn't have to look it up. Katherine herself answered.

'I've only just got back to the office,' he explained.

'Have you had any luck with your story?'

'Nope. No-one's talking.'

She paused dramatically. 'Would you like a surprise?'

Now what was she up to? 'All right.'

'We've had a visitation from a cousin of mine.'

He couldn't see how that was a surprise. 'Very nice.'

'No, no, you don't understand. Jack's with the navy, currently serving as signals officer aboard the *Destroyer*, one of the three submarines.'

Tim caught his breath. 'Where is he now?'

'Taking tea with Mama and Papa.'

'Can I meet him?'

'You don't have to. I've already found out everything you'll want to know.'

'You have?' he replied incredulously.

'I've just said so, haven't I?'

Now that *was* a surprise. A wonderful one! He hurriedly grabbed his notepad and snatched up a pencil. 'I'm listening.'

'Right, here we go.'

Ricketts laid down Tim's article and frowned at him. 'You're certain of this?'

'Absolutely, sir.'

'Where did you get your information?'

Tim shook his head. 'I can't say. It's confidential.'

'Hmmh,' Ricketts mused. 'But you are one hundred per cent certain this information is correct?'

'One hundred per cent, Mr Ricketts.'

Ricketts glanced at the article again, which stated that HMS *Destroyer*, *Demetrius* and *Dreadful* were bound for Spithead, where they were to take part in a massive mobilisation as preparation for a possible forthcoming war. It certainly wasn't the article he'd been expecting. It was far, far better.

Ricketts nodded. 'Well done, Wilson. This will be our lead story in the next edition.'

Tim swelled with pride. 'Will I get a by-line, sir?'

'Oh, I think so,' Ricketts replied drolly.

'Thank you, sir.'

Ricketts knew he was taking a risk in publishing the story. If the operation was supposed to be secret, then the navy wasn't going to be best pleased that it had become public knowledge. Still, that was their problem. There had been no official communication on the matter, which absolved the newspaper as far as he was concerned. Someone, somewhere, had opened his mouth. He just hoped the powers that be didn't discover who.

'All right,' Ricketts said, waving a hand in dismissal.

Tim took a deep breath – strike while the iron is hot, he told himself. 'I was wondering, sir.'

'Yes?'

'You're aware I've bought a motorbike?'

Ricketts nodded slowly. 'I've noticed it parked outside.'

'Would it be possible for me to claim petrol on expenses? I do use it rather a lot to get around on. For the job, that is. It makes everything so much easier and quicker.'

Ricketts considered that. 'Petrol, eh?'

'Yes, sir.'

He tapped the paper that the article was written on. 'Did you use it in connection with this?'

'Oh yes, sir,' he lied. 'In fact, I might go as far as to say I probably wouldn't have got the information without it.'

Ricketts was normally tight-fisted where expenses were

concerned, knowing only too well how journalists would take advantage, given half a chance. But he was in a good mood, a benevolent one even. Tim's article was something of a coup and the lad should be rewarded.

'Fine,' he muttered.

Tim couldn't believe his luck. 'Thank you, sir.'

'Now get out of here before I change my mind.'

Tim scurried away.

'My editor was delighted, Katherine. I can't thank you enough,' Tim said into the telephone a little later.

'I'm only pleased to have been of help.'

'Oh, you were. Believe me, you were.'

'There's just one thing, Tim.'

'What's that?'

'You must never mention any of this in front of Mama and Papa. Papa especially. He'd be furious. When Jack confided in us about the mobilisation he never dreamt it would go any further.'

'I understand. You have my word on that.'

'I wouldn't want him to get into any trouble, after all. The navy is his career.'

'Trust me, Katherine, our conversation will remain strictly between you and me. My solemn oath on it.'

'Thank you, Tim,' she breathed.

'No, thank *you*. From the bottom of my heart. You've put me in my editor's good books, which is no mean achievement.'

A warm glow spread through Katherine to hear that and she could feel she was blushing. 'I hope I'll see you again soon.'

'We'll arrange something.'

'Till then, Tim.'

'Till then, Katherine.'

As he made his way back to the office it was as though he was walking on air.

'You're quite stuck on him, aren't you?' Louise teased when Katherine had hung up.

Katherine became slightly flustered. 'What makes you say that?'

'It's obvious. Why, just look at your face, it's gone all beetroot.'

Katherine smiled. 'Maybe I am a bit,' she confessed.

'More than a bit, I think. Is he the one?'

That made her frown. 'The one what?'

'The one who'll be the man in your life. Your true love?'

'Don't be ridiculous,' Katherine snapped. 'I hardly know him. We've only met a few times.'

'Even so,' Louise sighed, her eyes taking on a dreamy, faraway look. 'It might have been love at first sight.'

Her friend really was talking nonsense, Katherine thought. Love at first sight indeed! How preposterous. 'I like him, and let's just leave it at that.'

'If you say so.'

'I do.'

Katherine gathered herself together. They'd better get back to Mama and Papa, who'd be wondering where they were. Jack was staying to dinner so it would be rude to absent themselves for too long.

'Tim is rather dishy,' Louise commented coyly.

Katherine didn't reply to that. She thought so too.

'Well?'

'He certainly hasn't got a hump and warts on his nose, if that's what you mean.'

Louise laughed. 'Far from it. Lucky old you, Katherine Coates.'

Katherine frowned. 'Why?'

'Meeting someone so nice. I wish I could.'

Katherine put a hand on her friend's shoulder. 'You will. It's only a matter of time.'

Not if you're as fat as me, Louise thought grimly. Porky, the girls at school had called her. Loathsome creatures. It wasn't as though she ate a lot, for she didn't. She was big-boned, her mother said, just like her father. She'd have given anything to have a figure like Katherine's. Katherine's figure and face. For Louise was under no illusions about her own.

'Now, let's get back on through,' Katherine declared.

Louise decided to play up to cousin Jack, who was single. He'd be something of a catch for the likes of her.

Think positively, she told herself. Anything was possible, after all. Jack might like his women on the chunky side.

Elyse was in despair. Mellon was up to his usual tricks and rehearsals had been a shambles. One week gone and to date the play, Bernard Shaw's *You Never Can Tell*, was a mess.

James, bless him, kept reassuring her that it would all come right, just as it had with *Trelawny*, but she wasn't so sure. It was going to take a miracle, in her opinion.

Sunday again, her most unfavourite day of the week. Especially in the provinces, where it was all so horribly boring. She'd already gone over her lines and would do so again later. In the meantime she would write to Benny.

Not that she cared all that much how he was getting on – very nicely thank you, if she knew him – but she hungered for some news of town, and the West End in particular. What was happening, who was doing what. Was there any gossip?

She'd tell him how much better she was feeling since coming to Torquay, the air here doing her the world of good. She wasn't coughing half as much.

But before getting down to that she'd have another cigarette and think about just what she was going to say.

A smile twitched her lips. She musn't mention James, except perhaps in passing as a member of the company. Benny was no fool and would easily read between the lines if she wasn't careful. Any undue reference to a specific man would quickly be noted.

As for James, things were bubbling along rather nicely there, their friendship deepening with every passing day. But would she take their friendship any further? That was one question she hadn't yet resolved. Perhaps. Perhaps not.

What James had achieved, without so far laying a finger on her, was to engage her sexual interest. Very much so, if she was honest with herself. Old appetites, and memories, had been reawakened. Why, only the other night she'd had the most erotic dream about him. Erotic! Obscene more like. It had been lovely.

Damn it, thinking like that made her want a drink. Crossing to a chest of drawers, she opened it and took out a bottle of gin. She poured a large one, thought about putting the bottle away again and decided not to.

What was James doing? she wondered. He was probably as bored as she. They should have arranged to do something together, but she hadn't thought of it and he'd never suggested it.

More and more she was becoming curious about him. Was he good in bed? Could he take her to the heights, as Benny once had? What bliss that had been. Sheer utter, abandoned bliss.

She felt a prickling in her stomach and a melting sensation elsewhere. With a laugh she realised that if he'd been present she'd probably have dragged him into bed there and then.

She despatched the gin and poured herself another, this one smaller. She didn't want to turn up sozzled at dinner. That would never do. What would Major Sillitoe, the old lecher, think? More importantly, what would Mrs Wilson make of it!

God, she was bored. To utter distraction. She drew smoke deep down into her lungs and was about to exhale when she burst out coughing, her entire body racked with violent spasms.

'Bloody hell!' she gasped when she was able to draw breath again. She was aware that tears were streaming down her face, which meant that her make-up would be ruined.

Chest heaving, Elyse collapsed into a chair. Would there be more coughing or was that it? It transpired that the spasm was over.

That was the first bad one today, she thought. There had been a couple of little ones earlier, but nothing to worry her. That one had come from the very depths of her being.

Instead of stubbing out her cigarette, as she should have done, she took another puff. Stupid of course, but there you are. She did enjoy smoking, even if that awful cough was the result.

Benny, she reminded herself – she'd better get down to that letter, in which she'd insist that he reply. She did so want some news of what was going on. She positively ached for it.

Tim was riding past the promenade when he spotted Mrs Davenport coming towards him. On reaching her, he pulled over and stopped.

'Good morning,' he greeted her a little shyly.

She gazed admiringly at the Royal Enfield, the first time she'd seen it. 'I say, that's a beauty,' she declared.

He literally swelled with pride. 'Thank you.'

'It must be fun to ride.'

'Oh, it is.'

'And dangerous. You're very brave.' She smiled inwardly at the effect that had on him, just as she'd intended.

'You have to be careful, that's all.'

'Then I hope you are.'

He thought of his mother, who'd have had the vapours watching him careering along the lanes outside Torquay, the bike revved up to maximum speed. He always felt like a god when he did that.

'I'm just having my daily constitutional,' Elyse explained. 'Though I must say it is a bit nippy today.'

'It's the wind off the sea that makes it even colder. We locals are used to it. We just don't take any notice.'

Elyse rubbed her hands together. 'I'd better get on. I'm due back at rehearsal shortly.'

'Before you go I've something to tell you,' he said quickly as she moved off.

'Oh?'

'My editor has asked me to do the review on your next play. I'm looking forward to it.'

'Really!' she exclaimed. 'I do hope you're going to be kind to me.'

'I'm sure I won't have to be kind. You're bound to be wonderful, just as you were in *Trelawny*.'

'How sweet,' she smiled. She certainly had a fan here. She wished she could be so certain about her performance. Mellon was still making a right hash of things, and his direction and ideas were simply appalling. If she did manage to shine, it would be against all odds and a tribute to her own natural talent combined with years of experience.

Thank goodness for James: he was a rock, a veritable tower of strength. He and Mellon were constantly bickering and it couldn't be too long before one of them erupted and there was a showdown. When that happened she prayed James won. It would be a catastrophe if James pulled out of the remainder of the season. That would be horrendous.

'Perhaps I'll see you later,' Elyse said, meaning before she left to go to the theatre.

'Perhaps. I'm not sure what my movements are.'

'Remember to be careful,' she declared, nodding at the bike.

'I will. Don't worry.'

And with that Elyse swept on her way, the wind ruffling the fur collar of her coat.

Tim watched her go, thinking what a good-looking woman she was. She must have been quite something when she was younger, about Katherine's age.

And then he had an idea. Of course! He wanted to take Katherine out somewhere, and the opening night of the play was the perfect opportunity. The play first and a meal afterwards.

Nor should it be too expensive. He'd naturally have to pay for the meal, but the theatre tickets would be free, thanks to his being there to review the play on behalf of the *Times*.

He decided to ring Katherine when he returned to the office.

The weather had really taken a turn for the worse. Tim shivered as he waited outside the theatre for Katherine's arrival, while all around people were streaming into the foyer. It was going to be another full house, just as the previous opening had been.

Suddenly a large black car hissed to a halt in front of him. The driver's door opened and a liveried chauffeur got out, then helped Katherine onto the pavement.

'Hello,' she smiled.

'Hello.' He'd have been lying if he'd said he wasn't impressed by the car and chauffeur. He most certainly was.

'I'll be here when the curtain comes down,' the chauffeur stated to Katherine.

'Thank you, Edward.'

She took Tim by the arm. 'So, how are you?'

'Fine. And you?'

'The same.'

He paused to look at her. 'I'm glad you're here,' he murmured softly.

'And I'm glad to be here.'

There was nothing more to be said for the moment. Arm in arm, they followed the crowd inside.

Chapter 7

Tim waited till they were both settled in the back of the car and purring towards The Imperial, where he'd booked a table, before asking, 'So, what did you think?'

Katherine hesitated in replying.

'Go on,' he urged. 'Be truthful.'

She shrugged. 'It was awful.'

'Exactly what I thought.' Even Mrs Davenport had been disappointing, Tim having expected far more from her.

'In fact, to be blunt, it was downright tedious. Several times I almost found myself dropping off to sleep.'

He nodded his agreement. 'If that's Shaw, than I can't say he appeals to me. Clever, yes, but so wordy. Some of those speeches went on for ever.'

'And ever,' she added.

They both laughed.

'I'd convinced myself it would be so good, too,' Tim declared. 'Now I'm just worried it'll put a dampener on the rest of the evening.'

'It won't.'

'Are you sure?'

'Positive.'

'That's all right then,' he beamed, relieved.

'What will you say about it?'

'Oh, I'll give it a nice review. That's the paper's policy. But I'll be muted in my praise.'

He glanced down at her hand, wondering if he dared take hold of it. He decided not to – it would be too forward. For now anyway. 'Are you hungry?' he queried instead.

'Quite.'

'Me too.' He was actually ravenous, not having eaten anything since lunchtime. He had thought of grabbing a sandwich when he'd gone home to change, but had found himself too nervous to eat anything. He only hoped his nerves hadn't been obvious when they'd met up.

They arrived at The Imperial and made their way straight to the restaurant, where the maître d' showed them to their table. Once they'd sat down, he produced the wine list with a flourish and handed it to Tim.

Tim cleared his throat. He was no expert on wine – far from it, the names meaning nothing to him. 'Red or white?' he asked Katherine.

'White, I think.'

Tim peered again at the list, trying to make up his mind, somewhat frightened by the prices, which were far higher than he'd anticipated.

Katherine rightly guessed the reasons for his uncertainty, having been surprised in the first place when he'd suggested they go to The Imperial, the most expensive hotel and restaurant in Torquay. She decided a little help was needed.

'Papa comes here a lot,' she smiled, 'and always swears by the house wine.'

The maître d's eyebrows shot up on hearing that. Mr Coates never ordered house wine.

'Then that's what we'll have,' Tim declared enthusiastically, the house wine being by far the cheapest.

'A bottle of house white,' the maître d' nodded, taking the list from Tim and moving off.

Tim glanced about him. The walls were a pale-green colour, the curtains brocaded cream. There was a magnificent chandelier hanging in the centre of the room. The word that sprang to mind was opulent.

'This is the first time I've been here,' he confessed.

She'd guessed that also. Next time – if there was a next time – she'd choose the restaurant. 'Do you like it?'

'It's very grand.'

She also glanced about. 'I suppose so.'

'It isn't your first time, I take it?'

Katherine shook her head. 'Papa has brought me often. It's quite a favourite of his when he's at home.'

He thought she looked enchanting in the ankle-length burgundy-coloured dress she was wearing, which was made of silk-embroidered Canton crêpe. The sleeves were straight, ending at the elbow, and the neck rounded. He was horribly aware that his suit had seen better days.

'I still think of it as a treat, though. Very much so.'

That brightened him. 'Good.'

'Anyway, it wouldn't matter where we went. It's the company that counts. That's what's important.'

This brightened him even more. He was about to reply when they were interrupted by a waiter with the menu. They both fell to studying it.

* * *

'Oh dear me, look who's just come in,' Tim exclaimed softly a little later as they were starting on their main course. Katherine was having *papillote de saumon*, while Tim had plumped for an *escalope de volaille*. 'It's Mrs Davenport, with one of the actors, called Erskine, whom I met at her first-night party after *Trelawny*.'

'Ah!'

'What will I say to them if they speak to us?'

Katherine reached across and patted his hand. 'You'll do the gentlemanly thing and lie. Tell them they were wonderful. That's what they'll want to hear, after all.'

That made sense to Tim, who resolved that was what he'd do. The gentlemanly thing and lie.

Katherine glanced sideways at the couple, who thankfully were being shown to a table on the other side of the room.

'It was dreadful. The play, I mean,' Tim said quietly.

'Truly. I wonder if they realise it.'

He had no idea. Perhaps they didn't. He thought back to his conversation with Mrs Davenport on the promenade and of how enthusiastic he'd been about her forthcoming performance, which, it now transpired, had been a stinker. Still, she hadn't been alone in that. All the performances had been appalling.

'Tell me more about yourself,' Katherine proposed, changing the subject. She was keen to listen.

Elyse was fuming. It had been an unmitigated disaster, as she'd known all along it would be. All down to that idiot Mellon, whom she could happily have strangled. Thank God no-one from London would be seeing the production. Her reputation as an actress would have been in tatters.

She'd already had three large gins before leaving the theatre, and now ordered another.

'Try and calm down,' James advised when the maître d' had left them.

Her eyes blazed. 'Calm down! How can I, after that fiasco? It was so humiliating.'

James couldn't but agree. The play had died a terrible death, just as he and Elyse had predicted. In fact, it had been even worse than they'd imagined.

'Fat little nonce,' Elyse breathed. 'He couldn't direct a shite out of an arsehole.'

James smothered a laugh, thinking that hysterical. 'Steady on, you might be overheard.'

Elyse bit back a comment that she couldn't give a damn if she was. That would be embarrassing for both of them. 'Sorry,' she apologised.

'That's all right. I feel exactly the same.'

'It's just . . . well, something has to be done about that man. We can't go through the rest of the season with him continuing to muck things up. That would be a total nightmare.'

'I wonder what he'll say at tomorrow's post-mortem,' James mused. That was the meeting held to discuss the night before, after which they started rehearsals on the next play. Notes were usually given, comments made and sometimes stage 'business' rearranged.

'I wonder too. It would be just like him to think it all went well. Especially his direction.'

Was Mellon that much of a fool and self-delusionist? James wasn't sure.

Suddenly Elyse smiled at him. 'I honestly don't know

how I'd be able to put up with this, if you weren't here.'

'Thank you.'

When her gin and tonic arrived she had to force herself to sip it slowly. Despite James' presence, and a good amount of alcohol, the anger stayed with her.

'I don't intend leading a life of idleness, you know,' Katherine confided to Tim. 'I'm going to do something positive.' Having talked about Tim, they were now discussing her.

'Like what?'

'A job, for a start.'

He stared at her in astonishment. 'But why? You surely don't need the money. And it's hardly common for well-bred young ladies of your background to go out and work. Not the done thing at all.'

'Do you object?'

'Not in the least,' he replied hastily. In fact he admired her for wanting to do so. 'It's just unusual, that's all. People in your position mostly involve themselves in charities and suchlike.'

'Well, that's not enough for me. I want to contribute, not be a parasite on the back of society.'

Tim hadn't realised there was this side to Katherine. He was intrigued. 'You're not a Socialist, I hope?'

That shocked her. 'Good God, no! That would be going far too far. If anything, I'm a Liberal, just like Papa.'

'And does he know about this?'

Katherine gave Tim the most disarming of smiles. 'Not yet.'

'I see. What do you think his reaction will be when you tell him?'

'It's not Papa I have to worry about,' Katherine replied. 'He's quite modern and forward-thinking. It's Mama. She'll have a fit. And I mean, a fit.'

Tim sipped the last of his wine. The bottle was empty and he couldn't afford another. Or liqueurs, come to that. Katherine had only had a glass and a half, while he had drunk the rest.

'I won't envy you when the time comes,' Tim commiserated.

'Which won't be for some while yet. I have "the Season" in London to do first.'

Tim thought about Katherine's coming-out, not liking the idea one little bit. It was a meat market, in his opinion – the debs and suitable young blades all thrown together for the purpose of matchmaking. He realised he was jealous.

'What sort of work do you have in mind?' he asked.

'I don't know, I haven't decided. Nothing too outrageous, though. Father would never allow that. Something suitable, whatever that is.'

Tim found himself wondering what it would be like to kiss Katherine. Perhaps he'd get the chance when they said goodnight. He certainly wanted to. That and more.

'Why are you blushing?' she queried with a frown.

'Am I?'

'Yes, you are.'

He could hardly tell her about the pictures that had suddenly flashed through his mind. Pictures involving her. 'I'm not blushing,' he lied. 'I just find it hot in here.'

She gazed at him in concern. 'Do you want to leave?'

Much as he wanted to stay, it was getting late. And he

certainly didn't want to make a bad impression on her family by keeping her out until all hours. Besides, he had the office to go to in the morning.

'Maybe we should.'

Katherine hid her disappointment. But Tim was right. Jeremiah would be waiting up for her.

'All right then.'

Tim summoned the waiter to ask for the bill.

Tim woke wondering why he'd done so, then realised that he needed to go to the lavatory. He cursed as he swung himself out of bed and reached for his dressing gown.

Many people kept a pot under their bed but he hadn't done so in years, hating the things. When younger he'd had the bad habit of missing the pot in the dark and peeing on the floor, which hadn't gone down well with Minna.

He was halfway along the corridor when there was a sound from below – someone moving around, he realised, as he heard steps.

A few moments later Mrs Davenport lurched into view, coming up short when she saw his outline in the darkness. 'Who's that?' she queried in a whisper.

'Tim.'

'Thank God. Help me to my room, will you?'

When he got close to her he could smell the alcohol. She absolutely reeked of it. 'Are you all right?' he asked, also whispering.

'I'm pissed as a rat.'

It mortified him to hear a woman use such language. But then, he didn't know actresses. 'Come with me.'

On reaching her room he took her inside and switched

on the light. She blinked as he did so. 'Thank you,' she nodded.

'My pleasure.'

'Your ma wouldn't have been best pleased to see me in this state.'

He didn't reply, knowing that to be true. Minna kept a respectable house, as she was forever saying. Mrs Davenport would undoubtedly have been given her marching orders.

'Have a nightcap with me,' Elyse said in a no-nonsense tone, collapsing into her chair.

'It's too late.'

'Sod the time. I want another drink and we've already been through the business of letting a woman drink on her own.'

Tim sighed. 'I'll have to go to the lavatory first. That's where I was headed.'

'Then hurry up and come back.'

When he returned he found her unsteadily pouring two gins, with a cigarette dangling from her mouth. He watched fascinated as ash fell into one of the glasses.

Elyse handed him the glass without the ash and then fixed him with a beady stare. 'I suppose you're going to crucify us in your review?'

Tim shook his head. 'I thought it rather good, actually.'

She laughed. 'You're either lying or mad. It was bloody terrible. A travesty. And that includes me. I can't remember the last time I gave such a dreadful perf.'

He frowned. 'Perf?'

'Performance, ducky. Performance. That thing actors give onstage.'

'Well, I thought . . .' he began gallantly, then broke off. He'd promised Katherine he'd lie, but now, in the light of what Mrs Davenport had just said, he couldn't. His heart went out to her because she was so obviously upset. 'It wasn't very good,' he confessed.

Elyse gazed gloomily into her glass. 'It's all that bastard Mellon's fault. Remember, the stage director who eyed you up?'

Tim nodded, remembering only too well.

'Something will have to be done,' she muttered darkly. 'It'll just have to be.'

'Mrs Davenport, I . . .'

She held up a hand to interrupt him. 'Why don't you call me Elyse? That's far less formal.'

'Oh, but I can't!' he protested. 'Ma would give me a right flea in my ear if she heard me address a guest by his or her Christian name.'

Elyse winked conspiratorially. 'Then just do so when we're alone. How's that?'

She really was a quite extraordinary woman, he thought. 'All right then,' he agreed, albeit reluctantly.

She beamed at him. 'Good. Let me hear you say it.'

'Elyse.'

'And again.'

'Elyse,' he repeated.

'Besides, continually hearing you call me Mrs Davenport makes me feel so damned old.' She stared intently at him. 'As a matter of interest, how old do you think I am?'

Tim gulped. Oh God! 'I have no idea. I'm terrible at guessing ages.'

'Have a try, though,' she urged. 'I'm curious.'

He had a swallow of gin while he considered this. What he mustn't do was err on the wrong side. And the all-pervading smell of her perfume wasn't helping matters. It was most disturbing. 'I really can't say,' he prevaricated.

Elyse, who'd stubbed out her previous cigarette, now lit another. 'You're not getting off that easily. Have a go.'

Tim took a deep breath. This was awful. 'Thirty?' He was certain she was more than that.

A wry, cynical smile curved Elyse's lips upwards. 'You are a sweetie, Tim. You should have been one of those diplomatic johnnies.'

'Am I wrong?' he queried, feigning innocence.

'By quite a few years. Now try properly.'

'But I was!' he protested.

'Now you're lying again.'

'I am not.'

She laughed. 'I'm thirty-nine actually. And right at this moment feeling every last day of it.'

Thirty-nine? Yes, that would be about right. In the harshness of daylight he might have put her at even more. 'Well, I am surprised.'

Elyse knew she should shut up, send Tim on his way. But she wanted company. She finished off her drink. 'Get me another of these and I'll give you a real surprise.'

He crossed and took her glass, trying not to stare at her straining cleavage. Voluptuous, he thought. That was what she was. Voluptuous.

'Do you like the name Elyse?'

'Very much so. It has a lovely ring to it.'

'I thought so too when I chose it.'

Now that *did* surprise him. 'Chose it?'

'It's not my real name, but the one I chose for the stage. Same with Davenport. Can you keep a secret?'

'Of course.'

'No, I mean it. You mustn't tell anyone.'

'I won't, Elyse. You have my word.'

She accepted the fresh drink that he gave her. 'I was born Elsie Tubbs in Clerkenwell, one of the poorest areas of London. I was a right little ragamuffin as a child, with my arse hanging out my knickers most of the time.'

He stared at her in amazement. 'Elsie Tubbs?'

'Dead common, isn't it? Not a proper name for an actress at all. Elyse Davenport is, though. Far more glamorous.'

Tim didn't know what to reply to that.

'Elsie Tubbs,' she repeated and shook her head. 'I even hate the sound of it, being associated with so many bad memories.'

Tim still didn't reply.

'Bad memories of the worst kind. Do you know my father, the rotten swine, used to . . .' She stopped suddenly and shuddered. 'No, I can't tell you that. Only Benny knows and he would have killed my father, if he hadn't already been dead.'

Tim had absolutely no idea what she was on about. Something distressing obviously. 'Did he hit you?'

Elyse shook her head. 'Far worse than that.'

He still didn't understand.

'Just forget it, that's all.' Elyse took a deep breath and changed the subject. 'That was a pretty girl you were with tonight. Is she your lady friend?'

Tim flushed. 'Her name's Katherine and that's the first time we've been out together.'

'Was it a success?'

'I think so. Well, it certainly was for me.'

'Very pretty indeed.' Elyse wagged a finger at him. 'What I wasn't impressed with was you sneaking out of the restaurant without saying hello. There again, I presume you were embarrassed at having been to the play.'

'It was a disappointment,' he replied quietly.

'And your review?'

'A good one. That's the paper's policy.'

'Well, just do me a favour and don't mention me in it. I'd appreciate that.'

He nodded. 'I won't. That's a promise.'

Tiredness washed over Elyse. It had been a long day, and a trying one. 'Will you see this Katherine again?'

'I hope to.'

'Very pretty girl,' Elyse repeated and yawned.

Tim immediately set his drink aside. 'I must be going. Truly. I have an early start.'

'And here's me keeping you up and boring you into the bargain. I must apologise.'

'You haven't bored me, Elyse,' he stated warmly. 'I've enjoyed our chat. And the gin.'

She came to her feet swaying slightly. 'Goodnight then, Tim.'

'Goodnight, Elyse.'

'And remember, Elsie Tubbs from Clerkenwell is a secret.'

He smiled. 'It'll never pass my lips.'

She saw him to the door and then leant against it when he'd gone. What on earth had got into her, telling him what she had? Gin, of course, and her current state of mind. Damn that Mellon. Damn him to hell!

Elyse closed her eyes, wishing that James was with her. If he had been she'd have taken him to bed and cuddled him all night long. She'd have liked that. Very much so.

And why had she mentioned her father? Another bloody pervert. He'd died an excruciatingly painful death, which was exactly what he'd deserved.

Elyse began to cry.

'You'd better stop daydreaming. Ricketts has been looking your way.'

Tim snapped out of his reverie. 'Thanks, Harry.'

'Thinking about that girl you were out with last night?'

Tim nodded.

'I thought so. I take it all went well?'

'Oh yes,' Tim enthused.

'Like that, eh?'

'Like that,' Tim agreed.

'Jammy sod. Now get on with that review or Ricketts will be calling you over.'

As Tim started to type he thought again of their parting, when the car had drawn up outside The Berkeley. He'd wanted to kiss Katherine, desperately so, but had been horribly aware of Edward, the chauffeur. That had put him right off. The last thing they'd needed was an audience.

Next time, he promised himself. He'd definitely do it next time.

James had had enough. Erupting with fury, he jumped to his feet. 'It wasn't everyone else's fault, as you're trying to make out, but yours alone. You're by far and away the worst director I've ever worked with. The blame for last night's fucking fiasco lies squarely on your fat shoulders,' he raged at Mellon.

'How dare you speak to me like that,' Mellon spluttered.

'I'm only telling the truth. You're about as much of a director as I'm a bloody deep-sea diver. And I can't even swim!'

'I say!' Paul Arthur, Mellon's boyfriend, exclaimed.

'I'll have you sacked for this impertinence,' Mellon shouted at James.

'Then go ahead and sack me. You'll save me the humiliation of being in any more of your amateur productions.'

Mellon's eyes bulged, that being the ultimate insult. '*Amateur!*' he shrieked.

'And that's being kind to you.'

'You . . . you . . . bastard.'

Elyse knew she had to speak up in support of James. Actors rarely stuck their necks out where work was concerned, but this was an exception. 'Everything James says is right,' she declared. 'You're absolutely useless, Mellon.'

The stage director was positively quivering from head to toe, his face having gone a bright shade of red. If looks really could kill, then Elyse would have expired on the spot.

Without uttering another word, Mellon wheeled about and strode from the room.

'Oh dear,' sighed Percy Moxton, who'd played O'Dwyer in *Trelawny*. 'The shit just hit the proverbial fan.'

Elyse went into the green room where an anxious cast were all waiting. There was no sign of Mellon or Paul Arthur. After James had been interviewed by Mr Peacock, the managing director, she herself had been summoned.

'Well?' James demanded.

'He wants to see you again.'

'Does he indeed,' James replied grimly. Well, here it was – the sack, as threatened.

A thin-lipped, apprehensive Elyse watched him leave.

'I've spoken at length to Mrs Davenport,' Peacock declared when James was once more standing before him. 'You'll be relieved to hear that she corroborates your accusation of Mellon's total incompetence.'

James *was* relieved, though he still believed that he was about to cop it.

'I didn't mention it earlier, but I saw the play last night,' Peacock went on. 'And I have to admit it was terrible. To be honest, I was quite stunned by the sheer awfulness of it.'

James didn't reply to that.

'I fully intended speaking to Mellon today, but hadn't got round to it before he was banging on my door. Most unpleasant chap, I have to say. Behaved quite disgracefully. Tried to tell me my job.' Peacock paused, then added softly, 'That was a bad mistake on his part.'

James began to think he might not be given the sack after all.

Peacock sat back in his chair and studied James. Elyse had impressed him because of her West End experience. Surely she knew what was what. And something she'd mentioned had given him the idea. 'I understand you've done some directing yourself?'

'That's correct, sir.'

'In which case, would you fancy taking over here?'

The unexpectedness of that completely threw James. 'You mean, in place of Mellon?'

'Actor and stage director. I'm afraid there wouldn't be any

117

more money in it for you. There again, it would have its obvious advantages.'

James thought fast. The extra work didn't bother him – in fact he'd rather relish it. Pity about the money, though. He could see from Peacock's expression there was no arguing about that. 'I accept, sir.'

'Good,' Peacock nodded. 'That's settled then. When you get back downstairs ask the ASM to find Mellon and send him to me. After you've done that you can tell the company.'

Peacock started humming after James had gone. He'd not only fired, or was about to, the odious Mellon, but had replaced him and saved a wage into the bargain. He decided he had every right to be pleased with himself.

Elyse was the first to congratulate James when he made his announcement. She couldn't have been more delighted.

Chapter 8

'What's wrong with 'ee, girl? You're white as a sheet,' Cook demanded of Daisy.

'She's been like that all morning,' a concerned Euphemia declared.

Daisy smiled wanly at Cook. 'I just don't feel well. I'm sort of dizzy and . . .' With a gulp she grabbed hold of the table to steady herself.

'Go find Mrs Wilson,' Cook ordered Euphemia, who immediately ran from the kitchen. Cook went to Daisy and placed a hand on her brow.

'You're burning up,' she frowned.

'But I feel cold.'

'You sit here in the meantime till Mrs Wilson arrives and I'll make you a nice fresh cup of tea.' The kettle hadn't boiled before Minna appeared. 'The maid's definitely sickening for something,' Cook informed her.

'I'm sorry, Mrs Wilson,' Daisy apologised.

'There's no need to be sorry. If you've caught something, you've caught something and that's all there is to it.'

Minna also felt Daisy's brow, thinking the girl's temperature very high. 'When did this start?'

'Late last night. I sweated a lot in bed and couldn't sleep very well. I kept tossing and turning.'

'Hmmh,' Minna mused. 'Any other symptoms?'

'I feel cold all the time and my head's spinning.'

'Well, it's back to bed for you, child. And I'm sending for the doctor.'

'Oh, don't do that, Mrs Wilson,' Daisy protested. 'There's no need. Whatever it is will pass.'

'Maybe so, but we're having the doctor nonetheless.'

'The cost . . .'

'Let me worry about that,' Minna interrupted. 'Now, Euphemia, you run and fetch Dr Shackle while I take Daisy up to her room.'

'I can manage,' Daisy protested.

'You'll just do as you're told.'

'I'll bring you some tea shortly,' Cook promised, thinking that Daisy looked even worse than she'd realised.

Minna helped Daisy upstairs and into bed, throwing an extra quilt over her when the girl began shaking.

'It's influenza,' Dr Shackle announced gravely to Minna, having completed his examination. The pair of them were standing outside Daisy's room with the door shut.

Minna's expression became grim. Influenza was very serious. 'I see.'

'I've already given her a powder, which is all I can do, I'm afraid. The powder is to try and bring her temperature down. In the meantime she must remain in bed and drink as much water as she can.'

'I understand.'

'I'm going to leave you a few more powders, which you're

to give her at four-hourly intervals. And I'll be back later on this evening.'

'Thank you, Doctor.'

His expression was as grim as hers. 'I wish there was more I could do, but there isn't. We simply don't have a cure.'

Shackle heaved his black bag onto the banister and delved into it. 'These are the powders,' he declared, handing them to Minna.

'Thank you.'

'Now, how about you and everyone else here? Have there been any signs?'

'Not so far.'

'Good,' he nodded. 'To minimise the risk of infection only one person should attend to her. That person should ideally keep themselves apart from everyone else.'

Minna considered that. 'Without Daisy I'll be short-staffed as it is. We'll just have to take a chance.'

'As you wish. But make sure whoever sees to her washes their hands thoroughly every time they leave the bedroom.' Shackle sighed. 'This is the sixth case I've been called out to this week. I only pray we haven't got an epidemic in the town.'

Minna knew exactly what he meant by that. People died from influenza. In the last outbreak some years previously there had been four fatalities in Torquay alone.

'I'll show you out,' she volunteered.

Tim wondered why he couldn't focus properly on the copy he was trying to read. Then he realised his hands were shaking.

God, he was dry, he felt as though he could drink a whole pailful of water. And he was sweating, even though it wasn't particularly warm in the office.

He took a deep breath and tried to stop his hands shaking, to no avail. They continued to waver. He had to lie down, he thought. He just had to. But he couldn't. He'd go to the lavatory instead and sit there.

He was rising from his chair when it suddenly happened without warning. Vomit spewed from his mouth to go flying and spattering everywhere.

Ironmonger, the photographer, who was passing at that moment, yelled out as his trousers were splashed. Tim meanwhile was clutching onto the desk for dear life, convinced that he was going to pass out.

'What the hell's going on?' a furious Ricketts thundered.

Ironmonger, seeing the obviously poor state Tim was in, grasped him by the shoulders. 'Are you all right?'

'Ill. Feel terribly ill,' Tim managed to mumble, grimacing at the taste in his mouth.

Ricketts came striding over. 'Have you been drinking, Wilson?'

Tim stared at him, Ricketts' face hazy. 'No, sir.' He groaned and bent over, thinking he was going to vomit again.

'Whatever it is, he's no use to me here. Take him home,' Ricketts instructed Ironmonger, his voice softening a little.

'Thank you, sir,' Tim managed to say.

The walk back to The Berkeley, with Ironmonger supporting him all the way, was a nightmare. When he arrived Minna took one look at him and, after thanking the photographer, helped Tim to bed.

Euphemia was despatched for the doctor, who confirmed what Minna had feared. Tim too had influenza.

* * *

Elyse was tired but elated as she let herself into the front hall. The new production, a play called *The Black Cat*, was a huge success, entirely thanks to James' inspired direction.

What a change after Mellon, she thought. James was an even more talented stage director than actor. With him everything was just so easy. It couldn't have been more so.

She was about to go upstairs when she glimpsed Minna sitting in the dining room, slumped with her head in her hands, clearly in some sort of distress.

'Mrs Wilson?'

Minna glanced up through weary eyes to find Elyse staring at her. 'Oh, it's you,' she said.

'I don't want to intrude, but is there anything I can do?'

Minna shook her head.

There was a half-drunk cup of coffee in front of her and a pot of the same on the table. 'That looks good,' Elyse smiled.

'Would you care to join me?'

'Please.'

Elyse sat facing Minna and poured herself a cup. 'I don't wish to be rude, but you look pretty ghastly,' she commented sympathetically.

'Is it that obvious?'

'I'm afraid so.'

Minna sighed, and ran a hand over her face. 'I'm just so tired. I've hardly slept a wink in the last three nights.'

'Oh?'

Minna studied Elyse, wondering whether or not to confide in her. In the end she decided to, for despite being an actress, Elyse struck her as being a common-sense sort of woman. 'I've got Tim and Daisy both down with influenza.'

Elyse was immediately filled with concern. 'That's terrible.'

'I can tell you it's worrying me sick.'

'Has the doctor been?'

'Oh yes, but there's nothing he can do except give them powders to bring down their temperatures, which hasn't seemed to work for either of them.'

'I thought I hadn't seen Daisy around,' Elyse frowned. As for Tim, she hadn't seen him either, but had presumed he'd been busy at the newspaper.

'People die from influenza,' Minna said very softly.

'Yes. I do know.'

Minna's shoulders shook. 'I've already lost a husband. I couldn't bear losing Tim as well.'

Elyse's heart went out to her. 'And you've been staying up nights attending to them, I take it?'

'That's right. I towel them down every so often and give them water. They need lots of that.'

'Can't anyone else help?'

Minna made a face. 'Euphemia is only young and needs her sleep. Don't forget the two of us are doing the work of three.'

'And what about Cook?'

'She doesn't live in and has her own family. She's got her parents to look after when she's finished here. Besides, I can't expose either of them unnecessarily to the risk of infection. Though heaven knows, if I get it, they probably will as well. We might even be infected already for all I know.'

'I presume you haven't informed the other guests?'

'No, most of them are elderly. You can just imagine their reaction, should they find out. The elderly, according to Dr Shackle, are more likely to succumb than the young. At least Tim and Daisy have age on their side.'

Elyse produced her cigarettes. 'Do you mind?'

'Go ahead. There's no-one to complain at this hour.' Normally smoking was forbidden in the dining room, but there was always the exception to the rule. And it wouldn't bother Minna.

Elyse lit up while thinking about the situation. Clearly Minna was at the end of her tether and desperately needed sleep. 'I have a suggestion to make,' she stated quietly.

'Which is?'

'I'll keep an eye on the two of them for a few hours while you get your head down. If you go on like this without a break you'll collapse and then you'll be no good to anyone.'

Minna stared at Elyse in astonishment. 'I can't agree to that.'

'Why not?'

'Well, you're a guest here for a start.'

Elyse laughed. 'So what? That doesn't make any difference.'

'It does to me. I couldn't possibly impose.'

'It wouldn't be an imposition, I assure you. Let's just say it's one human being helping another. And I repeat, if you collapse you won't be any good to either of them.'

Minna knew Elyse to be right. Just a few hours would make all the difference. The very thought of bed made her ache inside and her eyelids droop.

'Really, Mrs Wilson, I insist. It won't be any trouble – we actors are used to late hours. In fact, in our business it's almost obligatory.' This wasn't quite true, though actors, especially after a performance, often didn't go to bed until the small hours, needing that time to unwind.

'Are you absolutely certain about this?' Minna queried.

'Absolutely.'

'Look in on them every half-hour to wipe their brows and give them water.'

'Leave it to me. I'll do what has to be done.'

Minna reached across and laid a hand over Elyse's. 'This is very kind of you. I'm terribly grateful. But it's also exposing you to infection.'

'You can't always play safe in life. I learnt that a long time ago. If I was the sort who played safe, I'd never have become an actor in the first place. Now, why don't you show me their rooms.'

Tim was delirious, his face awash with sweat. His eyes were open but seeing nothing. 'Water,' he croaked.

Elyse cradled him in an arm, then held the glass to his lips and allowed some water to trickle down his throat, being careful to make sure that he didn't choke. When she removed the arm, the sleeve of her dress was sodden.

This was her fifth visit of the night, and so far they'd all been the same. Tim was a very poorly young man.

Being delirious, he hadn't recognised her. Once he'd called her Ma, another time Katherine, the name of his girlfriend. His temperature was excruciatingly high.

'Water,' he croaked again, and she repeated the previous procedure.

When she'd dealt with him and settled him a little, she was about to move on to Daisy's room when a sudden unmistakable smell assailed her. Luckily she knew, from past observation, where the linen closet was.

'Come in!' Elyse called out when there was a rap on her door.

An agitated Minna appeared. 'It's seven o'clock. You shouldn't have let me sleep so long. That wasn't what we agreed.'

'How do you feel?'

'Much better, thanks.'

Elyse took a deep breath. It had been a long night. What she needed now was a bath and a couple of hours' sleep herself before getting ready for rehearsal. Fortunately she had a latish call.

Getting out of the chair she'd been sitting in, she yawned and stretched. 'Completely uneventful, Mrs Wilson.' Then she smiled. 'Except for one minor thing.'

Minna frowned. 'What was that?'

'Tim soiled his bed, so I had to change it. I've put his dirty linen along with the other dirty linen waiting to be washed.'

Minna gaped at her. 'You changed his bed?'

'And pyjamas. Those I found in a drawer. Well, I could hardly leave him like that, could I?'

Minna was quite lost for words.

'Don't forget, Mrs Wilson, I'm a married woman. Changing a man's bed and pyjamas hardly holds any terrors for me.'

'I suppose not,' Minna replied with a half-smile, beginning to see the funny side. 'Tim will be beside himself with embarrassment if he ever finds out.'

'Then he mustn't. It'll be our little secret, eh? As will be the fact that I looked after him. Best that way, wouldn't you say?'

'By far,' Minna agreed.

Minna was impressed by Elyse. Very much so. She was a woman after her own heart.

Elyse had asked Fred, the stage doorkeeper, he being a local, if there was such a thing in Torquay, and he'd informed her that there was, giving her an address at the top of Union Street. He'd thanked her profusely for the shilling she'd tipped him.

After speaking to Fred, she'd had a word with James, who'd agreed to rejig some of the rehearsals so that she could have time off. He'd been most sympathetic when she'd explained the situation.

Now here she was in front of a shop with HERBALIST painted in large letters above the door. She had a look in the window before going inside.

'An old Irish tinkers' mixture?' Minna frowned.

'They used to swear by this. And I know for certain that it worked for a neighbour of ours when he was given it.'

'I don't know,' Minna prevaricated.

'Herbal cures have been around for centuries, Mrs Wilson, and there's no-one better at them than Irish tinkers and gypsies. They're past masters of the art.'

Mrs Davenport was certainly full of surprises, Minna thought. First last night, and now this. 'How do you come to know Irish tinkers anyway?' she queried.

Elyse laughed. 'Actors meet all sorts. You'd be positively

amazed at some of the people I've come into contact with.' What Elyse didn't say was that these particular Irish tinkers, ex-tinkers actually, had lived next door in Clerkenwell.

Elyse could see the uncertainty on Minna's face. 'Look at it this way, it certainly won't do any harm. So surely it's worth a try?'

Minna made up her mind. To her utter despair neither Tim nor Daisy was improving – if anything Tim was even worse than he'd been the previous day. She knew Dr Shackle was extremely concerned about the pair of them. And she'd found out earlier that someone in Torquay had now died of influenza.

'Then we will,' she declared bravely.

'I'll have to make it up. Can I use the kitchen?'

'Of course.'

Cook wasn't best pleased when Minna announced that Elyse was going to be using what she saw as strictly her domain. The thought of another person fiddling about there was most upsetting.

Elyse guessed what was bothering her. 'Perhaps you could help me, Cook? In fact, I can show you how this is done for future reference.'

Cook brightened a little at that. 'What does 'ee need?'

'Hot water for a start. Then a middling-sized bowl and a wooden spoon.'

Cook bustled off to collect these.

'Can I watch? I'm curious,' Minna requested.

'Certainly.' Elyse placed the paper bag she'd brought from the herbalist's on top of a work surface and started taking out the contents, seven items in all. She'd already gone over in her mind the correct proportions of each. It was many years since she'd learnt this, but thanks to her actor's memory she could recall quite clearly exactly what had to be done.

Cook returned with a white bowl and a wooden spoon and set them beside the ingredients. 'Water won't be long,' she informed Elyse.

'Thank you.'

'What's that?' Cook queried, pointing at what appeared to be a gnarled black root.

Elyse smiled at her. 'Mandrake.'

Cook's eyebrows shot up. 'That's poison, Mrs Wilson! *Deadly poison.*'

'You're quite right,' Elyse said quickly. 'But I shan't be killing anyone with it today. Once mixed in with the other things, the poisonous aspect of the root is nullified and only its beneficial qualities remain.' She hoped she was sounding reassuring, for what she'd just said was tosh.

Minna swallowed hard, wondering if she'd made a mistake in allowing this.

'There!' Elyse declared eventually when the preparation was complete. 'We're done. All I need now are two glasses.'

Cook provided those, with Elyse carefully tipping a measure into each. 'If this works I'll write down the recipe for you,' she said to Cook.

Cook immediately shot Minna a warning glance that said: don't tell her I can't read. Minna understood. She wouldn't have let on anyway, knowing only too well how sensitive Cook was on the subject.

'If you take one glass, Mrs Wilson, I'll take the other and we'll go upstairs.'

When the dose had been administered to both patients Elyse said that she'd have to get back to the theatre, informing

Minna she'd made enough for several doses and that they'd administer the second one that night when she returned.

'Don't worry. It can't do any harm, I promise you,' she said to Minna, again trying to reassure her.

All Minna could think of was the mandrake. A deadly poison, as Cook had pointed out.

'So how are the patients?' James asked when Elyse re-appeared at rehearsal.

'Very ill indeed. I'm only praying my concoction helps.'

'I'm sure it will.'

'Let's hope so.'

'I was wondering if you'd care to go out for some supper after the show tonight?' James smiled.

'I'd love to, honestly I would. But no. Remember I was up all last night.'

He'd forgotten that. 'Another time then?'

'Most definitely. I'll be looking forward to it.'

He stopped himself touching her as there were other cast members present, but wondered how long it would be before she gave in to him. For he knew she would. It was only a matter of time. And patience on his part.

He could wait.

'See for yourself – no change,' Minna said, as she and Elyse stood beside Tim's bed.

Elyse bit back her disappointment. Tim was still deliri-ous and Minna had told her on the way upstairs that he'd been thrashing about earlier. Hardly a sign of recovery.

'Let's get this mixture down him,' Elyse replied, which they managed to do between the pair of them. 'Here's what

I propose,' she declared when that was done. 'We'll split the night into two shifts. I'll do the first, you the second.'

'But you must be dead beat,' Minna protested. 'You only had a couple of hours this morning.'

'I'll cope, don't fear. And I'd rather do the first shift, as it will be easier for me just to keep on going. Anyway, I have lines to learn. So, is that agreed?'

'Now I am imposing,' Minna replied quietly.

'Nothing of the sort. It's my choice.' She heaved a sigh. 'If we're finished here let's go on through to Daisy.'

A clock was chiming 3 a.m. as Elyse let herself into Tim's bedroom. She helped him to some water and then mopped him down with a towel. Not that it did him much good for, with the sweat running off him in rivulets, he was sodden again within seconds.

Then a bulge in the bedclothes caught her eye, making her smile. If Tim was dreaming there must be a woman involved. She wondered who.

She couldn't help but notice when she'd changed his pyjamas what a big lad he was – considerably more so than Benny. Not that that sort of thing mattered, of course: at least she didn't believe it did, but it had been interesting.

She briefly toyed with the idea of having a quick peek, just for curiosity's sake, but decided not to. It would be undignified on both their parts.

Despite the gravity of the situation she found herself smiling again as she left the room.

'Mrs Davenport!'

Elyse came groggily awake to the insistent knocking on

her door. The voice was Minna's. 'Come in, Mrs Wilson.'

A flushed and excited Minna appeared carrying a cup of tea. 'I couldn't wait any longer to tell you. Both Tim and Daisy have taken a huge turn for the better. They're definitely on the mend.'

'Thank God,' Elyse breathed.

'I can't thank you enough, Mrs Davenport. Truly I can't. I've been out of my mind with worry.'

That had been obvious, Elyse thought. 'Is Tim talking?'

'Oh yes. Though he's still very weak. He can't remember anything of the past few days.'

Minna placed the tea on Elyse's bedside table. 'Take your time about coming down and there'll be an extra-nice breakfast waiting for you when you do.'

Elyse glanced at her alarm clock. She had two and a half hours before rehearsal, having another late call. 'All's well that ends well, eh?' she smiled.

'I must admit I doubted that magic potion of yours, but it's done the trick.'

Elyse shrugged. 'There was nothing magic about it. Simply a herbal cure, that's all.'

'Whatever, it worked, which is all I care about. If Tim had died . . .' Minna trailed off, a stricken expression on her face.

'I know,' Elyse murmured sympathetically.

'As agreed, I won't mention your part in this. Although I will tell both Tim and Daisy that it was your cure we have to thank.'

'If you wish, but it's really not necessary. I'm only pleased I was able to help.'

'Nonsense, you must get the credit. No doubt they'll both

want a word with you when I explain things to them.'

'But only *some* things,' Elyse replied with a conspiratorial wink.

Minna laughed. 'It would almost be worth telling Tim that you changed his pyjamas just to see his face.'

'Undoubtedly.' He'd be even more mortified if he knew about the bulge in the bedclothes earlier that morning and that she'd been witness to it. Or if he'd known what had run through her mind when she'd been thinking about it afterwards. So too would Minna, come to that.

'I simply can't thank you enough, Mrs Davenport.'

Elyse reached for her tea, intending to have a cigarette the moment Minna was out of the room. Disgusting to have one first thing, but it was the one she enjoyed most.

'I'll leave you to it then,' Minna declared.

'I'll be down after my bath and getting dressed.'

Eyes sparkling and with a spring in her step, Minna left, closing the door quietly behind her.

What a relief, Elyse thought. And how lucky she'd not only remembered the cure but the ingredients that went into it.

Now the crisis was over she could concentrate fully again on rehearsals. There was a lot to think about – more than enough – the play being a complicated piece.

She reached for her cigarettes and the ashtray alongside them.

Chapter 9

'I'm sorry you've been ill,' Katherine sympathised. 'I had no idea.' She and Tim were in the Café Addison, where they'd arranged to meet for coffee. Tim had been there first and she'd just arrived, Tim having told her the news over the telephone.

He was sitting drinking her in, thinking how gorgeous she looked. 'There's no reason why you should have known.'

He was so pale, she thought. So very pale and wan. There were dark smudges under his eyes and he'd definitely lost weight. 'Was it awful?'

'Pretty bad, I have to admit. Ma was convinced she was going to lose me.' He didn't want to be melodramatic, but that was true enough. 'And she might have done too, if it hadn't been for Mrs Davenport.'

Katherine frowned. 'How so?'

Tim explained about the Irish tinkers' cure and how it had worked wonders for both him and Daisy. 'I'm ever so grateful to her.'

'I can understand that.'

'But I'm better now, that's the main thing,' he declared heartily.

'Is this the first time you've been out of the house since it happened?'

He nodded.

'Then I'm jolly flattered.'

'The doctor says I've to take another week off work and then go back. I should be fully recovered by then.'

'Let's hope so.'

'Our doctor was most impressed by what happened and is using the tinkers' cure on other patients who've come down with influenza,' he informed her.

'That's good. There are three people in town who've died from it now. Did you know that?'

'Yes, I'd heard,' he acknowledged.

'It's horrible.' Her eyes opened wide. 'I pray I don't get it.'

'If you do, I'll be straight over to Oaklands with the magic cure, as Ma calls it.'

Katherine had wondered why Tim hadn't been in touch and had come to the conclusion that he was either busy or had lost interest. She'd wanted to contact him but of course couldn't – that wouldn't have been at all ladylike. And all the time he'd been ill. At death's door! Anyway, here they were now. She was so pleased he hadn't lost interest, for she certainly hadn't in him.

'How would you feel about going with me to the bioscope that's newly opened?' he proposed. 'That's a picture house called The Electric Theatre.'

Her face fell. 'Oh Tim, I'd love to, but I can't. I shall be in London.'

'London! Whatever for?'

'It's something we do every year. Papa attends to some

business there while Mama and I go shopping. We also usually take in a few shows and concerts.'

He was bitterly disappointed. 'How long are you away for?'

'A month.'

'A . . .' He broke off in confusion. Not to see her for a whole month!

'I'm ever so sorry,' she said softly.

Tim took a deep breath, trying to come to terms with this bombshell. 'Perhaps when you get back?'

'Of course.'

Well, that was something. 'Where will you be staying?'

'At The Savoy in the Strand. It's so central for everything.'

'Yes, it would be.'

Katherine made a face, his disappointment being all too obvious. 'It'll pass quickly. I'll be home again before you know it.'

Hardly, he thought. 'When do you leave?'

'The day after tomorrow. We shall be going up by motorcar. Papa prefers that.'

'I see. So this is the last time we'll be together for quite a while.'

'I'm afraid so.'

Hell and damnation, he raged inwardly. 'Lucky I rang when I did, otherwise I'd have missed you.'

They were interrupted at that point by the waitress. Tim ordered coffee for two and a plate of cakes. He stared morosely at Katherine when the waitress had gone.

'We could write?' she suggested, thinking that her parents surely couldn't object to that. Jeremiah had taken a great liking to Tim.

That cheered him up a little. 'I certainly will, if you will.'

'Then that's what we'll do.'

'Right then.'

They stayed in the café for well over an hour before Katherine declared that she had to leave, being expected back at Oaklands for lunch.

His heart was in his boots as he watched her being driven off by Edward, the chauffeur.

He'd write his first letter at the weekend, he decided.

It was in the middle of act two that Elyse suddenly dried. Her mind went blank and for the life of her she couldn't think what came next.

She turned and walked slowly in the direction of the prompt corner, expecting to see the DSM, or deputy stage manager, which should have been the case, but instead it was Ronnie standing in temporarily for the DSM, who'd been called away urgently.

Ronnie, realising that she'd dried, stared at her with frightened eyes, before hurriedly scanning the book, which consisted not only of the text but of stage directions and all the cues, lighting, sound effects and so on. He was in a complete panic, never having done this before.

Elyse swore to herself, wondering whether to ad lib or wait for the prompt. The silence seemed to stretch on for ever, although in reality it was only a handful of seconds.

Then Ronnie, totally flustered, dropped the book, and loose pages, plus additional sheets of instructions, were flying everywhere. Elyse would have laughed if she hadn't been so bloody furious with both herself and Ronnie.

James, who was also in the scene, took command. Expertly, and with the audience quite unaware of what was going on, he fed Elyse lines that brought her back to where she should have been.

One line in particular snapped her memory into place and she was away again.

The audience remained oblivious.

When the curtain closed for the interval James sought out Elyse, who'd come off before him, in her dressing room. 'What happened to you?' he asked amiably.

She shook her head. 'I don't know. I just went blank.'

'It happens to the best of us,' he commiserated.

She went to him and lightly grasped his arm. 'Thank you for getting me out of it.'

'You'd have done the same for me,' he replied softly.

'Nonetheless, I feel such an idiot. And that fool Ronnie didn't help. The stupid little bugger.'

James laughed. 'Don't be too hard on him. We all have to learn.'

'But he dropped the bloody book. Really!'

'To quote the next play we're going to do, "What's done is done and cannot be undone".'

That made her smile. 'Ah yes, the Scottish play.' Actors never mentioned the name *Macbeth* backstage as it was considered terribly unlucky. To do so was to invite disaster.

'Will you be all right for the next act?' he queried.

'Of course. I'm absolutely fine now. I simply have no idea why that happened. Most unlike me.'

He regarded her speculatively. 'Do you like omelettes?'

The total change of subject surprised her. 'Very much so.'

'Well, I do a particularly nice cheese-and-onion version. Light and fluffy, it just melts in your mouth.'

She was intrigued. 'Sounds delicious.'

'I, eh . . .' He paused and cleared his throat. 'I shall be making myself one after the show. Would you care to join me and sample my culinary expertise? I should also mention that I have in several bottles of not-bad claret.'

Elyse was frowning. 'You mean, back at your digs? What would your landlady say?'

'Ahhh!' he breathed, a twinkle in his eye. 'She wouldn't say anything because I haven't got a landlady. I've managed to rent a small house, nothing grand but adequate for the season.'

She knew exactly what this was leading to. 'By yourself, I take it?'

'You take it correctly, Elyse. There's only myself in residence.'

She turned away so that he couldn't read her expression. There was a lot more than an omelette and claret on offer here.

'Well?' he prompted softly.

She'd been considering this for some time. Would she or wouldn't she? There was absolutely no point in going with him if she wouldn't. That wasn't fair.

'It sounds lovely,' she answered at last.

He nodded. 'Good.'

'Now you'd better go, James,' she declared, suddenly businesslike. 'I have a costume change.'

He was smiling in anticipation as he closed the door behind him.

'Are you ready?'

'I just need a few more minutes.'

'Take your time. There's no hurry.'

Elyse fiddled with her hair, then dabbed on a smidgen more face powder. This was her last chance to change her mind, she thought. Unless she begged off now, she was committed.

She closed her eyes for a brief second, thinking of Benny and the love she'd once had for him. Well, that love was gone, there was no doubt about that. She might still be married, but in name only. And for years now Benny had had affairs all over the place, so why shouldn't she indulge? James had rekindled feelings and emotions in her that had long lain dormant. Slowly at first, but emerging more and more as time had passed and she'd come to know him better.

No, she was ready all right. And not just ready to leave the building.

The house was indeed small, poky even, and the furniture old and somewhat dilapidated. The carpet had certainly seen better days.

'So what do you think?' James asked wryly.

'It has . . . atmosphere.'

He laughed. 'Oh, it certainly has that. But it's quiet and peaceful, which suits me. I did consider sharing, to cut back on the expense, but decided against it. I'm used to being on my own and would hate to be tripping over someone else. I'm afraid I'm one of those rather neat and tidy sods – everything in its place, if you know what I mean. Bit of an old woman really.'

She stared at him, admiring his frank admission. 'Perhaps you've been a bachelor too long?'

He recognised that as a jibe, though one kindly meant. 'Probably.'

141

'I'm terrible round the house myself,' she confessed. 'Quite messy actually.'

He pulled a face. 'I don't believe that.'

'It's true. Why, does that disillusion you of me?'

'Oh no,' he replied softly. 'Not in the least. Anyway, I only invited you for a meal, not to move in.'

'I'm pleased to hear it. Think of the scandal it would cause if I was to. Tongues would wag furiously.'

He busied himself with a corkscrew. 'Why don't you sit down?'

'After you tell me where I can find an ashtray.'

The cork left the bottle with a satisfying plop. 'Don't have such a thing. We'll have to improvise. Give me a second and I'll get you a saucer. That'll have to do.'

Not for the first time she noted that he had a lovely bottom. The thought of it naked sent shivers coursing up and down her spine. Before long she'd find out all the things she'd ever wondered about James Erskine.

She tore her eyes, and her imagination, away from his back view and gazed about the room, which was lit by gas and mantle as opposed to electric, with the light shining from the mantle in a soft yellow glow that made the room look very homely.

'Shall we have a toast?' he asked, handing her a glass.

'If you wish.'

'Then what shall we toast to?'

She considered that.

'May I make a suggestion?' he went on.

'Go ahead.'

'How about, to us?'

There it was. His move. What happened next depended

on what she answered. She didn't hesitate. 'To *us*, James.'

He had a sip of wine, then laid his glass aside. Taking hers, he did the same.

She closed her eyes as an arm curled round her waist and his lips bore down on hers.

If she'd been a cat she'd have mewed with contentment. It had been so very long since she'd last felt like this. It was sheer, unadulterated bliss.

'A penny for them?'

She turned onto her side and smiled at him. 'I was just thinking how good that was.'

'For me too.' He traced an imaginary line along the length of her thigh. It had surprised and delighted him how passionate she'd been. There had been moments when he'd thought he was being consumed in a red-hot furnace. There was nothing whatsoever passive about Elyse Davenport. He'd liked that. In fact he'd liked it a lot. He disliked lovers who let you do all the work, content merely to lie there and receive without giving in return. Boring.

She grunted as a finger slid home, her smile widening as he began to gently massage her there. 'You are a glutton for punishment,' she breathed.

'Am I?'

'Oh yes,' she replied, her voice now a croak. She'd thought she was done, spent. But maybe not.

James leant across and kissed the swell of a breast. He was hungry, starving actually, but wouldn't be cooking yet. Not quite yet.

Elyse's breath started to come in short, sharp gasps.

* * *

Elyse let herself in as quietly as possible, easing the lock shut with the minimum of noise. She'd fully intended getting back earlier, before there was any possibility of the household getting up, but James, on hearing her stir, had other ideas. She was positively glowing from a surfeit of lovemaking.

She was gliding silently past Minna's parlour when its door opened and suddenly Minna was there. Damn, she thought. What now? This was precisely what she'd hoped to avoid.

Minna stared at Elyse in astonishment, taking in the fact that Elyse was still wearing the same clothes that she'd left in for the theatre.

'Good morning, Mrs Wilson,' Elyse smiled.

'Good morning, Mrs Davenport.'

'I've just been out for an early-morning walk,' Elyse lied glibly.

'Oh?'

'I had an awful headache and thought a stroll might clear my head.'

Minna kept a straight face. 'And has it?'

'Yes, I'm happy to say.'

What should she do? Minna wondered. Challenge such an obvious falsehood or pretend to be taken in by it? If it had been any other female guest . . . But Elyse was hardly that. She was the woman who'd saved Tim's life, for which Elyse had Minna's eternal gratitude. If Elyse had been out all night – and Minna could only think of one reason why – then that was her business.

'Shall we expect you for breakfast or will you be catching up on your sleep?' she queried in a neutral tone of voice.

'I'll be down.'

Without uttering another word Minna strode away, leaving Elyse staring after her.

She'd have to be far more careful in future, she told herself. For she fully intended paying further visits to James' house.

She smiled in memory of what had taken place there. The belief that you had to die to go to paradise was quite mistaken. As she could bear testimony to.

Elyse began to hum as she made her way upstairs. That had been a night to remember. A truly spectacular night.

And she'd been right about his bottom. The male variety didn't come any sexier.

'I don't think I approve, dear,' Ruth Coates declared to Jeremiah, who was engrossed in his newspaper. This was their fifth day in London, where they'd taken up residence in a suite at The Savoy.

He blinked. 'Pardon?'

'I said I don't think I approve.'

He couldn't for the life of him imagine to what she was referring. 'I'm not with you?'

'It's Katherine. I popped in on her a little while ago and discovered her writing a letter to that boy back in Torquay. You know, the one you so kindly gave the motorbike to.'

'You mean Tim Wilson?'

'The very chap.'

'And she was writing to him, you say?'

Ruth nodded.

Jeremiah laid his paper aside. A glance at the clock on the mantelpiece informed him that they should be leaving fairly soon, having booked seats for a musical revue he'd heard terribly good reports about. 'Is there something wrong with that? He's an awfully nice lad, after all.'

Ruth sighed. Honestly, men could be so dense at times. They had an irritating habit of not seeing what was right under their noses. 'I don't disagree,' she replied. 'But I wouldn't want their friendship to develop. He's quite unsuitable.'

Jeremiah frowned, still not understanding. 'In what way is he unsuitable?'

'The family may have been of good standing once, but that was before his father died. His mother now runs a boarding house, for goodness' sake.'

So that was it, Jeremiah thought grimly. Snobbery. He loved his wife, but was only too well aware of her faults, and snobbery was most certainly one of them. It wasn't a side of her he admired. Quite the contrary.

'Tim can't help that,' he replied slowly. 'What was the woman supposed to do, left almost penniless as she was and with a child to bring up? Starve?'

'Of course not. Don't be ridiculous!'

'Well then?'

She glared at him. 'You're being most obtuse, Jeremiah, completely missing the point altogether.'

'Which is?'

'As things are, he's simply not good enough for Katherine. It would be a most unsatisfactory match – not at all what I have in mind for her.'

Jeremiah was both cross and amused at the same time. 'Ruth, they're only corresponding. Don't you think you're reading far too much into that?'

'Perhaps,' she conceded. 'But it's not a relationship I wish to encourage. Little acorns, you know. Little acorns.'

'And what exactly do you have in mind?' he queried, trying to be patient.

'Someone she'll meet during the Season next year. A title maybe. Now that would be ideal.'

Jeremiah shrugged. 'If she did meet such a person and fall in love, and he with her, all well and good. I certainly wouldn't have any objections as long as Katherine was happy. That's all that counts.'

'There then!' Ruth acknowledged with satisfaction. 'We're agreed.'

'Oh, are we indeed?' he replied drily, thinking that if he was quick about it he could still get down to the bar for a drink before they left. And heaven knows, he needed one after this conversation. 'I wouldn't exactly say so.'

Her smug self-righteousness vanished. 'Why not?'

'We're only partially agreed. I think Katherine should be allowed to choose her own friends. Not have them specially picked and selected by us.'

'Nonsense! Of course they should be. It's how these matters have always been conducted.'

'Then perhaps it's high time they were conducted differently. This is the twentieth century, after all.'

'And you're being anarchic,' she snapped back.

He laughed. 'Anarchic! You make me sound like one of those political lunatics who sneaks around wearing a long black cloak and carrying a bomb.'

'You know what I mean,' she declared hotly.

Yes, he did, only too well. 'I still say you're jumping the gun. If Katherine chooses to write to that young man, then so be it. It's her decision. God Almighty, a few letters is hardly a life-long commitment.'

That further infuriated Ruth. 'I repeat, these things should be nipped in the bud before they have a chance to develop.'

Jeremiah had had enough of this claptrap. 'She's my daughter and as such can do as she wishes. Within reason, that is. You're not to do anything to her about corresponding with Tim, or say that you disapprove of him because he and his family are poor. Poor by our standards, that is. Do you understand?'

Ruth knew they'd reached an impasse. For now anyway. 'I understand, Jeremiah.'

He came to his feet. 'Good. I'm going out and shall return in twenty minutes when I expect you to be ready.' And with that he left her.

Ruth snorted. There were occasions when Jeremiah could be impossible. Honestly, where did he get his ideas from?

Katherine would have the sort of match she'd long ago decided was right for her daughter. She fully intended seeing to that, and bringing it about. No matter how manipulative she had to be.

James stretched languorously. It was Sunday afternoon and he and Elyse were in his bed, having just concluded an intense and energetic bout of lovemaking. On her side the bedroom fire crackled merrily, yellow and orange flames dancing in the grate.

'What are you doing over Christmas?' he asked. A local amateur company was in the theatre for three weeks during the festive season, presenting *Aladdin*. This meant that they had one full week off, while the second and third weeks would be taken up with rehearsals for *Macbeth*, which followed the panto.

'I shall go up to London,' she replied.

'To see Benny?'

She gave a low laugh. 'Not jealous, are you?'

'Green with it.'

She knew that to be a tease. 'It's not entirely Benny: it's more that I miss town and my chums there. Lovely as Torquay is, it's terribly quiet and parochial. I want to be back for a while amongst the buzz that only London has.'

'You mean the West End in particular?' he continued to tease.

'Of course. I'll want to put my face around, remind people of my existence. I'll also hear what's coming up in the future. Casting, that sort of thing.'

Now he was jealous, dreadfully so. 'I shall miss you when you're away, Elyse.'

'And I'll miss you.' She reached down and took hold of him. 'Especially that.'

'Brazen hussy!'

They both laughed.

His mood abruptly changed to become pensive and wistful. 'I wish I could come with you,' he sighed.

'But you can't. Where would you stay?'

'A cheap hotel somewhere, I suppose.'

She was tempted, toying with the idea in her mind. It was certainly an attractive one.

'You could introduce me around,' he said casually.

'To whom?'

'Managements for a start. Connections. People of importance and influence in the "business".'

She eyed him cynically. 'Is that what this is all about, James?'

His expression changed to one of innocence. 'Is what all about?'

'Us. Is it simply my contacts you're interested in, and not me?'

He sat upright and stared at her. 'Do you really think that?'

Elyse shrugged and didn't reply.

'Well, you couldn't be more wrong if you do. I wouldn't . . . couldn't . . .' He broke off and shook his head. 'I'm sorry I brought the subject up. I should have known better. But I'm also bloody angry that you could believe that I'd go to bed with you just to use you.' Suddenly he was all charm again. 'Well, use you, yes. In a certain sense. To make love to you. To do the things I enjoy doing to you. But never the other. I swear.'

He was an actor, she reminded herself. And a damn fine one too. But his tone and manner positively oozed conviction. Surely this was beyond acting? 'I'm sorry,' she whispered.

'Let's not mention it again, all right? As I said, I'm just sorry I brought the subject up.'

'Perhaps you could come with me and stay in that hotel you mentioned?' she said quietly.

He slipped from bed and into his dressing gown. 'Not now, Elyse. It was only a thought. A silly one really. How could you introduce me to people without Benny finding out? It simply isn't on.'

'I . . .'

'No,' he interrupted, holding up a hand. 'We won't speak

of this any further. Apart from anything else, I do have my pride, you know.'

Elyse bit her lip. She'd clearly been mistaken in suspecting him and his motives. The trouble was that the acting world, as she knew only too well, was a cynical one. What she'd suspected wasn't at all beyond the realms of possibility. Why, there had even been times in the past when she herself . . .

She paused and took a deep breath. But *never* going to bed with someone.

'I'll make coffee,' James declared.

He was smiling as he poured water into the kettle.

Chapter 10

Tim parked the Royal Enfield at the kerb and went into the office. A letter from Katherine had arrived just as he was leaving home and was burning a hole in his pocket. He couldn't wait to read it.

For once he was early and decided to nip into the lavatory where, in a cubicle, he could have absolute privacy. He gave Harry Nutbeam a brief wave as he hurried in that direction. It was going to be a busy day, for he had lots to do.

It amused him how childishly Katherine wrote, her handwriting no better than that of a ten-year-old. It was as if she'd only recently learnt to do joined-up writing.

She was well, thoroughly enjoying herself, though beginning to tire of big-city life. She described a concert they'd been to, then a visit to an art gallery, which she'd found excruciatingly boring.

Earlier that day she and her mama had gone for a stroll through Green Park, then had hurriedly to catch a cab back to the hotel when it started to pour.

There were five pages in all, each containing nothing but trivia. She ended by saying that they'd be returning to

Torquay the following week and she was looking forward to seeing him.

Tim sniffed the pages, which were lightly scented, with a sort of summery lemony smell. He thought it delightful.

Starting at the beginning, he read through the letter a second time.

You'd never have known what the house represented, Jeremiah thought as he mounted the steps to the front door. It was an establishment that he'd been using for years when he was in London, ever since Ruth had fallen ill and lost all interest in the physical side of their marriage.

A pretty young maid answered the bell. 'Come in, sir.'

The hallway was exactly as he remembered it. Heavy red-flock wallpaper, its skirting board and dado rails of dark wood. A lit chandelier glittered at the end of the hallway.

The maid took his coat and hat and asked if he'd been before. He replied that he had so she instructed him to go on through. In the ornate salon, this time hung with green wallpaper with lots of gold in evidence, he was met by the proprietor, Mrs Green.

Her face lit up on seeing him, in a professional greeting. 'Ah, Mr C., how wonderful. It's been a long time.' Clients were never referred to by their full names, unless in private, but by the first initial of their surname. That was the house's policy in order to safeguard its clients.

'Yes, I'm afraid it has been a while,' Jeremiah replied. Initially he'd been reticent about visiting a brothel, but in the end needs had forced him to capitulate. And the best thing was that Mrs Green's establishment catered only for the well-to-do and successful members of society. There was nothing sleazy or sordid here, everything being conducted in the very best of taste. Furthermore, the ladies were guaranteed to be clean. For him that had been a prerequisite.

'You've been busy elsewhere, I presume?'

He nodded. 'Abroad quite a lot. Though that's now mainly over. I shall be staying at home more with the family.'

'I recall you once mentioned that your poor wife doesn't enjoy the best of health?'

'Unfortunately no.'

Another maid appeared carrying a silver tray on which were an opened bottle of champagne and two glasses. She set the tray down, poured and handed a glass each to Jeremiah and Mrs Green. Mrs Green's glass contained only a token amount.

'Is Josephine still with you?' Jeremiah inquired. She was his favourite.

'Sadly not. She had to move on.'

Jeremiah wondered why, but didn't ask. That was none of his business.

'I do have some new girls who might appeal,' Mrs Green informed him.

'Oh?'

She knew Jeremiah didn't like them being too young, preferring the slightly more mature women. 'Kindly ask Henrietta, Sybil and Florence if they'll join us,' she instructed the maid. 'Shall we sit?' she then suggested to Jeremiah.

'It seems quiet,' he commented, making conversation.

'It's the time of day, Mr C. We're always busiest in the evenings.'

'Of course.'

They continued with their polite chitchat until the three

women sent for arrived, each in turn being introduced to Jeremiah, who'd risen at their appearance.

It always amazed him how well-spoken and seemingly educated these women were. There was never anything common about them. Not for the first time he found himself wondering what their backgrounds were.

In the end he settled on Henrietta, a dark-haired beauty whom he judged to be in her early thirties. Having made his choice, Sybil and Florence discreetly withdrew.

'Shall we go upstairs?' Henrietta suggested.

'Of course.'

'I'll have the rest of the champagne sent right up,' Mrs Green declared.

'And another bottle, I think.'

She nodded that that would also be done.

Side by side Jeremiah and Henrietta made their way up the long, winding staircase to where the bedrooms were.

Jeremiah had no intention of returning to The Savoy until it was time to dress for dinner.

'There you are! I wondered where you'd got to.'

Katherine glanced round at her mother, the pair of them being in Harrods. 'Did you get Papa's shirts?'

'A half-dozen that'll be delivered to the hotel later. Pure Egyptian cotton, just as he likes.'

'What do you think of this?' Katherine queried, showing Ruth the man's scarf she was holding. Behind the counter an attentive assistant hovered.

'Hmmh,' Ruth mused. 'Not really your father's colours.'

'Oh, it's not for him,' Katherine replied lightly. 'I was considering it as a Christmas present for Tim.'

Ruth's face tightened, and for a split second her eyes glinted. 'That's hardly necessary, Katherine. The lad is only an acquaintance after all, hardly the sort of close friend you'd give a gift.'

'But I want to,' Katherine protested. 'Even if he is only an acquaintance, as you put it.'

Ruth took the scarf from Katherine and laid it back on the counter. 'You'd just embarrass him, as I doubt he'll have anything for you.'

Katherine hadn't thought of that. 'I wouldn't want to embarrass or upset him.'

'Which is what would happen.'

'But what if he does give me something? Then I'll have nothing to give in return.'

'I shouldn't think for one moment he will,' Ruth replied dismissively. 'Apart from anything else, I'd be surprised if he has the money to lavish gifts on anyone other than immediate family.' Then, with heavy emphasis, 'Journalists, especially young ones, don't earn very much, my dear. It's a rather hand-to-mouth existence, I understand.' The latter was a downright lie, but Katherine wasn't to know that. 'Now,' Ruth declared, suddenly all smiles. 'I think we should visit the Food Hall, don't you? I always adore the sights and smells down there. It perks up my appetite every time.'

That was a laugh, Katherine thought. Her mother ate like a sparrow.

Tim twisted the throttle of his motorbike, trying to coax every last ounce of speed out of it. Damn that stupid old man he'd been sent to interview. Damn him, damn him, damn him!

Talk about slow speaking and not getting to the point.

Round and round in circles they'd gone, before at long last Tim had been able to winkle the story out of the bugger. At least it had proved to be a good one, which was something. But now he was late for his rendezvous with Katherine.

It started to rain, drizzle at first, then becoming heavier. He was going too fast for this weather, he warned himself. He should slow down. But didn't.

It was just outside Irelades, Booksellers and Stationers, that a beer-delivery dray appeared as if from nowhere, causing him to slam on the brakes and instantly slide into a skid. Tim's heart was in his mouth, thinking he must surely crash. Behind him two of the large dray horses had reared onto their hind legs, while the driver fought to bring them back under control.

More by good luck than skill he managed to bring the bike upright again and continue on his way unscathed.

Christ, that had been a near thing, he thought, aware that he was sweating all over. He'd already reduced his speed, which he kept down for the rest of his journey to the Old Torre Tearooms, where he and Katherine had agreed to meet. Hastily he parked the bike, took a deep breath, horribly aware of the scare he'd just had, and went inside.

'I'm terribly sorry for being late,' he apologised profusely to Katherine on reaching the table where she was sitting. He quickly explained about the old man, not mentioning the fact that he'd almost had an accident in his rush to get there. 'It's wonderful to see you again,' he declared on finishing his explanation.

'And you,' she replied somewhat coyly.

'I've missed you awfully.'

She didn't reply to that, but just smiled.

'Did you miss me?'

'Of course, silly. A good deal actually.'

That pleased him. Terribly. 'I enjoyed your letters. It sounded as though you had a fabulous time.'

'Oh, I did. As I wrote, we saw lots of shows and went to a number of concerts and galleries. I also attended the most marvellous party the night before we left.'

He frowned. 'Party?'

'Well, I'd call it that, though our hostess referred to it as a social gathering. It was wine and canapés, that sort of thing.'

'And who was your hostess?' he inquired politely.

'Lady Mary Crabthorne. She and Mama are old friends.'

'I see,' he murmured, wondering who Lady Mary Crabthorne was.

'I met oodles of jolly interesting people there. Time just flew by.'

Tim gestured to an approaching waitress that he'd have the same as Katherine. 'What kind of interesting people?' he asked casually.

'Oh, all sorts.'

'Many young folk?'

'Certainly. In fact, a good half of the company were young. Lady Mary's daughter Clarice was ever such fun. As was her brother.'

There was something in Katherine's tone that made Tim go cold inside. 'Brother?'

'Miles Crabthorne. He's in the Household Cavalry and was there with several of his fellow officers. There was also a flyer chap called Julian, who told the most hair-raising stories of going up in a kite, as he called it.'

Tim's jealousy was blossoming with every passing second. 'A flyer, eh?'

'With the Royal Flying Corps. He and Miles were at school together, apparently. Wellington in Berkshire.'

Tim didn't like the sound of any of this. All these no doubt handsome young chaps. How could he hold a candle to the likes of them? Especially a daredevil pilot – they didn't come more dashing than that. No wonder Katherine had been impressed; she had every right to be.

'Clarice said she'd come down and visit in the spring. Promised she would. I'm looking forward to that. As I said, she's such fun.'

'With her brother?'

'I shouldn't think so. He'll be far too busy with army business, I should imagine. He's forever on parade.'

Thank God for that, Tim thought grimly, already hating Miles Crabthorne and all his friends.

'Speaking of parties,' Katherine went on. 'Mama wants to know if you'd like to come to dinner a week on Saturday? There should be fourteen of us sitting down.'

'Dinner?' Tim repeated, momentarily taken aback by the unexpectedness of the invitation. 'Who else will be there?'

Katherine reeled off the names of various Torquay luminaries and a few Tim had never heard of.

'Do come, please?' Katherine urged.

'I shall be delighted to.'

'Good, that's settled then.' She beamed innocently at him. 'It's black tie of course.'

Ouch! he thought, wouldn't it just be. Drat his luck.

She noted his expression. 'Is that a problem, Tim?'

'No, no,' he replied quickly. 'I was just thinking I'll have to get mine out and brushed down. Haven't had it on for absolutely ages.'

She nodded her approval. 'We'll be sending you a proper invitation naturally.'

Before he could reply their conversation was interrupted by the arrival of his tea and scones.

Now who could he borrow black tie from? he wondered. For he didn't possess such a thing. And his father's, which he might have been able to have altered, had been chucked out years ago. He was going to have to give this some thought.

He brought his attention back to Katherine, who'd started speaking again.

Elyse was passing the Wilsons' parlour when she spotted Tim through the open doorway staring moodily out of the window.

'Tim?'

He snapped out of his reverie and turned to her. 'Oh, hello, Mrs Davenport.'

'Why so miserable?' she asked in concern. 'You look really down in the dumps.'

'Do I?'

'Yes, you do.'

He shrugged as he made his way over to her. 'It's simply that I've been invited to a black-tie dinner and I don't . . .'

'Have black tie,' she finished for him, causing them both to laugh.

'I was hoping to borrow from a colleague at work, but sadly he doesn't own one either.' The colleague referred to was Harry Nutbeam.

'I see. I suppose buying new is out of the question?'

'Quite,' Tim replied emphatically. 'Even if I wanted to, I just don't have the cash at present. Anyway, it would be a complete waste. How often am I going to be required to wear one of those? Once in a blue moon, I should think.'

'Isn't there somewhere you could rent it? We have outfitters that do so in London.'

He shook his head. 'This is Torquay, Elyse. We're hardly so sophisticated or well provided for.'

She had a sudden idea. 'Let me have a look at you,' she said and, taking a step backwards, eyed him from head to toe. 'Hmmh.'

'Elyse?'

'Can you manage to drop by the theatre later?' she asked mysteriously.

'What for?'

'I may be able to help.'

That baffled him. 'How?'

'Four o'clock would be ideal. I'll have a word with Fred, the doorkeeper, to let you in. Come to my dressing room and if I'm not there wait for me.'

'All right.' He nodded slowly. What on earth was she up to?

'Till then.' And with that she swept on her way, leaving an intrigued Tim staring after her.

It wasn't till she had gone that he became aware of her perfume lingering behind. A smell that he would associate for ever with Elyse Davenport.

Elyse breezed into her dressing room to find Tim already there. 'I think this should fit,' she declared, crossing to a wardrobe and throwing open its doors. From the hanging rail she lifted a dinner jacket complete with shirt, cummerbund and trousers.

She held the ensemble up against an amazed Tim. 'Looks about right. Nip behind the screen and try it on.'

'Where did this come from?' he queried.

'James. James Erskine. You've met him. I thought he was more or less the same size as you. When I explained the situation he was only too happy to lend it to you.'

Tim remembered Erskine, whom he hadn't particularly liked. He didn't know why, there was just something about the man. 'That's very kind of him. Please thank him for me.'

'I shall.'

'I'm only surprised that . . . well, he had one.'

Elyse laughed. 'All actors are expected to provide certain items of clothing when they start an engagement. It's part of the contract. And black tie is one. A corresponding frock, or frocks, in my case. Now on you go, get behind that screen. I haven't got all day.'

Tim accepted the coathanger from her and did as instructed. He felt most uncomfortable stripping off, as his head and shoulders were visible above the screen and Elyse remained in the room.

If she was aware of his discomfiture she ignored it. Men taking their clothes off and putting others on was hardly new to her. There were occasions when a quick change was required, which both actors and actresses did in full view backstage. No-one ever took a blind bit of notice.

'Tell me about this dinner you're going to,' she asked.

'It's being given by Katherine's parents at their home. From what I gather it's a real swanky do.'

'Sounds lovely.'

'It will be, with Katherine there.'

Elyse smiled to herself. Young love, what a marvellous thing that was. In a way she quite envied Tim.

Or did she? Maybe not on reflection. Young love – any love come to that – was all right as long as it worked out. The trouble came when it didn't. That was when you got hurt. And in the case of young love, probably for the first time.

'Can I come in?'

She glanced round to discover a smiling James already inside her dressing room. Normally, if they'd been alone, he'd have crossed over and kissed her, but didn't because of Tim's presence.

'Does it fit?' he asked.

'We're about to find out. How are you doing, Tim?'

'Almost there.' He found Erskine being in the room even more unsettling and embarrassing. Also the clothes smelt faintly of mothballs, which wasn't very nice. Beggars can't be choosers, he reminded himself. Elyse and Erskine were trying to do him a favour, after all.

Elyse lit a cigarette, she and James exchanging small talk till finally Tim presented himself. 'What do you think?' he asked anxiously.

Elyse eyed him critically. 'A couple of tucks are required in the trousers,' she mused. 'James?'

'I agree.' He went to Tim and tugged on the shoulders. 'Other than that I would say it's fine.'

'I'll do the tucks, then let them out again afterwards. That isn't a problem.'

'Can you do that?' a surprised Tim asked.

She laughed. 'Every actress I've ever met is a dab hand with a needle and thread. We're forever altering things out of necessity. It isn't all limelight and applause, you know.'

'Sorry,' Tim muttered.

'Do you have cufflinks?' James inquired of Tim.

'Yes, thank you.'

'Well, that saves me digging out a spare pair.'

Elyse had knelt in front of Tim and was fiddling with his trousers. Normally she would have chalked what needed doing, but as she didn't have any chalk handy she made do with visual measurements. 'I'll have these ready for you tomorrow morning,' she declared.

'There's no rush. The dinner's not till next week,' Tim protested.

'Whatever, you'll have them in plenty of time.'

'I hate to break this up,' James said to Elyse, 'but we have to get on.'

'I asked Mrs Davenport to thank you, but now you're here I can do so personally. Thank you,' Tim declared.

James stared Tim straight in the eye and smiled wolfishly. 'You're welcome, young man.'

Tim glanced away, fighting back the urge to shiver. What was it about Erskine? He was damned if he knew. Only that it made him uneasy to be in Erskine's company.

'We'll leave you to it, Tim,' Elyse informed him. 'Take the rest, but leave the trousers so that I can attend to them.'

'Goodbye then, and thanks again.'

Tim was relieved when they'd left the dressing room. Or, to be more precise, when Erskine had gone.

He went behind the screen again, delighted that his problem had been solved. To use Elyse's own phraseology, she was a real sweetie.

* * *

This time he did come off. Tim cursed vehemently to himself as he went tumbling over the cobbles, the Enfield finally coming to rest when it smacked into a lamp post.

It was all his own fault, he raged inwardly. He'd been far too cocky, his mind elsewhere and not on riding the damned bike. Sitting up, he gingerly felt himself, trying to find out if anything was broken. Thankfully nothing appeared to be. But when he ran a hand over his face it came away smeared with blood.

Passers-by had stopped and gathered round, all looking on anxiously. 'Are you all right?' an elderly man inquired.

Tim nodded.

'What happened?'

He didn't reply, but instead lurched to his feet, where he had to stand still for a few moments as his head was spinning.

'I'm just shaken, that's all,' he said to the passers-by as the vertigo died away.

'Your face?'

He gently touched it, wincing as he did so. 'Scraped, nothing more.' At least he hoped that was all it was.

Muttering amongst themselves, the passers-by began to disperse as Tim went over to where the bike lay against the lamp post.

He groaned when he saw the damage that had been done – considerable from a quick cursory examination. How much was that going to cost to get fixed? Heaven knows.

But he was in one piece, that was the main thing. Though his face was now beginning to sting like billyo.

'Stupid sod,' he grumbled to himself. No-one's fault but his own. Well, that would teach him.

* * *

'Ain't you the smart one right enough. A proper toff and no mistake,' Cook declared, admiring Tim, who was shortly off to dinner at the Coateses'.

Daisy giggled. 'I've never seen 'ee look more handsome, Master Tim. I'd hardly have recognised you.'

'Handsome, with a face like that!' Minna exclaimed. 'Your eyes need testing, girl.'

Tim had a deep purple discoloration under one eye and several strips of sticky plaster on his scraped cheek. He'd been lucky not to kill himself, Minna had declared on seeing him when he'd arrived home, having had to push the bike all the way. He'd told her there had been a patch of oil on the road and that was what had caused him to crash. A lie of course, but better saying that than telling the truth. It was the story he'd stuck to ever since.

'I think he looks like a pirate,' Daisy went on, and this time burst into a fit of giggling.

'No he don't,' Cook scolded her. 'Pirates were nasty men. Cut-throats and the like. Master Tim looks nothing like one of thae.'

'And how would you know about pirates anyway?' Minna queried, thinking that a bizarre thing for Daisy to have come out with.

'I saw a picture at the bioscope a few weeks ago, and that was about pirates,' Daisy explained. 'Master Tim reminds me of the hero.'

'What nonsense,' Minna muttered.

Tim glanced at the clock on the mantelpiece, hoping that the motor taxicab he'd ordered wasn't going to be late.

Minna came over to him and brushed an imaginary speck of dust off his lapel. She was quite bursting with pride to see Tim dressed like this. It brought back so many memories of when Redvers was alive. Dear Redvers, whom she missed desperately. He too would have been proud to see his son tonight.

'Don't drink too much, son,' Minna quietly advised Tim. 'You might make a fool of yourself.'

'I won't, Ma.'

'Remember, these people are the gentry and not the usual crowd you run around with.'

'Ma, you're making me nervous!' he protested.

'Well, I don't want to do that. Just watch your p's and q's, that's all.'

'Will you stop fussing, please!'

The kitchen door burst open and Euphemia flew in. 'The motor taxicab is here,' she announced breathlessly.

'That's that then. Time to be off.' Tim smiled, then immediately stopped because it hurt.

Minna couldn't help herself. Despite the staff being present she gave him a quick hug. 'Enjoy yourself, son.'

'I'm sure I will. Now goodbye everyone.'

'Goodbye,' Cook, Daisy and Euphemia chorused, Cook's eyes bright with tears, having always had a particularly soft spot for Tim.

It was a fine night, Tim noted before stepping into the taxicab. A million stars twinkling down from heaven. He hoped that was a good omen.

Pirate, he thought, as he settled back into the leather seat, and laughed.

Chapter 11

R uth Coates was furious, absolutely livid. Her planned showing-up of Tim had completely backfired. Rather than what she'd hoped for, he'd been the hit of the evening.

Everyone had taken to him, particularly the ladies, who'd declared him charming when they'd withdrawn while the men took port. How sympathetic they'd been about his injury, speculating on the dashing sight he must make on that wretched motorbike Jeremiah had given him. She'd found that especially galling.

She'd watched him like a hawk during dinner, hoping he wouldn't know which knife and fork to use, or that he'd handle them incorrectly. But no such luck. There had been nothing to find fault with there.

And he'd certainly held his own in the general conversation, proving both entertaining and funny. Why, he'd even made Maude Reece-Jones laugh, which was almost unheard of, Maude normally being of a most serious – almost sour, you might say – temperament. The old girl had actually flirted with him, and she at least forty years his senior!

Disaster, that was what the evening had been. A total

disaster. From her point of view anyway. Everyone else had enthused about how much they'd enjoyed themselves.

'I've asked you a dozen times not to smoke those smelly things in the bedroom,' she snapped viciously at Jeremiah, who was indulging in a cigar.

He looked at her in astonishment, wondering why she'd used so severe a tone for such a minor infraction. 'Sorry, darling, I clean forgot,' he apologised.

'Well, put it out this instant.'

For a moment he was tempted to remind her that he was still master in his own house and would do as he damn well pleased, especially when she spoke to him like that. But he didn't, instead complying with what could only be called a command.

'That better?' he smiled.

'Hmmh!'

He couldn't imagine what had suddenly got into her. 'Are you feeling quite well, Ruth?'

'I'm absolutely fine.'

'I just thought . . . well, one of your pains. I know how you suffer from them.'

She sniffed. The cigar smoke hadn't really been bothering her: she had simply been venting her ill humour. 'A touch of headache, that's all,' she lied.

His expression was immediately one of concern. 'Is there anything I can get you? A powder perhaps?'

'No, no, I'll be all right. A good sleep is all I need.'

Jeremiah had already taken off his jacket and now began to undress further. 'I must say, I thought young Tim was in splendid form tonight,' he chuckled, not realising that he was fuelling Ruth's anger and pique.

Her lips thinned, and it took all her will-power not to make a caustic retort.

'I was surprised you asked him, after our conversation in London – about him and his family being relatively poor, that is.' He smiled at her. 'I'm pleased that you took what I said on board.'

She turned her back to him so he couldn't see her scowl. She had nothing personally against Tim, it was simply that he was quite unsuitable for Katherine. She'd noted the way they'd been looking at one another earlier on: Katherine all gooey-eyed, Tim's gaze full of admiration. Admiration and more. Well, that relationship mustn't develop – it couldn't. She just wouldn't allow it.

'Well?' Jeremiah prompted, expecting a reply to what he'd just said.

Ruth took control of herself and forced a smile onto her face. 'As usual you know best, Jeremiah. Hasn't that always been the case?'

'Quite,' he replied, puffing out his chest a little.

Ruth was mentally counting off the months until she and Katherine returned to London for the Season, Katherine's coming-out. That was when matters would be sorted.

She'd already decided that Miles Crabthorne would be perfect. Not only was the family incredibly rich, but one day Miles would inherit his father's title.

Lady Katherine Crabthorne had a lovely ring to it, she thought.

Tim couldn't get to sleep, for he was still thinking about dinner at the Coateses'. Mrs Reece-Jones and her husband

Bertie had been terribly kind in giving him a lift back into Torquay, which had solved his transport problem.

How stunning Katherine had looked, with her hair swept up in a style new to her, or at least new as far as he was concerned. Her dress had been dark blue, and that was all he could remember. For the world of him he couldn't have described it. The girl inside the dress had had his full and rapt attention.

There had been a few sublime moments as he was leaving when she'd slipped her hand into his and squeezed, with him squeezing back. He'd wanted to kiss her then, but of course that had been quite impossible. He'd have given his eyeteeth to have been able to do so.

How upset she'd been to see his face when he'd arrived, and what a delightful fuss she'd made over him. To hear her go on, you'd have thought he was some brave soldier returning from war.

While holding his hand, she'd whispered that she'd ring him in the next couple of days and they'd make another arrangement to meet. He resolved to try and think of somewhere really nice.

He paused at the sound of footsteps outside in the corridor. That must be Mrs Davenport returning from the theatre. He'd tell her all about the dinner when he got the chance, for it was thanks to her that he'd been able to attend. He was terribly grateful.

When he finally fell asleep, it was to dream of Katherine. A dream that caused him to blush next morning when he woke up and remembered it.

Elyse stepped down onto the platform at Paddington

Station and drew in a deep lungful of air. London! There was no mistaking that distinctive smell.

Instantly she felt alive again, the blood singing in her veins. How she'd missed dear old London town, the very hub of the universe.

And she had six whole days here before she had to go back to Torquay and start the *Macbeth* rehearsals, for it was the Christmas break, with the amateurs opening that night in *Aladdin*.

James had come to see her off, fussing over her, ensuring that she was comfortable in the carriage. He'd bought her magazines for the journey and a fancy box of chocolates to spoil her. His last words had been to hurry back again, for his thoughts would be with her all the time she was away, which would seen like an eternity. What a gorgeous man he was.

Two nights previously she'd stayed over at his house and what a sensation that had been. She'd been positively glowing when she'd slipped into The Berkeley next morning long before Mrs Wilson or anyone else was stirring.

She heard a loud cockney male voice, as cockney as her own had been once upon a time. Turning, she saw that it belonged to a porter, whom she beckoned over.

Later on it would be the Salisbury pub to start with – that was always full of actors, in and out of work – followed by Kean's, *the* thespian club in town, and her great haunt.

When both she and her luggage were ensconced in a taxi-cab, she instructed the driver to take her to Seven Dials, where she and Benny lived.

* * *

Elyse put her hands on her hips and surveyed what could only be described as a complete tip. Benny could at least have made an attempt to clear up for her return home.

The first thing she did was open the windows, despite it being bitterly cold outside, for the place stank. Going through to the scullery, she sighed in exasperation when she saw the sink piled high with dirty dishes. The sheets in the bedroom didn't look as though they'd been changed in an age.

She threw back the topclothes to stare at the bottom sheet. Just as she'd suspected, Benny had been entertaining in her absence. It made her extremely angry that he'd used their bed – somehow that was a violation. The bed where they themselves had so often . . . in the past.

'Bastard,' she hissed. 'Rotten bastard.'

She found the letter she'd written telling him she was coming back, and when, unopened on the mantelpiece. Well, if it was there, then it hadn't arrived that day. Didn't that just tell her something.

Where to start? In the bedroom, she decided. That was her first priority.

Molly O'Malley, the wife of Kean's owner, let out a loud, raucous screech when she spotted Elyse. A large Irish lady, she charged across the floor to wrap Elyse in a bear-hugging embrace.

''Tis yourself, me fine darlin'. You're a sight for sore eyes, as God is me judge.'

Elyse laughed. She'd spent several hours in the Salisbury pub, chatting to old chums, hearing the news and catching up on the gossip. She was having a whale of a time.

'You'll squeeze me to death if you're not careful, Molly,' she declared.

Molly immediately released her. 'Sorry, I sometimes forget me own strength.' There were those who'd caused trouble in the club who'd felt the full weight of Molly's meaty fist. It was said she could throw a punch equal to any prizefighter's. 'Now, how long are you here for?' Molly demanded.

'Six days.'

The Irish woman pulled a face. 'Is that all?'

'I'm afraid so.'

'Well, we'll just have to see we make the most of them.' Molly grasped Elyse by the arm and steered her towards a vacant booth. 'I think we'll have a bottle of champagne to celebrate. My treat.'

'Oh, Molly, you shouldn't!' Elyse protested.

'Now, you be shutting that gob of yours. We're friends, aren't we? And 'tis Christmas, don't forget.'

When they were sitting, with Molly having had to manoeuvre her bulk carefully into the space available, she signalled to her husband Seamus behind the bar and mouthed the word 'bubbles'.

'Now, where was it you've been? My memory isn't what it used to be, which isn't surprising working in this bedlam night after night.'

'Torquay,' Elyse reminded her. 'In Devon.'

'Whatever, it sounds like the back of beyond.'

Elyse laughed. 'It is quiet, I have to admit, but very pleasant there. The sea air has been good for my cough.'

'Ah yes, that cough of yours. 'Tis the smoking that does it, to be sure. Speaking of which, I've left mine out back.'

'Then have one of mine.' Elyse produced a packet and a box of matches and they both lit up.

'There's something different about you,' Molly stated shrewdly. 'I can see it in your lovely face.'

'Different?'

'You're more relaxed, happier.' Molly broke off to study her. 'Would I be right in thinking there might be a man involved somewhere?'

God, was it that obvious? Elyse thought.

'Well?'

'There are times you frighten me, Molly. Positively frighten me.'

'Stop evading the question.' She leant forward. 'I've hit it on the nail. Go on, admit it. Is he a handsome darlin'?'

'Very,' Elyse replied quietly.

'See, I knew it! You can't hide anything from Molly O'Malley. 'Tis a gift I have. The all-seeing eye and no mistake.'

'He's an actor in the company, who's also stage director.'

'And does he look after you well? Treat you as a lady, like you should be treated, and not as that sod of a husband you have does?'

'He treats me very well. I certainly don't have any complaints.'

'Good. That's no more than you deserve. Now for the nitty-gritty – you've already said he's handsome, but is he a good shag?'

Elyse burst out laughing. That was typical Molly, completely outrageous. She would ask things other people wouldn't dream of, and somehow got away with it. Perhaps it was because she was Irish. 'None better,' Elyse replied.

'Ahhh!' Molly breathed. 'That's so terribly important. There are those who say it isn't, but I believe otherwise. A woman can put up with a lot if the bloke's a good shag.'

'And doesn't stray,' Elyse added softly, thinking of the stains on her bed. Final proof of what she'd known for a long time and one of the reasons she'd agreed to sleep with James. The goose and gander after all.

Seamus came over with the champagne and two glasses, which he set before them. 'I swear the place lit up when you walked through the door,' he declared and, bending over, pecked Elyse on the cheek.

'Get away with you, Seamus. The pair of you are so full of Irish blarney I'm surprised you don't burst from it.'

Seamus, a thin man, eyed Molly's bulk. 'Well, in her case that might still happen.'

Molly aimed a smack at him, which he neatly avoided by dancing away. 'We'll have less of that cheek from the likes of you, Seamus O'Malley,' she admonished, not in the least put out. The two of them were still as much in love, and devoted to one another, as the day they'd been married.

'It's grand having you back, Elyse,' Seamus called out and hurriedly returned to the bar where a group of thirsty customers were clamouring for refills.

'Have you seen Benny?' Elyse asked.

Molly shook her head. 'Seamus has several times, but not meself. You know he rarely comes in here, because it's not good enough for his high-and-almightiness.'

'That's not true. He goes elsewhere because I come here. There's no other reason.'

Molly poured the already opened bottle of champagne. Raising her glass, she said, 'Here's a toast to me good friend and customer. May you get to blessed heaven before the devil knows you're dead!'

They both drank.

'Now, tell me about this new chap of yours. I want to hear everything.'

'Everything?' Elyse teased.

'Indeed I do. Dirty prying bitch that I am.'

Elyse complied.

Elyse was beginning to think Benny wouldn't be returning home that night, for even by his standards it was extremely late. She was about to take herself off to bed when the outside door opened.

One look at his face told her he was drunk. But what shocked her was how much he'd aged in the relatively short time since she'd last seen him. There were streaks of grey in his hair where there had been none before, and the same hair was now clearly thinning. There were new lines round his eyes and two startlingly new creases that cut outwards from the corners of his mouth. In appearance he looked at least ten years older, maybe more.

'It's you,' he slurred, staring at her.

'None other.'

'When I saw a light under the door I thought maybe we had burglars.'

'And here it's only me. Your wife.'

He grunted. 'You might have let me know.'

'I did, Benny,' she replied sarcastically, lighting her umpteenth cigarette of the evening. 'Only you couldn't be bothered even to open the letter.'

His gaze slid sideways to the mantelpiece where her letter

still lay. 'I was going to get round to it. I just forgot.'

'Well, that just shows how important hearing from me is to you.'

Benny lurched over to a chair and sank into it. He desperately wanted a drink from his special bottle, but didn't want to have it in front of Elyse in case she asked for one too.

'So how are you?' he queried, a tinge of impertinence in his voice.

What had she ever seen in him? she wondered. Whatever, it was long gone. 'Fine. Yourself? You look a wreck.'

He glared at her. 'There's no need to get nasty.'

'I wasn't. Merely stating the obvious. Where have you been – out with some tart?'

'And why should I be out with a tart?' he snarled in reply.

'I've seen the evidence.'

He frowned. 'What bloody evidence?'

'The sheets, Benny. The sheets. I call that evidence.'

He leant back in his chair, a leery expression coming to his face, his mind suddenly less befuddled and racing. 'Well, that just shows how wrong you can be. Adding two and two and coming up with five.'

Now it was her turn to frown. 'How do you mean?'

He shifted his body into a pose of nonchalance, an old actor's trick. 'You're a woman of the world, Elyse. Can't you guess?'

She shook her head.

'A chap gets lonely at night. All on his own, like. He can do things to relieve the loneliness and frustration.'

The penny dropped. 'Are you saying that's how those stains got there?'

'I am. Embarrassing as it may be.'

Elyse took a deep breath. That was a possibility that had simply never entered her head. In all her years with Benny she'd never known him indulge in such a practice. On the other hand, that wasn't to say he didn't.

'Why hasn't the rent been paid?' she demanded.

'You're changing the subject.'

'For the moment. So?'

He shrugged. 'Every time I meant to I seemed short of money and put it off.'

'According to the rent book, it's only been paid once since I left.'

A smile curled his lips. 'Doesn't time pass quickly? It seems like only yesterday you were off to Torquay. My, my.'

He was infuriating her, but then that was nothing new. 'You earn good money, Benny – West End wages, far more than I'm getting – so why were you short of cash?'

'I clearly spent it. You know what I'm like with money, Elyse, it never stays long in my pocket. It just sort of disappears. Like magic, I sometimes think.'

'On booze and women, you mean.'

'*Women*, me?' he replied incredulously. 'What a lurid imagination you've got. You wrong me entirely.'

'In a pig's arse I do. You've been at it for years behind my back. I'm not stupid, Benny, all the signs have been there. Anyway, you've been seen on many occasions.'

'You mean with someone? So what! That doesn't mean I'm sleeping with them.' His smile was one of pure innocence.

This could go on all night with him denying, denying, denying. She'd thought she'd had him with the sheets, only for him to come out with that explanation. She didn't believe it for a moment, but the trouble was that it was entirely plausible.

'Well, I haven't enough to pay the back-rent,' she stated. 'It's taking me all my time to get by in Torquay as it is. You're going to have to find the cash from somewhere, otherwise we'll be out in the street.'

'You worry too much, Elyse,' he admonished, wagging a finger at her. 'Leave it all to me. I'll sort it out.'

'You'd better,' she snapped.

He closed his eyes, thinking of the young actress he'd been with earlier. What a piece that was, ripe as a bursting plum. Not like Elyse, who was . . . well, to put it kindly, past her best. Her body was nothing like it had once been.

'Benny?'

'What now?'

'Are you going to sleep?'

He opened his eyes again. God, how she irritated him, he'd forgotten how much. 'No.'

'Because when you do, you're on the couch. I've laid out a couple of blankets.'

That angered him. 'Have you now,' he replied threateningly.

'And that's where you're spending the nights while I'm here. We'll have no argument about that.'

He wanted to rush across the room and slap the slag, slap her hard. Cause her pain. 'And why should I be sleeping on the couch when there's a perfectly good bed through there?'

'Because I insist on it.'

'I told you how the stains came to be on the sheets, Elyse. Can't you take my word for that?'

'In a word, no.' She came to her feet. 'As you can see,

I've tidied the place. Try and keep it that way. It might not bother you living in a sty, but it does me. Understand?'

His look was one of sheer venom. He would leave her, he decided. Something he should have done years ago. He'd be well rid of her, the nagging cow. And when he went the rent would still be unpaid. She could deal with that herself.

Suddenly Elyse was terribly tired: it had been a long day after all. How she wished James was here instead of Benny. She was already missing him. Not just the lovemaking, but as a person, his company.

'Goodnight, Benny.'

He didn't reply, but continued glaring at her.

The bedroom door had no sooner clicked shut than he was over at the cupboard where he kept his special bottle. He swallowed a large gulp of its contents, then another. The familiar warmth and euphoria began to spread quickly through him. Christ, he'd needed that. Unimaginably so.

He had to hide the bottle where she'd never find it, he told himself. She need never know about this. It would only cause further trouble.

He took a final swallow before starting to think of a suitable place for concealment.

Tim found the summer house easily enough, for Katherine's directions on the telephone had been quite explicit. He slipped inside to wait.

He'd only picked up his motorbike from the garage the previous morning, the bill, thankfully, not being as high as he'd feared. The bike was now parked behind a bush on the edge of the Oaklands grounds.

He rubbed his hands briskly together, for it was a chilly day. He was supposed to be out on a story for Ricketts, which he'd get onto directly after seeing Katherine.

It had been a disappointment when he'd phoned her to learn that she couldn't get into Torquay before Christmas, hence this meeting, a compromise solution.

He watched her hurry across the lawn, the collar of her coat pulled up round her ears. He smiled in anticipation.

'Hello,' she greeted him on entering the summer house.

'Hello.'

'I'm afraid I only have a few minutes, Tim. We're having people arriving tomorrow to spend the holiday with us and there's still masses to do.'

A horrible thought occurred to him. 'Anyone I know or have heard of?'

Katherine shook her head. 'It's a family from outside Exeter, who are very old friends of Mama and Papa's.'

So it wasn't the Crabthornes or the flyer Julian, he thought with relief.

'You said it was important?' she prompted.

'Shall we sit down. Or is it too cold for that?'

'Not at all. But, as I said, I've only got a few minutes.'

When they were sitting on a cushioned wrought-iron sofa he stared into her face, wanting to take her hand but not daring to. Anyway, it wouldn't have felt the same, as she was wearing gloves.

'What are you doing for Christmas?' Katherine asked.

'The same as always, spending it with my mother and the guests. I'm sure it will be just as boring as last year, and the year before that, and the year before that.'

They both laughed.

'In the evening it's just Ma and myself. That's when we exchange presents, after which Ma usually falls asleep. It's not very exciting at all. I just wish . . .' He trailed off.

'Wish what, Tim?'

'That I could spend it with you.'

She was touched by that, deeply. 'It would be nice,' she whispered in reply.

'Yes.'

'But sadly can't be.'

Not yet, he thought. Not yet. There might come a time. 'Talking of presents, I've brought a little one for you.'

That caught her by surprise. 'You have?'

He delved into a pocket to produce a small, flat gift-wrapped package. 'Here.'

She accepted the package and stared at it, thinking of Harrods and the scarf she'd been going to buy. 'I'm afraid I've nothing for you,' she said, pulling a face.

'That's all right, I wasn't expecting anything.'

'Even though . . .' She was angry with herself for letting her mother talk her out of buying the scarf. She should have insisted that she did so. And now this.

'Go on, open it.'

Inside she found six wispy linen handkerchiefs edged with lace. 'They're lovely,' she declared, genuinely delighted.

'Hardly original, but when I saw them I thought you'd like them.'

'And I do. Thank you, Tim. Thank you ever so much.'

Tim swallowed hard, urging himself to say what had suddenly come into his mind. How could he possibly ask that, when he hadn't dared reach out and take her hand. Summoning all his will power he forced himself to. 'There is something you could give me for Christmas,' he husked. 'Something I would truly treasure.'

'And what's that?'

'A kiss.' There, it was said. His heart was hammering.

She nodded slowly. That was something she could give. Wanted to give. With all her being.

Leaning forward, her lips met his. Seconds later his arms went round her and he drew her close.

Chapter 12

E lyse stared down the length of Shaftesbury Avenue thinking what a marvellous and exciting street it was. So many theatres, so many good and successful productions running. With a little imagination you could actually smell the greasepaint.

All about her people were hurrying to and fro, most of them Christmas shopping. Well, that was something she didn't have to worry about as it was years since she and Benny had exchanged gifts. Benny whom she'd left snoring his head off earlier – what an unattractive and unappetising sight he'd made, with his thinning hair standing on end and his mouth agape. Rancid alcohol fumes had been emanating from him and he definitely needed a good bath.

Where to start? she wondered. She wished she could have a cigarette, but couldn't light up because of where she was.

Gordon Davis Management, she finally decided. She'd often worked for them in the past, the last time being a little over three years previously. Now, what was the name of his secretary again? Marion, that was it.

She headed in the direction of their offices, which were situated just off the avenue.

'Elyse, come in, me darlin'!' Molly O'Malley had answered her knock and now ushered her through to the premises at the rear of the club where Molly and Seamus lived.

'I was passing and wondered if there was any coffee going.'

'There's always that for you. And while you're here, why don't you stay for a bite of lunch? Nothing fancy, just shepherd's pie.'

'No, thank you, Molly. I've still got a lot to do.'

'Suit yourself. Park yer arse while I get the kettle on.'

An unshaven Seamus appeared wrapped in an ancient dressing gown with several rents and holes in it. 'So help me God, Elyse, you look like an angel descended,' he declared.

She laughed. 'Flattery will get you everywhere, Seamus.'

He winked salaciously at her. 'I was hoping that.'

Elyse knew only too well it was just a game, a tease. Seamus would no more have betrayed Molly than fly. Still, it did make her feel better.

Molly came bustling back from the kitchen. 'Kettle's on and won't be a tick. I've got a new blend of coffee that I picked up in Old Compton Street. Been buying it from one of those French delicatessens, as they call them. I swear on all that's holy 'tis sheer nectar. I go to bed dreaming about the first cup I'll have in the morning.'

'Must be good,' Elyse acknowledged.

'You'll find out for yourself.' Molly stopped to stare at Elyse. 'I didn't notice it last night but you've lost a lot of weight. Why, you're almost skin and bone.'

'An elephant is skin and bone compared to her,' Seamus commented quietly to Elyse.

'You shut your gob, you miserable old git! You don't say that when you want your evil way with me. Which is often enough, I have to say.'

'I never hear you complaining when I do,' he riposted.

'Only doing me wifely duty,' she sniffed, all three of them knowing that to be a load of drivel.

'Har har!' That positively dripped sarcasm.

Elyse always thoroughly enjoyed the O'Malleys' company, finding them such fun. They had the knack of making her feel totally at ease.

'Getting back to your weight, are you all right? Have you been ill or what?' Molly demanded.

Elyse shook her head. 'I'm fine. Absolutely fine. Honestly.'

'Do you think she looks peaky, Seamus?'

He studied Elyse. 'Can't say that I do. But then how can I tell when she's wearing slap?' This was the theatrical expression for make-up.

'It's your imagination, Molly, that's all.'

'Maybe, maybe not,' Molly mused, unconvinced. 'What isn't me imagination is how skinny you've become. 'Tis a right good feed you need. Are you sure you won't stay for lunch?'

'No, I must get on. I'm doing the rounds of the managements, those still open, that is. I want to find out what casting there'll be in the spring. Rep is work, I know, but it's not the West End, which is where I prefer to be.'

'And should be, a great actress like yourself. Isn't that so, Seamus?'

'Indeed it is.'

Great actress! That made Elyse smile. Yes, she was good, there was no denying that, but hardly great. That applied to the likes of Ellen Terry and Mrs Patrick Campbell, not Elyse Davenport.

'Here, have a gasper,' Molly said, offering a packet to Elyse.

Elyse's eyebrows shot up. 'Passing Cloud! Nothing but the best for you, eh?'

'Oh, to be sure. Except I didn't buy these. A pissed customer left them. Anyway, his loss is our gain.'

Elyse stayed for about half an hour, during which she agreed with Molly: the coffee truly was delicious.

What worried her slightly was that Molly thought she'd lost so much weight. She'd known she'd lost some, for she'd had to take her skirts in a while back, but that much!

She decided Molly was exaggerating, which, being Irish, God bless her, she was inclined to do.

The Salisbury pub was busy, Elyse instantly recognising a number of faces. She ordered herself a drink and then made her way across to where Pattie Browne was sitting on her own. She and Pattie had shared a dressing room during a production of a play whose title she couldn't now remember, probably because it had closed after only a few short months due to terrible reviews.

'Do you mind if I join you?'

'Elyse! Long time. How are you?'

Elyse sat down beside her friend. 'Are you working?'

'A cough and a spit at the St Martin's. Showy, mind, and it keeps the wolf from the door. You?'

'Rep in Torquay.'

Pattie frowned. 'That's Cornwall, isn't it?'

'Devon,' Elyse corrected her.

'So, why are you here?'

Elyse explained about the week she had off because of the amateur production of *Aladdin*. 'That's why I'm back home trying to find work for the spring. Know of anything?'

Pattie thought about that. 'Not really. Though I did hear there's a production of a Russian play opening in April. Or is it May? The whisper said it was provisionally booked for the Fortune.'

Elyse's heart sank. She loathed Russian plays and couldn't understand for the life of her what people saw in them. They were all so gloomy and heavy-going. Like wading through the proverbial treacle. Still, work was work.

'Who's the management?'

'A new one. Chap called Marcus Brierley, I believe. He's got offices in Southampton Street. Number fourteen, I think was the number mentioned.'

'Has he cast yet?'

'No idea. He might have. There again, maybe not. It could be worth a try.'

Elyse squeezed Pattie's hand. 'Thanks.'

'Wish I could help you further, but that's all I know.'

Elyse glanced at the clock behind the bar. There was no time like the present. She bought Pattie a drink before taking her leave.

Sure enough, Marcus Brierley Management was located at number fourteen Southampton Street, although unfortunately their offices were well and truly shut. Elyse stared at the door in dismay.

'Can I help you?'

She turned to find a well-dressed middle-aged man standing behind her, smiling sympathetically. 'I've come to see Mr Brierley, but it appears their offices are closed for the holiday.'

'And you are?'

She frowned. What business was that of this stranger? 'And who are *you*?'

He laughed. 'Excuse me. Perhaps that did sound rather rude. I'm Mr Brierley.'

'Oh!' Well how was she to have known?

'You're quite correct, we are closed till the New Year, but I've popped back for some papers that I left behind.' Recognition dawned. 'Of course, you're Elyse Davenport. I should have realised sooner.'

It pleased her that he knew who she was. 'You've seen my work then?'

'Many times, Mrs Davenport. I'm quite a fan.'

Better still, she thought.

'Let me open this door and then, please, come inside. We can talk in there.'

He led her along a narrow hallway into an office that was clearly his own. Old framed theatrical bills and posters lined the walls.

'Please, please sit down,' he requested, pointing to a chair in front of his desk. 'Now, how can I help you?'

He was neither good-looking nor ugly, she thought. A rather bland face really, but one dominated by sharp, intelligent eyes. She'd taken an instant liking to him. 'I hear you're doing a Russian piece in the spring and I was wondering if you're fully cast yet?'

'Ah!' he exhaled. 'It's *The Seagull* by Anton Chekhov. Do you know it?'

Elyse shook her head. 'Unfortunately not.'

'Well, that doesn't matter.' He studied her thoughtfully, twisting his head first one way and then the other to get a different view of her face. 'I think you would be right for Madame Arkadina,' he mused.

'Madame Arkadina?'

'An actress. Very flamboyant. Wonderful part.'

She smiled, but didn't reply to that.

'Have you ever played Chekhov at all?'

'No, I haven't,' she answered truthfully.

'Then you've been missing something. A treat, I assure you.'

Again she smiled and stayed silent.

He leant forward slightly. 'I shouldn't really ask an actress of your experience and reputation, but would you read for me? It would be a great help.'

She liked his tact. 'I'll be happy to read, Mr Brierley. My pleasure.'

'Good, good!' he enthused. Rising, he crossed to a shelf from which he took a typewritten manuscript. Going across to Elyse, he handed it to her.

'Why don't you have a look through first. And if there are any questions you'd care to ask, I'll be only too pleased to try and answer them.'

'Thank you.'

She was aware that his eyes never left her as she began flicking through the manuscript's pages.

Marcus Brierley sat back in his chair and sighed, Elyse having just finished her reading. 'The part was made for you, Mrs

Davenport,' he declared in delight. 'That wasn't a reading but a full-blown performance. Congratulations.'

This was beginning to look promising, she thought. And he was right, it was a superb part – one she'd give her eyeteeth to play. Particularly in the West End. Despite his enthusiasm, she warned herself not to get her hopes up too high, for she'd been in this position before, believing the part was hers, only to be let down when it eventually went to someone else.

'Now tell me, what have you been doing recently?' he queried.

He nodded while Elyse spoke about Torquay and the roles she'd already had there and about those to come, making special mention of Lady Macbeth, which she'd be tackling next.

'And when exactly does this engagement finish?' he asked.

'The end of March.'

He smacked his hands in approval. 'Couldn't be better. That means you'd be free to start rehearsals with us.'

'Which theatre do you have in mind?' she inquired, already knowing the answer.

'The Fortune.'

'Lovely little theatre. I did a Sheridan there once.'

'Indeed, I recall. I saw it. If I remember correctly, you got a round on every exit and a tumultuous ovation at the curtain call.'

Elyse flushed to be reminded of that. The Sheridan had been one of her biggest successes, with the *Times* critic, no less, being lavish in his praise.

'I tell you what,' Brierley declared. 'There's a little pub just round the corner where I usually drop by for a drink round about now. Would you care to join me?'

Elyse was taken aback. Where was the harm? she asked herself. Especially if a drink and a chat helped her land the part. 'That would be lovely.'

'Right then.'

They were about to leave the office when she said, 'Haven't you forgotten those papers you came for?'

He laughed. 'Bless me if I haven't. Thank you, Mrs Davenport.' He paused momentarily. 'May I call you Elyse? And you must call me Marcus. I'd feel far more relaxed that way. I may just have met you, but it's as if I've known you for years. Which, in a way, I have, considering the amount of times I've seen you onstage.'

There was an infectious enthusiasm about him that was most appealing. 'Then that's how it'll be, Marcus.'

He beamed at her before collecting the papers from a drawer in his desk.

One drink became two, which became three, the conversation flowing freely between them. Marcus was married with two almost grown-up children, the family living in Hampstead. All his life he'd been an ardent theatre-goer, finally deciding to give up his profession – that of a successful King's Counsel – to go into theatrical management. *The Seagull* was to be his first venture.

'Naturally I haven't used my own money,' Marcus went on. 'Having many rather well-off friends, I've roped a lot of them in as angels.' An angel was someone who invested in a play.

'Good for you,' Elyse replied. 'I would imagine the law must be a dreary sort of job.'

'It can have its moments, but in the main it's tedium itself. The theatre is far more exciting. So far I'm adoring every minute of it.'

'And does your wife approve of you changing over like this?'

He grinned. 'She had no option, Elyse. Once my mind is made up that's it. I explained my plans to her and she just had to go along with them, like it or not.'

A forceful man, she reflected. Used to getting his own way. 'When will you make a decision about the part?' she inquired casually, this being the question she'd been dying to ask since they'd arrived at the pub.

'Soon. I promise you that.'

'Before I return to Torquay?' Don't push him too hard, she warned herself. There again, it was best to strike while the iron was hot.

'I should imagine so,' he smiled. 'Now, would you care for another?'

It was time she went, even if she was enjoying herself. Enough was enough.

Marcus looked disappointed when she said she had to go. 'Pity,' he murmured.

She fished in her handbag for one of the cards she always carried and handed it to him. 'Unfortunately I'm not on the telephone,' she apologised.

He gazed at the card, then back at her. 'I really should see more of you, get to know you better during the next few days. I'd hate to make a mistake in the casting, Madama Arkadina being such an important part in the play. So, let me make a suggestion. Why don't we have lunch tomorrow?'

'Lunch?' Again she was caught on the hop. This was most unusual treatment by a theatrical management. At least for her. First drinks, now lunch. She didn't see how she could refuse in the circumstances. 'Where do you propose?'

'Ah, you accept. Good! Would The Savoy be agreeable?'

Elyse gulped inwardly. The Savoy! Lunch there would cost a fortune. Her mind was already racing, thinking what she might wear for such an occasion. Wait till she told Molly. 'More than agreeable, Marcus.'

'Shall we say one o'clock? I shall be waiting in the lobby for you.'

'One o'clock it is then.'

He finished the remainder of his drink, Elyse already having done the same. 'I'll escort you outside and call a taxi for you.'

She'd intended to walk as it wasn't that far, but no matter. 'Thank you.'

He leant across the table. 'If I may say so, you really are the most dashed attractive woman, Elyse. And please take that the way it's meant.'

'Thank you again.'

His eyes gleamed. 'Shall we?'

On hailing a passing motortaxi, he insisted on paying the driver. 'Till tomorrow,' he said once she was sitting inside.

'Till tomorrow,' she agreed.

Well, she thought, as the taxi drove off. Talk about being given the red-carpet treatment. Thank God she'd bumped into Pattie Browne.

'I think he fancies you, so I do,' Molly O'Malley declared after listening to Elyse's tale.

That had never occurred to Elyse. 'He's married, Molly, happily too by all accounts.'

Molly snorted. 'Since when has that ever stopped those randy buggers?'

'You're being far too cynical. Seamus would never look elsewhere, for a start.'

Molly's expression softened. 'That's true enough. But he's one in a million, the ignorant Irish sod.'

Could it be that Marcus did fancy her? Elyse wondered. What was it he'd said: a dashed attractive woman. Potential employers didn't usually make comments like that. Now that she came to think of it, Molly might well be right. It was a worry. One thing was certain – she wanted that part. Badly. A return to the West End in a starring role would give her career the boost it needed. Particularly if the play – and she in it – was a huge success.

'You see it all down here,' Molly commented, looking round. She and Elyse were in one of the club's booths. 'Married, single, it never seems to make any difference. You'd be shocked at what I hear behind the bar. The daft buggers on the other side forget you're there after a while and act, and speak, as if you don't exist. And it's not only men with women, either, if you understand my meaning.'

Elyse nodded. She did.

'There are chaps come in here whose wives and girlfriends have no idea they also have a taste for their own kind. Women, too. There's one I could name, a well-known actress, and I mean well-known, who's regularly on the lookout for a piece of female dalliance. I swear you'd never guess there was that side to her. So don't be naïve, Elyse. If your Mr Brierley is inviting you to The Savoy, he may have more in mind than simply discussing casting and telling you how much of a fan he is. It could well be that he wants to get between those legs of yours. And it wouldn't be the first time an actress has lain on her back for a part.'

Elyse would hardly have called herself naïve, but perhaps, in this instance . . . 'I'll have to give this some thought,' she declared quietly.

'Would you?' Molly's eyes were boring into hers.

'I never have. Though, to be honest, it's a decision I haven't had to make before.'

'That's not answering the question.'

Elyse took her time in replying. 'I simply don't know,' she confessed at last.

Molly knew that to be an honest answer, but before they could discuss matters further she was signalled by Seamus behind the bar that she was needed. Business was hotting up.

They didn't speak again on the subject as Elyse left shortly afterwards.

Elyse was woken abruptly out of her sleep by an almighty thump, as if someone had dropped a sack of coal on the floor in the lounge. She couldn't imagine what had caused it.

Getting out of bed, she slipped on a dressing gown and padded through to discover Benny lying flat on his back clutching a bottle in his hand. Despite having fallen off the sofa, he was still out for the count.

Pissed as a rat, Elyse observed bitterly. Well, he could lie where he was. She had neither the strength nor the inclination to help him back onto the sofa.

Her lips thinned in anger to note that alcohol had spilled from the bottle onto the sofa and carpet. Whether it stained or not depended on what sort of alcohol it was.

She went to him and prised the bottle out of his grasp, frowning to see that there was no label on it. She sniffed, and her frown deepened. Gin, she thought, but more than that. The smell was most odd. Tentatively she had a taste, and immediately spat out what had gone into her mouth.

Her eyes blazed in fury. How could he! How could the stupid bastard start on laudanum! It was not only highly addictive, but against the law unless prescribed by a doctor. And she doubted that was where this lot had come from.

She knew only too well about laudanum, for it had been a scourge in Clerkenwell when she was young. She'd had an uncle who was an addict – Uncle George, who'd died in his twenties thanks to the bloody stuff. Now here was Benny on it.

'You fool!' she hissed down at him. 'You stupid fool. How could you?' No wonder he was looking old. Laudanum knocked the stuffing out of a person, particularly if taken regularly and in quantity. It was a destroyer, far worse than alcohol, with which many people mixed it.

She poured the remainder of the bottle's contents down the sink before returning to bed.

Elyse stared up at The Savoy. It was precisely one o'clock. She'd chosen a one-piece, straight-line frock for the occasion, which was adorned with wool embroidery in a French knot design. The dress itself was all-wool French serge with a waist lining of batiste. Its neat tailoring was set off by a narrow tie belt, the entire ensemble being in royal blue.

Her black coat was enhanced by a fur stole round the shoulders, while the hat she had on was black velvet in a toque style, with a large bow of the same fabric set at a jaunty angle. Her gloves were cream-coloured with lace at the wrists.

Elyse took a deep breath before going inside, where Marcus, as he'd promised, was waiting for her in the lobby.

'How are your chops?'

'Fine,' she smiled.

'My veal is absolutely delicious. You know, in all the years I've been coming here, I don't think I've ever had a bad meal. Says a lot for its standards, don't you think?'

She nodded.

He picked up the bottle of Bordeaux he'd ordered and topped up her glass, then did the same to his own.

Elyse glanced about her, thinking what a grand place the Grill was. A grand place full of very important-looking people. It all screamed of money and class. In a subdued and refined way of course.

So far they'd been making small talk, mainly about the theatre and past productions they'd either seen, been in, in Elyse's case, or heard of. *The Seagull* hadn't yet been mentioned.

Marcus took a sip of wine, meanwhile studying Elyse intently over the glass's rim. He cleared his throat as he set it back down again.

'Such a shame you're only in town for a few more days,' he said.

She smiled, but didn't reply.

'I do so enjoy your company.'

'Thank you, Marcus.'

'And I hope you enjoy mine?'

'Very much so.' That wasn't a lie. So far he'd been most entertaining, easy to be with. And quite funny at times, with an amusing line in theatrical anecdotes. 'Tell me about your family,' she probed. 'You haven't mentioned them so far.'

His face clouded. 'There's not a lot to tell. We're quite ordinary really.'

'And your wife?' she pressed, wanting to see his reaction to that question.

Marcus shrugged. 'What's to say? Carolyn is two years younger than me, paints watercolours in her spare time and does rather a lot for charity. My elder son Peter hopes to follow me into the law, while Michael is considering a naval career. Though why that, I've no idea.'

'They sound nice.'

Marcus reflected on that. 'I suppose so. I'm very proud of the boys. They're both good sorts.'

'Do they like the theatre?'

'So-so. It's hardly their overriding interest, as it's always been mine.'

'What about Carolyn? If I may call her that.'

'She prefers light comedies, revues and such. But in the main I attend things on my own.'

'And you don't mind that?'

He shrugged again. 'Sometimes, sometimes not.' He paused for a second. 'Which brings me round to the fact that I have two tickets for *The Misanthrope* by Molière tomorrow night. I was hoping you might go along with me.'

'Tomorrow night?' she mused, as if she might have some prior engagement.

He watched her expectantly.

Drinks, an expensive lunch and now a proposed visit to the theatre. And they'd only met yesterday! It seemed Molly was right: this wasn't just about casting. It was personal.

'Well?' he prompted.

She thought of *The Seagull* and Madame Arkadina. Did he intend a simple visit to the theatre, or something else? She was torn.

He reached across and placed a hand over hers. 'Please, Elyse? It would mean a great deal to me.'

As Marcus had pointed out, there were only a few days left before her return to Torquay, so what could be the harm? None that she could see. And once she'd signed the contract, the part would be hers, no matter what. If it took humouring him in the meantime, then so be it.

'I'd love to,' she smiled in reply.

Chapter 13

'There you are, lads,' declared Ironmonger, the photographer, placing a tray of drinks on the pub table. It was the office Christmas party and he, Tim, Harry Nutbeam and Patsy were the only ones still remaining. It was now two hours since they'd arrived from work.

'Stout chap,' Patsy beamed, helping himself to a fresh pint. As always, he would be the last to leave.

Tim wasn't sure he could manage another, or that he even wanted to try. He'd already had more than enough.

'Are you all right?' Harry queried with a frown.

'Why, don't I look it?'

'No, you don't. You're suddenly all down-in-the-mouth. As if you're about to burst out crying.'

'Booze affects some men like that,' Patsy commented sagely. 'With me, I just eventually fall asleep, happy as Larry.'

'Excuse me, nature calls,' Ironmonger apologised and left them.

Patsy discovered that he'd run out of cigarettes and got up to go to the bar for a replacement packet.

'How's that girlfriend of yours?' Harry inquired amiably of Tim.

It was Katherine whom Tim had been thinking about and the fact that he wouldn't be seeing her again till sometime in the new year – the reason for him feeling miserable. 'Don't know,' he mumbled.

'And what does that mean?'

Tim explained the situation.

'Tough luck, eh?'

Tim nodded.

'You being so keen and all.'

'She's lovely, you know,' Tim slurred slightly. 'Really lovely.'

'I'm envious. Truly I am. I wish I could find someone like that.' Harry gazed disconsolately into his drink. 'I keep trying, but never do. I think I'm going to end up a male version of an old maid.'

'No you won't!' Tim protested. 'The right girl will come along. It's only a matter of time. You'll see.'

'Maybe,' Harry mused. 'Maybe.'

Patsy came ambling back. 'They've run out, so I'm nipping round to the shop.'

'I finally kissed her,' Tim stated quietly when Patsy had gone again.

'And?'

'I couldn't believe a pair of lips could be so soft. It was wonderful.'

Harry sighed with jealousy. The girls he kissed never had lips like that.

Ironmonger returned to join them. 'Who fancies an adventure?' he queried with a broad grin.

Tim brought himself out of his reverie. 'What sort of adventure?'

Ironmonger, who was older than Tim and Harry, though also a bachelor, leant forward and winked conspiratorially. 'I've just been having a word with a female I know. There's a whole group of them here having their Christmas party, same as us.'

'Where?' a suddenly eager Harry demanded.

'Don't make it obvious, but on the far side of the pub to your right. There's about a dozen of them and they're all out for a good time.'

'Really?' Harry replied softly. Surreptitiously he glanced round, searching the bar till he located the group that Ironmonger was talking about. 'Some of them aren't bad,' he observed.

'They're a bit rough, mind you. Females who work in one of the dockside gutting sheds. But usually a tremendous laugh.' The gutting sheds were where the Torquay fish catches were prepared for the onward journey. Other fish – those for local consumption – were sold whole.

'So what do you think?' Ironmonger demanded.

Tim shook his head. 'You go ahead, but leave me out of it. I'm not interested.'

'He's in love,' Harry teased.

'Shut up.'

'Well, aren't you?'

Tim glared at him.

'Well, I for one am going to chance my arm,' Ironmonger announced. 'I know for a fact that they're not averse to a bit of rumpy-pumpy if the fancy takes them. They're not shy in that department. Especially when pissed, which they will be shortly.'

'Come on,' Harry urged Tim. 'Maybe we can both find

out what it's all about.' Like Tim, he was a virgin.

'I said no thanks, and I meant it.' Despite himself Tim had a quick peep at where the women were sitting. Harry was right, some of them were lookers. A blonde with a large chest caught his eye in particular, his imagination immediately firing up at the thought of what lay beneath her blouse. He felt a familiar stirring.

'Harry?'

'I'm with you. But shouldn't we wait for Patsy?'

'He can come over if he wants. Meanwhile, we'll do the groundwork.'

Harry couldn't wait: this was going to be fun, he just knew it. 'Don't be a spoilsport,' he appealed to Tim one last time. 'It is Christmas after all. And Katherine will never know.'

'But I would,' Tim replied in a gritty tone.

'Just to keep us company?'

'No. Now on you go. And good luck. I'll send Patsy across when he gets back.'

'He's really got it bad,' Harry whispered to Ironmonger as they wove their way through the customers.

The girls from the gutting shed were only too happy to welcome Harry and Ironmonger among them, and soon shrieks of laughter were coming from their tables.

Tim left his beer and headed for the lavatory, only to slip out the back door. He walked home with shoulders hunched and hands deep in his pockets, not having taken his motorbike to the office that day on account of the party.

During the entire journey he kept wondering what Katherine was doing and wishing they were together.

* * *

Elyse had purposely waited in all morning till Benny awoke. A loud groan told her that was about to happen.

A few minutes later he sat up, bleary-eyed, and stretched himself, stopping in mid-stretch when he saw Elyse sitting staring at him. He knew what was coming next.

'Just don't start,' he snarled.

'Laudanum, Benny. How could you be so bloody stupid?'

'I said: don't start. What I do is none of your business.'

'Keep on with it, Benny, and you'll kill yourself. That's what usually happens.'

'Don't talk nonsense, woman. I know what I'm doing.'

She gave him a cynical, disbelieving smile. 'Do you really?'

'Yes, I do. Now go and make me a cup of tea. My throat's like sandpaper.'

'Look at you,' she admonished. 'What a state!'

He pushed his trembling hands under the blankets that he'd pulled over himself before going to sleep. It wasn't really tea he craved, but another drink from his special bottle, the one he'd bought to replace the liquid Elyse had poured down the sink. Knowing she'd done that, because he'd found the empty bottle by the sink, where she'd left it.

She shook her head. 'God alone knows what I saw in you. But the man I fell in love with certainly isn't the one you've become.'

'That's enough,' he said through gritted teeth.

It was too, she decided. She couldn't bear being with him a moment longer.

Hell mend him, she thought bitterly as she collected her coat, that being a favourite expression of her mother's when referring to her father. Hell mend him. The really sad thing was that she didn't even feel any pity.

It was early afternoon when a pale-faced Harry Nutbeam finally turned up at the office, having genuinely been out on a story, which he now had to write. He slumped into a chair beside Tim.

'Where's Ricketts?' he asked, the editor not being present.

'Down with the printers, I think.'

Harry took a deep breath. 'Christ, what a night! My head's bursting.'

'So?' Tim queried emphatically, it being obvious to what he was referring.

A smile lit up Harry's face. 'I did it, Tim. I actually did it.'

'You mean, you . . . ?'

Harry nodded.

'Where?'

'In the graveyard, would you believe? It was the only place we could think of. We certainly couldn't go to my house and we couldn't go to hers either, as she's married. So it was the graveyard.'

Tim could only think that must have been awfully cold, not to mention uncomfortable. 'How was it?'

Harry considered that for a few moments. Not a man usually lost for words, he now seemed to be. 'Better than I imagined. A lot better. Absolutely fantastic in fact.'

'You actually . . . the full thing?'

'The lot, Tim. Over a gravestone, which was her idea. She said she didn't want to ruin her clothes by lying down.'

Tim was incredulous. Over a gravestone! His mind boggled. 'And it was all right?'

'Oh yes. I fumbled a bit to start with, but she soon put me straight.' He laughed. 'She certainly put me straight all right, if you get my meaning.'

Harry glanced about. They'd been speaking quietly, but he was making sure they weren't being overheard.

If Harry had been jealous of Tim the night before, then Tim was now jealous of Harry. 'Are you seeing her again?'

'Don't be daft. I told you she's married. It was strictly a one-off thing. Which, I have to say, she made quite plain.' Harry shook his head in wonder. 'You should have seen the tits on her. They were enormous.'

Tim recalled the girl who'd caught his eye. 'Was she blonde?'

'Out of a bottle.'

It had to be the same one, Tim thought, part of him desperately wishing it had been him instead of Harry, but another part recoiling at the thought, because of Katherine. Well, when he first slept with a woman it would be on his wedding night, with Katherine. And there would be no gravestone either, but a soft, warm bed.

'As a matter of interest, what was her name?'

Harry looked sheepish. 'Hortense. She wouldn't tell me her surname.'

Tim found that funny – hysterical even. Hortense! How awful!

Their conversation was cut short by Ricketts returning, and the pair of them hastily got on with the job in hand so as not to invite the displeasure of their editor.

Every so often Tim stopped and smiled. Hortense! The more he thought about it, the funnier it was.

After the play Marcus had pressed Elyse to go to a supper and drinking club with him, insisting that was the only way to round off their evening.

In the taxi taking them there they discussed the play, a production neither had been particularly impressed with. The casting had been wrong in parts, Marcus declared, that being its main fault, in his opinion. They also agreed it had been lacklustre and short of energy, which was always so important. Vital even.

The Wellington was off the Cromwell Road and catered solely for well-to-do clientele. Elyse and Marcus were in the lounge, Elyse having declined his offer of a meal. They were drinking champagne cocktails.

'I wish you'd change your mind and have something to eat,' Marcus urged.

'I can't. Honestly. I have to get back shortly. I explained that to you before we came.'

Marcus toyed with his glass. 'I know what you said, but I was rather hoping you'd spend the rest of the night with me.'

There it was – what she'd been half-expecting and hoped wouldn't happen. She'd have been a liar if she'd denied not having already given this a lot of thought.

'I'm a married woman, Marcus,' she reminded him.

'And I'm a married man.'

She was curious. 'And where would we . . . ?' She trailed off with a raised eyebrow.

'I have a friend who has a small apartment not far from

here, a pied-à-terre. He's agreed to let me have it for tonight. The key's in my pocket.'

'You have been busy,' she commented with an edge in her voice.

He smiled thinly but didn't reply.

James – if it hadn't been for James she might have been tempted. But when it came to it she couldn't betray him, her feelings for him being too strong. Benny, despite being her husband, didn't come into it. That relationship was well and truly finished. But James was something else.

'And the role of Madama Arkadina. Does that depend on my answer?'

Marcus shrugged.

'Yes or no? I want an answer.'

'I do find you terribly attractive, Elyse. Something happened the moment we met. I knew I just had to have you.'

'Yes or no, Marcus?' she repeated doggedly.

'That's terribly blunt.'

'Is it? I'd call it a fairly simple question.'

He picked up his glass and had a deep swallow. 'If you were agreeable, it wouldn't just be tonight. We could come to some sort of arrangement. And don't forget I'm just starting out in management. *The Seagull* is, hopefully, only the first of many productions.'

Elyse glanced down at her lap and fought back the urge to cough. Damn the man! She was being offered an open ticket here, if he was being honest, that was, and she believed he was. The sincerity in his voice was only too real. If it hadn't been for James . . .

'I'm in love with someone else, Marcus. I couldn't betray him. Not for anything.'

'Your husband?'

'No. Another man.'

'I see.' The disappointment was etched clearly on his face. That and petulance at not getting his own way, for he was used to doing so.

'I'm sorry.'

'So am I, Elyse,' he replied softly. 'So am I. Maybe more than you might think. Would it help if we talked about what you'd be paid for the part?'

She shook her head.

'It could be substantial. Far more than I imagine you'd normally get.'

'No, Marcus. No. Please accept that.'

'I could always . . .'

'No,' she interrupted forcefully.

He knew then that he was beaten, that he wouldn't be going to bed with her after all.

'I think I should go now.'

He stared into his glass and didn't reply.

'Marcus?'

'I heard. I'm sure the doorman will hail a cab for you.'

So much for his being a gentleman, she thought. 'Are you staying here?'

He nodded without looking at her.

Elyse rose, picked up her clutch bag and walked away. She knew an opportunity like the one she'd just turned down would never again present itself.

'Did you have a good time?' Minna asked, having bumped into Elyse in the corridor.

'Yes, thank you.'

'When did you get in?'

'A few minutes ago. I'm on my way out again.'

Minna didn't comment on that, it was none of her business. She guessed correctly that Elyse was anxious to see her chap, the one she stayed out nights with. 'Will you be in for dinner?'

'I don't think so.'

'It's good to have you back.'

'Thank you. It's good to be back. I'm looking forward to starting rehearsals.'

'Good luck with them then.'

As Minna had surmised, it was James that Elyse was off to see. There was a terrible need in her.

James answered her knock. 'Hello,' he smiled.

'Hello.'

'When did you return?'

'I've only just. I haven't even unpacked.'

'And you came straight round here?'

She nodded.

'Then you'd better come in.'

The door was no sooner closed behind them than she was in his arms, her lips on his.

Still entwined, they made their way into the bedroom, where he immediately began undressing her.

Elyse closed her eyes. That had been glorious. The best yet, which she'd hardly thought was possible. How skilful he was, and considerate in the extreme. She sighed with contentment.

'Elyse?'

'What, darling?'

'Tell me about London? I'm dying to hear.'

One thing was certain – she wasn't going to mention Marcus. Not that it would have mattered if she had, for she hadn't done anything after all. She just didn't want to. It was as simple as that.

'What do you wish to know?'

'Where you went, who you met, what you did. Most importantly, did you manage to arrange any work for after here?'

'No, I didn't.'

'Not even a sniff?'

She thought of Marcus: that had been a lot more than a sniff. It had been a cast-iron certainty. 'Can I say something?'

'Of course.'

'Being away made me realise something.'

'Which is?'

'That I love you.'

He suddenly went very still, the hand that had been caressing her naked thigh stopping in mid-motion. He didn't reply.

'James?'

'Are you sure?'

'I've never been more sure of anything.'

There was a slight pause, then the hand resumed its stroking. 'It's a relief to hear you say that, because I love you.'

She twisted round to stare into his face, the face she'd dreamt of every night while in London. Dreamt of with longing.

'You do?'

'Oh yes,' he breathed. 'Very much so.'

'That's all right then.'

'I want to be with you, Elyse. Not just for the season but for ever.'

'Then you shall be.'

'What about Benny?'

James listened intently as she told him about the laudanum and the state Benny had got himself into. That and the women she knew Benny was seeing.

When she'd told him everything, with the exception of Marcus, James made love to her again. It was heaven.

'You seem happy this morning,' Minna commented to Elyse, who was making her way in to breakfast. 'I heard you singing in the bathroom earlier.'

'I am, Mrs Wilson.'

'You look quite radiant.'

'I feel it.'

Minna hesitated, then decided to say it anyway. 'Is he nice?'

Elyse knew she was referring to James. 'Very.'

'And he's the cause of your happiness?'

Elyse nodded.

The two women understood one another, with Minna clearly approving, which surprised Elyse. 'I'll tell you about him sometime, if you'd like?' she offered.

'I would.'

Now it was Elyse's turn to hesitate. 'It's not my husband. Our marriage has been in tatters for years. I'm lucky enough to have been given a second chance.'

'Then you must grab it with both hands. Will you divorce?'

'As you'll appreciate, Mrs Wilson, that's terribly expensive, and something of a social stigma. Though I can't say that applies so much in the theatre. We're, shall I say, more broad-minded in our outlook. Less judgemental.'

'The world is changing, Mrs Davenport, my Redvers used always to say that. Perhaps faster than we realise. He too was a very non-judgemental man, and a compassionate one. He used to quote from the Bible. "Let he who is without sin cast the first stone." There's a lot in that, don't you think?' The way Minna ran The Berkeley was in accordance with public mores and supposed morality. Her private views could, however, at times be quite different.

'Yes,' Elyse replied softly.

Minna's manner abruptly changed. 'Now, you go through for your breakfast. Euphemia is serving today.'

She'd liked Minna before, but now she liked her a great deal more, Elyse thought as the landlady hurried away.

And yes, she truly was happy. The happiest she'd been for a long, long time. Thanks to James.

Tim halted *en route* to his room as a familiar smell assaulted his nostrils. Minna had told him Mrs Davenport had returned, but he'd have known, even if she hadn't.

That perfume was unmistakable.

'What are you doing, dear?' Jeremiah Coates inquired casually of Ruth, who was busy at their bureau.

'Preparing Katherine's Season.' She glanced over at him. 'There's such a lot to organise you know, and it's only a few months away.'

That was true enough, Jeremiah reflected, for the new

year had passed and it was now almost February 1913.

He took a deep breath. God, he was bored, and restless. This staying at home was beginning to get on his nerves. Now that he'd retrenched his business interests, he could manage well enough from Oaklands, but the daily routine he'd fallen into lacked excitement and edge.

News from the Continent continued to be alarming. And not only there, but in the Balkans as well. The war in Turkey, which had been invaded by the Bulgarians and Serbs, also boded ill. If it was to spread, who knew what the result might be.

Jeremiah sighed. He badly needed distraction, but what? The answer, now he thought of it, was all too obvious. 'I'm thinking of taking a trip to London next week,' he announced.

'Oh?' said Ruth, who'd been about to resume writing.

'Business. A few things I need to attend to. You don't mind, do you?'

'Of course not, dear. I'd come with you, but as you know my chest has been playing up. Winter has never been agreeable to me.'

'No, it hasn't,' he sympathised, pleased that she wasn't coming, because that meant there would be no restrictions on visiting Mrs Green's establishment and being with the lovely Henrietta.

Ruth looked across the room to where the grandfather clock stood. 'Katherine's late,' she frowned.

Jeremiah also glanced at the clock. 'Hardly that, dear. It's only quarter to ten.'

Ruth's lips thinned in disapproval. 'Even so.'

'You wouldn't be saying that if it was Miles Crabthorne

she was out with instead of Tim Wilson,' he commented wryly.

Ruth couldn't deny it, knowing it to be so. She busied herself again with her plans for Katherine's coming-out.

'It was a lovely evening, thank you, Tim.' She and Tim had been to an amateur concert that he was covering for the newspaper, and then taken coffee afterwards. They were now staring out over the bay, where they'd come to say good-night. Edward, the chauffeur, was parked nearby.

'I enjoyed it too,' he replied softly. 'But then I always enjoy your company.'

She pressed herself closer against him and surreptitiously sought his hand.

'I wish I could kiss you,' Tim said.

'Well, you can't,' she replied, knowing that Edward might be watching.

Tim glanced back at the car parked under a street lamp, the outline of Edward's head and shoulders clearly visible. If only he could wave a magic wand and make the damned man disappear for a few minutes.

'I sometimes wonder whether or not your parents like me,' he said.

Katherine turned to him with a frown. 'Why do you say that?'

'I don't know. Just a feeling I get sometimes.'

Katherine was only too well aware that her mother didn't approve of the relationship. There had been too many remarks and comments for her not to be. Her father did, though. He was very fond of Tim.

'If we were to have a little stroll and end up behind that

building, you could kiss me then,' she suggested.

'What a good idea,' he breathed, a hint of laughter in his voice. 'Let's go then.'

They proceeded slowly, Katherine having taken her hand out of his. Then they were masked by the building, hidden from Edward's prying eyes.

Her lips were every bit as soft as Tim remembered.

Chapter 14

'I've been thinking,' Elyse declared from behind the screen where she was changing after the show.

James, already changed and having taken off his slap, was sitting nursing a glass of Scotch. 'I wondered what the noise was,' he said drolly in reply.

Elyse laughed. She was euphoric, which was nearly always the case when the play had gone particularly well. It had been a wonderful audience and a packed house. At the end there had been twelve curtain calls, including a solo for herself. James was very good at singling her out.

'Why don't I give up my room at The Berkeley and move in with you?'

'What a lovely idea,' he smiled.

'Far more convenient. And I'd get to sleep and cuddle with you every night.'

His smile broadened. 'Me too.'

'So, do you agree?'

He finished his whisky and, rising, crossed to where the bottle stood on her dressing table. Despite his calm, controlled exterior his mind was churning.

'I'm afraid not,' he replied eventually.

Elyse popped her head round the side of the screen. 'Did you say no?'

'I did, darling. Oh, it's not that I don't want you to move in. I'd carry your luggage there tonight myself, if it was possible. But, sadly, it's out of the question.'

Elyse hadn't been expecting this, thinking he'd jump at the chance. 'And why's that?'

'The owner, darling. He simply wouldn't allow it. This is Torquay after all, the *provinces*, dear. You staying the occasional night is one thing: actually taking up residence quite another. Before we knew it we'd both be out on our ear.'

She couldn't hide her disappointment, but James did have a point. 'I see what you mean.'

'If it was up to me, I'd move you in like a shot, but it isn't. Now, when we get to London, that'll be different. Nobody gives a fig there. We can call ourselves Mr and Mrs Whatever when we rent and no-one will be any the wiser.'

That was certainly true, Elyse reflected. Oh well, the end of the season would come round quickly enough. It wasn't that far away. 'What about tonight?' she queried.

He pulled a face. 'I'd rather you didn't. I have a tremendous amount of work to get through, which I won't if your tempting self is floating about.'

Probably just as well, she thought, for she too had lines to learn, since they had just started rehearsals for the next production.

'What I suggest is that we save it all for Sunday. We can spend the whole day in bed then, if you wish.'

'Oh, I like the sound of that,' she enthused.

'Thought you might. By the way, I'm helping myself to more whisky, is that all right?'

'Don't ask. I've told you not to. If it's there, just help yourself.'

There was a knock on the door. 'Who is it?' James queried.

'Ronnie.'

'Come in.'

'I thought you might be here, Mr Erskine. Is there anything else you want me to do before I go?'

James stared hard at the ASM, a glitter of amusement – and something else – in his eyes. 'No, that's fine, Ronnie. I'll expect you tomorrow at ten o'clock sharp.'

'Thank you, sir.'

Ronnie hesitated, glancing in the direction of the screen, then turning back again to James, who made a small sign. Ronnie nodded that he understood and left.

Elyse emerged from behind the screen and went straight to James. 'Why don't you kiss me?'

'Why don't I indeed.'

How warm he was, she thought, as their tongues entwined. And how damned sexy. There were times, like now, when she could hardly keep her hands off him. Wanted to eat him alive.

A kiss was all she got though, for they didn't go any further. Not in the dressing room – that would have been so squalid, although not unheard of.

She had a cigarette and a quick Scotch before James escorted her from the theatre.

Sunday, and all that promised, seemed an eternity away.

Elyse knew only too well why she couldn't concentrate: it was because she kept thinking about James, wishing that she was with him, that they were in bed together, making love.

She threw down her script on the chair. Hard as she tried, the lines just wouldn't go in. She'd been over that particular scene time and time again and still didn't know it.

She lit a cigarette, then poured herself another drink. Well, she was just going to have to keep at it, there was no question about that. She'd be expected to know these lines when she turned up for rehearsal in the morning. James wouldn't be best pleased if she didn't. Besides, she was a professional, and that was part of being one. Never letting the others down. At least in her book it was.

She thought about the conversation they'd had in the dressing room, and her disappointment at not being able to move in with him. As for finding a suitable place in London – well, she had an idea about that. She'd write to Molly O'Malley and ask her to keep an ear to the ground for somewhere. Molly heard all sorts at the club, not least about digs and apartments going cheap.

Elyse paused in her reflections when she heard someone outside in the corridor, instantly recognising the footsteps. He'd helped before, so why not again?

'Tim?'

He swung round to face her. 'Mrs Davenport?'

She beckoned him inside. 'Can you spare me half an hour?' she queried, closing the door behind him.

As on the previous occasion, Elyse was wearing a négligé over her nightdress. As far as Tim was concerned, these left little to the imagination. 'I suppose,' he replied reluctantly. He wasn't at all sure about this.

'It's lines, I'm afraid. Be a sweetie and help me. There's a good chap.'

'If you wish.'

She beamed at him. 'Care for a drink first?'

God, she did knock it back, he thought. He'd never known a woman like her. 'Please.'

'It's over here. I'll get a glass. So,' she said when the glass was charged and he'd had a sip. 'How's the romance coming along?'

'You mean Katherine and me?'

She nodded.

'All right. I don't see as much of her as I'd like, but there we are.'

Elyse wanted to tell him all about her and James, but didn't think it appropriate. 'Is it still serious?' she asked instead.

'Well, I am, and I believe Katherine is too.'

'Good,' she smiled. 'I'm pleased.'

He had to force himself not to stare at the swell of her breasts, which he found quite hypnotic. Despite his feelings for Katherine he couldn't help but imagine . . .

'Didn't you say Katherine is well-off?'

'The family is. They live in a large house called Oaklands. Her father's a businessman, now semi-retired because of her mother, who doesn't enjoy the best of health.'

'Poor woman,' Elyse sympathised. 'Are there any brothers and sisters?'

'No, Katherine is an only child.'

'Just as you are,' Elyse pointed out. 'That's something you have in common.'

'Yes.'

Love, Elyse reflected, the most wonderful thing in the world. And the most important, according to many people. A sentiment she wholeheartedly agreed with. The most important, but not always easy. But then the best things in life rarely were. She supposed you appreciated them more when it was that way.

'I played Juliet once,' she mused. 'Oh, a long time ago now. The irony of that part is that you don't fully understand it when you're young enough to be cast, and when you do, you're too old. It's therefore virtually unplayable.'

Voluptuous, Tim thought. That was the word he'd come up with before to describe her, and it still applied. She positively oozed sensuality.

'I wish you and your Katherine all the very best,' Elyse said. 'I hope it works out for you.'

'Thank you.'

She had a large sip of Scotch, then another. 'Anyway, enough of this chitchat. I asked you in to help, so we'll make a start, eh?'

'I'm ready when you are.'

He swallowed hard when she bent over to retrieve her script, her gorgeous backside pointing right at him.

He wondered what Katherine looked like in a nightdress and négligé. Well, he'd find out one day. And what she looked like wearing nothing at all.

The thought of that made his skin prickle.

Christ, she felt awful. Elyse had been awake for several hours and still couldn't summon the energy to get out of bed. She felt totally drained, lifeless. The stuffing had been knocked right out of her.

It was too much booze and cigarettes, she told herself. Had to be. Well, she was just going to have to cut down on both – there was nothing else for it.

During the night she'd had several horrendous bouts of coughing, bringing up masses of horrible green stuff. Her throat still ached from it.

She took a deep breath. If she didn't rouse herself soon, she'd be late for rehearsals and that would be unforgivable. She'd never been late for rehearsals in her entire life.

She tried to sit up, then sank back onto her bed again when the inside of her head began going round and round, the dizziness threatening to overwhelm her.

And then the coughing started once more.

'When do I get to meet this lady friend of yours?' Minna asked out of the blue. 'You're very secretive about her.'

Tim glanced up in surprise from the book he was reading. He and his mother were sitting in their parlour. 'Meet her?'

'That's what I said.'

'I . . . don't know,' he stuttered. 'I hadn't thought about that.'

'Well, isn't it time you did? You have been seeing her for some while, after all.'

Tim closed his book in confusion. The idea of Katherine coming to The Berkeley had simply never entered his head.

'You don't have to worry,' Minna went on. 'I'll be perfectly polite and charming, and promise not to embarrass you by telling her stories about when you were little.'

Tim coloured. That would be awful. He was almost squirming at the thought.

'Or show her pictures,' Minna added with a faintly malicious, though kindly, smile.

Now Tim was really alarmed. There was one picture,

Minna's favourite, taken when he was only a few months old. It was of him lying stark-naked on a rug with his bottom in the air. And another of him aged about three wearing the most ridiculous sailor suit and grinning into the camera like some demented idiot. Both equally cringe-making, in his opinion. Minna, of course, disagreed, thinking them ever so adorable.

'As her parents have met you, don't you think it's high time I met Katherine?' Minna went on quietly and ruthlessly.

Tim sighed. 'I suppose so,' he reluctantly agreed.

'Unless, that is, you're ashamed of me and our circumstances?'

'I'm nothing of the sort,' Tim protested hotly. 'Whatever made you think that?'

'Just asking, that's all.' Minna paused, then said, 'How about tea one Sunday? Just the three of us. Then I could get to know her and she me.'

Tim glanced about the parlour, suddenly aware of how shabby it was compared to the smart decoration and furnishings at Oaklands. What would Katherine make of this room and the rest of The Berkeley? What if he went down in her estimation as a result?

'But if you'd rather not . . .' Minna trailed off, intentionally forcing him into a corner. She was curious about Katherine Coates, having made inquiries about the family. Mr Coates was a respected and well-liked figure in Torquay, and everyone spoke highly of him. Not so of his wife. She had a reputation for being a snooty, high-handed bitch who was generally loathed. The question was: who did the girl take after?

'I'll speak to Katherine about it,' Tim conceded. 'Is that all right?'

'Any Sunday that suits her. Just let me know.'

Tim pretended to start reading his book again, but was actually wondering what Katherine's reaction would be when he put the suggestion to her.

'You promise no stories or pictures?' he said without looking up.

'I promise.'

Well, that at least was something.

James watched Elyse's face as she threw back her head and screamed, her body continuing to rock against his as the scream went on and on.

Finally she stopped and collapsed onto him, and he idly ran his fingers through her sodden hair. It gave him a feeling of enormous self-satisfaction when she screamed like that.

'Oh, James,' she crooned, 'I do so love you.'

'And I you.'

Gently, without disengaging, he rolled Elyse onto her back, smiling to see the river of sweat running between her breasts. He dipped his head to kiss each nipple.

'You spoil me,' she breathed, eyes glowing.

'And so I should.'

'Now it's your turn.'

'In a bit. I'm in no hurry. Are you?'

'No,' she confessed eagerly. As far as she was concerned the longer it went on, the better.

A little later he had her screaming again.

* * *

'Ma, this is Katherine. Katherine, this is my mother.'

The two women shook hands, Minna's expression not betraying the fact that she was sizing up the girl. So far she liked what she saw.

'How do you do, Katherine. Welcome to The Berkeley.'

'Thank you. I'm pleased to meet you, Mrs Wilson.'

Tim was agitated, on edge. But at least, despite Minna's assurances, he didn't have to worry about those silly pictures. He'd looked out the family album the night before and hidden it.

'Please take a seat.'

Expensive dress, Minna thought. Definitely bought in London, possibly Bond Street. There had been a time when she'd worn dresses from there, but no more. Those days were long past.

Good complexion, Minna further noted, and intelligent eyes. She could understand why Tim was attracted to her.

Katherine, for her part, was quite at ease and had readily agreed to meet Minna when Tim had rather nervously suggested it. She hoped they were going to get on.

'Tim, could you bring the trolley through from the kitchen while Katherine and I chat?' Minna smiled.

He shot her a warning glance before leaving the room. No stories of when he was little, please God, he prayed.

Katherine stayed for a full two hours before announcing that she had to leave, assuring Minna that she'd thoroughly enjoyed herself.

Tim saw her out to where Edward was waiting in the car.

* * *

'Well?' Tim demanded on his return.

Minna nodded her approval. 'She's very nice.'

'You two talked non-stop. I hardly got a word in edge-ways,' he complained.

That was true enough, Minna thought. She'd couldn't recall all they'd spoken about, but the conversation had certainly flowed, with hardly a let-up.

'She's pretty, isn't she?'

'Well, I can't disagree there.' Minna had searched – probed – for the qualities she'd heard about concerning Mrs Coates and simply hadn't found them. She could only conclude that Katherine took after her father, which was a relief.

'She asked if she can come again.'

'Any time she wishes. Though, being a guest house with all that entails, Sundays are best. I can give her time, and make her feel more at home, then.'

Tim slumped into a chair, the one Katherine had sat on, which was still warm from her presence. 'I'm glad you liked her, Ma. I was worried you wouldn't.'

'Oh?'

'Well . . . I mean. I've never brought a girl back before. I wasn't sure how you'd react.'

'I would always be pleasant, Tim. You should know that. I'd never let you down.'

'I appreciate that, Ma. It's just . . .' He shrugged. 'You understand?'

'Of course I do. I was your age once, don't forget. I well recall the first time my parents met Redvers. I was almost ill with anxiety for a week beforehand. Fortunately that also went well.' She smiled wickedly. 'Otherwise you wouldn't be here.'

Tim blushed. 'I suppose not.'

Minna rose from her chair. 'Now, I'd better tidy these things away.'

'Would you like a hand?'

That surprised Minna. Tim never offered to help with anything round the house, especially where washing-up and drying were concerned. He only did things when told to, so this was novel.

'Why, thank you.'

Minna washed while Tim dried, Daisy and Euphemia having got the afternoon off.

To Minna's amusement, Tim was full of the visit and what a great success it had been. Now it was he who chattered almost non-stop.

Elyse was appalled at what she was reading. Molly's reply to her letter had just arrived and contained disturbing news. Startling actually. Benny had been sacked from the play at the Duchess.

According to Molly, it was all round the West End and had been much discussed in the club, where gossip and rumour were always rife, theatricals loving both.

Twice Benny had missed curtain up, arriving just in time to get changed, made up and go on. The third time he'd arrived too late even for that and had been incoherently drunk. He'd been sacked on the spot, the understudy taking over his part.

Elyse couldn't believe it. This was virtually unheard of – actors simply didn't turn up late and never, ever drunk. According to Molly, the word was that he'd never be employed in the West End again. Indeed, he would be lucky to land another job anywhere in the profession.

Booze or laudanum – Elyse wondered which. Well, she had no sympathy for him, the stupid bugger had got what he deserved.

And yet, she'd loved him once. There was no getting away from that. There was a part of her that still cared, despite everything. What would he do now? That was the question. He had no trade or skills that she knew of, other than acting.

The other thing was: what did this mean for her? The house was full of her stuff – clothes, shoes, all sorts. Benny could hardly catch up with the rent now and would only be evicted in due course. Her guess was that she'd seen the last of what she had there. Benny would be down to the pawnshop with them, if he hadn't already been.

'Damn you, Benny Davenport,' she hissed, her voice filled with fury. If he'd been present she'd have slapped him as hard as she could.

The end of the letter was about her inquiry regarding possible accommodation. Molly knew of nothing currently going or coming up, but would keep her ear to the ground and be in touch again, should she hear of anything.

Elyse closed her eyes, thinking this was truly the end of an era. Thank God she had James. It would have been a lot worse without him.

Turning up incoherently drunk! Even she wouldn't have believed Benny would ever do that. Except that he had.

She couldn't wait to tell James of this latest development.

'Wilson, come here!' Ricketts barked from behind his desk. He watched Tim as he hurried over.

Ricketts eyed the reporter dyspeptically. 'Are you ready to cover your first murder?' he queried when Tim was standing before him.

Tim gaped. 'Murder?'

'Don't repeat me like a bloody parrot. That's what I said. Normally I'd send Patsy, but he's off ill again – another hangover no doubt. So it's got to be you. Are you up to it? If not, say and I'll send someone else. Though who, I don't know, as everyone's already out.'

'I'm up to it, sir.'

Ricketts nodded. 'Good. It's number nine Melville Lane, where a body's been discovered in a wardrobe apparently. A woman. The police are there now interviewing the husband.'

'I'm on my way, sir.'

'And take Ironmonger with you. Tell him I want at least one decent printable picture, preferably of the husband being led away. Failing that, the body being carried out. Understand?'

'I understand, sir.'

'Then hop to it. I want your copy on my desk by teatime at the latest.'

Ricketts sat back and smiled. The timing of this was excellent for tomorrow was publication day. He'd make it a banner headline. Murders were few and far between in Torquay. And in this case the wardrobe added spice. They might even double their circulation. Possibly even more.

Number nine had already been cordoned off, with two constables on duty outside, when Tim and Ironmonger arrived in Melville Lane. There was a car present that Tim assumed to be a police vehicle.

'Are the suspect and body still inside?' he asked the nearest constable.

The policeman stared at Tim, recognising him as an employee of the *Times*. He nodded.

'Set up your camera then,' Tim instructed Ironmonger, who hastily began doing so. 'Who discovered the victim?' he asked.

'Her mother, who called round, not having seen her for some while. The smell inside gave the game away.'

Tim wrinkled his nose in disgust. 'What's the deceased's name?'

'Greta Hervin.'

Tim noted that down. 'And the husband?'

'Bernard. Works in a local scrapyard.'

'Which scrapyard is that?'

The constable told him.

All this went into Tim's notebook. He was thankful the constable was being so cooperative. They weren't always. In fact some were real bastards to deal with, treating every piece of information as though it was a state secret.

'And was the body really hidden in a wardrobe?'

'Both parts of it, yes.'

Tim frowned. 'Both parts?'

'Her head had been cut off.'

'Jesus,' Tim whispered. That was gruesome. 'And how was she killed?'

'Stabbed with a kitchen knife, I believe. Many times. I can't give you a precise number, as that's still to be established.'

When he'd finished with the constable, Tim moved on to the onlookers to find out what they knew.

They had a long wait, but eventually they were rewarded with a picture of a blanket-covered stretcher being taken to an ambulance, followed by a blanket-covered man being led to the police car, which went roaring off jangling its bell.

Tim came up short, his face flaming scarlet with embarrassment. 'I'm . . . I'm . . . I'm ever so sorry,' he stuttered, transfixed.

Elyse was staring at him in astonishment, having been washing herself in the bath with a large sponge.

'I . . . I . . .' Tim trailed off, not knowing what to say next.

Suddenly Elyse smiled. 'Thank God it's you and not that dreadful Major Sillitoe. I must have forgotten to lock the door.' She made no attempt to cover herself in any way.

Tim's eyes looked as though they were out on stalks. He could see absolutely everything, there not being a great deal of soap floating on the water.

'If you close the door again behind you I'll get out and lock it,' Elyse said, a hint of laughter in her voice. She found this rather funny and not at all disconcerting, which she would have done had it been someone like the major.

'Of course.' Tim swallowed hard and finally, making a supreme effort, tore his gaze away from Elyse's nakedness. Without uttering another word, his forehead beaded with sweat that had nothing to do with the heat of the bathroom, he left.

Elyse was still smiling as she wrapped a towel round herself. Stupid of her to have forgotten to lock the door, but these things happened. She'd been busy thinking about a scene she was to rehearse that afternoon.

She was probably the first woman Tim had ever seen without her clothes on, she thought as she slid the door bolt home. Then she laughed. The expression on Tim's face had been absolutely priceless!

Chapter 15

'How did he cut off her head?' Ruth Coates queried. 'Your report didn't mention that.'

Tim had been asked to visit Oaklands for drinks, Katherine telling him that it was at her mother's request. All four of them were now ensconced round a blazing fire while Ruth quizzed Tim.

'With the same kitchen knife he used to stab her, apparently.'

Ruth nodded slowly. 'And the motive? Why did he kill her?'

Tim was finding Ruth's interest in the murder somewhat bizarre. He was also uncomfortable under her intense, bird-like gaze. 'Because of her nagging, I understand.'

Jeremiah laughed. 'Sorry, it's hardly a laughing matter,' he instantly apologised. 'But it does seem rather extreme. I mean, why not just leave her?'

Tim shrugged. 'I've no idea. Perhaps it had gone on and on for years and then on that particular day he just snapped. Done in the heat of the moment, so to speak.'

Eyes twinkling, Jeremiah turned to Ruth. 'Be warned. There's a lesson there for every woman.'

'Don't be ridiculous, Jeremiah,' she snapped back. 'I don't nag. Never have done.'

That wasn't exactly true, he reflected. There were times in the past that he could remember all too clearly.

'Now, tell me about the wardrobe,' Ruth went on. 'Why there?'

'It seems that, after he killed her, he wrapped her up in a sheet and took her in a handcart out into the fields somewhere and dumped her. A day later, according to the police, he went back again, reloaded the body onto the same cart and returned to the house, where he put it in the wardrobe out of the way.'

Katherine shivered. 'That's horrible.'

'It was then, it seems, that he cut off her head.'

'How strange,' Ruth murmured.

'The man's insane, if you ask me,' Jeremiah declared. 'That last act certainly wasn't done in the heat of the moment.'

'She'd been there a fortnight before the mother came round and discovered her. The stench was unbelievable, I was told.'

Katherine had gone white and now held a hand to her mouth. She couldn't understand why Ruth wanted all these gory details.

As though reading her daughter's mind, Ruth said, 'If I'd been born a man I'd love to have been a detective. At Scotland Yard of course – they usually get the best cases. The most interesting and difficult to solve.'

Jeremiah was regarding her curiously. 'You've never mentioned that before.'

'Well, I am now, dear. Perhaps I thought you'd laugh at me. Think me potty.'

'Not in the least,' he replied quickly. 'Not at all. A bit unusual maybe, but hardly potty.'

Tim had a sip of his wine. He wasn't enjoying this at all, except for Katherine's presence. It was all too morbid. In a way Ruth frightened him.

'I wonder if they'll hang him,' Ruth mused. 'They might not, if Jeremiah's right and he's declared insane.'

Tim glanced at Katherine, noting how pale she was. He wished they would change the conversation, though he doubted Ruth was finished yet.

'I thought your piece in the *Times* very well written,' Jeremiah complimented Tim.

'Thank you.'

'Perhaps one day you'll be employed in the real Fleet Street, and not the one of the same name here in Torquay.'

Tim smiled. 'That would be nice.'

'Are you ambitious in that department?'

He considered that. 'I suppose so. I haven't really thought about it all that much. I'm still learning my trade after all. And believe me, there's a great deal to be learnt.'

'No doubt,' Jeremiah nodded.

'Did you actually speak to the man?' a frowning Ruth asked.

Here we go again, Tim thought. She wasn't going to leave it alone. He continued to be quizzed for the best part of the next hour.

'I'm sorry about that,' Katherine apologised, having accompanied Tim to the front door.

'It can't have been very pleasant for you.'

'It wasn't. Why Mama has such a fascination with these

matters is quite beyond me. And Papa, too. She just adores her crime and mystery novels and can't get enough of them. She has a standing order at the bookshop for every new one when it comes out.'

'It is rather odd, I have to say. She wanted to know every last detail that I could provide.'

A worried expression came over Katherine's face. 'I hope that doesn't put you off me.'

He had to smile. 'Not in the least. Nothing would put me off you. Certainly not that.'

'Truly?'

He reached up and touched a corner of her lips. 'Truly. Believe me.'

'That's all right then.'

'When will I see you again?'

'I don't know. There's such a lot of planning to do for my Season, but I will be in touch as soon as I can find some free time. I promise you.'

Tim's heart had sunk when she'd mentioned the Season. She'd be away for months, socialising with all those dashing young men. He was quite green with jealousy at the thought. What if she met someone she liked more than him? What if that actually happened! He'd be devastated, heartbroken. But it wouldn't, he reassured himself. It just wouldn't. It couldn't.

'There's been a change of plan,' Katherine went on.

'Oh?'

'Originally Mama was going to stay here while Papa and I went to London. Now she's coming as well.'

'What about her health?'

'She's been so much better since Papa decided to stay

home more, which she puts down to his being here. She insists she's strong enough to cope. Don't forget, it's not that long since we were up there and she was perfectly all right then.'

Tim couldn't help but wonder if Ruth's illnesses came and went as it suited her. He wouldn't have been at all surprised if that was the case. Though, in all honesty, he had to admit she never appeared to be a well woman. And thin! Incredibly so.

'It's going to be terrible when you're away,' he said softly.

'For me too.'

'You'll be enjoying yourself. Parties nearly every night, balls. Not to mention all the attention you'll get. You'll love every minute.'

'But I'll be thinking of you.'

'Will you?'

'Oh yes. Unless you're deaf, dumb and blind, I'm very keen on you, Tim Wilson. Or hadn't you noticed?'

'I'd noticed,' he grinned. 'It's the same with me about you.'

'I know. Isn't it lovely?'

'More than that. It's heaven.'

She squeezed his hand. 'Now you'd better go. And thank you for coming and answering all Mummy's questions. I'm afraid she was rather boring on the subject.'

'Relentless more like. But no matter. It gave us the chance to be together, which is all that counts.'

She kissed him, quickly and briefly. 'Now go.'

He hesitated, then said earnestly, 'There'll never be anyone else for me, Katherine. Never.'

That moved her to the very depths of her being. 'I feel like that too.'

It was freezing outside, and perishing cold during the ride back on his motorbike, but Tim never noticed. He was ecstatically in love.

James placed his pint on the table and sat down, having purposely chosen a quiet part of the pub with no-one else around.

He'd considered inviting Elyse, but decided not to. He wanted to be alone with his thoughts.

London! He'd dreamt of it for so long. Appearing on the West End stage, the applause, the acclaim. Now it was all within his grasp, thanks to Elyse.

In the past he'd often toyed with the idea of going there, but knowing what undoubtedly lay ahead had always stopped him. He was a provincial actor without friends or contacts in the capital. It could take him years to break in, and what in the meantime? Menial jobs to make ends meet, to pay the rent and feed himself. All the while hoping, praying, with never a certainty that he'd make that all-important breakthrough.

Now he had Elyse and her many connections, which he'd exploit to the full. A few months with her by his side and he was bound to land a part – months during which he'd subsidise himself with money he'd already saved.

'London.' He whispered the word to himself, tasting it, enjoying it, revelling in the thought of what it meant, what it held in store for him.

Soon. Oh, very soon, for the run at the Pavilion was fast drawing to a close. He just had to ensure that she never guessed his secret. That would be disastrous.

* * *

'You're ever so lucky going up to London to be presented at Court,' Louise Youthed declared enviously. 'I wish I was.' Her father was a local solicitor and, although moderately well-off, the Youtheds were hardly in the same social or financial bracket as the Coateses.

'I wish you were too. I could use a friend there,' Katherine replied.

Louise sighed, trying to imagine what it was going to be like for Katherine. What fun she was going to have! All those gorgeous men she was bound to meet.

'Are things still thick between you and Tim Wilson?' Louise asked, not having seen Katherine for a while.

Katherine's eyes lit up and she nodded.

'I spotted him in the street the other day,' Louise went on. 'But I don't think he recognised me.'

'I'm going to marry him one day,' Katherine announced.

Louise squealed. 'Are you really?'

'Yes, I am. I've thought about it a lot and I'm decided. He's the one for me. We'll be terrifically happy together, I'm certain of it. Happy, with masses of children. Four at least.'

Louise was delighted. 'Oh, Ka, I'm so pleased for you. Does your mother know?'

'Not yet.'

'What do you think she'll say?'

'She'll be furious and totally against it, of course. She wants me to marry someone with pots of money and preferably a title. She makes no bones about it. Tim just doesn't fit the bill as far as she's concerned. He's too poor, and he certainly doesn't have a title.'

'What about your pa?'

'He'll approve, I think. He's fond of Tim, admires him.

Anyway, all that's in the future. I've made another decision – in the autumn I'm going to apply to train as a nurse.'

Louise's eyebrows shot up. 'A nurse! You are full of surprises today.'

'You know I've always said that I'm going to do something worthwhile with my life. Well, nursing's what it's going to be. I can't think of anything more worthwhile than that.'

'Again I ask: what about your mother?'

Katherine laughed. 'Vesuvius erupting will be nothing compared to how she'll greet that news. But she won't stop me or persuade me otherwise. I'm determined about that. My mind is quite firmly made up. I shall be a nurse and eventually marry Tim.'

'Good for you!' Louise enthused, thinking that she might be a nurse as well. Perhaps they could even train together! Now that would be a laugh.

'You keep this to yourself,' Katherine warned her. 'Promise me?'

'I promise.'

'I mean it, Louise. Not a word to anyone.'

'Cross my heart, Ka.'

Both girls suddenly giggled, Louise going up to Katherine and hugging her.

Later, when Louise was leaving, Katherine reminded her of her promise and again Louise assured her that it was strictly between the pair of them.

'We shouldn't really,' a worried Tim said to Harry Nutbeam. 'What if Ricketts smells it on us? You know how disapproving he is of drinking during working hours.'

'Damn Ricketts. I've had a bellyful of that man. I've never

known anyone more odious. So are you coming or not?'

Reluctantly Tim agreed.

'I'm thinking about leaving Torquay,' Harry declared as they strode along the street.

Tim was appalled. 'Leave Torquay?'

'Why not? There are lots of other newspapers, you know. The *Times* isn't the only one, or Ricketts the only editor.'

Tim considered that. He couldn't imagine himself leaving Torquay while Minna was still alive. And then there was Katherine. Sometime perhaps, but not in the foreseeable future. 'Won't you miss it? Torquay, that is. After all, you were born and brought up here, same as me.'

'I suppose I will. Bound to. All my friends, relatives. There are certainly a lot of worse places to live and work in. But I just can't take Ricketts any longer. If I thought I'd get away with it I'd strangle the bastard with my bare hands.'

'I have to admit he can be pretty awful on occasions.'

'Awful! That's the understatement of the year. Earlier on, when he was yelling at me, I found myself wishing he'd have a heart attack and die there and then.'

Tim had witnessed the incident, which had been pretty grim, and humiliating for Harry. Over nothing really, but enough to incur one of Ricketts' rages.

'Will you take my advice?' Tim queried.

'Depends. What is it?'

'Don't do anything rash while you're still angry. Wait till you've calmed down and can see things in perspective.'

Harry knew that made sense. 'All right.'

They arrived at the pub, not one they normally visited, and disappeared inside.

* * *

Elyse opened a second letter from Molly O'Malley and started to read. Molly still hadn't heard of any suitable accommodation, so she and Seamus had talked it over and wanted Elyse and James to stay with them until such time as they could sort themselves out.

How kind, Elyse thought. And just like the O'Malleys. They were such good friends.

Molly went on to say that there was a room they'd never bothered with, mainly using it to store boxes and tinned provisions. They'd decided, at long last, to do something about that room, which they would decorate and furnish, to be ready when she and James arrived.

The next item of news was even more interesting. According to the rumour going round the club, Benny had fallen on his feet in meeting a rich widow with whom he'd taken up. Molly didn't have a name yet, but the woman was supposedly loaded and a lot older than Benny. If the rumour was right, the widow was completely hooked on Benny, indulging his every whim.

Elyse laughed – trust Benny! As Molly had said, it would appear that he'd fallen right on his feet. Which made her wonder about their house and its contents. Perhaps she might still be able to rescue her belongings after all. She sincerely hoped so.

The rest of Molly's letter was general chitchat about the goings-on at the club.

Elyse laid the letter aside and lit a cigarette. That was one worry out of the way. She and James were now fixed up, thanks to the O'Malleys. As for Benny – a rich older widow who doted on him! Well, the widow, whoever she was, was welcome to the bastard.

Yet in a way, because of what he'd once meant to her, she was pleased for him. She only hoped the widow realised what she was taking on. A laudanum addict, as she presumed Benny had become, was no joke.

Ruth Coates smiled as she helped herself to another chocolate. Jeremiah was in London viewing a house they were considering renting for the Season, and Katherine was out. She wouldn't have been indulging herself like this if there was a chance of being caught.

She smiled further, thinking how readily Jeremiah had accepted the explanation that her recent upturn in health was due to him being home more. How easily men were fooled. As long as you said it with a straight face and sincerity in your voice they'd believe almost anything.

Of course there was nothing wrong with her, and never had been. Her various illnesses had started off as an excuse, a device, to stop having sex with Jeremiah.

She shuddered, remembering what a nasty, messy business that had been. She'd hated every moment of it. As for childbirth, after the horrors of having Katherine, she'd sworn never to go through that again, which was when – and why – the sex had stopped.

She knew she was being cruel to Jeremiah in denying him his marital rights, but as far as she was concerned that was just too bad. He simply had to cope, and always had.

That lack of physicality had never affected their marriage, which was still as strong as the day they'd wed. He was a good man, her Jeremiah, and most understanding.

But the thing worrying her of late was whether she had made a mistake in persuading him to stay at home with her.

It had been terribly lonely without him – long periods of desperately trying to fill the day, missing his company and having him about. The trouble was that now he was about far too much, forever under her feet, it seemed. She sighed. Well, she couldn't have it both ways. Or could she?

She dipped again into the box of chocolates while she racked her brain. There must be some sort of solution, some compromise – there usually was.

And then she had it. Of course! If he agreed, and she was certain he would, then she could have her cake and eat it, too. The best of both worlds.

My God, but at times she was clever. There again, didn't she always get her way!

James turned full upstage to face Elyse, who was sitting behind him, and slowly crossed his eyes while at the same time poking out his tongue. To the audience, who could only see his back, he appeared stricken with grief.

Elyse fought back the laughter bubbling inside her. He'd been like this during the entire act, trying to make her 'corpse', which was what actors called breaking out of character and grinning, or laughing, onstage.

Elyse delivered the next line with all the gravity that it required, her expression one of utmost concern. James was now rolling his eyes, his tongue flicking in and out.

Elyse's sides began to ache from the effort she was making to contain herself, but she wouldn't corpse. She was damned if she would. No matter what he tried or did.

A little later he was supposed to hold her gently by the neck as she comforted him in his grief. But instead of holding her, the bugger was tickling, knowing full well, from intimate experience, the effect that tickling that particular spot had on her.

She broke away, which wasn't how they'd plotted it in rehearsal, to stop the tickling. A few more lines and she was able to make her exit into the wings.

She immediately fled into the corridor, where she was finally able to burst out laughing. Bloody sod! He'd come within an ace of getting her.

Ronnie, the ASM, appeared to stare at her, wondering what on earth was going on.

'I'll murder him,' Elyse choked. 'When he comes off I'll murder him.'

'Who, Mrs Davenport?'

'Mr Erskine of course.'

She had to compose herself, she thought, and quickly. She was due back on again shortly.

Elyse took a deep breath, then another. There, that was better. She was back in control.

When she made her next entrance the first thing she saw was that James' eyes were twinkling mischievously. Then she noticed that two of the buttons on his flies were undone.

James poked his head round Elyse's dressing-room door. 'Still talking to me?'

She picked up a shoe and threw it at him, James laughing as it bounced harmlessly away.

'Missed!' he teased.

'Get lost!'

'Now you don't mean that.'

'Yes I do.'

'No you don't.'

'I do.'

'*Oh no you don't!*' That a strictly pantomime delivery.

She suddenly smiled. 'Idiot.'

'Beautiful lady.'

'You're still an idiot.'

She wasn't really angry with him. It was all pretence, as he well knew. Nonetheless she was pleased she'd won, that he hadn't been able – and how he'd tried! – to corpse her.

Elyse crooked a finger. 'Come here.'

He went to her. 'What for?'

Rising from her chair, she put her arms round him. After Benny, she'd never thought she'd find true happiness again. And then James had come along. Dear, lovely, adorable James.

'Are you still staying at my place tonight?' he asked softly.

'If you want.'

'Oh, I want, Elyse. I want very much.'

And so did she. Very much. She already knew what her revenge was going to be. When he was fully roused she'd prevaricate. Making him wait and wait, and then wait some more, before finally giving herself.

'You're awfully nice, you know,' Henrietta said from the bed where she was lying watching Jeremiah get dressed. This was his fourth visit on the trot to Mrs Green's establishment since arriving from Torquay. 'Believe me,' she went on. 'It's rare to come across that in my profession. Most men, even so-called gentlemen, are far from it.'

'I'm flattered,' Jeremiah replied slowly.

'Will you come again tomorrow?'

'Probably.'

'And ask for me?'

'Haven't I every time so far?' She was a prostitute, he reminded himself. He mustn't get too fond. 'Do you really like me?' he asked casually. 'And remember, that's not part of the service.'

'I've already said, haven't I?'

He glanced sideways at her reflection in the mirror. She had a tremendous figure – cracking, in fact. It reminded him of Ruth's before she'd become ill and lost so much weight. But it wasn't only her figure. She was intelligent too, and could hold a good conversation.

'I have to go away again at the end of the week,' he declared. 'But I'll be back soon, and this time for several months.'

She didn't reply to that, just continued watching him, with a look of expectation on her face.

'What is it you want, Henrietta?' he asked.

She shook her head. 'Nothing.'

'Yes you do, out with it. And don't lie. I can't bear liars.'

She seemed to have a change of mind. Getting up, she shrugged herself into a wrap. 'I'll see you tomorrow, if you turn up.'

He caught her by the arm. 'Tell me, I want to hear.'

She glanced down at the carpet for a few seconds, then up again at him. 'If you report this to Mrs Green I'll be for it. Believe me, there's a side to her you've never seen.'

'I'm waiting,' he urged.

'Do you think I enjoy working here? Because I don't. I have dreams, Mr C.'

'And what are they?'

'That someone might come along one day and take me

away from this. Someone to look after me. And I don't mean marriage, either. I wouldn't expect that. Just look after me.'

'Set you up, you mean?'

She nodded. 'Exclusively. I wouldn't cheat. I promise you that.'

He let her go and returned to getting dressed. 'That's impossible, I'm afraid. At least where I'm concerned. If I lived in London it might be different, but I don't.'

'I've no idea where you live, but couldn't you . . .'

'No,' he interjected harshly. 'I couldn't.'

Her shoulders slumped. 'Pity. I still think you're nice.' And with that she padded from the bedroom.

Yes, it was a pity, he thought. A great pity. What she'd been proposing would have suited him down to the ground.

As they were in the middle of the last play's run there weren't any more rehearsals. With her days now free, Elyse could therefore do as she wished.

She'd decided to call in at the Pavilion to collect a scarf she'd inadvertently left in James' dressing room the night before. She didn't really need it, but it gave her something to do. There was also the chance she'd run into James and, if she did, she intended suggesting lunch.

She didn't bother knocking, but simply opened the door and went straight in. The next moment she was reeling in shock.

Ronnie, the ASM, was bent over the dressing table, his trousers and pants round his ankles. James, in a similar state of undress, was hunched over him. There was a space of several seconds before either man realised she was standing there.

Elyse had gone numb, for it was blatantly obvious what they were doing. Bile rose up in her throat and she thought she was going to vomit.

'Oh, Elyse,' James whispered, 'I'm so sorry.'

The next thing Elyse knew she was out in the corridor again and running.

Fred, the stage doorkeeper, gaped in astonishment as she went hurtling past.

Chapter 16

'M rs Davenport! Whatever's wrong?'

Elyse, having just returned to The Berkeley, stared blankly at Minna. 'What time is it?' she frowned.

'A little before five.'

Elyse tried to digest that. She must have been walking for hours, though where she'd been she couldn't recall. 'Thank you.'

Minna was most concerned, for Elyse looked terrible. And judging from the state of her make-up, she'd been crying. 'I think you need a good strong cup of tea. Come into my parlour and I'll fetch us one.'

'I don't want to trouble you,' Elyse mumbled.

'It's no trouble at all. Now come on through and have a seat.'

When Elyse fumbled for her cigarettes she noted that her hands were shaking. She was going to have to pull herself together for curtain up for, despite what had happened, there was no question of her not going on that night. Though how she was going to act with James was beyond her.

Minna was soon back with a tray. She poured and handed Elyse a cup. 'Biscuit?'

Elyse shook her head.

'Has something happened?'

Elyse looked at Minna through tortured eyes. 'Yes,' she whispered.

'Do you want to talk about it?'

Elyse tasted her tea and tried to think about that. How could she possibly relate what she'd witnessed, and the awful hurt it had caused her?

Minna waited patiently.

Elyse decided she wanted to say something. It must help to confide in someone. Though God knows what Minna would make of it. 'It's James,' she said in a small voice.

'Your chap?'

'Yes.'

There was a long silence during which Elyse stared into her cup.

'Have you broken up?' Minna queried. 'Is that it?'

Elyse gave a sudden hollow laugh. 'We've broken up all right. I found out, quite by accident, that . . . that . . .' She swallowed hard. 'He's been seeing another person.'

'Ah!' Minna sank back in her chair. That explained it. Poor Mrs Davenport. 'And you were so keen on him too.'

'I loved him,' Elyse whispered. 'And for him to do that to me!' She shuddered.

'I appreciate this is a bit personal, but when you say "seeing", do you mean . . . ?'

Elyse nodded.

'That's despicable!'

'For how long I don't know. Anyway, that doesn't matter. What does is that I found out. I walked in on them. It was horrible.'

'Oh dear.' Minna couldn't have been more sympathetic,

trying to imagine what that must have been like for Elyse.
'Do you know her?'

Elyse smiled wryly. 'It isn't a woman, Mrs Wilson.'

Minna didn't understand.

'It's a man.'

She was stunned. She knew about such things of course,
but she had no direct experience of people like that. She
considered it nauseating.

'A man. A young man to be precise. He works at the
theatre.'

'And they were . . . ?'

'When I walked in on them. Over a table, of all things.
I was nearly sick.'

Minna just didn't know what to say. 'Is there anything I
can do?'

'Not really. I'll just have to come to terms with it, I
suppose. Though how I'm going to do that I've no idea.'
She paused, then said, 'I did love him ever so much.'

That was obvious, Minna thought.

'And he swore he loved me. So how could he . . . ?'

Elyse broke down and started crying again. Minna quickly
crossed over and did her best to comfort her.

It was nearly an hour before Elyse left and went upstairs
to get changed.

James avoided her before the performance. Nor did he say
anything when they were together in the wings just prior to
curtain up. She never looked in his direction, but simply
concentrated on the nightmare performance that lay ahead.

Being the professional she was, she somehow got
through it.

* * *

Elyse was just about to start removing her slap when there was a knock on the door. She said nothing, guessing who it was.

He knocked again, and again she said nothing. Her eyes were icy, her expression glacial.

'Elyse, can I come in?'

She remained mute.

'Elyse, please?'

She began massaging cream into her face.

She caught her breath when the door opened and James appeared. 'I must speak to you, Elyse. Try and explain.'

'Get out!' she shrieked.

'Elyse, I . . .'

'GET THE FUCK OUT!'

James closed the door quietly behind him.

He was persistent, she'd give him that, for she found him waiting, hovering, just outside the stage door. She was about to walk straight past when she had a better idea. Halting momentarily, she gave him an almighty smack before continuing on her way.

Thankfully he didn't attempt to follow her.

'Here's the train now, ma'am,' the porter with her luggage declared.

Elyse glanced off into the distance and saw a ribbon of smoke far down the line. The train taking her to London was dead on time.

It had been a sad morning for her, having to say goodbye to Minna, Daisy, Euphemia, Cook, the other guests and of course Tim. She'd enjoyed her stay at The Berkeley, where everyone had been so kind.

The traditional end-of-season party had been held the night before but she hadn't gone. Which was a shame, for the cast had been a good one, with everyone getting on and working well together. She simply couldn't have faced it, with James there.

She was also sad to leave Torquay itself. It might be quiet compared to what she was used to, but in a way she'd come to enjoy that. And the mild climate had certainly suited her, since she wasn't coughing half as much as when she arrived.

The train was looming large now. Another few minutes and she'd be gone. How different she'd thought this would be. She and James leaving as a couple, she and James . . .

Well, that was over, finished. She would never see him or hear his voice again. Men, she thought bitterly. Bastards!

And then the train was pulling into the station and the porter was helping her aboard.

Torquay and James Erskine were left behind in a great cloud of smoke and hissing steam.

'I shall miss her, you know,' Tim declared to his mother.

'Mrs Davenport?'

'She certainly brought a bit of life and colour to this place.'

Minna couldn't disagree with that. She too was going to miss Elyse, and could only wonder what would become of her after the dreadful thing that had happened.

Tim was suddenly morose. Mrs Davenport had left, and Katherine was shortly to follow. The months he and Katherine would be apart were going to be agony.

'Perhaps she'll come back and do another season here.

Mrs Davenport, that is,' Tim speculated.

Minna doubted it. Torquay would hold too many bad memories for Elyse to want to return. No, they'd seen the last of her.

Tim yawned. He always felt tired on Sundays. He didn't know why, probably because they were so boring. 'I helped her with her lines a couple of times, you know.'

This was news to Minna. 'Oh?'

'I read the other parts, cueing her in, as she called it. That was fun.'

'And where did this take place?'

Damn, Tim thought. Him and his big mouth. Would he never learn to think before speaking. 'In her bedroom,' he replied casually. 'With the door open, of course. All very right and proper, Ma, I can assure you.'

Minna nodded. 'We both owe her your life, I'll never forget her for that. If she hadn't been here . . .' Minna trailed off and shrugged, not wanting to complete the sentence.

'Yes,' Tim agreed quietly. He hadn't forgotten about that either, just put it to the back of his mind. His nearly dying from influenza wasn't something he wished to dwell on.

'God bless her,' Minna whispered, a lump in her throat. God bless her indeed. 'Now, I'd better get on.' And with that she hurried off.

Tim wondered what Katherine was doing. They'd arranged to meet the following lunchtime. What a painful parting that was going to be.

On the one hand he was looking forward to it, on the other dreading it.

'It's the same lock, it hasn't been changed!' Elyse exclaimed in delight to Seamus O'Malley, who'd escorted her to the house in Seven Dials where she'd lived with Benny. Did that mean her things were still intact?

'What if he's home?' Seamus queried.

Elyse thought about that. 'I doubt he'd try and stop me taking my stuff, with you here. He'd be too scared of what you might do to him. Benny's never been the physical type.' In that respect anyway, she smiled to herself. He certainly was in another.

'In you go then.'

She inserted her key and the door opened. She immediately noted that the hallway was just as she'd left it – nothing had been removed. A good sign.

'Do you want me to go first?' Seamus asked.

'Maybe you'd better.'

Seamus had never been in the house before, but the layout was obvious enough. They went into the living room, where the furniture and everything else remained.

'I think you're in luck,' he declared.

There was a stale smell about the place, as if no-one had been there for quite some time. Certainly the windows hadn't been opened recently.

It took them less than a few minutes to discover that the house was indeed empty. 'I'm surprised he hasn't been kicked out by now,' Elyse commented. 'Or been down to the pawnshop. Either he's found some sort of a job or his lady friend has been giving him money.' Knowing Benny, and remembering what Molly had said in her letter about the widow, she would bet it was the latter.

'Right then, I'll have to go back for the handcart. Do you want to come with me?'

'I'll stay and start packing,' Elyse replied. 'And don't worry, I doubt very much that Benny's going to show up suddenly. It's probably weeks since he's been here.'

'Are you sure?'

'I'm sure, Seamus. And thank you for your help.'

'You're welcome, Elyse. Now I'll be on my way.'

'Don't be too long. Just in case.'

He smiled. 'I won't. And if Benny should appear and so much as lay a finger on you, then he'll have me to deal with in spades. Tell him that.'

'I will.'

She went into her bedroom, where the bed was unmade and rumpled, and began collecting a few items together. There were old theatre programmes that she dearly prized, plus other mementoes and a couple of bits of real jewellery, not the stage kind that Daisy and Euphemia had been so captivated by. There were also clothes, shoes, several coats and a cape she occasionally wore.

She piled everything on the floor, not wanting to put them on the bed.

'This is it then,' Tim said to Katherine, giving her a strained smile. As agreed, they'd met up in Addison's for coffee.

'I'm afraid so. We're off early tomorrow, as you know.'

Tim felt wretched. In the short space of time he'd known Katherine she'd come to mean everything to him. 'Will you write as you did before?'

'Of course.'

'And I will too. And you can always telephone me at home or in the office. I'd like that.'

'I've brought you something,' she announced.

That surprised him. 'What?'

'A small gift. Well, I never gave you anything for Christmas, so this is instead of that.' From under the table she produced a box that she'd brought in with her and handed it to him. 'For you.'

He gasped when he opened the box and saw what was inside. A pair of silver men's hairbrushes.

Katherine laughed at his incredulous expression. 'They're not solid silver, silly, just silver-plated. Do you like them?'

'They're . . . they're wonderful,' he managed to get out at last. 'Even plated, they must have cost a fortune.'

'Hardly that,' she teased. 'Anyway, I can afford them, so let's say no more about that.'

He ran the tips of his fingers over the back of one, then the other. 'I'll treasure them for ever,' he stated quietly.

'Good.'

'Katherine, I can't thank you enough. I'm quite overwhelmed.'

'Just think of me every time you use them.'

'I will. I'm always thinking about you anyway, but now I'll never fail to when I use these. That's a promise.'

Their remaining time together flew by and all too soon she had to go. Reluctantly he walked her outside, where the car was waiting.

Ruth replaced the telephone on its cradle. How she hated the beastly thing. Though she had to admit, it did come in useful.

She smiled in quiet satisfaction. That was a good start. They'd all been invited to tea with Lady Mary Crabthorne this coming Thursday, and Mary had promised that, army duties permitting, Miles would be there.

Ruth intended doing everything in her power to ensure that Katherine and Miles were thrown together as often as possible during the Season.

She waited till Katherine had gone to bed before speaking to Jeremiah, who was enjoying a whisky and soda. Everything was packed ready to be taken by train to London in the morning, while she, Jeremiah and Katherine would be travelling by car. Jeremiah wished the car to be available while they were in town.

'I've been thinking, darling,' she smiled.

'That sounds ominous,' Jeremiah replied drily.

She laughed. 'About you actually.'

'Oh?'

'You're not really happy being home all the time, are you? I mean, you're forever prowling around the house like a bear with a sore head looking for something to do. I've often noticed it.'

He regarded her keenly over the rim of his glass. 'I came home because of you, Ruth.'

'And hasn't my health improved ever since! You must agree that's so?'

He nodded.

'I appreciate the gesture, Jeremiah, truly I do. Having you around has been absolutely marvellous. Cheered me up no end. I thought you would settle, find hobbies and other sources of amusement. Things to keep you busy. But that simply hasn't happened.'

Jeremiah sighed. 'I have to admit you're right. Time seems to hang so heavily nowadays, which is why I'm looking forward to the next few months in town.'

Ruth's eyes were fixed intently on her husband. Putty in her hands, she thought, he'd always been that. It never ceased to amaze her just how easy he was to manipulate. There again, if she said so herself, she was rather good at that sort of thing. 'I have a suggestion to make,' she stated simply.

'Which is?'

'I don't want you travelling abroad like you used to. I certainly don't wish us to go back to that. But it seems to me there's a compromise that would be ideal for our situation.'

Jeremiah felt a flutter of excitement. Was there to be a way out of this tedium that he'd come to loathe? 'I'm listening, Ruth.'

'Why don't you buy a small house in London, a base from which to carry on more business. I know you manage some from down here, but that's minimal and not at all keeping your mind fully occupied.'

The excitement was growing within him. This was almost too good to be true. 'A house?'

'Oh, nothing too grand. I thought you might stay a week there, and then similar here. Ten days or a fortnight – whatever.'

He considered that. 'What happens if you have a relapse?'

'Then we'll reconsider the arrangement. But it's you I'm thinking about, Jeremiah. I want what's best for you. And it's now all too evident that you're a man who needs to work. Obviously it wouldn't be on the scale it was before, but a trimmed-down version so to speak. That way we'd have the best of both worlds. I'd see you far more often than I did previously, and you would be happy again.'

'It's certainly worth considering,' he mused, already knowing what his answer was going to be.

'I had thought of putting it to you when we're in London, but decided that now would be better. This way you have lots of time to look for somewhere.'

He couldn't help but think of Henrietta and the suggestion she'd made, a suggestion that he'd ruled out because it seemed impossible. Suddenly all that had changed.

'Are you sure about the health thing?' he queried.

'Sure enough to believe we should give this a try. Now, what do you say?'

'I say I'll begin looking later on in the week.'

She beamed at him. Putty in her hands. He'd no longer be perpetually under her feet, but home enough of the time to stave off the loneliness that had so bothered her.

Jeremiah began eagerly to discuss possible areas where he might buy.

'I'm sorry I didn't visit you in the spring as I promised. I simply wasn't able to get down,' Clarice Crabthorne apologised to Katherine when the Coateses arrived for tea.

'That's all right.'

'But now you're here, and that's wonderful. We shall have such fun you and I. I just know it.'

Katherine gazed about her. The house in Farm Street was certainly a splendid one, and the drawing room they were in now was quite sumptuous. Ruth was already deep in conversation with Lady Mary, while Jeremiah was studying a Gainsborough, a painter he much admired.

'Pa can't be here, I'm afraid,' Clarice went on. 'Tied up in the City, but Miles has promised to drop by for a short while. You remember my brother Miles, of course?'

'I thought him positively charming.'

'He's a great admirer of yours. Spoke often of you after the last time we were together.'

'Really?'

'Quite taken. He'll be at a number of the balls and parties we'll be attending. He and many of his colleagues from the Household Cavalry.'

'Sounds very exciting.'

'Oh, it will be, Katherine. I can't wait.'

A little later tea was served, during which they all sat and made small talk. Lady Mary and Ruth were old friends, having known one another as children in Suffolk where Ruth originally came from. In the middle of all this Miles arrived.

He said hello to the guests then sat down beside Jeremiah after having accepted a cup of tea from Lady Mary. He declined the sandwiches.

Ruth and Lady Mary exchanged glances, for Lady Mary was in on the conspiracy and thoroughly approved of the potential match.

Every so often Miles looked over at Katherine and smiled. She was even more gorgeous than he remembered.

'Any luck?' Molly O'Malley demanded of Elyse, who'd just let herself in through the back door.

Elyse shook her head. 'Not yet.'

Molly was instantly sympathetic. 'Don't worry, a nice juicy part will come along soon. You'll see.'

'I certainly hope so. The sooner, the better. I can't go on living off you and Seamus for ever.'

Molly wagged a finger at her. 'None of that now. You'll stay here as long as it takes and that's all there is to it.'

'You're a godsend, Molly. I don't know what I'd have done without the pair of you.'

'Something, no doubt. Something.'

Elyse hesitated, then said, 'I've been wondering, Molly.'

'About what?'

'Do you think I should try Marcus Brierley again? I hear he'll be casting directly after *The Seagull* opens.'

Molly sat and stared hard at her friend. 'Are you willing to sleep with him this time?' she queried softly.

Elyse blushed and glanced away.

'Well?'

'There was James before. Now he's out of my life.'

'That isn't answering the question,' Molly persisted.

Elyse took her time in answering by lighting a cigarette. 'I just don't know,' she confessed eventually.

'Well, you'd better before you go and see him.'

Elyse didn't reply to that.

'As I said to you once, you wouldn't be the first actress to get a part by lying on your back.'

'It's just . . .' She trailed off.

'Just what, Elyse?'

'Prostitution, I suppose,' she whispered.

'Is it indeed?' Molly smiled thinly to herself. 'Well, you could call it that. There again, haven't women been doing it down the ages to get what they want? And I include many married women with their husbands. It all depends on how you look at it. You wouldn't exactly be hawking your body for money, like some common street tart who'll go with anyone. There's a huge difference in my opinion.'

Elyse raised an eyebrow. 'You approve then?'

'I never said that. What I suppose I *am* saying is that I'm of a practical nature. He has what you want: you have what he wants. It would simply be an exchange of wants.'

'That's true enough,' Elyse mused. 'Though it is being somewhat simplistic.'

'Life can be like that. And let's face it, you need work, which he can possibly provide. In the end it's up to you.'

'I'm going to have to think further about it.'

'You do that.' Molly rose and sighed. 'I'd better get out front. I'm expecting the draymen, and Seamus has gone out. No rest for the wicked, eh?'

Wicked? Elyse thought. Was that what sleeping with Marcus Brierley would be? She'd slept with James, so why not with him? The difference was that she'd loved James, and she didn't love Marcus, whom she'd be sleeping with purely for gain.

Yes, love was the difference.

'There!' Katherine exclaimed, having signed her name with a flourish. The latest letter to Tim was written and ready to be sent.

According to Tim's last he was fine, though missing her enormously. Most of his news had been about work, the stories he'd been on, and so on.

She'd been trying not to paint too rosy a picture of London, though the truth was she was having a whale of a time. She'd already been to two balls and five parties, where she'd met all sorts of interesting people.

Miles had been present at all but one of the parties, which he'd been unable to attend because of army duties. She'd come to like Miles a lot. He had a terrific sense of humour, made her laugh a great deal and was incredibly attentive.

She'd sensibly not mentioned Miles, or any of the other young men, in her letters, not wanting Tim to get jealous, which, knowing him, he surely would.

She sealed the envelope and wrote his name and address on the front, thinking how different life in London was from life in Torquay. Different, and far more exciting. She loved Torquay, and Oaklands, with all her heart, but there was a part of her that had come to think she wouldn't mind living in London, where there was so much more to do and see. How alive she felt here. How very alive.

'I believe this dance is mine.'

Katherine pretended to study her card, knowing full well that the next name on the list was Miles Crabthorne. Earlier in the evening, if she'd allowed it, he'd have booked every single dance with her.

How handsome he looked in full dress uniform, Katherine thought. He positively shone. Like a prince out of a fairy tale.

'I do believe it is,' she smiled in reply.

Moments later the band struck up and she was in his arms, whirling off in a polka.

From where she was watching Ruth gazed on approvingly.

Chapter 17

'So you're not going to leave us after all?' Tim said to Harry Nutbeam. The pair of them were in the pub after work, it being a Friday night.

Harry shook his head.

'Well, I for one am pleased to hear it. But why the change of mind?'

Harry had a swallow from his pint. 'Call it sheer bloody-mindedness.'

'Oh?' That wasn't a trait Tim would normally have associated with Harry.

'Why should I let that bastard Ricketts push me out? I'll go, but only when I'm good and ready. And I've decided that time isn't yet.' His explanation wasn't the whole truth. He'd sent off four inquiries to other local newspapers, with all four replies saying that there was nothing available at present. He'd somehow lost heart after that.

'Good for you.'

Harry sniffed. 'I still hate him, mind you, him and his tyrannical ways. But I refuse to let him get the better of me. From here on his tempers and insults will just wash over my head. I'm determined about that.'

Tim looked at Harry with new admiration, vowing that he'd try and adopt the same attitude.

'I still wish he'd have a heart attack and drop down dead,' Harry declared vehemently, which made Tim laugh. 'But I doubt it'll ever happen. No such luck. Anyway,' he went on. 'Enough of that and of me. Have you heard from the girl-friend recently?'

Tim's face darkened. 'I haven't had a letter for days, almost a week actually. During that time I've tried to ring her twice and on each occasion she's been out.'

'I take it she hasn't rung you?'

'No,' Tim stated quietly.

Harry was about to tease Tim, then thought better of it. He could see this wasn't a teasing matter, being far too sensi-tive an area. 'She's just busy, that's all.'

'I suppose so,' Tim sighed.

'Well, think about it. I don't know much about these things – debutantes, coming out and the like – but her calen-dar must be extremely hectic. I wouldn't worry about it if I was you.'

'I'm not,' Tim lied.

'She'll be back soon enough and it will be just as it was. Take my word for it.'

Tim fervently hoped that was true. But there was still the present to cope with, and it was hard.

Jeremiah pulled out his pocket watch and flicked open the case. Henrietta was now twenty minutes late. What was keeping her?

She had jumped at his proposal when he'd put it to her. Once he'd found a suitable house, and furnished it, she would move in as his combined housekeeper and mistress. In the meantime he'd decided he didn't want her continuing at Mrs Green's. The plan was therefore that she'd sneak away early one morning, join him in a cab and he'd spirit her off to a hotel that he'd already chosen. She was to remain there until such time as the house was ready.

He took out his watch again – twenty-five minutes late now. Something must have gone wrong, in which case what did he do? Knock on the door and demand that she leave with him? Out of the question. Mrs Green must never know who she'd gone off with.

And then suddenly there she was, carrying a carpetbag and hurrying towards the waiting cab.

Jeremiah opened the door and she slipped inside. 'Drive on, man,' he immediately instructed and the hansom moved off down the street. 'I was beginning to think you weren't coming,' he said to her, noting how flushed she was.

'For once Mrs Green was up and about early, pottering around in the kitchen where the back door is. I just had to wait for my opportunity and pray you'd still be here.'

The overhead flap snapped open. 'Where to, guv?'

Jeremiah gave the cabbie an address and the flap snapped shut again.

'It's a small hotel between King's Cross and Islington,' he explained to Henrietta. 'Not exactly first-class but comfortable enough. You'll be fine there.'

She placed a hand over his. 'I still can't believe this is happening. It's like a dream.'

'It's happening all right,' he assured her. 'You're safe now, with me.'

Henrietta momentarily closed her eyes, then opened them

again. 'You won't regret this, Jeremiah, I swear.'

He could hear the ring of sincerity in her voice. She meant what she said.

'I'll be with you as long as you want me,' she added in a whisper.

He stroked the side of her face, then brushed his lips over hers. This was a whole new chapter in his life, he thought. It made him feel young again.

And that was a lovely feeling.

'My father thinks there might be war in Europe,' Katherine said to Miles as the pair of them strolled in Kensington Gardens.

Miles glanced at her. 'He could well be right. There are many who believe that.'

'Do you?'

He shrugged. 'To be frank, I'm not sure. Though I have to say, the Germans and Austrians would be mad to take us on. They'd be on a hiding to nothing, I can guarantee you that.'

'If there was a war, would you be involved?'

'Rather!' he laughed. 'You couldn't keep me away. Think of all the glory to be won, not to mention advancement in rank. Our lot would be among the first to fight. We'd insist on it.'

She stared at him in admiration. 'You're very brave.'

'Not really,' he replied dismissively. 'I'm a soldier, Katherine, and that's what soldiers do. Fight wars. We're trained for it, look forward to it even. Why else be a soldier after all?'

'Nonetheless, I still think you're brave.'

They walked a little way in silence. 'I shan't always be in the army, you know. I never joined to make it my career, more for the adventure and comradeship. But the time will come when I'm tired of that and then I shall be a civilian again.'

'Will you work?'

'Probably, though at what I've no idea. I could follow Pa and be an underwriter with Lloyd's, though I would imagine that's a bit stuffy for my taste. One thing is certain: I shan't be vegetating in the country. As far as I'm concerned, the country is fine in short doses – weekends and all that sort of thing. But London is where I'll live. Wouldn't have it any other way.'

'The more I'm in London, the more I like it,' she said. 'Torquay is going to be dull as dishwater after all this.'

'Never been there, but hear it's quite pleasant. A holiday sort of place.'

Katherine had never thought of Torquay in that light before. But yes, Miles was right. That was exactly what it was.

How old was he? she wondered. Twenty-five, twenty-six? Somewhere round about there. Despite herself, she couldn't help but compare him to Tim. Miles was a man – and an experienced, sophisticated one at that – while Tim . . . well, he was still a young man, a boy in some ways, with little experience and certainly no sophistication about him.

'I know it's impolite to make remarks like this, but my mother mentioned that your family's terribly rich. Is that so?'

'Frightfully so, I'm happy to say,' Miles beamed at her. 'We have pots of the stuff. An estate in Scotland and another in Ireland, which we hardly ever go to, Pa being an urban creature like myself. Our money was made several hundred years ago in the wool trade. The family lived in Yorkshire then. Wool and afterwards tea, both incredibly successful.' He eyed her keenly. 'Why do you ask?'

'Curiosity, I suppose. In Torquay we're considered extremely well-off, but I don't imagine we could hold a candle to you.'

'Is that important?' he queried softly.

'Not to me personally, but it does seem to matter to my mother.'

He laughed. 'Well, that's honest.'

'I hope you're not offended by this?'

'Not in the least. We should know what's what between us.'

That jolted her. 'Should we?'

'Oh yes, Katherine. I think it's important.'

She didn't reply to that. And when she spoke again it was to change the subject.

'Elyse!' Marcus exclaimed. 'Do have a chair, please.' He indicated one set in front of his desk. 'I was about to have a glass of sherry. Will you join me?'

'That would be nice.'

She watched him as he poured from a decanter. He seemed genuinely pleased to see her, which had to be a good sign. Her hopes rose a little.

'Back from Torquay, I presume?' he declared, handing her a glass.

'That's right.'

'And looking for fresh challenges?'

'Work, in other words, Marcus.'

He smiled and sat down facing her. 'Quite. So how can I be of help?'

She suddenly knew he was going to make this difficult for her, the glint in his eyes betraying the fact. Well, she'd come this far, so she might as well get on with it. But she was damned if she was going to beg. If he wanted that, he was due for a disappointment. She'd conduct herself with the utmost dignity.

'I understand you might be casting shortly?'

He leant back in his chair and stared at her. 'Where did you hear that?'

'From a friend.'

'Male or female?'

'Female actually.'

'Ah!'

She had a sip of her sherry and then placed the glass on his desk. A sip was all she'd be having.

He took his time in going on. 'As it happens, I do have a play in the pipeline. A comedy.'

'Oh?'

'A new piece.'

She nodded.

'Called *Ship Ahoy!*. A potboiler, but it will make money. Or so I'm convinced.'

She thought it sounded dreadful. 'And would there be a part for me?'

'Possibly.'

This was like drawing teeth. 'What sort of part, Marcus?'

'A character role. Not at all glamorous, but she does have a few good lines.'

Elyse was dying for a cigarette but decided she'd wait until she'd left. She felt instinctively that, in the circumstances, smoking would make her appear vulnerable. 'Sounds interesting,' she lied.

'Hardly the lead, but I'm afraid you're just a teensy bit old to be considered for that.'

Bastard, she thought. He was enjoying this. 'An ingénue?'

'No. A young woman in her prime.'

Elyse winced inwardly. He really was driving the knife home. Driving and twisting it. She was now sorry she'd come. 'I see.'

'Anyway, I haven't even begun on the casting yet. It's still all up in the air. I shan't be getting down to it till after *The Seagull* opens.'

She swallowed hard. 'I hope that's going well.'

'Brilliantly in my opinion.'

She anticipated what was coming next. Another twist of the knife.

'The actress playing Madame Arkadina is superb, quite superb. I fully expect her to get rave reviews in all the newspapers.'

'That's Mrs Jordan, I understand.'

'Ah, you've taken an interest then?'

'Of course.'

'Do you know her?'

'We've never met, but I know her by reputation. A fine actress by all accounts.'

'I'm glad she meets with your approval.' The sarcasm in that was thinly disguised.

Will he ask about James? she wondered. And if he does, what should she reply? Certainly not the truth. She wouldn't give him the pleasure of that. And by truth she meant that they'd broken up, not the reason why.

'So, you're not casting at present,' she said.

'Unfortunately that's how things stand. But I will keep you in mind. That's a promise.' He reached for a pen. 'If you'll give me an address where I can contact you.'

He had no intention of casting her, she thought, none whatsoever. What he might do was ask her to read or, worse still for someone of her standing, audition. Whichever, she wouldn't get the part. She'd simply love to rake the bastard's face with her nails.

'I'm staying with friends who own Kean's. I can be reached there any time.'

He wrote that down. 'Well, I must say it's lovely seeing you again, Elyse. You're looking tremendously fit. Your provincial seaside stint has obviously done you the world of good.'

Another barb. She rose. 'Thank you for your time, Marcus. And don't bother getting up, I know the way out.'

He remained seated, smiling all the while as she left his office.

Elyse gazed morosely into a large Scotch, her third since entering the Salisbury. She just couldn't get over how awful – not to mention humiliating – that had been. One thing was certain: she'd never get work from Marcus Brierley. His revenge for her turning him down.

'Christ!' she whispered to herself. Talk about putting your head on the chopping block. She'd certainly done that. But how was she to have known he'd be so spiteful? The utterly unspeakable bastard.

'Mrs Davenport?'

The face of the man who'd addressed her was vaguely familiar. 'Yes?'

'You may not remember me, but I was ASM on a play you did some years ago. My name's Alan West.'

Now she had him. 'At the Vaudeville?'

He smiled. 'That's right. May I join you?'

She'd didn't really want company, but she didn't want to be rude either. From what she recalled of Alan West, he'd been a very pleasant young man and good at his job. 'Feel free.'

He pulled out a packet of cigarettes. 'Have you stopped?'

'No,' she laughed and accepted one, which he lit for her. 'Are you working at the moment?'

She shook her head. 'Unfortunately not.'

'Then I'm in luck.'

She gave him a puzzled look. 'How so?'

'I'm deputy SM on *Lady Windermere's Fan* at the Haymarket, which has been running for eighteen months. Have you seen it by any chance?'

'I haven't, I'm afraid,' she confessed. 'But I've heard it's a first-class production.'

'We're about to change the cast, as per some of the original contracts. The thing is that the director is ill and can't manage to do the rehearsals. So I've been asked by the management to recast the play and rehearse them in.'

'Congratulations!' she exclaimed. 'Is it your plan to be a stage director then?'

'Oh yes,' he enthused. 'That's always been my aim. The management have intimated that if I make a success of this, then I'll get my own play sometime in the near future.'

'That's good news, Alan. I'm delighted for you.' And she meant it.

'Thank you, Mrs Davenport. Now the thing is, would you be interested in taking over the part of Lady Windermere?'

She hadn't dared hope he was about to ask her something like that. Elation filled her.

'Perhaps you feel it's beneath you to step into someone else's shoes? I would fully understand.'

Beneath her! At the moment that was a joke. 'Alan, I'd be delighted to accept. When do I start?'

He breathed a sigh of relief. 'I know you'll be smashing in that part, Mrs Davenport. It's a cracker. Rehearsals start a week on Monday and will take place on the set. Now,' he paused to take a breath, 'can I buy you another drink before we get down to the details?'

She wanted to hug Alan, kiss him. He was a lifesaver. And such a wonderful role, play and theatre too! 'It's Scotch.'

'Coming up.' And with that he went to the bar.

Back in the West End in a leading role. Her prayers had been answered, and in such an unexpected way. A foul day had miraculously turned into a glorious one.

'This calls for a bottle of bubbles,' Molly declared after Elyse had burst in and told her and Seamus the news.

'At this time of day?' Seamus queried with a frown.

'Oh, don't be a miserable old fart all your life. Fetch a bottle this instant, Seamus O'Malley. It's an occasion to be sure.'

A grumbling Seamus lurched to his feet. 'Thank God we only pay trade prices,' he said. That was a joke, getting at his wife. He was just as pleased for Elyse as Molly was.

'I must go and see the production before I start rehearsals,' Elyse declared, fired with enthusiasm.

'Good idea,' Molly nodded.

'A script will be arriving here within the next few days, which will give me plenty of time for study before rehearsals begin.'

'And Marcus Brierley can go fly a kite, eh?'

'Nasty bugger. To think I even considered . . .' She broke off and shook her head.

'It's an escape you've had, Elyse. No mistake about that.'

'He was so awful, Molly. And enjoyed every moment of it. Well, he can stick his *Ship Ahoy!* right up . . . Not that I would have been offered a part, there was never any chance of that.'

Seamus arrived with the champagne and quickly popped the cork.

'To Elyse and her new role! May she excel in it, as I know she surely will,' he toasted.

Now that she was about to earn again she'd have to find accommodation of her own, Elyse reflected. Kind as the O'Malleys were, she didn't want to outstay her welcome.

'I understand from Lady Mary that you and Miles are getting on extremely well,' Ruth said to Katherine over breakfast, Jeremiah having already had his and gone out on business.

'Yes, we are, as a matter of fact.'

'Good. I was hoping you would.'

Katherine was only too well aware of that. Of all the young men she'd met so far, Miles was the nicest and most attractive. They were very much at ease in each other's company. 'Did Lady Mary say anything else?'

'That he's quite smitten. So what do you make of that?'

Katherine blushed. 'Is he really?'

'Very much so, apparently. I know he's talked to his father about you.'

Katherine had met Sir Rafe on several occasions. He was more or less an older version of his son. 'And?'

'He approves, Katherine. As of course does Lady Mary.'

Katherine knew where all this was leading. That was why the debs attended all these balls and parties after all, to find themselves a suitable husband. And vice versa for the young men. A cattle market, she'd heard one deb call it, who'd then burst into braying laughter.

'How do you feel about that?' Ruth asked softly.

Katherine thought of Tim, whom she'd mused about a lot recently. She'd been so convinced that he was the one for her, but now, if she was honest, she was beginning to have doubts. Then there was the fact that she intended working before marriage. How would Miles react to that? Tim was all for it of course, but Miles might be a different proposition.

She realised then that she hadn't written to Tim the previous night as she'd meant to, it having completely slipped her mind. She would do so later that day without fail.

'I asked you how you felt about that,' Ruth repeated.

'I'm not certain yet, Mama.'

'He's a tremendous catch you know.'

'So you keep saying,' Katherine almost snapped in reply, wishing her mother wouldn't be so pushy about this. It would be her decision, and hers alone, whatever was decided.

'A lot of girls will be setting their caps at him. If they haven't already. You're lucky he's paid you so much attention.'

'Well, he would if he's smitten,' Katherine retorted. 'If he truly is.'

'Oh, he is all right. Thinks the world of you.' Ruth ate some toast, then asked, 'Are you seeing him today?'

'He'll be calling at ten o'clock to take me to lunch.' Miles had suggested a Greek restaurant, which had sounded terribly exciting, most exotic. She had no idea what Greek food was like, but presumably very different from the English variety. She just knew it was going to be fun.

A smile of satisfaction creased Ruth's face. The pot was bubbling along very nicely indeed.

'This is it. What do you think?'

Jeremiah had found what he considered to be a suitable house in Wilton Crescent, SW1, and had brought Ruth along to see it before he finalised matters.

'It's rather small, isn't it?'

Jeremiah shrugged. 'I'll mostly be on my own, darling. Apart from staff, that is. Anything larger and I'd be rattling around like a pea in a drum.'

'That's true,' she mused. 'Does it get plenty of sun?'

'So the agent assures me.'

'And it is central.'

'Personally I consider it ideal and exactly right for my purposes.'

She gazed about her, wondering when the place had last had a lick of paint. She mentioned this to Jeremiah.

'I shall be calling in interior decorators, Ruth, to revamp the entire house. I shall also instruct them to choose furniture and fittings – everything necessary – so that I can just move in.'

She nodded her approval. 'Well, if you're happy with it, dear, then so am I. I think it will be a splendid town residence when finished.'

'Yes, I am pleased with my find,' he beamed. 'You and Katherine will of course be staying here too whenever you are in London.' Which, he presumed, wouldn't be too often.

Her ploy had worked well, Ruth congratulated herself. She'd got what she wanted. Jeremiah out of her hair for at least some of the time. A most gratifying arrangement. She'd urge him to hurry the legalities through as quickly as possible.

Katherine didn't know how it happened. One moment she and Miles were on the verandah talking, taking refuge from the latest party they were attending, and the next she was in his arms and they were kissing, she kissing him just as eagerly as he was kissing her.

'Oh, my love, my angel,' he crooned in her ear when it was finally over.

She snuggled into the front of his uniform, thinking how marvellous that had been. She felt so safe, so secure with Miles. And now here he was, with his arms wrapped round her, holding her close.

'Katherine?'

She looked up at him. He was smiling in the moonlight. Then they were kissing again, with Katherine almost in a swoon of emotion.

* * *

Tim knew he shouldn't be making this telephone call. He'd been in the pub most of the evening and as a result was drunk. But he just had to try and speak to Katherine, know what was going on, be told why she'd been so long in writing.

'Hello?'

Instantly he recognised her voice. 'Katherine, it's Tim.'

She sucked in a breath.

'Katherine?'

'It's good to hear from you, Tim. How are you?'

'I've rung and rung, but you've never been there,' he accused her petulantly.

'I'm sorry, Tim. It's just I've been so busy.'

'And haven't written.'

'I said I'm sorry.' His tone was making her cross, the guilt she was feeling rapidly dissipating.

'I expect it's all those swanky shindigs you've been going to. Is that it?'

'As I said, I've been busy.'

'Huh!' he snorted.

'I should have written more often, I know, but there simply hasn't been the time.'

'I've missed you.'

'And I've missed you.'

'Have you really?' he slurred.

'Tim, are you all right? You sound strange.'

'Of course I'm all right. Except for missing you, that is,' he replied bitterly.

'Well, I can't keep saying sorry,' she retorted, anger creeping into her voice.

'When are you coming home?'

'Not for a few weeks yet.' In fact it was longer than that.

'Can't you come sooner?'

'No, I can't,' she replied, trying to be patient.

'Are you sure?'

'Quite sure.' She didn't like this Tim, not one little bit. Where was the kind, understanding young man she'd left behind in Torquay? 'Tim, I have to go.'

'Why?' he demanded.

She couldn't think of a reason, but knew she wanted this conversation to finish. 'I just have to.'

'Have you met someone? Is that it?'

'You're talking nonsense now,' she lied.

'That's it, isn't it? You've met someone else,' he shouted.

'Go to bed, Tim. It's late.'

'No it's not.'

'We'll speak again.'

Suddenly he was contrite, ashamed. 'Yes, we'll speak again,' he mumbled.

'Goodbye.'

'Goodbye, Katherine.'

He'd lost her, he thought in despair as he hung up. He'd lost her!

Still in the depths of despair he strode from The Berkeley, slamming the door behind him, not caring that it might disturb the guests, and headed back to the pub, hoping Harry was still there. If he was going to get drunk, he might as well make a proper job of it.

Chapter 18

'It's a glorious party. Your parents have done you proud,' Miles said to Katherine as the pair of them waltzed. Ruth had arranged for the occasion to be held in the Connaught Rooms, and no expense had been spared. The turn-out was even better than they'd hoped.

'Well, I'm enjoying myself,' she replied, having danced with no-one but Miles all evening.

'Me too. And let me say again, at the risk of repeating myself to the point of tedium, that you look absolutely ravishing.'

'Why, thank you, kind sir.'

Her dress was an all-silk crêpe satin, its colour marron glacé. It boasted Parisian characteristics in the cut, with a curved yoke and cuffs of rich ecru lace faced with silk georgette. Crystal-like buttons trimmed the bodice, while a jaunty pin set off the georgette-faced tie.

Katherine knew many of the people present, having met them at other parties and balls, while others were new to her. A large contingent of Miles' colleagues was there, all resplendent, as he was, in dress uniform.

Clarice and her partner passed close by, Clarice giving

Katherine a small wave. Her partner was Julian, the flyer, whom Katherine had met during her previous visit to London.

'Happy?' Miles teased.

'Very much so.'

'Good.'

'And you?'

'Positively ecstatic.'

She laughed at that. But then Miles had a way of making her laugh. He was enormous fun to be with.

Katherine spotted her father standing alongside one of a number of punch bowls, with glass in hand. Judging from his complexion he'd had quite a few already.

Ruth was somewhere about, though for the moment Katherine couldn't see her. Probably behind the scenes checking that everything was going according to plan. What a tremendous effort her mother had put into this evening, Katherine reflected. She hadn't appreciated just how much hard work had been involved.

But everything was going swimmingly and couldn't have been better. The party was a huge success. She was now well and truly launched into society.

And the day after tomorrow was the pièce de résistance, her presentation at Court. It gave her butterflies even to think about it. She could only pray that she did everything as Ruth had primed her and didn't make a mess of things.

When the dance was over Miles led her from the floor. 'I want to speak to you in private,' he said. 'And I know just the place, a small anteroom off one of the corridors.'

She wondered what this was all about. The twinkle in his eyes told her something was up. Perhaps he was about to give her a surprise gift. In the circumstances that was entirely possible.

'If you like.'

They made their way to the anteroom, which was fortunately empty. Miles closed the door behind them.

'So what's this all about?' she queried.

Instead of replying he went straight to her and kissed her, and she melted into his arms.

'Well!' she exclaimed when the kiss was over.

'I love you, Katherine.'

She opened her mouth, then closed it again. She hadn't been expecting this.

'I don't know when it happened,' he went on softly. 'But it has. And that's why I'm asking you to marry me.'

She was absolutely stunned, having been caught completely on the hop. 'I'm lost for words,' she finally managed to say.

He smiled as he delved into his trouser pocket to produce a small blue box. 'This is for you.' He opened the box and showed her the contents, a magnificent single diamond atop a platinum band. 'An engagement ring,' he stated unnecessarily.

Katherine's thoughts were suddenly racing. How stupid of her, how naïve! She should have guessed what was coming when he'd asked her to leave the party for an anteroom where they could be alone.

'Of course I'll have to ask your father for your hand before you can wear it,' Miles continued. 'But I don't think he'll refuse me.'

Katherine couldn't help herself. She took the ring from its box and slipped it onto the appropriate finger, where it gleamed and flashed as though the stone contained a thousand tiny suns.

'Katherine?'

'I, eh . . . I . . .' She broke off in confusion.

'Will you marry me?'

She'd been expecting a surprise, but nothing like this. As for the ring, it would have graced a princess' hand. 'It's a bit of a shock,' she stated quietly.

'Not a nasty one, I hope?' he joked.

'Not at all. But a shock all the same.'

Suddenly Miles frowned. 'Have I got it wrong, Katherine? Have I made a fool of myself?'

'Not in the least,' she retorted quickly. 'That's the last thing you've done.'

'Then why are you hesitating?'

'Because . . .' She drew in a deep breath. 'Miles, I have to think about this. I know that's not the answer you want, but it's the only one I can give. I simply have to think about it.'

'I see,' he murmured.

'No, you don't. I just want time to consider. For one thing, I want to work before getting married, as a nurse.'

'A nurse?'

'That's my intention.'

'You've never mentioned that before.'

'I suppose I haven't. You see, I want to do something with my life, Miles, something useful. What I don't want is to become some pampered wife sitting around the house all day with nothing to do but gossip and occasionally some charity work.'

It pained her to see the hurt in his eyes and how his shoulders had slumped.

'You are refusing me then,' he said stiffly.

'I am doing nothing of the kind. I said I want to think about it, and that's exactly what I mean.'

He paused before replying, 'Then time you shall have. Within reason, though. Don't keep me on tenterhooks for ever.'

'I won't,' she promised.

'I do love you, Katherine,' he repeated. 'We'd be an ideal couple. Quite perfect. As for your working, I would have thought bringing up children was hard enough work for any woman.'

Children! She smiled at the thought of that. 'I'll give you my answer soon, Miles. You can rely on it. In the meantime . . .' She removed the ring from her finger and replaced it in its box. 'Hang on to that.'

He cleared his throat. 'We'd better get back to the party, I suppose. They'll be wondering where we are.'

'Yes,' she agreed.

He closed the box and returned it to his pocket. 'Shall we make a move then?'

'Miles?'

'What, Katherine?'

'Kiss me again before we leave. Please?'

It was another five minutes before they rejoined the party.

'I don't think it could have been more successful. You did a wonderful job, dear.'

'Thank you, Jeremiah. I must say, I was highly delighted with the result. And so many people! Far more than at many of the other parties.'

Ruth glanced sideways at Katherine, who was staring out of the car window, apparently lost in thought. Edward, the chauffeur, was driving them home.

'You're very quiet, Katherine,' Ruth smiled.

Katherine brought herself out of her reverie. 'Sorry, Mama. I suppose I'm just exhausted.'

'Hardly surprising,' Jeremiah commented. 'You danced all evening.'

'With Miles,' Ruth added softly.

'Thank you both again.'

Jeremiah considered lighting up a cigar, then decided to wait for a while. Ruth was sure to complain if he smoked in the car. At least he didn't have that problem with Henrietta. There again, she was hardly in a position to complain.

Katherine turned away from her parents and went back to staring out of the window.

Ruth tapped on Katherine's bedroom door. 'Can I come in?'

'Of course, Mama.'

Ruth found her daughter in her nightclothes, brushing her hair. 'Shall I do that for you? Like I used to when you were a little girl.'

'That would be nice.'

She took the brush from Katherine and positioned herself behind her. Slowly, and with great care, she began to brush.

'I have to ask, darling, but what did you reply to Miles' proposal? I presume you accepted him.'

Katherine gave her mother a startled look in the vanity-table mirror. 'You know about that?'

'Lady Mary told me last week that Miles was going to ask you on the night of your party. Make a special occasion into a memorable one was his idea, I believe.'

Katherine blushed.

'But so far you've said nothing, which is worrying me.'

Katherine was aware of her mother's eyes boring into hers. She glanced hurriedly down.

'I'm waiting, Katherine.'

She took a deep breath. 'I said I wanted time to think.'

Ruth hesitated in her brushing for the briefest of moments, then continued. 'And what was his reply?'

'To take that time. Within reason, as he put it.'

Ruth was angry and doing her best not to show it. Anger would get her nowhere in a situation like this, she told herself. Gentle but firm reasoning was the answer.

'It's Tim Wilson, I presume?' she probed.

Katherine didn't reply to that.

'He's a pleasant lad, I have to admit. Your father certainly likes him. But there's a gulf between the pair of you, a gulf that would eventually destroy a marriage.'

Katherine frowned. 'What gulf, Mama?'

'I'm an older – and wiser – woman, I hope. And as such I understand human nature far better than you.'

Katherine was listening intently.

'We're a rich family,' Ruth went on patiently. 'And neither your father nor I will live for ever. When we're gone you'll inherit everything.'

'Tim's not interested in my money,' Katherine protested. 'Nor will I have you imply that he is.'

Ruth smiled angelically. 'I wasn't trying to say he'd marry you for your money, for he's not the gold-digger type. But that eventually the money would breed resentment, which would come between you.'

Katherine considered that. 'Go on.'

'I'm talking about pride, Katherine, and your young Tim is full of it. I've seen it in his face. Let's take his circumstances for a start. His family were once well-off, but no longer. As a result he earns his living as a reporter – or journalist, if you will. An admirable enough profession, I suppose, but one that will never bring in a large remuneration. Even if he became an editor one day, he would still be on, more or less, a working man's wage.'

Ruth paused to let Katherine digest her argument so far. When she thought Katherine had, she continued. 'So there he is, bringing in a relative pittance while married to a woman who is wealthy in the extreme. Now, if it was the other way round – a wealthy husband marrying a poor girl – it wouldn't matter. No trouble there. But a wealthy woman with a poor husband, especially living in a house like Oaklands, and it wouldn't be long before resentment set in, particularly if you wished to maintain the lifestyle you've been used to.'

Katherine hadn't thought about any of that.

'On the other hand,' Ruth went on relentlessly, 'that problem certainly wouldn't exist with Miles, as his family is far richer than ours. It would be a marriage of "haves", not of a "have" and a "have-not".'

'I suppose so,' Katherine admitted at last.

'Believe me, Katherine, I know what I'm talking about. Resentment, jealousy and in time possibly even hatred, an ever-growing canker eating away at the relationship. He may love you now, but wouldn't it be horrible if one day he ended up hating you through no fault of your own?'

Katherine recalled Tim's phone call and how childish he'd been. Admittedly he had been right about there being someone else, but his tone, his manner, his belligerence! She hadn't been at all impressed with the Tim she'd spoken to that night.

Ruth was watching her daughter keenly in the mirror and could see the confusion and uncertainty in her expression. 'Why settle for second best, and probable unhappiness, when the alternative is Miles Crabthorne who positively worships you? I can't believe you'd be that big a fool.'

Like her telephone conversation with Tim, Katherine now wanted this conversation to end, for her head was buzzing with what her mother had said. 'I'm tired, Mama. I have to go to bed.'

Ruth stopped brushing. 'You told Miles you needed time to think. Well, that's what you'd better do. Though it seems an easy enough decision to me. A choice between happiness and eventual unhappiness.'

It was hours before Katherine eventually managed to drop off into a troubled sleep. Her final conclusion, arrived at reluctantly, was that a lot of what Ruth had pointed out made sense.

'Well, well!' Molly O'Malley exclaimed, coming up short. She and Elyse were shopping in Oxford Street.

Elyse also halted. 'What is it?'

'Look who's just got out of that car up front. And him

dressed like a dish of fish, if you don't mind. That coat alone he's wearing must have cost a pretty penny or two.'

Elyse wasn't interested in Benny's clothes, but in who he was with. She watched as he opened a door and helped a woman out onto the pavement.

'Holy bejesus, she's old enough to be his mother!' Molly exclaimed.

Not quite, Elyse thought, but she was certainly a lot older than Benny. Somewhere in her mid-fifties, she judged.

'Do you want to say hello?' Molly teased.

'Don't be ridiculous. Knowing Benny, that would be far more embarrassing for me than for him.'

'Look at the jewellery, she's positively dripping in the stuff.'

That was true, Elyse now observed, taking great satisfaction that the widow, for it must be she, was no beauty. And never had been. She continued to watch as the woman took Benny's arm. He whispered something in her ear.

Elyse turned round. 'Let's go back. I don't want to go on, if you don't mind.'

'Of course I don't.' Molly peered at her friend's face. 'Are you all right?'

'I'm fine, Molly. It's just . . . well, seeing them like that was a bit of a shock.'

Molly glanced back to where Benny and the widow were now entering a shop. 'Good riddance to bad rubbish, I say. You're well shot of him, Elyse. Take my word for it.'

'I know that. She's welcome to him, whoever she is. And to show there's no hard feelings on my part, I wish them well.'

'He seemed sober enough. If you can tell at that distance.'

'Perhaps he was. Not that I care. He could be rolling around in the gutter and it wouldn't interest me one whit. He's out of my life forever, and for that I'm damned glad.'

'That's the spirit, girl. He wasn't any good anyway. I never understood what you saw in him.'

'Oh, he had his good points,' Elyse declared and winked salaciously.

The pair of them burst out laughing.

'There is something else I didn't mention the other night,' Ruth said to Katherine over breakfast. This was yet another morning when Jeremiah had gone off early on business.

Katherine glanced across at her mother, reluctant to hear any more on that particular subject. She didn't reply but went on eating instead.

Ruth dropped her voice, assuming a conspiratorial tone. 'This is delicate, Katherine. Strictly between you and me. You must promise me you won't breathe a word of it to anyone, particularly your father.'

Katherine was intrigued. 'Why not Papa?'

'Because it would cause him great distress, which I don't want to do. Do I have your promise?'

Katherine nodded.

Ruth took a deep breath, then went on in the same conspiratorial tone. 'Both you and your father are aware I've been ill these many years. Well, what nobody knows, apart from me, is that last year I was told I probably have only a short time left to live.'

Katherine's jaw dropped open.

'Since we've been in London I've visited a specialist in Harley Street for a second opinion and he agrees with the diagnosis. I could literally go at any moment.'

'Oh, Mama,' Katherine whispered. This was terrible.

Ruth had decided to resort to this lie to force Katherine's hand where Miles was concerned. Of course it was despicable, but sometimes needs must. When she continued to survive she'd say that the doctors must somehow have got it wrong.

'Now you can understand why your father must never learn of this. He would be beside himself, which I want to spare him. It'll be bad enough for him when the time comes. But rather that than the ongoing agony of waiting for the inevitable.'

Ruth hoped she wasn't overdoing it. She didn't think so.

'Is there nothing that can be done, Mama?'

'Unfortunately not.'

Katherine reached across the table and clasped her mother's hand. 'So why are you telling me now?'

Ruth sighed. 'It would give me a great sense of peace to know everything is rosy for your future. That you're well married and happy.' She paused dramatically. 'I know that would be the case if you accept Miles' proposal. He's a good man, who loves you and can look after you. I would die contented knowing you and he are together. Whereas . . .' She trailed off and shrugged.

'You mean Tim?'

'Yes, I do. I just can't believe, for all the reasons I've already given you, that that would work in the long term. I'm utterly convinced it would be a ghastly mistake.'

Katherine fought back tears, her mind simultaneously numb and whirling She didn't know what to say.

'But the final decision is yours, dear. You know that. I

simply wanted you to be aware of exactly what was what before you made your choice.'

There, Ruth thought triumphantly. If that didn't do it, nothing would. She hadn't enjoyed lying to her own daughter, but the silly girl just had to see sense: marrying Tim Wilson would be a total disaster.

'Have you any idea at all how long . . . ?' Katherine broke off, unable to complete the question.

'None whatsoever. It could be next week, next month, whenever. The doctors simply couldn't be specific.'

Katherine pushed her plate away, her appetite having vanished. She'd never felt so close to her mother as she did at that moment.

'Now, what do you plan to do today?' Ruth smiled bravely, changing the subject.

Katherine got the message. Ruth didn't want to talk any further about this.

After breakfast Katherine went to her room and sat there for well over an hour. Every so often she'd burst into tears as the full import of her mother's looming death sank in.

'Nervous?' Alan West asked Elyse. It was opening night for the new cast and he'd dropped by her dressing room to wish her luck.

'A little.'

'You'll be a knockout, Mrs Davenport. They'll love you.'

He was such a sweetie, she thought. And a good director too. He should go far.

'Let's hope so.'

He kissed her on the cheek. 'I'll see you afterwards. I'll

be spending the entire performance in the audience taking notes.'

'Not too many in my case, I hope?' she joked.

'Probably none at all where you're concerned.'

Elyse re-examined her make-up when Alan had gone off to visit other cast members on the same errand. It was perfect, she decided. Best not to fiddle with it any more.

Then she remembered a few cards that had been delivered earlier, which were lying by the side of her dressing table. She picked up the top one and opened it.

The signature at the bottom made her go cold all over, for it was from James Erskine.

He'd written that he'd read about the change of cast in *Stage*, the actors' trade newspaper, which had also given the date of the new opening, and that he wanted to wish her well. He was currently in Worthing for a short season, after which he thought he might try London at long last. Would it be possible for them to meet up? He'd enclosed his current address, hoping that she might contact him.

Again he apologised profusely for what had happened and felt dreadful at letting her down so badly. Could she please, please forgive him?

And please write.

Elyse slowly tore the card into two, then into quarters. A flick of the wrist and all four pieces fluttered into her bin.

'I have to go to Glasgow for a week, possibly longer,' Jeremiah announced to Henrietta. They were in her hotel room.

'Glasgow?'

'There's a steelworks in trouble up there, which I'm

considering buying. If war does happen, then steel will be in great demand, so it seems a good investment to me.'

'I would imagine so.'

'In the meantime . . .' He pulled out his wallet and extracted some notes. 'Here's thirty pounds. If you're going to act as my housekeeper you'll have to look the part. Get the appropriate clothes, and spend what's left on whatever you fancy.'

Henrietta accepted the six large white fivers. 'You're very generous, Jeremiah.'

'Perhaps,' he smiled. 'The other news is that the house is now mine and the interior decorators will be starting work next Monday. It shouldn't be too long before we can move in. After my wife has returned to Torquay of course.'

'Of course,' she nodded.

He hesitated. 'Any regrets, Henrietta? If so, tell me.'

She put her arms round him. 'No regrets, none at all.'

'Good.'

'And you?'

'No.'

She rested her cheek against his chest, her face a picture of contentment.

Jeremiah sighed with sheer pleasure.

'Oh dear!' Harry Nutbeam exclaimed and laid the latest edition of the London *Times*, which he'd been reading, on the desk in front of him.

'Something wrong?' Tim queried without looking round, being busy on a story.

'No, nothing.'

Harry glanced surreptitiously at Tim, then picked up the

paper again to reread the announcement that had caused him to exclaim.

It was one of the rare occasions when Ricketts was off ill, with Patsy deputising for the editor until his return.

Harry chewed a fingernail, wondering what to do. If anything. Finally, reluctantly, he decided there was nothing else for it but to show the announcement to Tim.

'I think you'd better see this,' he declared and passed the paper over.

'See what?'

Harry took a deep breath, then pointed. 'That.'

Tim read the first line and went white. The announcement concerned the engagement between Katherine Isobel Coates and Miles Peregrine Charles Crabthorne.

'I'm so sorry,' Harry sympathised.

There was such a lump in Tim's throat that he was sure it was going to choke him. There it was, in black and white – confirmation that she'd not only met someone else but got engaged to the bastard. He noted absent-mindedly that his hands were trembling.

'Get lost for a couple of hours,' Harry whispered. 'If Patsy asks for you, I'll say you're out doing an interview. Go on.'

Tim turned a stricken face to his friend.

'The pubs are open,' Harry urged. 'Go on.'

Without uttering a word, Tim rose and, as if in a trance, walked out of the office. He was totally and utterly heart-broken.

It was almost midnight when Tim reached the inner harbour wall. The tide was in, as he'd known it would be.

He stood for a little while staring out over the water,

thinking, remembering, full of hurt and pain.

Eventually he reached into both jacket pockets and pulled out the matching pair of silver-plated hairbrushes that Katherine had given him, which had been his most treasured possessions.

The first one arced through the air to disappear with a splash, then the second.

That done, with all it symbolised, he returned home.

Chapter 19

1914

Ricketts replaced his telephone receiver on its cradle and stared thoughtfully at it for a few moments. Then, with the grimmest of expressions, he came to his feet.

'Could you all please gather round,' he requested in a loud voice.

Tim glanced at Harry and pulled a face, the pair of them wondering what this was all about. They joined the rest of the staff assembling in front of Ricketts' desk.

When everyone was there the editor held up a hand for silence. 'I've just been informed that Belgium was invaded this morning. Mr Asquith, the Prime Minister, has announced in the House of Commons that as a result we are now at war with Germany.'

There was a deathly hush, broken when someone cheered. A cheer that was taken up by others, including Harry. A shocked Tim remained mute.

War had been talked about, endlessly discussed, since the start of the year, but in their heart of hearts many – Tim among them – hadn't really believed it would actually happen, but that somehow the situation would blow over.

Ricketts held his hand up again. 'Obviously this will be the banner for our next edition, with most of the lead story coming from the wire services. As a local paper, I want local reactions.' He named four reporters including Tim. 'Start right away. Local tradesmen, the fishing fleet, the man and woman in the street, etc., etc. That's all for the moment.'

'Bloody hell,' said Harry as they returned to where they'd been sitting. 'Isn't it exciting?'

Tim was appalled. 'What's exciting about it? People are going to get killed, Harry. Probably an awful lot of them. I don't see anything exciting in that.'

'Of course it's exciting,' Harry enthused. 'We'll thrash the Hun good and proper. Our ships will blow theirs out of the water, while on land they won't be able to hold a candle to us. A couple of months and they'll be hoisting the old white flag and begging for mercy. You'll see.'

'I doubt that,' Tim protested. 'This won't be short and sharp, but long and bloody. You mark my words.'

'Nonsense,' Harry replied dismissively. 'Anyway, it's high time those Jerry bastards were taught a lesson, and our boys are the very ones to do it.'

Tim shook his head, thinking that Harry couldn't be more wrong. One thing he knew for certain: this was going to affect their lives far more than any of them realised. And what if the unthinkable happened and Britain and the Empire should lose? What then?

'Oh Tim!' Minna exclaimed later that night when he arrived home, and rushed into his arms. 'Isn't it terrible?'

He could see she'd been crying. 'Are you all right?'

'It's been an awful day. Apparently thousands of young

men have already been to the recruitment offices to join up.'

She pulled herself slightly apart and stared him straight in the eye. 'Promise me you won't do anything so foolish?'

'I can't do that, Ma,' he replied after a few moments' hesitation. 'It may be that I have to.'

'Tim!' she wailed. 'Promise me? I couldn't bear it if you did.'

'Let's see how things go, eh? My joining up might not be necessary. Harry at work thinks it won't last than a few months and maybe he's right.'

'Pray God it doesn't. That's all I can say. Pray God it doesn't.'

He hadn't heard about the thousands joining up – that was new to him. 'Now, what's to eat? I'm starving. It's been a long hard day, as you can imagine.' He managed a light laugh. 'It's not every day we go to war after all.'

Minna's reply was to burst into tears.

'Now you're not to worry, Katherine. I'll be safe as houses.'

'Of course I'll worry. It would be stupid not to,' she snapped back, instantly regretting her tone. 'I'm sorry, Miles.'

'I understand, darling. It's natural to be concerned after all.'

She turned away from him so that he couldn't see her face. They'd only been married for five months and now he was off to war. It just wasn't fair. 'If only you didn't have to leave so soon.'

'Katherine, you know we've been on stand-by in case this happened. We've been ready for weeks, just waiting for the off. Even the ship taking us over has been berthed at Tilbury for a fortnight. And I did warn you a long time ago that our regiment would be in the thick of things as soon as possible, which is exactly what's going to happen.'

'But so soon,' she whispered and started to weep.

Miles crossed over and put his arms round her, savouring her sweet scent. He was going to miss her dreadfully when he was away, but that was a soldier's lot. As, indeed, it was the lot of a soldier's wife.

'Don't make me feel even worse, Katherine. It's bad enough as it is.'

'I can't help it. Sorry.'

He hugged her tight. 'I'll be thinking of you all the time. And who knows, when I do get back I might be a captain or even a major. Wouldn't that be wonderful?'

'Yes,' she husked, saying that just to try and please him.

'Now, no more tears. I have to return to the barracks, so come on, cheer up. It isn't the end of the world.'

'Shall I come and see you off tomorrow?'

'It would be a waste of time, Katherine. Believe me. The whole thing will be pandemonium. There will be thousands of troops embarking and further thousands of civilians there to wave goodbye. Chances are you wouldn't even catch a glimpse of me. We'll say our goodbyes in the morning. That'll be best.'

'If you wish.'

He turned her round and ran the palm of his hand over her face, wiping away the tears. 'You're so lovely, my darling. So very beautiful. I'm the luckiest of men to have met and married you. That's something I remind myself of every day.'

She attempted a smile. 'Do you?'

'Yes, I do. Every single day.'

'I just wish . . .' She trailed off.

'That this war hadn't happened?' he prompted.

She nodded.

'Well, it has, I'm afraid. And my job is to go and fight it. Do my duty for King and Country. And do it I shall, to the very best of my ability.'

'I know you will.'

'You'll be proud of me, Katherine. I swear it.'

'I already am,' she replied softly.

'And I'm proud of you. Bursting with it. So, no more tears and heartache. It has to be done and that's all there is to it.'

'You won't take any unnecessary risks?'

'None whatsoever. I shall be brave, I hope, but not stupid. I fully intend coming home again, you can rest assured about that. Home again to you.'

She prayed that would be so.

It was early and still dark outside as Miles silently got dressed. When he was ready he went to stand beside Katherine's side of the bed, where she lay sleeping.

He smiled in memory of the night before. He'd never known her so passionate or demonstrative. It had been as if some sort of wild demon had possessed her.

How angelic she now looked, he thought, with her hair spread out in a golden halo on the pillow. Reaching down, he placed the tips of his fingers lightly against her cheek.

He wouldn't wake her, he decided. He didn't have the heart to. Besides, he didn't want a tearful parting, with her clinging to him, not wanting to let him go, for he was sure that was how it would be.

'Goodbye for now, my darling. I do love you,' he whispered. Moments later the door clicked shut behind him.

As it did Katherine opened her eyes, having only been pretending to be asleep. Staring into the darkness, she wondered how long it would be before she saw him again.

Miles stood on the deck of the SS *Pride of Liverpool* and watched the English coastline slowly vanish over the horizon. Within a few short hours they'd be in France and it would all begin.

He could only imagine what lay ahead.

'What's the audience like?' Elyse asked Alan West, who'd popped into her dressing room for a quick hello.

'A good house. What I'd expect for a Tuesday night.'

'Many tickets bought at the box office?'

'More or less the same as usual. If this keeps up we shouldn't have anything to worry about.'

Both cast and management had feared that with the declaration of war their audiences would fall away to the point where they might have to close. But so far that hadn't happened.

'Let's hope so,' Elyse said. The last thing she wanted was to be thrown out of work, for in the present circumstances it was uncertain how the theatrical profession would be affected. If there was a general lack of audiences and theatres went 'dark', or shut, then unemployment among actors would be even worse than usual.

'Are you all right, Alan?' Elyse asked in concern. They'd been on first-name terms for some time now, and she'd been thinking how pale and drawn he looked. Not at all his usual self.

He hesitated, then said, 'I had a bit of a shock today.'

'Oh, darling! Can I help?'

Alan smiled and shook his head. 'It's my younger brother. He's gone and volunteered. Apparently six of them at the bank where he's a clerk went down together to the recruitment office and joined up.'

She pulled a sympathetic face. 'And of course you're worried for him.'

'Extremely. He's only eighteen, you see. The impulsive little bugger.'

'There seem to be a lot of young men doing that,' Elyse mused. 'The whole thing doesn't bear thinking about.'

'No,' Alan agreed.

'Tell you what,' she declared, having had an idea. 'Why don't you come to Kean's with me after the show? That'll cheer you up.'

'Thanks, Elyse, but I can't. I've other plans.'

'Well, if you change your mind just let me know. I shall be going.'

'You're very kind. Now I'd better get on.'

'Five minutes please!' the call boy shouted through her open doorway.

The audience that night turned out to be one of the most receptive imaginable. Perhaps it was the patriotic fervour that had gripped so many people, but they laughed and cheered almost non-stop, with the applause quite deafening at curtain call, of which there were twelve.

Almost manic, was how Elyse later described it to Molly.

* * *

'I've laid on a little light supper for you,' Henrietta said to Jeremiah, taking his coat and hat and hanging them up. For the past three weeks he'd been in Torquay.

'I'd have come sooner, but Ruth has been in a right old state since learning that Miles, our son-in-law, has been sent to France.'

Jeremiah paused and sucked in a deep breath. How good it was to be here again with Henrietta, how comforting. More and more Ruth was irritating him by her coldness, her aloofness at times. A complete contrast to the intimacy he had with Henrietta.

How he enjoyed the nights they spent alone together. Not doing anything in particular, but sometimes reading, talking, having a quiet drink.

And then bed, where they'd snuggle up, he with his arms wrapped round her, fondling her during the night, caressing her naked body. She was always willing and enthusiastic when he desired her. It was a totally different world from that of Oaklands, where he slept by himself, as did Ruth. He hadn't realised how very alone he'd been until setting up house with Henrietta, who'd become more of a wife to him than Ruth had been in many a long year.

'Shall I get you a whisky?' Henrietta smiled. 'I'm sure you could use one after your long journey.'

'Please.'

'And those cigars you ordered arrived yesterday. I opened the box and put some in the humidor.'

'Thank you.'

He took her by the hand and stared at her. 'It always amazes me how different you look dressed up like that.'

Henrietta was wearing a severely cut three-quarter-length black dress with her hair tied back in a bun. There wasn't a trace of make-up on her face.

She laughed. 'I'm simply being the housekeeper.'

'And a very efficient one you are, too. I couldn't ask for better.'

'Or I a better employer.'

His smile faded. 'I hope I mean more to you than just that.'

'Of course you do, Jeremiah,' she replied softly. 'You should know that by now.'

He drew her close and kissed her. 'After I've eaten will you get changed?'

'If that's what you wish.'

'Something attractive.'

'A dress or simply underwear?'

His smile returned. 'Why not the underwear? I have been away for a while after all. I deserve a treat.'

'And one you shall have.'

Hand in hand they walked through to the dining room where a place had been set, Jeremiah having told her the previous day by telephone what time he expected to arrive.

After she'd served him, starting with the whisky, he brought her up to date with all his news of what had been happening while he'd been away.

'Listen to those guns,' Jeremy Bull said. 'They just don't stop.'

It was night and Miles was sharing a bivouac with three other equal-ranking officers. They were camped not far from the Belgian border, within striking distance of the battle now raging. In the morning they'd be going into action.

Rodney Cecil-Tapwood, who'd been packing his pipe, now lit up. 'Ours or theirs, I wonder?'

'Ours, I should think,' Miles replied.

'Probably both,' Philip Maidens chipped in.

Miles shivered despite the greatcoat he had on, for it was a bitterly cold night, even if it was only the end of August.

'Coffee, gentlemen?' asked Miller, the batman, materialising out of the darkness.

'Thank you, old boy. I certainly shall,' Rodney replied.

When it was agreed they'd all have coffee, Miller disappeared off again to fetch it.

'Anybody worried about tomorrow?' Philip asked casually.

'Looking forward to it actually,' Jeremy declared. 'Give the Hun a taste of cold steel, what?'

'That's the spirit,' Philip stated.

'Why, are you?' Miles queried.

Philip looked across at him. 'Worried?'

Miles nodded.

'Apprehensive more like. Just don't want to let the side down.'

'You won't do that,' Jeremy assured him. 'None of us will. Anyway, once it starts you won't have time to be worried, apprehensive or anything else. The blood will be up and all you'll be able to think about is killing Germans.'

Miles wasn't at all sure about that, but didn't contradict his friend. When the order came it would be the moment of truth for all of them. He hoped Jeremy was right.

'Christ! What was that?' Rodney exclaimed when a massive explosion went off.

They all peered into the distance where they could now see a raging inferno where none had been before.

'Possibly an ammo or fuel dump has been hit,' Miles speculated, unable to think of anything else that could cause that size of explosion.

'It's upset the horses,' Philip observed. From nearby came assorted whinnyings and the stamping of hooves.

'They'll settle down again,' Jeremy remarked, confident that the well-trained and disciplined beasts would soon do so.

Miller reappeared carrying a pot of steaming coffee.

'Ah!' Miles exclaimed, reaching for his tin cup. 'The very thing.'

When the time came Miles was able to fall asleep, which he'd thought, what with the noise of the guns and his own pent-up emotions, he would be able to do.

The guns continued throughout the night without let-up, but there were no further massive explosions.

'This battle at Mons doesn't seem to be going too well for us, according to the reports coming in,' Harry said to Tim. The pair of them were ensconced in the pub.

'So I understand.'

'Lots of casualties.'

Tim drank some of his pint, his sixth of the evening. He'd go home after he'd finished this one, he decided.

'I wish I was there,' Harry declared.

Tim stared at him in disbelief. 'You must be mad!'

'I'm nothing of the sort.'

'You'd like to be in the middle of a battle where men are being killed and hideously maimed?' Tim queried incredulously. 'I'll bet there's not a soldier there who wouldn't happily swap places with you right now.'

Harry glared at him. 'I don't think I like your attitude. It's defeatist talk.'

Tim realised then just how drunk Harry was. 'I don't care what you think. I'm only saying what I consider to be the truth.'

'Defeatist talk,' Harry repeated and hiccuped.

'Nonsense.'

'Oh yes it is.'

'You yourself just said the battle wasn't going too well for us,' Tim protested.

Harry blinked. 'I was merely stating a fact, that's all. And I still wish I was there.'

'Bloody insane,' Tim muttered.

'At least I'm not a coward.'

Tim caught his breath. 'Are you accusing me of being a coward?'

'Well, aren't you? Otherwise you'd want to be over there too. Doing your bit.'

This could easily turn nasty, Tim thought. He should just walk away.

'I want to do my bit,' Harry declared proudly.

'Good for you. Now shut up before I lose my temper. You're beginning to get on my wick.'

Harry laughed. 'Big talk! It's easy to do that when you're tucked up safe in the pub.'

Tim had had enough. He quickly drained his pint and stood up. 'I'll see you at work in the morning.'

Harry laughed again, this time mockingly. 'The yellow streak showing, eh?'

Tim clenched his hands into fists. This was so unlike Harry, or he might have done something about it. 'Goodnight.'

Harry's mocking laughter followed him out into the street.

This is it, Miles thought, his horse trembling in anticipation beneath him. It was now early afternoon and they been at the ready for hours. They'd just been told the order would shortly be given, as German cavalry – dragoons – had been sighted.

Reaching down, he gently patted his horse's neck, the animal throwing its neck back and snorting in reply.

Philip Maidens was on his left, Rodney Cecil-Tapwood on his right. Both appeared quite calm and Miles could only wonder if that was how they really felt. Like himself, this was their first taste of enemy action. Their blooding.

'I can see the bastards,' Philip said quietly to Miles. 'Over by those trees.'

'Which trees?'

'The ones by the side of the road.'

Miles spotted the Germans, the dragoons who had been sighted earlier, moving among the trees. It was impossible to make out how many there were.

'Let's get this over and done with,' Rodney muttered. 'I'm getting desperate for a pee.'

Miles smiled, finding that funny. Here they were, about to engage the enemy, and Rodney was worried about having a pee. Then it struck him that might be because of nerves.

When the order came it almost took him by surprise. Suddenly they were advancing at a trot, quickly breaking into a canter.

The Germans were moving out of the trees now and they were doing likewise. They would meet somewhere in the middle of the distance that had been separating them.

When the canter became a full-blooded charge Miles had never felt so exhilarated in his life, or more alive.

He was yelling like a banshee when the two forces clashed.

It was late in the afternoon before Harry made an appearance in the office. He sauntered in and headed straight for Ricketts' desk, giving the watching Tim a wink as he passed by.

'Where the hell have you been?' Ricketts demanded.

Harry leant forward to place both hands on the desk and stared Ricketts straight in the eye. 'Don't talk to me like that,' he said softly.

Ricketts was taken aback. 'I'll speak to you any way I wish, when you come strolling in here late as this.'

'Get stuffed.'

Bloody hell, Tim thought.

'I beg your pardon?'

'You heard me, get stuffed. With bells on.'

Ricketts was no fool – there had to be a reason for this. 'Getting brave, are we?'

'And about time too. You're a tyrant, Ricketts. A bad-tempered, irascible, mean-minded tyrant who's made my life a misery all the time I've worked here. I think you stink.'

Ricketts began to see the funny side. 'Do I take it you're leaving us?'

Harry nodded.

'May I ask where you're going?'

'To France. I've joined up.'

Ricketts rose to his feet and came round the desk to stand facing Harry. 'Good for you, Nutbeam. I'm proud of you. Here, let me shake you by the hand.'

This wasn't at all the reaction Harry had been expecting. He stared in bewilderment as his hand was grasped and pumped.

'And let me say,' Ricketts went on, 'you're a damned fine reporter. You'll be missed. And oh, when you come back after the war's over, your job will be waiting for you, should you want it.'

Harry was speechless.

Oh, Christ, Elyse thought, hastily stubbing out her cigarette as a coughing fit seized her. Soon her body was racked with spasms, her face puce. At one point it was so bad she thought she must surely choke.

On and on it went, the longest bout by far she'd ever experienced. Staggering to the dressing-room sink, she poured herself a glass of water, hoping that would help.

But before she could drink it she spat out a dollop of evil-looking phlegm, then another and another. To her horror she noted that all were shot through with blood.

Finally it was over. Chest heaving, forehead beaded with sweat, she sank onto her chair.

She really should give up smoking, she told herself. She really should. But she knew she wouldn't. Couldn't. Her will power just wasn't strong enough. She'd been smoking for so long it was a very part of her, nicotine ingrained in every fibre of her being. She simply couldn't imagine life without cigarettes.

Perhaps she could cut down. Yes, she'd try that. Make a conscious effort. Force herself.

She'd never coughed up blood before, she reflected. That was new. And very worrying.

God, she felt awful! Drained of energy, washed out. And it was curtain up in about fifteen minutes.

She began repairing her make-up.

Katherine was luxuriating in a hot bath scented with her favourite crystals when there was a knock on the door. 'Yes?'

'A telegram, madam.' The voice belonged to Jessie, one of their maids.

Katherine's brow furrowed. A telegram – who'd be sending her one of those? 'Just slide it under the door and I'll read it in a minute.'

'Yes, madam.'

Katherine got out of the bath and wrapped herself in a huge pink Turkish towel. She then scraped some hair away from her face, reminding herself to make an appointment with the hairdresser, before bending down and picking up the telegram. It still hadn't dawned on her what it might be.

Moments later a piercing scream rang out. Miles had been killed in action.

Chapter 20

Jeremiah was there to meet Ruth when she stepped off the London train. 'How was the journey?' he asked, signalling to the porter he'd buttonholed to collect her luggage.

'Long and tedious, but that's by the by. How's Katherine?'

'More or less as you'd expect, I'm afraid.'

'Poor child,' Ruth sympathised, pain in her eyes. 'Poor child. I must go to her immediately.'

'We'll go straight there.'

Jeremiah checked the luggage, ensuring that everything had been accounted for, while an agitated Ruth looked on. When that was done they made their way to where the car was parked.

Jeremiah poured himself a hefty whisky and downed it in one swallow. He shuddered, then poured himself another.

Henrietta came into the room. 'I saw you arrive from upstairs. How was it?'

'Pretty bad. Pretty damned bad in fact. Katherine's in a terrible state. However, at least she now has her mother with her, which must be a help.'

'And Ruth will be staying with Katherine?' They hadn't

been sure what Ruth's plans were, the telephone calls having been somewhat hurried and emotional.

Jeremiah nodded. In other circumstances Ruth would have stayed at the house with him, but she'd insisted it was best that she was with Katherine, which he'd agreed made sense.

Henrietta went over and placed a hand on his arm. 'You look done in.'

'I feel it. I've hardly slept a wink, as you know, since the news came.' He paused, then said softly, 'You feel so useless, impotent, at a time like this. I've always been able to give Katherine anything she wanted, but even I – with all my money – can't bring back the dead.' He had a sip of his drink. 'You should see her, Henrietta. It's as if all the devils from hell were tormenting her. I found myself glancing away because I couldn't bear to look at her face.'

Tears welled in his eyes.

'My little baby. Sweet Katherine. Only married a few short months and now a widow.'

Henrietta put her arms round him and hugged him tight. 'Would you like a lie-down?'

Jeremiah thought about that. 'I believe I would.'

'May I suggest something?'

'Of course.'

'I have some sleeping pills. Why don't you take one?'

'No, I promised to go back in a few hours and I don't want to oversleep or be groggy.' Suddenly he frowned. 'Why do you have sleeping pills anyway? You don't have trouble in that department. At least not to my knowledge.'

She smiled thinly. 'I used them at Mrs Green's. There were nights when . . .' She broke off and took a deep breath. 'There were nights when I'd lie awake thinking about my situation, what I was doing. Haunted by the men who I had to . . .'

He stopped her with a peck on the lips. 'I understand. It must have been terrible.'

'You've no idea, Jeremiah. There were a few like you who were kind and respectful. Most treated you as if you were dirt, a commodity simply to be used and then discarded without a further thought. While some of them wanted things that were quite disgusting, and which I had to comply with as it was part of the service. Disgusting and obscene, with me pretending it was fun and wonderful. Others would hurt you, cause you pain. In a way those were the worst.'

'Oh, Henrietta,' he crooned. 'At least that's all over and done with now.'

'Thanks to you, Jeremiah. I owe you more than you will ever realise, and for that I'll be forever grateful.'

He smiled at her. 'If I lie down, will you lie down with me? A cuddle would be nice.'

'You don't have to ask, Jeremiah. You know that.'

'And if I do drop off, make certain you wake me in a couple of hours.'

'To go and see Katherine again? Of course I will.'

How lucky he was, he thought. How very lucky. He only wished he'd met Henrietta years ago.

'What's wrong with you? You're ever so restless.'

Tim stopped pacing to stare at his mother. 'I suppose I am.'

'Come and sit down, for goodness' sake. You're making me quite dizzy.'

Tim pushed his hands deep into his trouser pockets and slumped onto a chair.

'Well, what's bothering you?' Minna demanded. 'Something clearly is.'

'It's not bothering me exactly,' Tim replied. 'It just seems strange, that's all.'

'What does?' she persisted.

'Harry left today. He was ordered to report to Regimental Headquarters in Plymouth. So that's him gone, for God knows how long. And two of the young apprentice printers have joined up as well and they too will be away shortly. I just don't know how we're going to manage at work.'

Minna brought her attention back to her knitting, which was a jumper for Tim. Although she'd only met Harry Nutbeam on a few occasions, she'd liked him. And now the lad was off to war. Icy-cold fingers clutched at her heart. There had been rumours during the past few days of conscription being introduced. If that happened then Tim might be called up. The thought made her feel sick inside.

'He was a good friend,' Tim went on. 'I mean, *is* a good friend. I'm going to miss him a lot.'

'Just don't you do anything stupid, you hear me? For my sake, if nothing else. Oh, I know I'm being selfish in asking that, but you're all I've got.'

Tim didn't reply.

'Damn the Kaiser!' Minna suddenly exclaimed. 'Why couldn't he just let things go on as they were?'

Tim had no answer to that.

'And why is everyone so excited about the war, as if it was something wonderful? No war is. They're all horrible, and needless in my opinion.' Minna stopped knitting and laid it aside. 'I think I'll make a cup of tea. How about you?'

'No thanks, Ma.'

'Damn the Kaiser!' Minna repeated in a murmur as she left the parlour. If she'd been able to get hold of him, she'd have told him a thing or two. Yes, indeed.

'Where do you want to set up your camera?' Tim asked Ironmonger. Under the cover of night HMS *Iron Duke*, *Marlborough* and *Lord Nelson* had slipped into the bay and dropped anchor. Ricketts had sent Tim down to cover the event, which was of course of great local interest.

Ironmonger gazed about him. There must have been at least a thousand people present, all of them having come to see the ships. The atmosphere was a holiday one, like a carnival even. Many folk had small Union Jacks on sticks that they were waving, their faces radiating pride and exultation.

'Quite a turn-out,' Ironmonger commented.

'You can say that again.'

From somewhere over to their right a rousing cheer went up, though nothing in particular seemed to have happened.

Tim looked out at the three ships. 'They're an awesome sight, aren't they?'

Ironmonger nodded. 'I only wish they were closer in. Even if I take photos from the end of the pier, they're all going to be distance shots.'

'So it's the pier then?'

'Not yet. I want some photographs of this lot first.' He pointed to the Clock Tower. 'I think that will be my best vantage point.'

They moved to the Clock Tower, where Ironmonger began setting up. While he was doing so Tim interviewed several of the passers-by, asking them what they thought of the ships.

'Best damned navy in the world,' an elderly man enthused. 'Wish I was young again. I'd sign up in a flash.'

A housewife said that her son was in the navy, although not serving on any of those ships. She also declared that, according to her son, morale was sky-high in the navy and that there wasn't a single soul aboard his vessel who couldn't wait to give the Hun what for.

When Ironmonger had what he needed, they packed up and made their way to the pier, which was so thronged that it took them ages to get to the concert pavilion at the end.

'What about that?' Tim suggested, indicating the harbour wall lined with what appeared to be acres of sightseers.

'Good idea,' Ironmonger nodded.

Tim stared out at the three ships. Impressive was hardly the word, for they were far more than that. He noted the many bristling guns and sheer menace they exuded. He would get information on the ships themselves from *Jane's*, a publication that detailed every known warship right down to the last rivet.

He wondered where the ships were bound, and why they'd stopped off in Torquay. Even if he'd known or been able to find out, he couldn't have printed that, as such information would be classified. No, his article would be about the ships' arrival and the local reaction to it.

Was there a sea battle in the offing? he wondered. Were these ships part of an assembling fleet? He put such speculation in the article and, much to his surprise, Ricketts allowed it to remain.

But it was almost two years before the great sea battle that Tim had speculated about finally took place at Jutland. An indecisive encounter that cost many lives and which both sides claimed to win. HMS *Iron Duke* was heavily involved, playing a crucial role as flagship of the Grand Fleet.

'And this is Mrs Webb, my housekeeper.'

Ruth stared Henrietta up and down. She'd been expecting someone older, more motherly. This female didn't at all fit the description – albeit a vague one, she had to admit – that Jeremiah had given her.

'Pleased to meet you, ma'am,' Henrietta said, and gave a small bobbing curtsy.

Ruth nodded.

'Shall we go on through?' Jeremiah smiled.

Henrietta took hats and coats and hung them up. 'Would you care for tea or coffee?' she inquired.

'Ruth?'

'Not for me, thank you.'

'Nor me, either. That's all for the moment, Mrs Webb.'

'As you wish, sir.'

Ruth waited till they were in the drawing room. 'Close that door, Jeremiah.'

He raised an eyebrow before doing as he was bid.

'She's rather young, don't you think?' Ruth accused.

'Mrs Webb? Yes, that did cross my mind when I interviewed her. But she did come with excellent references and is rather good at the job. I certainly don't have any complaints.'

'And she lives in?'

'At the rear. She has her own room and facilities. Quiet as a mouse when not attending to her duties.'

'And where's Mr Webb?'

Jeremiah, knowing Ruth only too well, had been

expecting something of an interrogation and was fully prepared. 'He deserted her. Ran off leaving her with twins, a boy and girl. Her sister looks after them while Mrs Webb works to pay for their keep. She assures me it's a quite satisfactory arrangement.'

'Hmmh,' Ruth mused. 'I'm not sure I approve.'

'Whyever not?' he queried.

'Because of her age – people might talk.'

Jeremiah laughed, pretending to find that funny. 'I doubt it very much, darling. It's well known that I'm a devoted family man. And if I was going to have an affair, I'd have far more sense than to install the female in my own house. Besides, I don't wish to be cruel, but Mrs Webb is plain as the proverbial pikestaff. I'd have thought that was obvious.'

It still amused him how plain Henrietta could make herself. The complete lack of make-up and the clothes helped of course, as did the bun in which she did her hair up. In the evening when she changed the transformation was quite startling. The ugly duckling became a swan.

'I'm glad you think so,' Ruth replied, a little mollified. 'Two children, you say?'

'Twins, boy and a girl. The scoundrel of a husband just disappeared leaving her in the lurch. I have to take my hat off to the way she's coped.'

'She's still rather young,' Ruth muttered.

'Well, I'm certainly not holding that against her. She's absolutely first-class at her job and that's all I care about.' He decided it was time to change the subject. 'Now, let's discuss the matter of Katherine and what's going to happen to her.'

When Ruth left an hour later she'd come to accept Henrietta, despite her youth, as Jeremiah's housekeeper.

* * *

Ironmonger sat back in his seat and sighed. He and Tim were in the pub, having nipped in for a quick one before going home. 'I can't get those warships out of my mind,' he declared.

Tim stared across the table at him. 'Why's that?'

Ironmonger shrugged. 'I don't know. They were simply so magnificent. Beautiful even. I've been thinking about them ever since.'

Tim had a sip of his pint and didn't reply.

'I can just visualise them in action. Guns blasting, great spouts of flame and smoke, the scream of shells.'

'Coming in as well as going out,' Tim reminded him.

Ironmonger, who'd been lost in a reverie, blinked. 'Beg pardon?'

'I said shells coming in as well as going out. Don't forget that, while you're merrily firing at the Germans, they'll be doing the same to you.'

'True,' Ironmonger reflected. 'But I'd much prefer that to fighting on land, as Harry intends. He's welcome to that.'

Tim considered the two options. 'My preference would be the land. Besides, any time I've ever been out on a boat I've been dreadfully sick. Even when the water's calm as can be I'm decidedly unwell.'

Ironmonger laughed. 'Really?'

'Really.'

'My family have been fishermen for generations and I'm the first to break the mould by becoming a photographer. Forgetting my aberration, the sea must be in my blood.'

'So are you thinking about enlisting?' Tim queried.

'Possibly. Let me put it this way: rumours of conscription

keep on persisting and, if that happens, I might not get the choice of which service to go into. If I enlisted I'd be certain.'

'I'd rather go to France myself,' Tim mused. 'It's supposed to be a beautiful country by all accounts.'

Ironmonger sneered derisively. 'From what I hear, the French – allies or not – are a filthy people who hardly ever wash. And their toilets are just holes in the ground, which I find quite disgusting. No, you can keep France and the French, as far as I'm concerned.'

Tim had never heard about the holes in the ground, or that the French were an unhygienic lot. He found it hard to believe.

Ironmonger drained his pint. 'Another?'

'It was supposed to be a quick one.'

'Suit yourself.'

'All right then,' Tim relented as Ironmonger started to move away. 'I will.'

'And Scotch to go with it?'

'Why not? In for a penny, in for a pound.'

Ironmonger laughed. 'A man after my own heart.' He hesitated. 'You know, I think I'll have rum. Navy rum.'

Tim was left wondering how long it would be before Ironmonger was in uniform.

'Come in, Jeremiah,' Henrietta called out when there was a tap on her bedroom door.

He appeared with a sheepish look on his face. 'I wasn't sure whether or not you'd be asleep.'

'Well, I'm not. What's wrong?'

He crossed over and sat on the side of her bed. 'Don't laugh, but I'm lonely.'

She couldn't help but smile. 'A big grown man like you,' she teased. 'You'll be telling me next that you're afraid of the dark.'

'Don't be ridiculous, Henrietta. Of course I'm not. It's just . . .' He took a deep breath. 'I know we agreed not to sleep together while Ruth was in town, but the fact is, I've become used to having you in bed with me.'

She took his hand. 'That's sweet.'

'All those long years with Ruth in one bed and me another. All alone, no comfort, no companionship. Then I met you and we came here, and it all changed, became what it should have been all along. Now, and I know it's only temporary, I'm forced to be by myself again and I hate it. Positively loathe it.'

She was coming to love Jeremiah Coates, Henrietta realised. To begin with it had been simply a business arrangement, but now it was more than that. There was something inside her that softened every time she was in his presence.

'Am I being pathetic?' he asked.

'Not at all.'

'I wouldn't want you to think that of me.'

'I don't. I assure you.'

'Can I get in?'

She pulled back the bedclothes and he went round to the other side of the bed, removed his dressing gown and slipped in alongside her. He immediately put an arm round her waist and rested his head on her bosom.

'Better?'

'Oh yes,' he crooned.

'Just as well you bought me a double bed and not a single.'

'If I had, I'd take you up to mine, so that wouldn't have

been a problem. My bed, where you usually are and where you belong.'

Belong? It sent a thrill through her to hear that. She began stroking his hair.

'Can I ask you something, Henrietta? And I want a truthful answer.'

'Go ahead.'

'What did you think of Ruth when you met her?'

Shit, she thought. Not that. Anything but that.

'Well?' he prompted.

'It's not my place to comment, Jeremiah. She's your wife after all.'

He glanced up at her. 'I said a truthful answer, Henrietta. Don't prevaricate.'

Henrietta sighed. How could she be truthful when it would be both hurtful and insulting. 'Please, Jeremiah, don't press me.'

'But I am,' he replied softly.

Henrietta knew there was nothing else for it – she would have to say what her impression had been. 'You told me she was a cold woman, and I could see you were right. It came off her in waves.'

'What else?'

'Jeremiah, I . . .'

'What else?' he demanded.

'She was so old-looking, and appallingly thin. To be honest, she might have been your mother.'

Jeremiah winced. Perhaps it was because he'd become used to Ruth over the years that he hadn't realised that was so. 'She was very pretty when I met her, you know. Quite beautiful really, with a wonderful figure. Full of fun and laughter.

And, as I discovered after we were married, extremely libidinous.'

Henrietta shook her head. 'I don't understand that word, Jeremiah.'

He chuckled. 'It means she liked sex. Lots of it. The more, the better.'

Henrietta just couldn't imagine the woman she'd met ever being that way.

'Then Katherine came along,' Jeremiah went on. 'And it all changed. Drastically so. She was ill after the birth and never really recovered her health. First it was one thing, then another. Then yet another. A positive litany of illnesses. But still I kept on loving her – seeing her, I suppose, as she'd once been and not as she'd become. But now . . .' He trailed off.

'Now what?'

'Now I find her irritating. Self-centred, spoilt and irritating. There's no joy in her or in being in her company.' He ran a hand down Henrietta's naked thigh. 'Since meeting you I've become a man reborn, alive again.'

'Oh, Jeremiah,' Henrietta whispered, tears in her eyes.

'I'll never leave her, that's out of the question. As you said, she's my wife and the mother of my child, which is how it'll remain. I just don't want to be with her any more. I want to be here with you. And it's not just bed, either, wonderful as that is. It's a lot more than that.'

Henrietta was choked, and her reply stuck in her throat. Her tears had become a steady stream.

'A lot more than that,' he repeated.

'Dear Jeremiah,' she managed to get out after a while. 'Dear, dear Jeremiah.'

'And lovely Henrietta.'

She started stroking his hair again and soon he was fast asleep, snuggled up tight against her, his head still on her bosom. Anyone seeing them after she too had fallen asleep might have been reminded of two babes in the wood.

'Bye, Ma, I'm off!'

Minna stuck her head out of the kitchen door. 'There's a postcard for you.'

'Thanks, Ma.'

He picked the card up from the tray where mail was placed after delivery and glanced at the signature of the sender. He smiled to see it was Harry's.

According to Harry, he was well and quite enjoying training, though it was blinking hard physical graft. He felt fitter than he'd ever been and was champing at the bit to be 'over there'. He finished by saying he'd be due a week's leave when his training was over and hoped to meet up with Tim, preferably in the pub!

'Good news?' Major Sillitoe inquired, having come to check the mail, which he did regularly every morning despite rarely receiving any.

'It's from a chum of mine in the army,' Tim replied.

The major's eyes lit up. 'In the army, eh? Good show! That's the ticket. Volunteer?'

Tim nodded.

'Excellent. The country needs all the volunteers it can get at the moment. Tried to reactivate my commission myself, but the fools wouldn't have me. Said I was too old. Well, I argued you could be getting on a bit but still run a desk to release other chaps for the Front. But they wouldn't listen.'

'Too bad,' Tim sympathised.

'Idiots!' Major Sillitoe drew himself up to his full height, which wasn't very tall. 'Anyway, what about you, young lad? You're just the stuff they're looking for. I suppose you'll be joining up soon?'

'Oh no he won't!' Minna's tone was sharp as steel and sliced through their conversation like a thrown knife.

The major turned to find Minna, arms folded over her chest, eyes blazing, glaring at him. 'I beg your pardon, Mrs Wilson?'

'I said he won't, and that's all there is to it. And I'll thank you, Major Sillitoe, to mind your own business and not go putting ideas into my son's head.'

The major spluttered with indignation, not used to being spoken to like this. 'I say, steady on!'

'They can fight their stupid war without my Tim. He's all I've got and is staying safely at home. Understand?'

Tim, initially taken aback, now smiled. It was rare to see his mother this roused. It was a splendid sight.

'I just thought . . .' the major frowned.

'Well, don't think where Tim's concerned,' she interjected cuttingly. 'Now hadn't you better get along, Tim, before you're late for work.'

That wasn't a suggestion or a reminder, it was a command. 'Yes, Ma.'

'And I'm sure you have other things to do, Major,' she added.

'Retreat, I think,' the major muttered to Tim and hurried off.

Tim was grinning broadly as he shut the front door behind him, feeling amused but also somewhat disturbed by what the major had said.

* * *

'That cough of yours is terrible,' Molly O'Malley said to Elyse. 'It's getting worse all the time. You must go and see a doctor.'

'It's only the fags,' Elyse protested. 'That's all.'

'I still think you should see a doctor. You've lost weight again, you know. If you're not careful you'll soon be down to skin and bone.'

'It's not that bad,' Elyse shrugged.

'Oh yes it is. Now who's your doctor?'

Elyse had to think about that, for it had been years since she'd been to one. 'Doctor, eh . . .' For the life of her she couldn't remember his name.

'Right!' Molly declared emphatically. 'You'll go to mine. And a finer doctor you'll be pushed to find.' Suddenly she winked. 'He's dishy too. Take my word for it. I always say, but not to Seamus of course, that he can examine me any time he likes.'

Elyse laughed, a laugh that quickly broke down into a hacking cough.

'Leave it to me. I'll arrange the appointment for you,' Molly declared. 'And make sure you keep it.'

Chapter 21

'Now there's something I want to discuss with you,' Ruth stated firmly, replacing her mid-morning cup of coffee on its saucer.

Katherine glanced across from the flowers she was arranging. 'And what's that, Mama?'

'I shall be returning to Oaklands in a few days and I think you should come with me.' Ruth made an expansive gesture. 'I can't leave you here rattling around on your own. That wouldn't do at all. You would only get morbid, with nothing to do all day long except brood.'

'There,' smiled Katherine, the flowers now as she wanted them. Crossing over, she sat down facing her mother. 'And what would I do at Oaklands except exactly what I'm doing here?'

'You'll have company for a start,' Ruth declared. 'And I'll be able to keep an eye on you.'

'But this is my house, Mama, where I belong.'

Ruth nodded. 'And a lovely house it is, too. I can't deny that. Quite splendid really, though hardly a patch on Oaklands.'

'It's a town house, Mama,' Katherine pointed out. 'Of course it isn't a patch on Oaklands.'

'Precisely. I've talked this over with your father and we both agree. You should come home.'

'My house, Mama, and my home now. It became that when I married Miles and we moved in.'

'Of course, of course, I understand. But you know what I mean. It's in your best interests to come back with me.'

Katherine glanced down. Her mother was formidable when in this kind of mood, but her mind was made up and there would be no changing it. No matter what Ruth said or did. 'I shan't be rattling around, as you put it, Mama. I shall be working a lot of the time.'

Ruth gaped. 'Work? I can't believe you're serious. Why on earth should someone in your position want to work?'

'To be useful. I want to contribute something to society, not just – and I say this with all respect – live off it.'

'Nonsense!' Ruth exclaimed. 'I won't have it, you hear? No daughter of mine is going out to work. Why, the whole idea is preposterous.'

'I spoke to Miles before he left and, somewhat reluctantly, I have to admit, he agreed with me. The plan was that I should become a nurse until such time as I fell pregnant, when I would stop. That was the compromise we reached. Only now I shan't be falling pregnant, as he's dead.'

'I see,' Ruth murmured. 'But that doesn't make it right. I shall never agree to this.'

Katherine sighed. 'I don't need you to agree, Mama. I'm a grown woman who's been married and now widowed. I make my own decisions.'

Ruth's lips pursed into a thin line. 'Being a nurse is such a menial job, Katherine. You have to deal with all sorts of things . . .' She swallowed hard. 'Bodies and the like. How could you possibly even consider putting yourself in such a position?'

'What you say is true enough,' Katherine replied slowly. 'But look on the positive side. You're bringing hope and comfort to people, looking after them when they're ill. Helping them recover their health. I can't think of anything more worthwhile than that.'

'Even so,' Ruth demurred.

'Then let me put it this way, Mama. Miles died doing his duty for this country. Well, I can't fight as he did, but I certainly can do my bit. Or have you forgotten there's a war on? I believe all sorts of folk are going to be doing things they've never done before.'

She'd lost her, Ruth suddenly realised. All those years Katherine had been hers, but no more. Her baby had indeed grown up and, judging by this conversation, developed a mind of her own. In a way she couldn't help but approve.

'I had thought to train as a proper nurse,' Katherine went on. 'But that takes years. There's a new professional body been formed called the VAD, Voluntary Aid Detachment, women who assist the nurses after a minimum of training. I shall be one of those, providing they'll have me, that is.'

Lost her, Ruth thought. Well and truly. 'In that case I may as well return to Oaklands right away. It seems you don't need me here any more.'

Katherine joined her mother on the sofa. 'I can't thank you enough for coming here when I needed you. You've been a pillar of strength.' And with that she kissed Ruth on the cheek.

'I'll leave first thing in the morning. That would be best.'

'Thanks again, Mama. You've been an absolute brick. I was in pieces when you arrived. Absolute pieces.'

'I know.'

'I still hurt a great deal. But as they say, life goes on. The best thing for me is to keep busy and that's what'll happen when I join the VADs.'

'Your father's not going to be pleased, you know.'

Katherine knew that to be a fib, a last-ditch attempt to get her to change her mind. 'I'm sure he'll understand, Mama. If he wishes I'll sit down and talk it through with him.'

Ruth took a deep breath, finally admitting defeat. She pulled away from Katherine and stood up. 'I think I'll go and have a lie-down. I feel a headache coming on.'

'You do that, Mama. I'll knock when it's time for luncheon.'

Katherine hung her head when Ruth had gone. Closing her eyes, she pictured Miles as she'd last seen him, at their final farewell. As it had turned out, it truly had been a final farewell.

She wouldn't cry, she told herself. She was past that. But she did.

Sweat beading his forehead, Tim woke from a nightmare to sit up in bed.

Harry had been in the nightmare, a drunk Harry calling him a coward, just as he had done that night in the pub. Major Sillitoe had been in it too, asking him over and over again when he was going to join up. Then Major Sillitoe had also branded him a coward.

Harry's mocking laughter still echoed in his brain. Harry at a distance pointing, chanting the same word again and again. Other people had appeared and then disappeared, Katherine among them. She too had taunted him.

Tim groaned and clasped his head. That had been simply awful. A horrible, horrible nightmare.

News from the Front wasn't at all good, and now Kitchener was appealing for 500,000 additional volunteers. All over the country young men of his age were answering that appeal, signing up in droves. In some instances literally hundreds at a time.

He flopped back onto his bed and stared at the ceiling. It was early days yet, for the war was still in its infancy. Who knew? Perhaps those who said it wouldn't last long were right and soon it would all be over. If that was the case, then why rush into things when he needn't bother?

Except that the war wasn't going well – no rout of Germany and Austria, as many had predicted. If anything the Germans and Austrians were gaining the upper hand. Pushing the British back in many places.

No, no, this war wasn't going to be over quickly. He was kidding himself if he believed that. Kitchener wasn't calling for half a million additional men for nothing.

But he wasn't a coward, deep within himself he knew that. He'd fight if he had to, no matter what his mother said. Or how much she pleaded with him to stay out of it.

But not yet. Not yet. For he knew only too well that if he did enlist it would break Minna's heart.

Jeremiah instructed the porter where to put Ruth's suitcases, the pair of them waiting patiently on the platform until this was done. He tipped the man a handsome shilling for his trouble.

'I do wish you were coming with me, Jeremiah,' Ruth said when the porter had left them.

'I simply can't, darling. I have far too much on my plate at the moment. The steelworks I bought in Glasgow is taking up a lot of my time. As are other things.'

He kissed her on the cheek. 'You have my word I'll be down to Oaklands just as soon as the opportunity presents itself. I miss it, and you, terribly.'

'And you will speak to Katherine about this ludicrous idea of hers?'

'I'll drop by this afternoon. I promise.' What he didn't say was that he thoroughly approved of Katherine becoming a nurse, or VAD. It showed spunk and initiative on her part, and was a far better thing to do than hanging around the house moping. Besides, it was helping the war effort and that was entirely laudable. He applauded any young woman – no matter what her station in life – doing her bit.

'Now you'd better get aboard,' he declared.

He assisted Ruth into the carriage and shut the heavy door. She tugged at the window strap and the window slid down.

Jeremiah took her proffered hand. 'Have a good journey, dear. I'll ring tonight when you're home again.'

'Don't work too hard, darling. That was never the intention. Part-time was what I had in mind when I made my suggestion about the London house.'

'It's the war, Ruth, it's affecting all of us. And I'm no exception. Only in my case it's profitable.' As he'd foreseen, steel – and many other commodities – were suddenly hugely in demand.

'But you will come as soon as possible, like you promised?'

'You have my word on that.' He spotted the guard preparing to wave his green flag. 'Now pull that window up again. The train's about to start.'

Jeremiah waved as the train chugged and clanked away. He had absolutely no intention of returning to Oaklands for quite some while. As long as he could possibly put it off, in fact.

He'd much rather be with Henrietta.

Dr Rathbone removed his stethoscope from Elyse's chest, rolled it up and replaced it in its box. He then sat back in his chair with a puzzled frown on his face to study her.

'Can I get dressed now?'

'Sorry, please do.'

Elyse went behind the screen and put her top garments back on. It had been a most thorough examination of her upper body area.

When she was finished she rejoined the doctor, who was sitting in exactly the same position as she'd left him. Her left arm was stinging a little from where he'd taken a blood sample.

Molly hadn't lied about the doctor being good-looking: he was most certainly that. He had black hair, a neatly trimmed, matching-coloured moustache and grey eyes. She judged him somewhere in his early forties.

Leaning forward, he picked up the notes he'd made and studied them, his expression still quizzical.

'Well?' she demanded.

'Have you ever heard of X-rays?'

Now it was her turn to frown. 'Yes, I believe I have.'

'A machine takes a sort of inner picture of your body. Well, that's what I'd like you to have.'

Panic swelled in her. 'Are you saying it's more than just a bad smoker's cough?'

'That certainly isn't helping matters. But somehow . . .' He paused. 'I feel it's more complicated than that. The soundings I was getting were strangely irregular, though exactly how I'm not quite sure. One thing I can say is that you've had bronchitis, which I suspect has been recurring at intervals.'

Now thoroughly alarmed, she thought about that. 'I wasn't aware I had bronchitis.'

'As you told me, Mrs Davenport, you haven't been to a doctor in years, so how could you have known?'

He was right of course. 'Whenever I've had trouble with my chest I've always blamed the fags and sometimes the weather.'

'Both undoubtedly contributory causes, but I can't help feeling there's more to it than that, which is why I want you to have an X-ray. To be on the safe side, so to speak.'

'Will the . . .' She hesitated. 'Will the X-ray hurt?'

He smiled. 'Not in the least, I assure you. And it'll be over in a few brief seconds.'

That was a relief, Elyse thought. Nonetheless, she didn't like the sound of this X-ray one little bit.

'Now,' he went on. 'I'm going to request an appointment for you at St George's, where they have the necessary facilities. Are there any limitations on when you can attend?'

Elyse shook her head. 'I'm not rehearsing, so my days are quite free. Any morning or afternoon will be suitable.'

'Good. They should be in touch shortly.'

'Thank you, Doctor.'

He rose and ushered her to the door. 'When I have the results of your X-ray I'll contact you to arrange another visit here so that we can discuss matters further.'

'Thank you,' she said again.

Once out in the street she halted and took a deep breath. It was all right for him to tell her not to worry, but that was easier said than done.

She hurried on her way.

'Christ, I've missed the beer!' Harry Nutbeam declared, having just downed nearly half a pint in one swallow.

'I can see that,' Tim observed drily.

Harry beamed at him. 'It's good to see you again, me old fruitcake, I've missed you.' He glanced around. 'In fact I've missed Torquay far more than I imagined I would.'

'You look really fit.'

'I should be with all the training and physical jerks I've done. Sadistic bastards some of those sergeants and NCOs. You wouldn't believe how sadistic. However, that's all over now. It's the Front for us.'

'When do you leave?' Tim asked quietly.

'No idea. But the rumour in camp was directly after our leave's over, which would make sense. Personally speaking, I can't wait to get to grips with the bloody Jerries. Just let me at them.'

Tim laughed. 'Well you're certainly keen enough, I'll say that for you.'

'We all are in the Devons. Keen as mustard.' Harry picked up his pint and saw off what remained. 'Another?'

'Hold on,' Tim protested. 'I've hardly started mine.'

'Then I'll just get one for myself.'

Tim watched Harry swagger up to the bar, incredibly proud to be in uniform. Even if it wasn't a particularly good fit, Tim couldn't help but feel a teensy bit jealous.

'Here's a laugh,' Harry said on sitting down again. 'There's an aerodrome close by our camp where they train pilots. Daft buggers, that lot. You should have seen some of the things that have happened to them during their spell there. Crashes, flying upside down and not knowing how to get right side up again. Why, one idiot actually fell out of the sodding cockpit.'

'Was he killed?' Tim asked.

Harry shook his head. 'He was lucky. Just got up and walked away without even a scratch.'

'I've never seen an aeroplane,' Tim mused. 'Pictures, of course, but not the real thing.'

'Scary things, if you ask me. But enormous fun too, I should think. And not too difficult to fly either, once you get the hang of it, that is. Or so I'm told. No more difficult than that motorbike of yours, I would imagine. How is the bike, by the way?'

'Fine.'

'Still using it for work?'

'Weather permitting. I get great enjoyment out of it.'

'Then you'd like the planes. Same sort of idea, after all. They're both just machines that go fast. Only in the case of the aeroplane up in the air and not on the ground.'

That caught Tim's imagination. So far he'd thought of

war from the infantry or naval point of view, but this was different. He wondered what it would be like to fly and decided that it had to be even better than riding his bike.

'A jammy lot too, those pilots,' Harry went on. 'When they're "over there" they lead the life of Riley. Up once a day, I'm led to believe, do a spot of observing over enemy lines and then back again to a nice warm meal and your own mess. I hear those chaps get pissed nearly every night.'

'Really!' Tim exclaimed.

'Oh yes. They each have their own cosy little room, a batman to look after them, three squares a day and bathing facilities whenever they wish. What more could you ask for?'

Tim was becoming more and more intrigued. 'And all they do is a bit of observing once a day?'

'So I was led to understand. Jammy, eh?'

Tim could only agree. And surely Harry was right: flying an aeroplane couldn't be that much more difficult than riding a motorbike. Except, as Harry had pointed out, that you were in the air of course, which must make it a fantastically exciting thing to do.

'Ready for another yet?'

Tim gaped, noting that Harry's glass was empty again. He hadn't even noticed Harry drinking that one.

Harry laughed at Tim's incredulous expression. 'Well, I told you I've been missing the beer. I've a lot of catching up to do.'

Tim hurriedly swallowed his.

'What!' Ricketts exploded.

Ironmonger repeated what he'd just said.

'But you can't leave. If this goes on I'll have no bloody staff left!'

Ironmonger shrugged. 'Not my business, Mr Ricketts. I'm sure you'll manage somehow.'

So Ironmonger had joined up, Tim thought, watching this exchange. No doubt it was the navy.

'What are you staring at, Wilson!' Ricketts roared, having caught sight of Tim. 'Haven't you got something to do?'

Tim swiftly brought his attention back to the story he was writing about the local Women's Institute, who'd now voted to add sweets, cigarettes, tea, coffee, and so on to the boxes of knitting they were already sending the troops. The knitting invariably compromised socks, gloves, sweaters and balaclavas.

That was five now who'd enlisted from the newspaper, Tim calculated. No wonder Ricketts was furious – the staffing situation was becoming critical.

When he looked up again Ironmonger had disappeared and a stunned Ricketts was gazing vacantly into space. Tim couldn't help but feel sorry for the man, and for himself come to that. His own workload had increased enormously since Harry had been the first to go.

'Well, Mrs Davenport,' Dr Rathbone said. 'As you know, I've called you in because I have the results of your X-ray.'

He wasn't smiling, Elyse noted, fear clutching at her insides. It must be bad.

'And what are they?' she asked, her face an expressionless mask.

Rathbone pulled the X-ray from a brown manila folder and held it up to the light. He stared at it for a few moments and then indicated her lungs. 'Do you see that shading?'

She wasn't sure that she could. 'Yes.'

'That's scarring.'

Elyse frowned. 'Scarring?'

'From consumption. Or tuberculosis as it's now called.'

She caught her breath. Consumption! Dear God in heaven. 'I have consumption?'

'Not now, but you have had.' He shook his head. 'It's rare, at least to my knowledge, for it to heal itself like this. But in your case it somehow has. You're a very fortunate woman, Mrs Davenport.'

Relief whooshed through her and she sagged where she sat. Consumption had been rife in Clerkenwell when she'd been a child, many people there dying from it. She offered up a silent prayer of thanks.

'It may have healed,' Rathbone went on softly, 'but that doesn't mean it can't return. We have to do everything we can to prevent that happening.'

'Return?' she croaked.

'I'd hazard an educated guess and say it's been on the verge of it several times, but for some reason hasn't developed further. I'll repeat myself, Mrs Davenport. You're a very lucky woman, considering your lifestyle.'

She stared grimly at him.

He laid the X-ray on his desk. 'You're going to have to make some changes to how you live, Mrs Davenport. Starting with cigarettes. You have to stop smoking immediately.'

When Elyse left Rathbone's surgery twenty minutes later she headed straight for the Salisbury pub.

'Consumption!' Molly O'Malley breathed. This was terrible news.

'Have had it,' Elyse pointed out. 'I'm clear for now.'

'Praise be to the Lord and all his blessed saints. 'Tis a miracle to be sure. Isn't that so, Seamus?'

He nodded.

Elyse gave a faint laugh. 'The joke is that to stop it coming back I have to completely change my lifestyle – that's the word Rathbone used.'

'In what way?' Molly queried.

'Give up smoking and drinking, for a start.'

'Bloody hell,' Seamus muttered.

'But it gets worse. I've to stop work and leave London for somewhere in the country, where I can have total peace and quiet.'

Molly was perplexed. 'How are you going to manage that?'

Elyse made a dismissive gesture. 'I simply can't. I mean, I work to live. If I give up work I'll starve.'

'But why the country?' Seamus asked.

'London's bad for me apparently: too much smoke and grime, which irritates my lungs. Then there are the fogs in winter, they're another irritant. And I've especially to stay out of places like pubs and clubs for the same reason.'

'And the theatre?' Molly asked.

'Same sort of thing, I imagine. What I should be doing is just lying around all day without doing a hand's turn, eating fresh food and breathing pure air. That way the consumption, or tuberculosis as he says it's now called, might just stay away permanently.'

Seamus shook his head. 'So what are you going to do?'

'What can I do, Seamus? Rathbone's asked the impossible. I must work to keep myself and that means staying in London.'

'There are always the provinces,' Molly suggested hopefully.

'Most rep theatres are in big cities, Molly. I'd just be swapping one big city for another. There's no point in that.'

'Well, what about the smoking and drinking?' Molly went on.

Elyse shrugged. 'I can try. But how long would it last? Come on, you know me. How long would that last?'

''Tis a dilemma, sure enough,' Seamus sighed, feeling desperately sorry for her.

Absent-mindedly Elyse took out her cigarettes and lit up. 'All I can do is soldier on as I am and hope the consumption stays away. There's nothing else for it.'

They continued chatting for a while and then Elyse announced that she had to get home, as she always tried to have a lie-down before the evening performance.

'Poor bitch,' Seamus said when she'd gone. 'She's between the devil and the deep blue sea right enough.'

'Amen,' Molly added with a choke in her voice.

The first thing Elyse did on reaching the rooms she was renting in Bloomsbury was to get stripped and changed into an old and very comfortable dressing gown. The second thing, despite Rathbone's warning, was to pour herself a glass of Scotch.

She needed to think about all this, she told herself, settling into a chair. What the doctor had said had been a bombshell.

Give up work, live in the country? Fat chance! Even if she'd been willing to do that, it just wasn't possible. As for smoking and drinking, she'd cut down on both. At least she could do that. Difficult, yes, but she'd make the effort.

Consumption – the very word made her go cold. Their next-door neighbour in Clerkenwell had died from it and she could remember all too clearly what a pitiful sight he'd been at the end. When he'd finally died, after a long and painful illness, there had been hardly anything left of him.

'Christ!' she muttered. The last thing she felt like doing was giving a perf that night. But of course she would do so. That was the way actors were. You always went on.

Suddenly she found herself laughing, laughing until the tears were running down her cheeks. It was funny really. It just depended on how you looked at it. For after all wasn't comedy merely the other side of tragedy?

'What's wrong?' Tim demanded, seeing his mother's expression. He'd just got in from the newspaper, having had a long and gruelling day.

'Euphemia's brother's been killed in France,' she explained. 'The girl's in a terrible state.'

Hell's teeth, he thought. 'Is there anything I can do?'

Minna shook her head. 'Cook's comforting her as best she can, while Daisy has taken over her duties.' Minna paused, then added, 'It was the brother she was closest to, apparently, which makes it even worse.'

Tim didn't know what to reply to that.

Anger flared in Minna. 'This war! Well, you know my feelings on the subject.'

Going to Tim, she threw her arms round him and held him tight. For a few moments he thought she was going to break down, but thankfully she didn't. He knew only too well what must be going through her mind.

'There,' she said eventually, releasing him. 'Now I suppose you're starving?'

'I am rather.'

'Things are a bit topsy-turvy at present. Go on into the parlour and I'll fetch you something there. It's best you stay out of the kitchen right now.'

'I understand, Ma.'

Minna bustled off to get his meal.

Chapter 22

Tim was reading about the appalling loss of life on board the Cunard liner *Lusitania*, which had been sunk by German torpedoes, when Ricketts came over.

'I've got a job for you, Wilson,' Ricketts declared.

Tim jumped to his feet. 'Yes, sir?'

'Apparently a group of women have been going round Torquay handing out white feathers to young men. As you no doubt appreciate, a white feather is the sign of cowardice. Now, I want you to interview a few of these ladies and get the whys and wherefores. What's prompting them to take such action, and so on.'

White feathers, Tim thought with a sinking feeling. That was awful.

'I'll expect . . .' Ricketts broke off when he noted the look on Tim's face. Of course, he should have thought! How damned stupid of him. 'Perhaps not,' he demurred. 'Let's give Gladys this one and see what she makes of it.' Gladys was a new trainee reporter, Ricketts having had to hire women now that there was such a shortage of men available.

'I'm willing to do it, sir,' Tim stated in a quiet voice.

'No, no, Gladys it is.' Ricketts glanced around. 'Now where is she?' He spotted her in one of the telephone boxes at the far end of the office. 'Send her over to me when she gets out of there,' he instructed Tim.

'Yes, sir.'

And with that Ricketts returned to his desk.

Mightily relieved, Tim sat down again wondering how he was going to react should a white feather be given to him. It was a ghastly prospect and would be humiliating in the extreme.

He was pleased that Gladys would be handling the story.

Tim laid down the latest article on aeroplanes that he'd managed to find and briefly closed his eyes. Since that night with Harry in the pub he'd read a great deal about aeroplanes, and the more he read, the more knowledgeable he became about them. And liked the idea of flying one.

He thought again of the *Lusitania* and the outcry that its sinking had caused. Twelve hundred people had reputedly died, including women and children, some of them babes in arms.

According to reports, 128 Americans had been among those lost, one of their number being Alfred Vanderbilt, the millionaire yachtsman. President Woodrow Wilson was said to be outraged, and the hope in Britain was that the US would now join in the war.

Other headline reports in the newspapers were about the great battle being fought at somewhere called Ypres, where a major offensive was taking place. Britain claimed to be winning this offensive, but the casualties being inflicted on them were horrendous. Tens of thousands had already died, with many more wounded. The French losses were even worse than the British.

Those who'd said the war would be over by Christmas had been sadly wrong. It was now nine months since the declaration had been made and the end of the conflict was nowhere in sight.

Tim had known for weeks now what he was going to have to do, but it was this white feather business that finally made up his mind.

It would be the Royal Flying Corps for him.

Katherine wondered what she'd done wrong to be summoned to Matron's office. For the life of her she couldn't think of anything.

'Enter!' Matron called out when she knocked.

Matron was a thin North Country woman who ruled with a rod of iron. There wasn't a single nurse, or VAD, under her jurisdiction who wasn't terrified of her. Most of the doctors too, come to that.

Katherine, who'd already checked her uniform to ensure that everything was as it should be, took a deep breath and went in.

'You sent for me, Matron?'

'I did indeed, Coates. Just wait a minute till I finish this.'

Katherine stood patiently while Matron continued writing. Finally she finished with a flourish and laid down her pen. She fixed Katherine with a beady, penetrating stare.

'You've done well. Sister Spicer is pleased with your work, as I am.'

No ticking-off, but praise! 'Thank you, Matron.'

'I've been charged with putting together a party of nurses

and VADs to go over to France. Would you be interested?'

Katherine's eyes widened. 'France?'

'That's what I said, girl, France. I warn you it'll be no bed of roses, but sheer bloody hard graft. And I mean bloody, in its literal sense. You'd be right at the front. So what do you say?'

Katherine gulped. This was completely out of the blue. She hadn't had an inkling that anything like this might be in the wind.

'Perhaps you want some time to think it over? If you do, I fully understand. But I do need an answer by Monday next.'

'No, Matron, I'd love to go,' Katherine replied hastily, her mind still whirling.

'Are you sure? There will be a great deal of privation and, depending on where you're sent, the possibility of being hurt, even killed. This is not a matter to agree to lightly. I want you to appreciate that.'

Katherine's face clouded over. 'I lost my husband at Mons, Matron. If I can help save any of our boys "over there" then it's my duty to my country and his memory.'

'I didn't know,' Matron replied sympathetically. Then, briskly, 'Right, you shall be included in the party, which will be leaving in several weeks' time – the exact date not set yet. Thank you, Coates.'

'Thank *you*, Matron.'

Outside in the corridor Katherine paused to catch her breath. France! Part of her was thrilled at the prospect, while another part, if she was honest, was scared stiff.

It seemed to Tim that there were recruiting offices

everywhere, except for the RFC. He'd made all sorts of inquiries but hadn't been able to locate a single one.

He'd now decided that the only thing for it was to write direct to the War Office in Whitehall.

He stared down at the blank sheet of paper in front of him and wondered what to say.

When he had finally finished he addressed the envelope, neatly folded the letter and slipped it inside. After closing the envelope he stuck on a stamp.

There, he thought. It was done. And there was no time like the present to post it.

His heart was hammering and he was filled with exultation when a little later he dropped it into the letterbox. There was no turning back now, he told himself.

When he returned to The Berkeley he ran into Minna, speaking to her briefly, but unable to look her in the eye.

He was dreading the moment when he had to tell her what he'd done.

God, that was going to be awful.

Henrietta ushered Katherine into the hallway. 'I'm afraid your father isn't home, Mrs Crabthorne, but I expect him shortly.'

Katherine smiled at the housekeeper, having instinctively liked the woman the first time they'd met. 'In which case I'll wait.'

'Then let me take your hat and coat. Would you care for tea or coffee?' Henrietta went on as she disposed of those.

'Coffee would be lovely.'

'I'll have some for you in a tick.'

While Henrietta took herself off to get that, Katherine

went into the drawing room. Gazing around, she thought, not for the first time, what a find Mrs Webb was. Not only was everything spick and span, but the housekeeper had the knack of adding homely touches, which made the room far more comfortable and attractive than it might otherwise have been.

How was her father going to react to her news? she wondered. And, more importantly, Ruth? She'd already decided that her mother wasn't to be told, providing her father agreed, until after she'd left. Easiest that way.

Henrietta was soon back carrying a tray. 'I've brought a slice of Madeira cake and some Eccles cakes, should you be hungry,' she informed Katherine.

'Eccles cakes! Papa adores those!'

'I know,' Henrietta nodded. 'That's why I make them.'

'You spoil him, Mrs Webb.'

Henrietta gave Katherine a strange glance. 'Oh, I don't think so. He's very good to me, so I'm only returning his kindness. He's a great man, your father, one to be admired.'

Katherine thought that an odd thing for the housekeeper to say, but took no further notice of it.

About twenty minutes later Jeremiah arrived back. Henrietta, who'd been listening out, immediately went to him. When the door was shut he swept her into his arms and made to kiss her.

'Katherine's here,' Henrietta hissed.

Instantly he released her. 'I see.'

'In the drawing room.'

He looked puzzled for a moment. 'What does she want?' he mouthed.

Henrietta shook her head. 'Didn't say,' she mouthed back.

He strode into the drawing room. 'Katherine! What a lovely surprise. To what do I owe the honour?'

Katherine noticed that her father was putting on weight. A tribute to Mrs Webb's cooking, no doubt. 'I want to speak to you,' she said as he pecked her on the cheek.

'Oh?'

'I suggest you sit down.'

'That serious, eh?' he teased.

'That serious, Papa.'

'Now then,' he declared when he was comfortable. 'Out with it.'

Katherine recounted her conversation with Matron and the fact that she'd agreed to go to France.

Jeremiah was shaken. His daughter in France. Possibly even working close to the front line! He was shaken all right.

'Well, Papa?' she prompted when she'd finished.

His expression was grim. 'Are you asking my permission to go?'

'No, Papa, I don't need that. I've come for your blessing, I suppose. And to let you know my intentions.'

He rose and crossed to where the tantalus was kept and poured himself a large brandy. This was the last thing he'd expected. If she'd been a son, yes. But it had never crossed his mind that his daughter would want to go to France in the middle of a war. 'You do know nurses have been killed?' he asked quietly.

'Yes, Papa.'

'And that the same could happen to you. Killed or, worse, horribly maimed?'

She dropped her gaze. 'I've considered those possibilities and am willing to take the risk.'

He sighed. 'You're determined then?'

'Quite.'

'Then there's nothing else for it but to give you my blessing. And pray God keep you safe.'

'Thank you, Papa.'

He laid his untouched brandy down, went to Katherine and raised her to her feet. He kissed her on the forehead, then held her close. 'I can't imagine what your mother's going to say.'

'I did tell her I was going to be a nurse, but she'll go potty, no doubt.'

He smiled at the phrase. 'No doubt.'

'Which is why I don't want her to know until I'm gone. I'll write to her the day I leave.'

'She's bound to ask if I knew.'

'Explain the situation to her. Tell her I swore you to secrecy.'

Jeremiah laughed. 'I'll still be for it.'

'Only a little bit, if you stay in London.'

'And what if she wants to come up here?' he queried.

'Why should she, Papa? It would be pointless.'

'Or wants me to go down there?'

'Lie – say you have to go to Glasgow again. For several weeks at least.'

He shook his head in wonder. 'I never knew you could be so conniving.'

'I'm a woman, Papa,' she replied with amusement in her voice. 'Aren't we all?'

'True,' he conceded. 'Very true.'

'Now I must return to the hospital. I'm on duty in a little over an hour.'

He was disappointed. 'Can't you stay for lunch?'

'I'd like to, but it's impossible I'm afraid.'

'Then so be it,' he answered with an understanding nod.

Jeremiah escorted Katherine to the front door and helped her into her coat. 'Will I see you again before you leave?'

'Of course you will. I promise.'

'Don't break that promise, Katherine.'

'You know I won't.'

This time it was she who kissed him. 'Try not to worry. If that's possible.'

'I'll try.' But of course he would. He'd worry himself sick every day she was in France.

When she was gone he leant against the door and closed his eyes. In his mind's eye he was seeing her as she'd been when she was young. Pictures of her growing up flashed past him – her first party dress, the pony he'd bought her, the time she'd fallen over and broken an arm. The occasion when he'd discovered, quite by accident, that she'd become a woman. And now she was off to war. Not to fight, but still to be in the thick of it. At risk, every moment of the day and night.

He groaned.

'What is it, Jeremiah?'

He hadn't been aware Henrietta was awake. 'I can't sleep.'

'Is it Katherine?'

'Yes,' he sighed. A soft, tortured sound.

Henrietta turned to face him. 'It's her decision. There's nothing you can do about it.'

'I know that. Which doesn't help one little bit.'

They lay for a while in silence, then Henrietta slipped from the bed.

'Where are you going?' he queried, hating her being from his side.

'Nowhere.' She padded over to a chest of drawers, opened it and took out a bottle of scented oil. 'I'm going to do your feet,' she declared, well aware how much he enjoyed that and how relaxing he found it.

She pulled free the covers at the bottom of the bed and then sat with a foot on either side of her.

'Shall I put the bedside light on?'

'Please.'

He reached across and pressed the switch. How elegant her back was, he marvelled. If he'd been a poet he might have described it as a work of art. Her hair was unpinned and hung down to below her shoulders. He couldn't have imagined any woman being more attractive.

Henrietta poured a little oil onto the palm of one hand and slowly, expertly, began to massage. This was something she'd been taught to do at Mrs Green's.

'How's that?'

'Sheer heaven.'

Henrietta laughed. 'That good, eh?'

'Oh yes,' he breathed.

Henrietta continued to rub and knead, smoothing away all the tension that was there.

'In all the time we've been together you've never asked me how I came to be at Mrs Green's,' she stated quietly. 'You told your wife that cock-and-bull nonsense you made up about my husband deserting me and leaving me with twins. But not once have you asked me what the true story was.'

'That's because I felt you'd tell me when – and if – you wanted to,' he replied slowly.

She glanced at him over her shoulder. 'Would you like to hear?'

'Naturally I'm intrigued. But it's your business, Henrietta. Only tell me if you want to.'

She continued to massage his feet for a few seconds, then said, 'I'm a country girl from Cambridgeshire. One of a family of nine.'

'Really?' He was surprised, for she didn't have a country accent. Not even a trace.

'My father's a farmer, in a small way, and we all worked the land. In the case of the women – there were three of us, including my mother – the house *and* land. Cruel work, Jeremiah, hard grinding graft in all weathers. I hated it. Hated, loathed and despised it. Life was unending back-breaking toil and poverty. From sunrise to sunset, always on the go, with precious little ever to show for it.'

Henrietta paused and took a deep breath.

'I was married at nineteen to a chap called Alan Buck. A nice enough man, but . . . well, boring beyond belief. He couldn't talk about anything other than crops and weather, farming things. Whereas I wanted more than that.

'If anything, and I wouldn't have believed it possible, the work was even harder, there being only two of us to manage his piece of land. Every night I'd fall exhausted into bed, praying that he'd leave me alone as I simply didn't have the energy for that. Sometimes he did, and at others didn't. Then I fell pregnant.'

'So you do have a child?' Jeremiah queried softly.

She shook her head. 'I miscarried.'

'Oh, I am sorry.'

'So was Alan, especially when it happened for the third

time and the doctor told us I'd probably never be able to have children. Alan wanted them, you see, particularly boys, to carry on after he'd gone. But more importantly to look after him in his old age. That was when I began to suspect he was planning to get rid of me.'

This was a sorry tale indeed, Jeremiah thought. He couldn't have been more sympathetic. 'How do you mean, get rid of you?'

'Well, divorce was out of the question – far too expensive for the likes of us. And he couldn't just chuck me out, for my da and brothers would have had something to say about that.' She hesitated, then went on. 'You must remember, farms are dangerous places, and accidents happen all the time. And occasionally fatal ones.'

Jeremiah was shocked. 'Are you saying you thought he was going to murder you?'

She nodded. 'We farmers are practical people. If a cow is barren, you kill it. So why not a wife? It's easier done than you might think.'

'Dear God!' Jeremiah exclaimed. This was appalling.

'I'd never been content with the farming life anyway. When younger I'd taught myself to read from *The Bystander*, copies of which the vicar's wife used to give me when she was finished with them, so I thought that at least might stand me in good stead for what I had in mind.'

'Which was?'

'Running away.'

'I see,' Jeremiah murmured. That made sense, considering that her husband had been thinking of killing her.

'And so I did. One market day I told Alan I was ill and didn't want to leave the farm to go with him, so he let me stay. He'd no sooner gone than I put a few things together and took the little savings we had, which he kept hidden under a stone in the hearth. He went one way and I the other, eventually ending up in London, which I'd decided to head for.'

'And how did you get in tow with Mrs Green?'

Henrietta laid aside the foot she'd been massaging and started on the other. 'Quite by chance really. I was working in a pub when this regular told me that I was wasted there and he knew where I could get a far better job. The way he described it, it sounded wonderful. A real opportunity. So one night after the pub had closed he met me and took me to Mrs Green's. What happened next isn't very nice at all.'

'I'm still listening,' he said, wondering what on earth he was about to hear.

'Mrs Green interviewed me and I obviously suited her purposes. She asked me to follow her, which I did, downstairs into a sort of cellar area. There Bert, the regular from the pub, hit me hard, stripped me naked, threw me onto a bed and repeatedly raped me. That was the beginning of it.'

Jeremiah sat up, pulling his feet away from Henrietta, to stare at her in horror. This just got worse and worse. 'Raped you?'

'Repeatedly. Then I was tied to the bed and left.'

'Naked?'

'Totally. I must have been there for a week, though it's all a bit hazy. From time to time someone would appear – always male – and give me a little food, after which I'd always be raped and sometimes beaten.'

Henrietta stopped and sobbed. Jeremiah instantly slid down the bed and took her into his arms. 'There there,' he crooned. 'It's all over now. You'll never see Mrs Green again.'

'She's the most evil bitch, Jeremiah. You've no idea. Shall I go on?'

'Only if you want to, my angel.'

'I feel I have to, Jeremiah. Get it off my chest. Tell someone. And you're the obvious person.'

He gently stroked the back he'd been admiring so much, thinking what a horrendous ordeal it was for any young woman to go through. It was simply mind-boggling.

'Eventually I was released from the bed and taken upstairs, where I was allowed a bath and a dressing gown to put on. Mrs Green then sat me down and told me what was expected of me. I'd be taught, she explained, all manner of things, including how to satisfy a client's every whim.' She hesitated. 'I don't think I need go into that. You can use your imagination. But when I say every whim I mean exactly that.' Henrietta shuddered. 'It was disgusting, Jeremiah, absolutely disgusting. I never knew people did such . . . things to one another.'

He held her even more closely. He could have wept for her.

'I was watched all the time, and at night was locked in my room so I couldn't even try and escape. Mrs Green herself taught me how to dress, conduct myself at the table and speak properly. Luckily I turned out to have a good ear and learnt quickly. She was pleased about that.

'After a while, when she considered me properly trained, I started work. I was clothed, fed and given a roof over my head. Nothing more. I never ever touched money, as the clients always had to pay Mrs Green. Every night or morning I was searched, as was my room, in case a client had given me a tip. If you were found to have hidden one then Bert was called and you were viciously beaten. That's how it was and how I came to be there.'

Jeremiah was thoroughly ashamed of himself for having used Mrs Green's establishment. He'd had no idea.

'She's evil, Jeremiah, completely evil. Occasionally she does things to the girls after Bert has beaten them, for stepping out of line in some way. Not satisfying a client, for example, or when the girl has a complaint lodged against her. There was one particular punishment we all dreaded. Fortunately I never had it done to me.'

He knew from the tone of her voice she was going to tell him what that was.

Henrietta gulped in air. 'Apparently she'd have the offender tied naked face down on the bed. Then she'd . . . she'd . . . Sometimes a carrot, sometimes . . .' Henrietta broke off. 'The girl was then left there in agony for hours on end until Mrs Green decided that she had had enough.'

Jeremiah swore viciously. 'Thank God I saved you from that hellhole.'

'I knew I could rely on you, otherwise I'd never have dared it. If you're caught trying to escape from Mrs Green . . .' Henrietta's voice suddenly choked to the point where she couldn't go on.

'No more,' Jeremiah said firmly. 'No more.'

'Oh, darling,' she whispered. 'Dear, sweet Jeremiah. Now you know what you rescued me from and why I'll be eternally grateful and never let you down.'

'Hush,' he crooned, continuing to stroke her.

'I'm so happy being with you. So very, very happy.'

'And I'm happy being with you,' he responded, thinking

how true that was. Even during the good times with Ruth, when they'd first been married, he'd never been as happy as he was now. He had Henrietta to thank for that. 'Now you get under the covers and get warm,' he instructed. 'And just remember, I'm here to take care of you.'

She buried her face in his chest, then looked up into his eyes, her expression one of adoration and sheer gratitude. He couldn't help but be profoundly moved on seeing it.

'You were right,' he stated softly. 'It was best to get that off your chest. And now we'll never talk about or mention it again. Agreed?'

'Agreed,' she smiled.

He kissed her lightly on the lips, then helped her snuggle back under the covers.

For the rest of that night Henrietta clung to him like a limpet.

Since sending off his application to the War Office Tim had been the first downstairs every morning, even before Minna and the maids, for he wanted to pick up the post as soon as it arrived. If Minna spotted an official War Office-stamped envelope addressed to him she'd demand to know its contents.

He was dog-tired, having had a late night, but despite that he was down for the mail delivery as usual. That morning there was only one letter, the one he'd been so eagerly awaiting.

He snatched it up off the floor and stared at it for a few seconds before hurriedly stuffing it into a pocket. Then he ran back upstairs to his room, where he ripped the envelope open.

The tone was curt and very businesslike. On Tuesday of the following week he was to present himself at Room 613A in the War Office to be interviewed. The time of the interview was 4 p.m. A reply wasn't necessary unless he was unable to attend.

Tim read the letter again, then carefully folded it and replaced it in his pocket. He had an interview! That was the first hurdle over.

The next thing was to think of a suitable excuse for Minna to explain being out of town for a night.

Chapter 23

T im thought the War Office a most awesome place. An intimidating commissionaire requested that he fill out various buff-coloured forms, and while he was doing that a series of blue-clad messengers hurried to and fro, all seemingly on terribly important missions.

Eventually Tim was instructed to follow one of these messengers, who silently led him up a great staircase, through endless corridors, up more smaller staircases and down further corridors. Finally they arrived at a door bearing the legend 613A.

'Please wait here,' the messenger declared rather pompously and hurried away, reminding Tim of the white rabbit in *Alice in Wonderland*.

To his surprise, although he couldn't think why it should be unexpected, there were other applicants already waiting. He joined the queue by sitting at the end of a long, narrow bench. No-one spoke, so he didn't either.

One by one the applicants vanished inside, stayed for a spell, then emerged again to try and find their way out. At long last it was his turn.

Lord Henry Stamforth, staff captain, looked up as Tim

entered the sparsely furnished office. He was a small, bald man with kindly eyes.

'Good afternoon. You are?'

'Tim Wilson, sir.'

Stamforth ferreted through some papers and came up with Tim's letter. 'Ah yes.' He indicated a wooden chair in front of his desk. 'Take a seat.'

'Thank you, sir.'

Stamforth studied Tim's letter. 'This school you mention, haven't heard of it.'

'It's a very minor public school, sir.'

Stamforth grunted. 'Did you play games there?'

'Yes, sir. Rugger and fives. I got my house colours in the latter.'

That clearly impressed the staff captain. 'You have a good eye then?'

Did he? He didn't know. 'I suppose so, sir.'

'Hmmh. Important that. Any hobbies?'

He didn't really, unless you counted going to the pub. And he didn't think he'd better mention that. 'I ride a motor-bike, sir.'

The kindly eyes lit up with enthusiasm. 'What sort?'

'A Royal Enfield, sir.'

Stamforth nodded. 'Nippy machines those. Quite sporty.'

'Yes, sir.'

'I have a Rudge myself. Grand machine.'

'I'm afraid I don't know that one, sir.'

'Bit of a beast,' Stamforth smiled. 'Sadly I haven't had much chance to ride it of late, thanks to the war. Far too busy.'

'I understand, sir,' Tim nodded, thinking that there was

a stroke of luck, Stamforth also being an enthusiast. Surely that must count in his favour.

'I see you work as a reporter on a local rag,' Stamforth went on.

'Yes, sir. A jolly interesting job.'

'Occasionally do a spot of scribbling myself. Nothing published, mind you, but maybe one day.'

Even better, Tim thought jubilantly. Now they had several things in common.

Stamforth cleared his throat and sat back in his chair. 'Now, Mr Wilson, why do you want to join the RFC? Let me just mention that to date most of our people have come from the army. Cavalry officers, those sorts of chaps.'

That explained the lack of recruiting offices, Tim thought. 'The navy doesn't attract me at all, sir, nor the army. It did seem to me, however, that I might enjoy flying just as much as I do riding my bike. They're both similar in a way, I think, each merely a different type of machine. I like machines and seem to understand them.'

'Hmmh. Have you ever been up in an aeroplane?'

'No, sir. Never had the opportunity.'

Stamforth studied Tim for a few seconds, then appeared to come to a decision. Picking up a pen, he jotted down several notes on the top of Tim's letter.

'Well, that's it, Wilson. Thank you for coming. You'll be hearing from us in due course.'

Tim bit back his disappointment: that had been short and sweet. He'd somehow imagined he'd be told there and then if he'd been accepted or rejected. He stood up. 'Thank you, sir.'

'Send in the next chap, will you?'

'Of course, sir.'

Tim hesitated at the door. 'How long is "in due course" likely to be, sir?'

Stamforth's lips crinkled in amusement. 'Fairly soon, I should think.'

'Thank you, sir.'

Despite being given various directions, it took Tim all of twenty minutes to eventually find his way out of the building and back into Whitehall.

On leaving the War Office Tim headed for a Lyons Corner House that he'd noticed on the way there and had a coffee plus a bite to eat. After that, this being his first time in London, he decided to take in the sights.

He was booked into a cheap bed-and-breakfast in Paddington, where he'd spend the night, going straight from there in the morning to the station and home.

He stood in Piccadilly Circus for a while, marvelling at the grandness and bustle of it, then strolled to Leicester Square and on to Covent Garden. From there he made his way to the Strand and walked the length of that. Feeling a little tired by now and somewhat thirsty, he decided to call into a pub for a pint.

It was in the pub, while propping up the bar and listening to the strange London accents, that he noticed the poster. The name Mrs Davenport leapt right out at him.

Crossing over, he studied the poster, which informed him that Elyse was in a play called *Lady Windermere's Fan* at the Haymarket Theatre. Why not? he thought. He had nothing better to do that evening. And perhaps he might be able to speak to her afterwards.

The friendly barmaid gave him explicit instructions on how to get there.

'Come in!' Elyse called out when there was a knock on her dressing-room door. Her face was covered in cream, for she was busy removing her slap.

Freddy, the call boy, popped his head round. 'There's a Mr Wilson here to see you, Mrs Davenport. Says he knows you.'

Elyse paused in what she was doing to frown. She didn't recall any Mr Wilson of her acquaintance.

Freddy's head ducked away and then reappeared. 'A Mr Tim Wilson from Torquay.'

'Tim!' Elyse squealed.

Freddy ushered him inside and then hurried off.

'Excuse the state I'm in, but what are you doing here?' she laughed, thinking this a right turn-up for the book.

'I was in the audience tonight. You were fabulous, Elyse, quite fabulous.'

She preened. 'Why thank you, kind sir.'

'No, no, I mean it. Truly I do.'

Going over to him, she pecked his cheek. 'It's so good to see you again, Tim.'

He rubbed off the grease mark she'd left. 'And you, Elyse. How are you?'

'Fine. Absolutely tiptop.' That was a lie, but she wasn't about to tell Tim about her health problems. 'So why are you in London?'

Her eyes widened when he told her about Whitehall and applying to join the Royal Flying Corps.

'I see,' she murmured. Sitting down, she went on

removing her slap. 'And what does your mother think about that?'

'She doesn't know,' he admitted, rather shamefaced. 'She believes I've gone to Totnes to do a story there.'

'Uh-oh.' Minna wouldn't like that. 'Where are you staying?'

'Paddington. A B&B. I'll be catching the eight thirty-five tomorrow morning.'

Tim thought Elyse had lost weight which, in a way, made her even more attractive in his opinion. The smell of the perfume that he remembered so well was everywhere.

Elyse picked up a small towel and wiped her face clean. 'Do you have to get back there for any special time?'

He shook his head. 'They gave me a key in case I was late.'

'Good. I intend going on to a little club I know called Kean's. Why don't you come with me? My treat.'

A London club! That idea certainly appealed. 'Are you sure?'

'Of course I'm sure. You can be my escort for the evening.'

He flushed slightly at the thought of that, suddenly remembering the time he'd walked in on her when she'd been in the bath. 'Then I'd love to come.'

'Excellent. You'll have to wait for a while till I get ready, though. Is that all right?'

'Do you want me to leave the room?'

She laughed. 'Don't be silly. I'll change behind the screen. In the meantime why don't you pour us both a drink.' She indicated with the stab of a finger. 'The Scotch and several glasses are over there.'

Tim thought things had turned out even better than he'd

dared hope. A night on the town with Elyse Davenport! Someone somewhere was smiling down on him.

'Molly, I'd like you to meet Tim Wilson. I stayed at his mother's boarding house in Torquay.'

'Ah, to be sure,' Molly enthused. 'You've mentioned him a number of times. But what you never said was that he was such a handsome devil.'

Tim almost squirmed with embarrassment. Handsome devil indeed!

'And Tim, this is Molly O'Malley. She and her husband Seamus own the club.'

'How do you do, Mrs O'Malley,' Tim said, extending a hand.

'None of that Mrs stuff, me lad. It's Molly to all my customers. And put that hand away. 'Tis a kiss you'll be getting.' And with that she planted a wet smacker on Tim's cheek.

He was quite taken aback, at a loss how to respond. And, in truth, somewhat overwhelmed by his surroundings and the people there. He'd never seen such an outrageous bunch. Actors in the main, Elyse had explained on their way there.

'Are you hungry, Tim?' Elyse asked.

'A little, I suppose.'

'Then we'll eat.' She pointed to a huge blackboard on which the menu had been chalked. 'Choose whatever. As for me, an omelette I think. And a bottle of champagne to start with. It is an occasion after all.'

In the end Tim decided on Irish stew, he and Elyse settling themselves into a booth while Molly bustled off to place their order and fetch the champagne.

'What do you think?' Elyse smiled.

'Of what?'

She fluttered a hand. 'All this.'

'It's, eh . . . unusual.'

That amused her. 'A bit different from Torquay, eh?'

'A bit,' he admitted.

Elyse produced a packet of cigarettes and lit up. She'd been trying to cut down on them and on alcohol, succeeding with both, but only up to a point. Life was too short to be an ongoing martyr, she'd decided. It was to be enjoyed, not trudged through in a hair shirt.

'How's your mother?' she demanded. 'And the others at The Berkeley? And Torquay itself? I want to hear everything.'

Before Tim could reply, an attractive-looking woman of roughly Elyse's age stopped at their table. 'Why hello, Elyse. Cradle-snatching I see.'

Elyse smiled wickedly. 'Jealous, Emma?'

'Not in the least. Why don't you introduce me?'

'Eff off, Emma, there's a nice ratbag.'

Emma's face contorted with fury. 'Charming!' Having spat that out she walked stiffly away.

'Who was that?' an incredulous Tim asked. He'd never heard women speak to one another in such a manner.

'Emma Sinclair, a bitch of the first order. And a man-eater. Be thankful I didn't introduce you. She'd have been trying to get inside your trousers in no time.'

Tim went scarlet, struck quite speechless.

'Here you are, my darlings,' Molly declared, having threaded her way through the crowd. She placed glasses and a bottle of champagne on their table. 'Shall I?'

'No, Tim will do that. Thanks all the same, Molly.'

'Your food won't be long. Speak to you both again later.'

Tim watched the huge Molly waddle off, her enormous backside wobbling from side to side.

'Molly and Seamus are good friends,' Elyse explained. 'Probably my best friends.'

He glanced about. 'Do you come here a lot?'

'All the time. Why, don't you like it?'

'It just . . . I suppose, takes a little getting used to, that's all. I'm only a country boy, don't forget.'

'Well, can the country boy open champagne?'

'Of course.'

'Then get to.'

He managed it without too much difficulty, although it was only the second such bottle he'd ever opened, which he certainly wasn't going to admit to, and filled both glasses.

'A toast,' Elyse declared, picking up hers.

'To what?'

She thought about that and the fact that he was trying to join the RFC with a war on. 'Long life,' she said, suddenly very serious, thinking about herself as well.

'Long life,' he repeated, and they both drank.

'Now,' she smiled. 'Torquay. You promised to tell me everything.'

'I'll try to.'

She listened avidly as he spoke, occasionally prompting him with a question.

James Erskine apart, it surprised Elyse how nostalgic she was about the place.

It was just past two o'clock when they left Kean's and both of them were well tipsy.

'I thoroughly enjoyed myself, Elyse. I haven't had so much fun in a long time,' Tim declared.

'I'm glad. I enjoyed myself too. You're good company.'

'As are you.'

She took hold of his arm. 'I'm afraid you're not going to get much sleep before your train.'

'That doesn't matter. I'll nod off during the journey and catch up that way.'

Tim spotted an approaching motor taxicab and hailed it. 'You should have let me pay, Elyse.'

'Not at all. It was my treat, remember?'

'Even so.'

The motor taxicab drew up alongside and Elyse gave the driver her address. 'I'd drop you off, Tim, but I'm going the opposite way. And don't worry about getting back – there'll be another cab along in a minute. There always is.' She stared at him. 'It's goodnight then. And good luck with the RFC.'

'Goodnight to you too, and thank you.'

On a sudden impulse she quickly kissed him on the mouth. 'You look after yourself now.'

'I will. I promise.'

'It was terrific seeing you again.'

'And you, Elyse.'

He helped her into the taxicab and closed the door. She gave him a wave as the cab drew away.

Tim was left with that unmistakable, and unforgettable, odour of her perfume strong in his nostrils.

It was a month now and still no word from the War Office. Tim was beginning to despair, thinking it didn't look at all good. If he'd been accepted surely they'd have contacted him by now? There again, no news was good news. He hadn't been rejected either.

The rumours about conscription continued to cause speculation, with many people saying it would be coming in any day now. If that happened then it would be the army or navy, which he didn't want, particularly the navy on account of the seasickness.

And those damned women were at it again, handing out white feathers to young men not in uniform. Thankfully Ricketts had declared it an old story, so it hadn't been run a second time.

Only the previous week he'd had a lucky escape, spotting three of the harpies outside Williams & Cox's furniture shop berating some unfortunate they'd pounced on. He'd dodged up a side street to avoid them.

When was he going to hear? he raged inwardly. When?

'Don't cry, Ma, please,' Tim pleaded. This was turning out to be just as awful as he'd feared.

'You promised me, Tim. You swore you wouldn't join up.'

'I'm sorry, Ma, but I had to.'

Minna wiped the tears away with a handkerchief. Her whole world had suddenly collapsed around her. 'Why did you have to?' She fought back the urge to slap him.

He mentioned the forthcoming conscription and the ladies with white feathers, Minna having been only too horribly aware of both.

'It'll be jammy in the RFC, Ma. All I have to do is one flight a day to observe and then back again to safety.

Harry Nutbeam assured me of that. He took his training next to an aerodrome where new pilots were also being taught.'

That mollified her a little. 'Are you certain?'

'God's honest truth, Ma. One flight a day over the lines and that's it. Home to tea and crumpets and my own room. There will be no trenches for me, or enemy guns blasting away. That's why I joined the RFC before being forced into the army or, worse still, the navy.'

She could still have hit him. Tim was all she had left – her entire life now that Redvers was dead. But she could see his point.

'I'm really sorry for going behind your back, Ma, but it couldn't be helped. I could only tell you once the deed was done and there was no getting out of it.'

For a few moments there she'd thought she might faint, but that had passed now. 'When do you leave?' she asked coldly.

'Next Monday. I've to report to Brooklands.'

'Next Mon . . . so soon?'

'I'm afraid so.'

That was only five days away, no time at all. Not for the first time, Minna inwardly cursed the Kaiser. If it hadn't been for him none of this nightmare would be happening. When it was his turn to die she hoped he went straight to hell and stayed there for all eternity. Because of him so many young men, on both sides, had already died. How many more before it was all over? A single one would be too many.

Minna put a hand to her brow. This was just so hard to take in. Tim going off to war – it made her feel sick inside. Worse than that.

'Ma, do you want to sit down?' Tim asked anxiously.

'I think I'd better.'

She shrugged off his hand when he went to help her. She was angry with him, as angry as she'd ever been. And yet his argument made sense. If conscription came in, which was bound to happen – the only question being when – then he would have to go anyway and there wouldn't be a thing she could do about it. At least this way, as he'd pointed out, he had the choice of which service to join.

'Can I get you something, Ma?'

'A glass of sherry.'

That startled Tim. Minna drinking during the day! It was almost unheard of, Christmas apart, that is. And she rarely tippled at night, being fairly abstemious.

'Right!' he declared and rushed off to get some.

She dabbed again with her handkerchief, her face wet from tears that had now stopped. What a shock this was! It had left her stunned.

'Monday.' She said the word as though it was something obscene. To her, in a way, it was. All too soon it would be upon them and she'd be bidding him farewell, not knowing if she'd ever see him alive again.

Tim, her son. Her beloved son.

'Here you are, Ma.'

She accepted the glass and took a swallow. Then she took a long, deep breath.

She stared up at him, seeing Redvers in his face. Redvers and herself. She would have done anything to stop Tim leaving – gone in his place if that had been at all possible.

'Is there anything else I can get you, Ma?'

'No. Just leave me for a while. I want to be alone.'

Tim bit his lip. He'd hated hurting Minna. But as the local expression went, 'it had to be done'. The only alternative was to sneak off next Monday without telling her why, and that was unthinkable.

He closed the door quietly behind him.

'Will you please stop pacing, you're making me giddy!'

Jeremiah immediately halted. 'Sorry.'

'You're like a lion in a cage,' Ruth admonished. 'Up and down, up and down.'

He crossed to a chair and sat down. He was hating being back at Oaklands, only being there out of duty and because Ruth had insisted. He couldn't wait to return to London, and Henrietta. That was where his real home was now – not here.

Ruth shook her head. 'I still can't believe what Katherine's done, the ungrateful child. Had she no thought at all for her parents?'

Jeremiah stared at his wife, thinking how much he'd come to dislike her. She was selfish and completely unsympathetic. How could he have loved her all those long years? It was a mystery. Now the less time he spent in her presence, the better.

'She's a grown woman, Ruth, capable of making her own decisions. You'll just have to accept that,' he replied caustically.

Ruth glared at him. 'You sound as if you actually approve.'

'I do. The country's at war and she's doing her bit. Good for her, I say.'

'I can understand her wanting to help, but why volunteer for France, where she'll be in danger? I ask you that!' Ruth snapped waspishly.

'Because that's where she's needed. I would have thought that was obvious.'

'There are plenty of other women who could go. It didn't have to be her.'

'Those other women are someone else's daughters, Ruth. Parents who'd be just as worried about them as we are about Katherine.'

'Other parents are no concern of mine. I only care about my own daughter.'

'There comes a time, Ruth,' he went on patiently, 'when you have to let go. Katherine has her own life to lead and how she does that is completely up to her.'

Ruth snorted. 'Poppycock.'

'It's nothing of the sort.'

'I thought she'd come back here when Miles died. That seemed right and proper to me.'

'But clearly not to her.'

'She has an obligation . . .'

'Katherine has nothing of the sort,' Jeremiah cut in, beginning to lose his temper. 'At least not in the way you mean. What you are advocating is pure and utter selfishness on your part. What you want is a companion round the house, nothing more.'

Ruth blinked in shock, unable to believe her husband was speaking to her like this. Why, he was actually criticising her. 'Jeremiah?' she almost squeaked.

'Well, it's true, isn't it?'

'Not at all.'

'Yes, it is,' he insisted.

Her eyes brimmed with tears. 'Why are you being so horrible?'

'I am being nothing of the sort. I'm merely stating the blindingly obvious. Of course you care about Katherine, but you care about yourself and your own needs a great deal more. That's the long and short of it.'

Ruth put a hand to her chest. 'I feel faint. I think I have an attack coming on.'

'No you haven't. You're just making it up. And I'm beginning to suspect that a lot of your illnesses in the past have been exactly that – something you've made up.'

Ruth was horrified that he'd guessed her secret. 'It's not so. On my life it isn't.'

He stared grimly at her, thinking how pathetic she looked. Had he gone too far? An inner voice told him he was right and hadn't. It was something he'd given a lot of thought to of late. It was as if a veneer had been stripped away and he was able, at long last, to see the real Ruth. And he didn't like what he saw. A conniving, manipulative woman who was only after her own ends.

'If it isn't so, then how is it that you're always well enough when it suits you. Eh? I hadn't realised that until recently. Katherine's coming-out and wedding, for example. Not a trace of illness on either occasion because you wanted to be involved, right there at the centre of things.'

Ruth came to her feet. She had to get out of here, away from this. 'I'm going to bed,' she declared. 'And I suggest you don't speak to me again until you're ready to apologise.'

He laughed. 'You'll have a long wait then, I'm afraid. For I shan't do that.'

'I don't know you any more, Jeremiah, you've turned into a . . . a monster.'

'Have I indeed?' he queried. 'Perhaps all that's happened

is that I've come to my senses where you and my marriage are concerned. Both an utter sham.'

She swept past him and out of the room feeling extremely sorry for herself.

Jeremiah decided he'd leave for London straight away. That very night he'd be back in bed with Henrietta, with all the love and affection he'd find in her arms.

Chapter 24

'Are you Wilson?'

Tim, still in civilian clothes, having only arrived at Brooklands the previous night, snapped to attention, which he presumed he was supposed to do. 'Yes, sir.'

The man eyed him up and down. 'Well, I'm Sergeant Iveson, your instructor. I understand you've never been up. Is that correct?'

'Yes, sir.'

'Then there's no time like the present to remedy that.'

Despite himself, Tim gulped. He hadn't expected things to happen quite this fast.

Iveson pointed to the machine in front of which they were standing. 'This beauty is a Farman MF11, mainly used for reconnaissance and safe as houses to fly. Initially you'll be training on it. Understand?'

'Yes, sir.'

Tim stared in wonder at the plane, which seemed to have what looked suspiciously like piano wires strung everywhere. He thought it appeared as flimsy as hell.

'Right then, you get in the front cockpit and I'll be in the rear. You'll find a helmet and goggles there – put them on. And for heaven's sake don't touch anything either on the ground or in the air. Is that clear?'

'Perfectly, sir.'

'Fine, let's go.'

Tim glanced up at the sky. It was a gorgeous August day with only a few wispy clouds in evidence. Nor was there any wind worth mentioning.

Once in the cockpit he sucked in a deep breath, savouring the smell of the Farman: a combination of oil, fuel and grease. It reminded him of his Enfield, which smelt almost exactly the same. He found that most comforting.

Iveson tapped him on the shoulder. 'Ready?'

Tim nodded.

'Strapped in?'

'Yes, sir.'

'Then here we go.'

Seconds later the engine, a Renault 8 cylinder air-cooled, in-line V 100hp, roared into life. Next thing they were bumping along the ground.

The one worry Tim had was that he might react to aeroplanes in the same way he did to boats, which was by feeling sick. He'd soon find out, he told himself, praying that wouldn't happen.

Tim never even felt the plane taking off. One moment they were still on the ground, the next in the air. The only difference was that the bumping had stopped.

They began to climb, quite steeply, Tim thought, staring over the side in delight. Air was whipping against his face and the higher they went, the noticeably cooler it became.

Houses below had become the size of matchboxes, while a field full of sheep was in miniature. There was a railway track, the same one that had brought him to Brooklands, and far off a tiny train and carriages.

He'd never known such exhilaration, which was far better and more heightened than he felt on his motorbike. He wanted to stay up there for ever.

Sergeant Iveson took the Farman in a circle at about 4,000 feet. When the circuit was complete, it was time to land again.

More bumping and a bit of jolting, with Tim loving every thrilling moment of it. He sighed in disappointment when the Farman finally came to a halt.

Iveson gripped Tim's shoulder. 'How was that?'

'Simply wonderful, sir. When can I go up again?'

Iveson laughed. 'Not today, I'm afraid. But possibly tomorrow. Now, look at the controls in front of you and I'll go through them.'

Tim drank in every word.

'Do you mind if I sit with you?'

Tim glanced up at the speaker, a young blond chap of about his own age and also dressed in civilian clothes. They were in the mess, where an evening meal was being served. 'Please do.'

He sat and extended a hand. 'Paul Greville, pleased to meet you.'

'Tim Wilson, likewise.'

'I heard you speaking to your instructor earlier. The accent's Devon, isn't it?'

Tim nodded. 'I'm from Torquay.'

'Well, there's a spot of luck. I'm from just outside Exeter, a little village called Silverton. That makes us both Devonians.'

'Well met,' Tim acknowledged.

'First day?'

'Yes.'

'Me too. I arrived early this morning.'

'I was late last night.'

Paul regarded the plate in front of him. 'Well, the food doesn't look disgusting, I'll say that.' They both fell to eating. 'Did you go up?' he asked.

'Indeed.'

'So did I. What did you think?'

Tim smiled. 'Like a bird, or an angel, or something similar. I didn't want to come back down again.'

'Were you nervous?'

'Not in the least. You?'

'I must admit I was,' Paul confessed. 'But I'm sure that will soon pass.'

'I thought . . .' Tim's eyes took on a faraway, dreamy look. 'I don't know what I thought. It was as if – and don't laugh – I'd been born to fly.'

Paul stared at him in amazement. 'Really?'

'Really. I was at home up there, completely and utterly at home. I can't wait to go up again.'

'Well, good for you,' an impressed Paul replied. 'Despite my nervousness I enjoyed it, but I can't say I felt at home. To be honest, I was only too pleased to get my feet back on *terra firma*.'

They continued chatting, developing a friendship, and at the end of the meal when Paul suggested that they have another meal together, Tim instantly agreed.

That night Tim dreamt of his flight, over and over again.

* * *

The stage doorkeeper ran after Elyse, having been busy and almost missed her as she went past his cubicle. 'Mrs Davenport! Mrs Davenport!'

She stopped and turned to him.

'There's a letter for you.'

Typewritten, she noted as she accepted it. Hardly a fan letter then. 'Thank you.'

'My pleasure.'

And so it should be, she thought. She tipped him half a crown every week.

Once in her dressing room she took off her hat and coat, disposed of them, sat down and lit a cigarette. It was a good hour before curtain up.

She used a fingernail to slit open the envelope and took out the single sheet it contained. To her surprise she saw it was from a firm of solicitors called Bloom, Taylor and Kempinski. She'd never heard of them.

The letter was brief and to the point. Mr Kempinski requested that she contact their office and make an appointment to see him. There was no indication why he wanted her to do so.

'How odd,' she muttered, laying the letter aside. What was this all about?

She had absolutely no idea.

Jeremiah shook his head in disbelief. He had just completed his books for the week and was amazed at the profits he was making. It was an incredible amount of money.

Slowly he closed the ledger and stared thoughtfully at the green-and-brown cover. The steelworks in Glasgow was working to full capacity on a round-the-clock basis, with the demand for steel growing more and more urgent with every passing day.

He had to admit that he felt guilty at what some might see as profiteering, his argument for doing so being that if he didn't, someone else would. It was as simple as that.

And he wasn't setting the price of steel: he merely charged the going rate, never more. He could only reflect that if this continued then he was going to be rich beyond his wildest dreams.

Taking a cigar from the humidor on his desk, he clipped it, then lit up. The main thing was to produce goods for the war effort, he told himself. And if he made a tidy profit into the bargain then so much the better.

He was a shrewd enough businessman to know that this insatiable demand was only a temporary thing. When the war was over there was bound to be a slump. It stood to reason. But in the meantime . . .

Quite by chance he'd recently learnt of a small steelworks just outside Newcastle that had been shut down some years previously. As far as he knew the doors had simply been closed, leaving everything inside just as it was. If true, and he could acquire the property and restart production, it could only be to his financial advantage. And further help the war effort, of course.

He decided it was time to make inquiries.

'For you,' Jeremiah said to Henrietta, handing her a large, gift-wrapped box.

'Me?'

He laughed at the expression of incredulity on her face. It really tickled him.

'What is it?' she queried.

'Open the box and find out.'

Henrietta gently shook the box, hearing something moving about. 'Is it breakable?'

Jeremiah shook his head.

'I can't think what it might be,' she said.

'I doubt you'll guess. So go on, find out by opening it.'

She placed the box on a nearby coffee table and began unravelling the huge pink bow decorating its front. When it was finally undone she pulled free the ribbon and carefully wound it, before laying it aside.

She glanced at Jeremiah before undoing the matching pink paper in which the box was wrapped.

'My God!' she gasped when she saw what was inside. 'A fur coat.'

'Mink. Try it on. If it doesn't fit, we can take it back and have it altered. That won't be a problem.'

She pulled the coat free and shook it out. 'It's beautiful, Jeremiah. I can't tell you how much. It must have cost a fortune.'

He shrugged. 'Nothing I can't afford.'

She regarded him quizzically. 'But why?'

'Buy it for you?' He considered that for a moment. 'Because I wanted to and because you deserve it. Call it a token of appreciation, if you will. My appreciation of how much happiness you've given me.'

She opened her mouth, then shut it again. 'No more than you've given me,' she eventually husked.

He recalled how life had been before Henrietta. How dreary, how dull, how unloved he'd been. Being with her, it was as though a fiercely hot, blazing sun had burst out on a winter's day, completely transforming everything.

'I've never owned anything like this before,' she went on, staring at the coat in awe. 'Nor ever expected to.'

That truly touched him. 'Well, it's only the first of many things I'm going to get you. That's a promise.'

She gazed again at the coat. 'I'll never dare wear it. It's far too valuable.'

'Yes, you will, for I shall insist. Now, how about a kiss to say thank you?'

She hesitated. 'You don't have to buy me presents, Jeremiah. I'm not here for that.'

'I know,' he replied softly. 'I know.'

In the event he got far more than the kiss he'd asked for.

'Where have you been? I haven't seen you all week,' Molly asked Elyse.

Elyse slumped onto a stool beside the bar. 'I haven't been up to coming. I've been so tired that all I can do after the show is go home to bed.'

Molly stared at her friend in concern. 'You're not getting ill again, are you?'

'I don't think so. Perhaps I've just got a cold coming on. There's a lot of it about.'

'Maybe,' Molly replied, her eyes narrowing, remembering what the doctor had told Elyse.

Elyse sighed. 'I'll have a large Scotch. That'll buck me up.'

'Are you sure?'

'Of course I'm sure. I won't be staying long, though. I just popped in to tell you something.'

'Oh?'

Elyse recounted the story of the mysterious letter she'd received.

'And you've no idea what it's about?'

'None at all. I'm completely in the dark. I can't help feeling, though, that it must be bad news of some sort.'

'And why should it be that?' Molly frowned, pouring Elyse's whisky.

'Because it's from a solicitor, I suppose. You only go to them in times of trouble.'

'Not necessarily,' Molly responded. 'I wouldn't say that at all.'

'Well, I would.'

'Have you made the appointment yet?'

Elyse shook her head. 'To be honest, I'm rather reluctant to do so. I've been putting it off for days now.'

'Well, I think you should make it as soon as possible,' Molly counselled. 'I certainly would. It might be something to your advantage.'

Elyse laughed. 'I doubt that. Pigs will fly first.'

She had a sip of Scotch, closing her eyes briefly as it slid down her throat. She was right – it did make her feel better.

'Well, it has to be about something!' Molly declared.

Elyse knew she'd eventually have to pay this Mr Kempinski a visit. If nothing else, her natural curiosity would compel her to.

But she didn't like the prospect one little bit.

'I find it all so difficult,' Paul Greville grumbled to Tim as they left the lecture room. 'The theory of aileron control, hundred-horse Mono, Pitot tubes – where does it all end?'

Tim gazed at his friend in sympathy, all too aware of how

much of a struggle it was for Paul. 'You'll just have to stick with it, that's all. You'll get there in the end.'

Paul pulled a face. 'It's all right for you to speak. You find it easy.'

True enough, Tim reflected. The lectures were meat and drink to him. He seemed just to soak up what they were being taught. 'You know I'll help you as much as I can,' he offered.

'Thanks, I appreciate that. You're a pal.'

'Look!' Tim suddenly exclaimed, pointing skywards. 'It's the Nieuport that arrived yesterday. I wonder who's putting her through her paces?'

They watched as the pilot did a loop followed by a roll. Then he stood the machine on its head and dived, only pulling out of the dive at the last moment. Whoever it was, he certainly knew how to fly. Tim stared enviously, wishing it was him up there.

'It's got a ceiling of fifteen thousand feet and is as nifty as they come. We're having great success with it at the Front, I understand,' he informed Paul.

When the plane landed they discovered that Sergeant Iveson had been at the controls.

Later Tim spent some time with Paul trying to explain some of the things he was having trouble understanding.

'Ah, Mrs Davenport, delighted to meet you!' Kempinski beamed as Elyse entered his office.

The man was obviously Jewish, Elyse noted. Add a suitable wig and make-up and he had a wonderful face for Shylock. She'd have cast him any day.

Kempinski shook her by the hand. 'Will you please take a seat.'

'Thank you.'

The solicitor sat down facing her across his desk. 'You must be wondering why I've asked you here?'

She nodded, horribly aware of how apprehensive and nervous she was, having convinced herself it had to mean bad news. As she'd thought, it was her curiosity that had finally prompted her into making the appointment.

Kempinski made a pyramid with his hands while he studied Elyse. 'The first bit is difficult,' he stated slowly.

She found herself holding her breath. This was awful.

'Did you know that your estranged husband is dead?'

Elyse stared blankly at the solicitor. 'I beg your pardon?'

'Your husband, Mrs Davenport, was killed some while back in a motor-car accident.'

'Benny?'

'Killed along with a companion. Both died instantly, I'm led to believe.'

For a moment Elyse thought she was going to faint. No matter how it had ended, they'd been married and she'd loved him once.

Seeing her stricken look, Kempinski was instantly on his feet and round his desk to stand beside her. 'Can I get you something? A glass of water perhaps?'

'I didn't know,' she croaked.

'I wasn't sure. Some of the newspapers did carry the story, but only in a small way.'

Benny dead? She simply couldn't take it in. 'Do you have anything stronger than water?' she asked in a cracked voice.

Kempinski always kept alcohol in his office, it being surprising the number of times it was needed or requested. 'I have sherry and a single malt whisky.'

'The whisky, please.'

Elyse ran a hand over her brow while Kempinski attended to her drink. She remembered Benny the last time she'd seen him. He and that woman getting out of a car.

'Was the companion female?' she queried as Kempinski handed her the drink.

'Yes. Mrs Villiers, a client of mine.'

'A widow?'

'That's correct. She and your husband were – again I apologise if you didn't know – cohabiting.'

'Yes, I did,' she admitted. 'What I didn't know was the woman's name. Only that she was a widow and rich.' Elyse shook her head. 'I'm sorry, but all this is rather a shock.'

'Of course. I understand.'

She took a swallow of whisky. 'Do you mind if I smoke?'

'Not at all. Please go ahead.' He fetched an ashtray and placed it on the desk in front of her.

Elyse noted that her hands were shaking as she lit up. Benny dead? She still couldn't believe it.

'So what has Benny's death got to do with you, Mr Kempinski?' she eventually inquired.

'It was I who drew up his will.'

'His will!' Again Elyse shook her head. 'What would Benny want a will for? He had nothing to leave anyone.'

'Quite the contrary,' Kempinski corrected her. 'There are personal items, plus a sum of money. All to come to you, as his sole beneficiary.'

Another revelation. 'Where would Benny get money from? He was an actor, living from job to job, as we all do. I've never known him have any spare money to put in a bank. What he earned he more or less drank, and that's the truth of it.'

'I can only think Mrs Villiers must have been quite generous with him. I know from personal experience that she had
quite a generous nature. Especially with those she was fond
of.'

Elyse smiled wryly, recalling only too well how good
Benny had been in bed when he wanted to be. No wonder
Mrs Villiers had been fond of him.

'I still find it incredible that he made a will,' Elyse stated.
'He wasn't the kind even to think of that.'

Now it was Kempinski's turn to smile. 'Let me explain.
Mrs Villiers often consulted me on business and other
matters. In fact she was a regular visitor to my office. It was
on one such occasion, your husband being with her, that
she suddenly asked him if he had made a will. When he
said he hadn't, she insisted – she was a very forceful woman,
believe me – that he had one drawn up there and then,
which I know he found rather amusing. Nevertheless, he
complied with her wish, staying on with me while Mrs
Villiers went shopping. She insisted that he acted alone on
such a personal matter.

'And I'm the sole beneficiary?' Elyse queried.

'Your husband said there was no-one else to leave anything
to. As I told you, he found it all highly amusing. Of course
it never entered his mind – and why should it have done,
after all? – that he had such a short while left to live.'

Elyse took a deep breath. 'So what exactly has been left
to me then?'

Kempinski opened a drawer in his desk to produce an
ebony jewel case. 'These are the personal items I mentioned,'
he declared, sliding the case over to Elyse.

It was a beautiful case, she thought. Far more tasteful

than anything Benny would have bought himself. Beautiful, and expensive.

'Bloody hell!' she exclaimed when she saw its contents. The gold fob-watch that she lifted out was exquisite, the back hallmarked. Next came a signet ring, also of hallmarked gold, the stone being one she didn't recognise. His cufflinks were gold, inset with diamonds. The last items were a matching set of shirt studs, each a single diamond mounted on gold.

She glanced across at Kempinski, who was studying her intently. 'It's all real, Mrs Davenport.'

'I'm aware of that. I know enough about stage jewellery to appreciate the genuine article when I come across it. How, eh . . .' She swallowed. 'How much do you think all this is worth?'

'To be honest, I've no idea. But a tidy sum, I should imagine. I can have them valued for you if you wish.'

'Please.' Then she had a thought. 'Could you also have them sold for me? I wouldn't know where to begin to do that and could easily be cheated.'

He nodded his approval. 'Leave them with me and that shall be done. I know just the firm.'

She replaced the items in the case, closed the lid again and pushed it back to Kempinski. 'Don't think ill of me for not keeping them for sentimental reasons but, apart from anything else, they must have been given to him by your Mrs Villiers.'

Kempinski flashed her a smile. 'What you're doing makes perfect sense to me. I shall ensure you get the best possible price.' The case disappeared back where it had come from. 'Now the cash sum,' he declared.

'How much?' she whispered.

'A little over eleven thousand pounds.'

'Eleven thou . . .' She sat back in her chair and gulped.

'Eleven thousand, three hundred and ninety-six pounds to be precise,' Kempinski qualified.

'That's a fortune,' she croaked. 'There must be some mistake. Has to be.'

'Happily not. Happily for you, that is. The amount is what was in the deceased's account when he died.'

Elyse finished off her whisky and held out the glass. 'Can I have another?'

'Of course.'

She was stunned beyond words. She was dreaming, she thought. This wasn't real. Couldn't be.

But it was.

'Holy bejesus!' Molly O'Malley exploded. 'You're joking?'

Elyse shook her head.

'Eleven thousand quid. 'Tis a king's ransom, girl. You're rich as Croesus.'

'Mr Kempinski is ever such a nice man,' Elyse went on. 'He's going to arrange a bank account for me and pay in the money. The eleven thousand, plus what he gets for the jewellery. He's taking care of everything.'

'And you thought it was bad news!' Molly laughed, delighted for her friend.

'Bad and good, don't forget. Benny is dead after all.'

Molly stopped laughing to stare at Elyse. 'He was a rotten swine, no matter what your feelings once were. You know that.'

'I wouldn't have wished him dead though. Never.'

Molly shrugged. 'Man proposes, God disposes, as they say. He is dead and that's all there is to it. And if you benefit as a result, then so much the better. It couldn't happen to a nicer or more deserving person, in my book.'

'Thank you,' Elyse smiled.

'Of course you know what this means, don't you?'

'What?'

'Remember the doctor's advice about leaving London for the peace and quiet of the countryside? Well this gives you the wherewithal to do just that.'

'So it does,' Elyse frowned. 'That hadn't crossed my mind.'

'You can buy yourself a nice little house somewhere and never have to worry about another penny. You're set up for life, so you are.'

Stop being an actress, leave the theatre? The very idea was appalling. Heresy!

'Your health is the most important thing after all,' Molly said softly.

She might not want to admit it, but Elyse knew that was true. 'I'll give it some thought,' she replied.

Knowing Elyse as she did, Molly wisely left it at that and didn't pursue the subject any further. Eleven thousand pounds, not to mention the gold and diamonds! She wished that would happen to her.

'So tell me more about this Mr Kempinski and what he said,' she urged, dying to hear every last detail.

Chapter 25

Sergeant Iveson cut the engine, then hoisted himself out of the cockpit and dropped to the ground. Having removed his goggles and helmet, he turned to Tim who was doing the same. 'Very good.'

'Thank you, sir.'

Tim was showing real promise, Iveson thought. The lad was a 'natural' if ever there was one. 'How do you feel about going solo?'

Those were the words Tim had been impatiently waiting to hear. 'I think I'm ready, sir.'

'I think so too. Now remember, take plenty of room to get off. Got that?'

Tim nodded. 'Yes, sir.'

'Get your tail well up before you do take off. Forty-five is when you start to climb, not before, and then stay at a steady fifty-five until you decide to land.'

'I understand, sir.'

'I hope you do, for I don't want you smashing the plane to bits. That would make me very angry.'

Tim smiled. Only the previous week another cadet had done just that. The stupid sod had been jammy to walk away alive from a total wreck.

'On you go then. And good luck.'

'Thank you, sir.'

Iveson turned and strolled away, not wanting to put pressure on Tim by remaining and watching. He'd be watching all right, but from a distance.

This was it, Tim thought, as he climbed back aboard. His heart was pounding and the roof of his mouth had gone dry. He mustn't let himself down, he thought, reaching for the body straps.

The first thing he did was take a deep breath. Then he began to run through the procedures in his mind, going over them several times before touching the controls.

The engine roared into life and then ever so slowly the plane began to move forwards.

Suddenly any nervousness he had vanished. Throttle full open, elevator forward. Speed? Thirty, now thirty-five. More speed. Gently ease back the stick. And . . . and . . . he was airborne.

Elation thrilled through him. What a fantastic feeling! At long last he was up there alone with the birds and angels.

Iveson vanished from view as Tim brought the plane round. Climb higher. Yes, that was it. Fifty-five now. That was where to stay.

Oh, the joy of it. The sheer blissful joy! The smell of fuel was strong in his nostrils as he continued on what would be only a brief flight.

How he wished it could have been longer. Alone as he was, he could have stayed up there all day. Flown a thousand miles, if he could have got that far. Just fly and keep on flying.

Don't get carried away, he warned himself. This was

neither the time nor place. A circle round the airfield was all that was required. But how he wished it could have been otherwise.

All too soon he was bringing the plane down again, concentrating like mad on trying to make a good landing. Mustn't muck that up. Mustn't.

There was a bump, and another, then a rumble followed by a second, and that was it. He and the Farman were back in one piece.

He was smiling with pleasure as he switched off. He didn't need Iveson telling him to know that he'd done well.

Elyse gasped for breath, her body racked with coughing. Would it never stop? If it didn't, she would surely choke.

And then it was over, leaving her limp, with tears streaming down her face. She sucked in lungful after lungful of air while holding on to a chest of drawers to steady herself.

That had been terrible. Absolutely terrible. By far the worst bout yet. Then she noticed the spots of blood on her handkerchief – dark, some almost black.

In that moment she made up her mind. Molly was right, her health was the most important thing. She had to do as the doctor had recommended. No matter if it meant leaving the theatre and completely changing her life. It simply had to be done. And now, thanks to Benny's money, she had the means to do it.

The blood, especially the black spots, frightened her. Staggering through to the kitchen, she poured herself a glass of water. It was matinée day too, which meant an afternoon performance as well as an evening one. She prayed that she had the strength to get through them, for she was damned if she was going to ask for an understudy to go on.

Now that her mind was made up she decided to speak to Alan West at the earliest opportunity.

'The worst thing about all this is how much I miss my fiancée,' Paul Greville said to Tim. The pair of them were having a drink to celebrate Tim's having gone solo.

Tim raised an eyebrow. 'You've never mentioned a fiancée before.'

Paul coloured slightly. 'No, I haven't. It just seemed a bit personal, that's all. I mean, I don't know all that much about you, either. We rarely talk about such things.'

'That's true,' Tim acknowledged. 'What's her name?'

'Fenella. We've been engaged for ages and had planned to get married next year.' His expression became morose. 'Fat chance of that now. I'll undoubtedly be in France by then.'

Tim was curious. 'What's she like?'

'A smashing girl. Blonde, willowy figure, has a lovely laugh. She and I get on like a house on fire. We're going to be very happy together. I couldn't find a girl more right for me.' He had a sip of beer. 'What about you. Do you have anyone?'

Tim immediately thought of Katherine, as he often did. Well, not as often as he had, but still often enough. 'There was someone once, but that's over now.'

'I'm sorry,' Tim commiserated.

'So am I.'

'Can I ask what happened?'

Tim's mouth twisted into a cynical smile. 'I don't think I was good enough for her. She went to London for the

Season – you know, coming out, that sort of thing – and met another chap whom she married. That's it.'

'Rotten luck, old boy,' Paul sympathised.

'Yes, it was rather.'

They were both silent for a few moments.

'Do you know what I've been thinking about recently?' Tim said.

'What?'

'A bit morbid really.' He glanced around to make sure they weren't being overheard. 'It's about women in general and this war.'

'Oh?'

'Once we're in France we could easily be killed. You only have to read the newspapers to appreciate that. Well . . .' He paused, then dropped his voice. 'I'd hate to die without having ever . . .' He gave a small, conspiratorial nod.

'You mean . . . ?'

'Exactly. It's something I can't get out of my mind.'

'I already have,' Paul whispered back.

'With Fenella?'

'Good heavens, no, there's never been any question of that until we're married. It was a maid at a chum's house actually.'

Tim wasn't quite sure what to say next. 'Was it good?'

Paul's face lit up. 'I'll say. She was no looker, mind you, rather a plain thing. But at the time I didn't care. All that mattered was that she was willing.'

Envy stirred in Tim. When would his turn come? 'How did it happen?'

Paul shrugged. 'I'd been aware of her occasionally giving me "the eye" during the week I was there. Then one night going up to bed, somewhat tipsy I have to admit, I ran into her in the corridor. We got chatting, and the next thing I knew we were in my room and that was that.'

'Was it only the once?' Tim queried.

Paul nodded. 'I was leaving the next day, unfortunately.'

Tim found himself thinking of Harry Nutbeam and that night in the pub when Harry had gone off with a girl. How long ago that seemed now. How very long ago. He wondered how Harry was and hoped he was all right.

'I could use something stronger than beer,' Tim declared. 'What about you?'

'No thanks. Spirits and I just don't get on.'

Envy and depression were both gnawing at Tim's insides as he made his way across to the bar. Paul's admission had somehow ruined the occasion for him.

'I just know you've done the right thing,' Molly declared to Elyse. 'But I am going to miss you.'

'And I'll miss you and Seamus. Not that I'll be gone for ever. I'll be back every so often to see people, shop, go to a play. And maybe you can come and visit me from time to time?'

'Of course I will. You can rely on that. But visit where? Have you decided?'

'Yes, I have,' Elyse replied slowly. 'I know the doctor recommended the country, but I rather fancy the seaside. Torquay to be precise.'

'Torquay! Where you were last in rep?'

'That's right. I did enjoy myself there. It's ever so relax-ing, with lots of sea air. And it's a town, don't forget, albeit a small one. I couldn't bear being stranded in a village. At least in a town I can get out and about. Have people round me, go to the shops. Stop and have a cup of coffee if I want.'

Molly nodded her approval. It sounded ideal to her.

'Alan West was most understanding when I told him,' Elyse went on. 'I swore him to secrecy before explaining. I felt I owed him that. He'll find a suitable replacement as soon as possible and I shall go when she is rehearsed in.'

Elyse dropped her gaze to stare at the table in front of her.

'I still can't believe I'm doing this. The theatre has been everything to me for so long. I can't imagine what it's going to be like without it.'

Molly patted her friend's hand. 'You'll get by, Elyse. You must just try and look at it as one door closing and another opening. And who knows what lies through the new door? To be sure, it could be the most wondrous thing.'

Elyse smiled bravely. 'Let's hope so.'

Molly's eyes filled with tears. ''Tis a sentimental lot we Irish are and no mistake. Here's me blubbing like a baba when I should be happy for you. And happy I am, 'tis just that you'll be sorely missed. Not only by Seamus and meself, but lots of others too.'

'As I said, Molly, I will be back from time to time. Wild horses couldn't keep me away.'

Elyse closed her eyes. She was gasping for a cigarette but was putting off having one. She'd coughed up black blood again that morning.

Tim stood staring proudly at himself in the mirror. His brand spanking new uniform had arrived earlier, for he was now commissioned, a second lieutenant in the Royal Flying

Corps. He didn't have his coveted wings yet, but that event was only a short way away. Sergeant Iveson had assured him of that.

For the present there was some leave coming up, which he was looking forward to. He'd been promised a whole fortnight, after which he was being transferred to Gosport to learn how to fly Avros and BE 2cs. There was even mention of being trained for a Nieuport. Now that would be something!

It was odd wearing a uniform, he reflected. It somehow changed him. Made him look older, for a start. More mature. And he needn't worry about the ladies with white feathers when he returned home. None of them would be accosting him now, which was a relief to say the least.

He came to attention and saluted his reflection. Then burst out laughing. 'Idiot!' he teased himself. 'Bloody idiot!'

It was a special moment he'd always remember.

'Well,' Minna declared, coming into the kitchen. 'You'll never guess who that was on the telephone.'

Cook glanced up from the pastry she was rolling. 'Who?'

'Do you remember Mrs Davenport, the actress?'

Cook nodded. 'Of course I do. She helped Tim when he had the influenza that time. Nice woman, quite liked her. Drank like a fish.'

'That's the one,' Minna smiled. 'She's coming back to stay with us for a while. Apparently she intends buying a house down here.'

That surprised Cook. 'Do you mean she's moving to Torquay? Whatever for?'

'I've no idea. She didn't say and I didn't like to ask. And

I agree, she is a nice woman, even if she does drink like a fish, as you put it.'

'When is she arriving?'

'Next Monday evening. She'll come here straight from the station.'

'Well, she'll add a bit of excitement to the place,' Cook commented. Then, with a chuckle, 'Major Sillitoe will be pleased. He thought she was wonderful and still occasionally mentions her, I believe.'

'So I understand,' Minna replied drily. 'Now, where's Daisy? I have a special job for her.'

'About somewhere.'

Well, that wasn't much of a help, Minna thought as she turned and hurried off in search of the girl. There was a load of ironing urgently needing doing.

Katherine flopped onto her cot and groaned. She'd just come off an eighteen-hour stint and wasn't even going to bother changing before going to sleep.

'You look awful,' Mary Allen, one of the five other VADs with whom she shared the bell tent, observed.

'I feel awful. Are you due on?'

'In about ten minutes.'

'Then good luck. Casualties have been pouring in. Truckloads of them.'

Mary shook her head in despair. The Casualty Clearing Station, or CCS as it was commonly known, that they were assigned to was only half a mile from the Front and was constantly busy. Before the war she'd never even seen a dead body: now she'd seen literally thousands. There wasn't a single day went by but some poor Tommy died on her. She still wasn't used to it and didn't think she ever would be.

A few moments later when Mary went to speak to Katherine again she found her fast asleep. She covered her with a blanket before leaving the tent.

Well, that was it, Elyse reflected. The last wellwisher had gone, the last goodbye been said, the last curtain call taken. All that was left now was to pack up and go home.

She poured herself a glass of champagne and lit a cigarette. The end of an era. When she left the theatre it would be to start a new life.

Elyse smiled in memory, remembering plays she'd been in, people she'd known and worked with, incidents that had occurred.

When later she walked past the now dark stage there was ghostly laughter and applause ringing in her ears.

'Hello, Ma. Surprise!'

Minna's jaw literally dropped open as she stared at Tim in disbelief. Then, with a shriek of joy, she flew across the kitchen and into his outstretched arms. Cook, Daisy and Euphemia all beamed, their delight only too evident.

'Hello, everyone,' Tim smiled at them. Daisy and Euphemia chorused a reply, while Cook had turned away to hide her tears.

Minna was close to tears herself. 'You should have let me know,' she gasped, scrutinising his face.

'I thought a surprise would be better.'

'You nearly gave me a heart attack there,' she admonished.

'Well, I wouldn't want to do that,' he teased, hugging her

again. 'It's good to be home, Ma,' he said softly.

'How long for?'

'A fortnight.'

She wished it was longer. 'We'll have to make the best of the time then,' she declared. 'Are you hungry?'

'Starving.'

'I'll see to that,' Cook declared, still with her back to them and wiping her face with the hem of her apron. She thought of Tim as almost her own.

'Now sit down and tell me everything,' Minna instructed, once more in control of herself.

Everyone listened intently as he recounted stories of life at Brooklands.

Tim was halfway up the stairs when he caught an unmistakable whiff of perfume. He stopped and frowned. Elyse? It couldn't be. Someone else must be wearing the same brand. It wasn't until later, when he happened to mention it to Minna, that he discovered that Elyse actually was staying at The Berkeley, and why.

'You look very smart in your uniform,' Elyse complimented Tim, who'd knocked on her bedroom door, Elyse having been out all day.

He grinned at her. 'Thank you.'

'Quite the man.'

That pleased him enormously. 'It's the uniform, it makes me appear older.'

'Oh, I think it's more than that. In fact I'm sure of it.' She made a dismissive gesture. 'I'd offer you a drink, but I'm afraid I don't have any here.'

'That's all right. I have to say, it's lovely seeing you again, Elyse. I've often thought of that night we had at Kean's. It was terrific fun.'

'Yes,' she agreed. 'It was.'

'Perhaps we can go out again while I'm back?'

'I'd like that.'

'Good. Give me a few days to settle in and then we'll arrange it.' He was thinking how gorgeous she looked, if slightly pale. He put that down to having been in London. A few weeks in Torquay would soon put the colour back into her cheeks.

'Ma says you intend living here?'

Elyse sat on the edge of the bed. 'That's right. I'm trying to find a house to buy.'

He frowned. 'And you're giving up the theatre?'

'Right again,' she smiled. She'd tell him the same story she'd given Minna, which was the truth, if not all of it. The real reason – because of her health – was strictly her own business. 'I came into money, quite a lot actually, and decided to retire. Why work when I don't have to, after all? I suppose I just got tired of everything, the uncertainty of the profession, and opted for a life of ease. So there you have it.'

Tim shook his head in wonder. Elyse had been such a dedicated actress, so committed and enthusiastic. This was certainly a turn-up for the books.

She laughed. 'Anyway, if I get too bored I can always go back to it.' That was a lie, but he wasn't to know that. She'd merely added the rider to make her story sound more plausible.

'Of course.'

'That's the plan anyway.'

'I, eh . . . I'd better go,' he said, recalling the time. 'I want to go round a few of the pubs and see if I can meet up with some of my old pals. If there are any to be found, that is.'

'You enjoy yourself then.'

'I'll try.'

'Probably see you tomorrow.'

He nodded.

'And Tim . . . you do look smart. Very dashing.'

He coloured slightly. 'Tomorrow then.'

'Tomorrow.'

He closed her door behind him, inordinately pleased to have seen her again.

It was the same, yet different, Tim thought, gazing round the newspaper office, having decided to pay a visit. Then he realised why it was different. Apart from Patsy and Ricketts, they were all women. He could guess the reason for that.

'I hope you don't mind me dropping by?' he queried on arriving at the editor's desk.

Ricketts stared at Tim, seeing the change in him. 'You look well, Wilson.'

'Thank you, sir.'

'Very well indeed. How's the flying going?'

'I'm thoroughly enjoying it.'

'Been to France yet?'

'Not yet. I still haven't got my wings. But I should think I'd be off shortly after that.'

Patsy came bustling up, face wreathed in a huge smile. 'Tim! How the hell are you?'

They shook hands. 'Absolutely tiptop. And you?'

'Never better. Overworked and underpaid, mind you, but what else is new?'

They both laughed. It was an old cry.

Ricketts dug in his pocket to produce a crumpled ten-shilling note, which he laid in front of Tim. 'Why don't you have an early lunch, Patsy.' He indicated the money. 'Have a drink on me, Wilson.'

Tim was astounded. Ricketts buying him a drink! Wonders would never cease.

'Thank you, sir. I will.'

'Let's get to it then,' Patsy declared enthusiastically, hooking an arm round one of Tim's.

'Oh, Wilson,' Ricketts said softly as they were turning away.

'Yes, sir?'

'I hope to see you again next time you're home.'

A chill ran through Tim, for he knew exactly what Ricketts meant. That he hoped Tim did come home again.

'So, what do you think?' Elyse demanded. She'd been telling Tim earlier about the cottage she'd found and then insisted that he see it and give her his opinion.

'It's very nice, Elyse. Or could be, rather. There's an awful lot needs doing.'

'I appreciate that, which in a way is why I'm so keen. I've never owned a property before, always rented. This gives me the chance to do it up exactly as I choose.'

'In that case I like it,' he nodded.

'It's small, I admit. But then I don't need anything bigger. Also it has a garden, which is something I've always wanted.'

He laughed. 'I can't imagine you as a gardener somehow.'

'I can learn,' she pouted. 'Anyway, it will give me something to do.'

Just then the room they were in was flooded with light as the sun broke through what until then had been an overcast day.

'I do believe I'm already in love with the place,' Elyse declared, much to Tim's amusement.

'It's for you,' Minna said, holding out the telephone receiver to Tim. 'Someone from Brooklands. I didn't get his name.'

A frowning Tim took the receiver. 'Hello?'

'Is that you, Tim?'

'Speaking.'

'It's Paul, Paul Greville. I've got great news. I did my first solo today and will soon be joining you at Gosport. How about that, eh?'

Tim laughed. 'Congratulations. I'll look forward to seeing you there.'

'The solo went well. Bit of a bumpy landing, mind you. I did bounce a few times. But I got down safely in the end.'

Tim could just visualise the landing. A dicey old business, no doubt. But Paul had done it and that was all that mattered.

They chatted for a couple more minutes before Tim hung up.

At least he'd have a friend at Gosport, he thought. That pleased him.

'Cheer up, you've got a face as long as my arm.'

Tim grinned sheepishly. 'Sorry, I was just thinking about the day after tomorrow, that's all.'

Elyse nodded her sympathy, for that was when Tim was leaving for Gosport. 'Time does fly when you're enjoying yourself,' she joked.

They were in The Imperial, where they had almost finished dinner. Gazing round, Tim recalled the last time he'd been here, with Katherine. He hastily put that from his mind.

They had a brandy after the pudding, then another. It was the third occasion that Tim had taken Elyse out since arriving back, each one having been thoroughly enjoyable and great fun into the bargain.

Outside again, Tim glanced up at the sky. 'Look at that!' he said, pointing.

'I can't see anything.'

'There isn't a single star in the sky – no moon, either. Just a black velvet canopy stretching from horizon to horizon.'

Elyse stared in astonishment. 'I've never seen that before. It's spooky.'

Tim agreed with her. It was. He couldn't recall seeing a night sky like it either.

When they reached The Berkeley Tim let them in and they both went upstairs.

'Thank you for a lovely evening,' Elyse said on reaching her door.

'Thank *you*.'

Her eyes suddenly narrowed as she stared at him and her nostrils dilated ever so slightly. Tim found himself holding his breath, aware of how the atmosphere had changed between them – become charged.

'You can kiss me goodnight if you wish,' she said levelly.

He pecked her on the cheek.

'I said kiss, Tim.'

She flowed into his arms and their mouths met, her tongue a living snake twisting and entwining with his. He'd never known a kiss like it.

On and on it went, until finally Elyse pulled her face away and smiled radiantly at him. Next second she was gone, the door snicking shut behind her.

He was in a daze as he continued along the corridor.

Chapter 26

Tim sighed and laid aside the obituary that Minna had cut from the *Torquay Times*. Harry Nutbeam, dear old Harry, was dead, killed in action at Ypres. The obit had mentioned that Harry had been a former, and much-valued, reporter on the newspaper.

Another one gone, he thought in despair. How many more before this insane war was over? It was summer 1917 and he'd been in France for over a year now, the sole survivor in his squadron of all those who'd been there when he'd arrived fresh from Gosport.

He smiled, recalling Paul Greville, who'd turned up a month after him. Poor Paul, never had been much of a flyer. He hadn't even lasted a day, shot down on his very first patrol.

Harry Nutbeam, who'd convinced him to join the RFC by telling Tim how much safer and easier it was than being in the army or navy. A single observation flight every morning, then home to tea and crumpets.

Well, that had been true once, but certainly not for a long time now. The old chivalry had vanished too. Now it was dog eat dog, no quarter asked or given. Once you were in the air, it was kill or be killed. Vicious.

He closed his eyes, trying to recall all the dead faces. So many, hundreds of them. There were names he could no longer put a face to, and faces he could no longer put a name to.

All young men in their prime, singing their hearts out when they got here, thinking it was all going to be great fun, a superior game of cricket or rugger. Well, as they soon found out, it was no game, but deadly serious, with a grave inevitably at the end of it.

'Are you all right, Mr Wilson?'

Tim brought himself out of his reverie to stare at Sergeant Smallbone, his batman. 'I beg your pardon?'

'I said are you all right, sir?'

Tim nodded. He was so tired, so very tired. In spirit as well as body. If only the nightmares would go away. The terrible, incessant nightmares. He'd died a thousand times and more in those.

Smallbone lifted the bottle of Scotch from the table beside Tim and poured some into a glass. He'd long since stopped being amazed at how much many of the officers drank, especially the experienced ones. They seemed to live on it. And no wonder, considering that every flight might be their last. It was all down to maintaining their nerve and not cracking up.

'Get that down you, sir.'

Tim took the glass and emptied it. 'Another.'

Smallbone poured without comment. 'Are you ready for breakfast, sir?'

'Please. What can you tempt me with today?'

'A fresh egg, sir. Straight from the nest. Collected it myself earlier.'

'Jolly good. Lightly boiled as usual. Can't stand them overdone, as you know.'

'Of course, sir.'

'And what about jam, is there any jam yet? It's been over a week now since we ran out.'

'No jam, sir, but I do have marmalade. An entire pot.'

'Excellent!' Tim enthused. 'Where did you get that from?'

Smallbone coughed. 'Don't ask, sir.'

'I see.'

'I'll get on with that egg, sir.'

Major Brown, Tim's immediate superior, appeared. Before the war he'd been a lecturer in philosophy at Cambridge, a mild-mannered, soft-spoken man who'd certainly never have stood out in a crowd. He had nineteen kills to his credit and was deadly in the air. An ace.

'How are you this morning, Wilson?' he queried cheerfully.

'Fine, sir. Tiptop. And you?'

'The same.'

Brown sat down and lit up a cigarette. He smoked cigarettes during the day, a pipe at night.

'Smallbone has managed to get hold of some marmalade,' Tim informed him.

'Oh, I say, that's wonderful. I much prefer marmalade to jam myself.'

'I like either.'

'My mother used to make her own marmalade,' Brown went on. 'Runny stuff, could never get it to set properly. Tasted wonderful all the same.' He indicated the bottle. 'Mind if I join you?'

'Help yourself, sir.'

Brown got up and did just that. 'The weather seemed a

bit threatening when I looked outside. I think there's a storm on the way.'

'Good news if there is, sir. I could use a day off.'

Brown laughed, knowing that wasn't what Tim really meant. If the squadron was grounded then there was no flying, no dicing with death. 'Yes,' he agreed, 'that would be rather pleasant.'

Tim glanced at the obituary Minna had sent him. Harry Nutbeam, a good friend and great sport. Gone west, as they said.

Gone west.

Smallbone marched into the room, their headquarters being located in what had been a deserted farmhouse, and saluted. 'Replacements from the pool, sir.'

Brown didn't bother saluting in reply. 'Let's see them then,' he declared, coming to his feet.

'First-rate egg,' Tim complimented Smallbone.

'Thank you, sir.'

'And boiled just right. Spot on.'

'Thank you again, sir.'

They all made their way outside as a lorry drew up. The replacements always sang, Tim reflected. This time it was 'It's A Long Way to Tipperary'.

'Commanding officer present,' Smallbone barked as the replacements jumped from the rear of the lorry. They immediately fell quiet.

Three, Tim counted. Brown had requested five. That meant that, yet again, they were under-strength.

'I'm Major Brown and this is Captain Wilson,' Brown declared affably.

Boys, mere boys, Tim noted grimly. They just got younger and younger. This lot should still have been in short trousers.

The three replacements snapped to attention and saluted, all three clearly keen as mustard.

'Names?' Brown asked.

'Jenkins, sir.'

'How many hours?'

'Eight, sir.'

Tim groaned inwardly. A lamb to the slaughter.

'Smedley-Pratt, sir. Twelve hours.'

A little better, Tim thought.

'Stamp, sir. Six hours.'

Tim stared at the last lad. Sending him was criminal, but no matter how often Brown complained, the answer was always the same. They were being allocated the best available.

'Have you had breakfast?' Brown inquired.

'Yes, sir,' the three chorused in reply.

'Good.' He glanced at his wristwatch. 'You'll be taking off in about forty minutes. Come inside and meet the rest of the chaps, they're a friendly bunch.'

'Good luck, Wilson.'

'Thank you, sir.'

Brown clutched Tim's arm. 'I wish I was coming with you. You do know that?'

Tim stared into Brown's eyes and saw the most terrible anguish there. As officer in command, he wasn't allowed to fly with the squadron, something that went completely against Brown's temperament and character. He was the sort of man who'd much rather have been up there with them, at the sharp end.

'I know that, sir.'

'Bloody orders.'

'Yes, sir.'

Tim climbed aboard his Sopwith F1 Camel, the very latest fighter, which was proving an incredible success, thinking that Brown said the same thing at least once a week. From what Smallbone had told him, Brown would now pace endlessly up and down his office until they returned.

Those who did return, that was.

'Jeremiah?'

He looked up from his newspaper and frowned. What now?

Ruth gave him a thin, twitchy smile. 'Is there someone else? I'd like to know if there is.'

It was one of Jeremiah's infrequent visits to Oaklands. He only occasionally made the journey down from London, for appearances' sake. He felt he owed Ruth that much.

'Don't be ridiculous,' he snapped. 'I've never heard such nonsense.'

Her eyes were glinting as she studied him intently, trying to work out whether or not he was telling the truth. But Jeremiah's expression gave nothing away.

'It's just that you come home so rarely nowadays. That was never my intention when I suggested you stay in London. Several weeks there, then several weeks back here was what I thought it was going to be.'

Even her voice annoyed him now, he reflected. There was a whine to it that got under his skin. 'We're at war, dear, don't forget that. I'm only doing my bit for King and Country, same as everyone else.'

'Even so. There is me to consider after all.'

Another day to go, he groaned inwardly. His time here seemed interminable. A lot of it was spent trying to keep out of Ruth's company.

'The war takes precedence over us all, dear. You must try and remember that. What I'm doing is of the utmost importance. The utmost.'

Ruth sighed. 'I get so lonely, Jeremiah. It was bad enough some years ago when you travelled a great deal, but now . . . I hardly ever see you, and then only fleetingly.'

'It's a cross for me to bear as well,' he lied.

She was still as thin as ever, he thought. Pitifully so. Which might improve if she ate more. He knew from quizzing the staff that her health had improved greatly, and according to them she was almost never ill of late. That only bore out what Henrietta had guessed about her – that the majority of her illnesses had been a sham.

In a way he pitied her and couldn't even begin to imagine what went through her mind. It was obvious now that sex might have been the root of it all. Not wanting to have sex with him. Putting him off again and again, until eventually he'd rarely suggested it. And when she had indulged, what a lacklustre performance! No enthusiasm whatsoever, no eagerness. No enjoyment.

How different it was with Henrietta. For the umpteenth time he thanked God for meeting her. She'd brought colour back into a life completely devoid of it.

'I thought I might come to London soon and do some shopping,' Ruth declared.

That alarmed him. 'What sort of shopping?'

'Clothes mainly. I desperately need a new wardrobe.'

'You'd be wasting your time,' he replied dismissively.

'And why's that?'

'There's nothing stylish to be found any more. That's if you can find anything at all. Everything's scarce, including clothes. All needed for the war effort. Take my word for it.'

'I find that hard to believe.'

'Well, it's true,' he snapped. 'You'd be completely disappointed. Besides, you're safe here. The Germans have taken to bombing London. It's been in the newspapers, if you'd bothered to read them. I'm sure you don't want to be blown up.'

She had read that, Ruth reflected. But she hadn't thought it serious enough for her to stay away from the capital.

'So let's leave things as they are for the moment,' Jeremiah said, his tone one of finality.

He laid his newspaper aside and stood up. 'I'm going for a walk before lunch. Work up an appetite.'

Without waiting for a reply he strode purposefully from the room.

Christ! Where had that come from? Tim thought, as ack-ack opened up. All around him 'Archies' were peppering the sky. A damned heavy barrage too.

They'd been over the exact same spot yesterday and there hadn't been any anti-aircraft batteries. They must have been brought up since.

He swivelled round in the cockpit, visually checking the other planes in the flight, some of which were being buffeted by close explosions.

He saw Smedley-Pratt get hit, his entire tail section

disappearing into a puff of fragments. He watched helplessly as the Camel plummeted earthwards.

Moments to go and they'd be safe, he told himself. Next thing there was a thump and his plane yawed violently. Instantly he knew he'd been hit, but how badly? His controls were now horrendously sluggish, hardly responding at all. But, as far as he could make out, the Camel was still in one piece.

He gestured to the rest of the flight that he'd been hit and was turning back. It was a struggle, but somehow he brought the plane round in a semi-circle and headed home.

He could only wonder grimly if he'd make it. In a peculiar way he didn't really care whether he did or not.

Tim brought the Camel down and taxied to a halt. He switched off and immediately slumped over the controls, horribly aware that he was shaking from head to toe.

When he managed to look up Brown and some mechanics were racing towards him. Pull yourself together, he told himself. Pull yourself together.

Brown was the first to reach him and climbed up on the lower wing. 'Are you all right, old boy?'

Tim gave the semblance of a smile. 'Spot of bad luck. Copped a bit of "Archie". Damned nuisance.'

Brown had often played this game himself. Brave face, stiff upper lip and all that. Despite the pretence he could see how shaken Tim was. 'Here,' he said and produced a silver hip flask, which he never went anywhere without. 'Take a swig of that.'

Tim had a large swallow, then another. He was pleased that somehow his shaking had stopped. 'Thank you, sir,' he declared, returning the flask.

'You'd better come on in and tell me all about it.'

'I saw Smedley-Pratt go down, sir. Lost his tail to "Archie".'

Brown seemed suddenly to lose his temper. 'But there isn't any ack-ack where you were going! You must have been off course,' he almost snarled.

'No, sir,' Tim replied levelly. 'We were not. The batteries must have been brought up since yesterday.'

The two men stared at one another, then Brown's shoulders slumped. 'Damn,' he swore and took a gulp of whisky himself. 'I'd better phone through to General HQ and inform them.'

'Yes, sir.'

The pair of them returned to the farmhouse, and Brown's office, in silence. Smedley-Pratt had been just eighteen, no age at all.

Elyse paused outside the Pavilion to stare at the entranceway. Not once since returning to Torquay had she visited it, or seen a production. To begin with she'd had every intention of going, but had found herself putting it off again and again. Then it had finally dawned on her that she simply didn't want to go.

Her theatrical career was over, finished. To go and watch other actors would merely be rubbing salt into a still open wound. She'd hate it, wanting to be up there onstage with them, yet at the same time knowing she'd never tread the boards again. To have gone would have been sheer and utter torture.

A lump rose in her throat. How desperately she missed it all. Everything, even the bad bits. Never again would she put on slap, glue a wig into place, know first-night nerves, bask in applause. All that was now lost to her. In the past. Gone for ever.

The lump was still in her throat, and remained there for some while, as she went on her way.

Tim was deep in thought as he walked down the hospital corridor having just been to see the young lad Stamp, who'd had a foot amputated, the result of it being riddled with gunfire during a dogfight.

Lucky little sod, Tim thought. Stamp was now out of it, the war was over for him. The jammy blighter. He envied Stamp with all his heart.

'Tim?'

He blinked and turned towards the female voice that had addressed him. A nurse, he now saw, whose face was vaguely familiar.

'It is Tim Wilson, isn't it?'

He nodded.

She smiled. 'You don't remember me, do you?'

'I'm afraid not,' he apologised. 'There is some vague memory, but I can't put my finger on it.'

'Don't worry, I'm not offended. It was a long time ago and we only met a couple of times. I'm Louise Youthed, Ka's friend.'

Recognition dawned. She'd slimmed down considerably from the plump girl he recalled. 'Of course. I have to say you do look quite different in a nurse's uniform,' he replied tactfully.

'I'm not exactly a nurse,' she explained. 'But a VAD. That stands for Voluntary Aid Detachment. We help the nurses.

And *I* have to say how very dashing you look in *your* uniform. A captain too, I see.'

'You're working here, I take it?' he queried.

'Have been for the last six months. I became a VAD shortly after I heard Katherine had become one. I know she too is in France, but so far I haven't run into her.'

Katherine in France? That stunned him. 'I thought she was married, and imagined she'd have a brood of children by now.'

'You haven't heard then?' Louise queried softly.

'Heard what?'

She took a deep breath. 'Listen, Tim, I'm on a break and was on my way for coffee. Would you care to join me?'

What news hadn't he heard? It seemed that he was about to find out.

'Killed at Mons?' Tim repeated dully.

'Right at the beginning of the war. They were only married a short time before it happened.'

'Poor Katherine,' Tim mumbled, feeling desperately sorry for her. 'Are there any children?'

'No. None.'

He tried to digest this information, which came as quite a revelation. Any bitterness he'd once felt had long since evaporated. He wouldn't have wished any ill on either Katherine or her husband. 'I had no idea,' he stated quietly. 'None whatever. I knew she'd married of course, but that's all.'

Louise shook her head in wonder. 'Imagine bumping into you like this!' Her face suddenly clouded. 'You haven't been wounded, have you? I mean, this is a hospital after all.'

Tim laughed. 'No wound. Not even a scratch. I'm here to visit someone. One of my pilots, who's lost a foot. I should be flying, but we've been closed in by fog and general bad weather for days now. So I took the opportunity to hitch a lift and come here to see Stamp. That's the pilot. Young lad, I only hope . . .' He stopped himself going any further, having been about to say that he hoped Stamp knew how lucky he was.

'Hope what, Tim?'

He shook his head. 'Nothing really.'

'Do you mind if I smoke?'

That surprised him. 'I didn't know you did.'

'Ah well,' she sighed. 'Blame the job. I took up smoking because I suppose there's some comfort in it.'

He could well understand that. Didn't he drink to excess for more or less the same reason?

'How long have you been out here?' Louise asked.

'Over a year now.'

She stared at him, knowing only too well the high mortality rate among pilots. 'You've done well,' she acknowledged. 'You must be good.'

He shrugged. 'Fortunate, more like.'

She didn't believe a word of that. 'Where exactly are you based?'

They continued talking for another ten minutes, then Louise announced that she had to get back on duty, otherwise Matron would read her the riot act. 'She's the battleaxe to end all battleaxes,' Louise confided to Tim and they both laughed. 'It was lovely bumping into you,' she said as they were about to go their separate ways.

'And you. Thank you for telling me about Katherine.

Should the pair of you ever meet up, give her my regards.'

'I'll do that. You can rely on it.'

'Goodbye, Louise.'

'Goodbye, Tim. Stay fortunate, as you put it.'

'I'll try.'

On a sudden impulse she kissed him on the cheek, then hurried swiftly away.

Tim touched the spot she'd kissed, appreciative of the gesture. He'd almost forgotten what a kiss was like.

'Mrs Crabthorne!' Henrietta exclaimed in surprise, having been wondering who was knocking on the door at this time of night, as it was almost eleven o'clock.

'Can I come in?'

Henrietta immediately stepped aside. 'Of course. Please do.'

Katherine hadn't instantly recognised the housekeeper, who was wearing make-up and had her hair down round her shoulders. She'd never seen Henrietta wear make-up before or realised how pretty the woman was, having until then thought her quite plain. She also noted that Henrietta had on what appeared to be a very expensive housecoat, something that might well have come from Bond Street.

As Katherine moved into the hallway Jeremiah appeared at the top of the stairs tying his dressing gown.

'Who is it . . . ?' He stopped in amazement when he saw her. 'Katherine! What are you doing here?'

'I've come to stay for a few days, if that's all right?'

'Certainly it's all right.' He came quickly down the stairs and took her into his arms. 'How wonderful.'

'I hope I didn't get you out of bed.'

'Not really. I'd just gone up.'

His eyes sought Henrietta's. This had caught them completely on the hop. They'd been in bed together.

'There's a small suitcase outside,' Katherine explained.

'Let me,' said Henrietta.

Jeremiah escorted Katherine through to the drawing room. 'You must be freezing, it's bitter out there. Are you hungry?'

'I could eat something.'

Henrietta joined them, her gaze sweeping the room for telltale signs that they'd spent the evening together. Brushing past, she picked up two brandy glasses and put them away, but not before Katherine had noted what she'd done.

'So let me see you properly,' Jeremiah declared, holding Katherine at arm's length. 'You look tired.'

'Well, it is late and it has been a long journey. I should have been here hours ago but my train was delayed.'

With a shock Katherine spotted a small smudge of lipstick on her father's neck. What was going on?

'How about a drink to warm you up?' Jeremiah suggested. 'I have a rather splendid bottle of vintage port open.'

'To be honest, I'd prefer hot chocolate if you have any.'

'We do indeed, Mrs Crabthorne,' Henrietta stated. 'Would you also care for a slice of ham and some scrambled egg?'

'Perfect. Thank you.'

Not just pretty but rather beautiful, Katherine mused. It was quite a transformation from the plain-faced woman she recalled. And how had Mrs Webb been able to afford a housecoat like that on a housekeeper's wages? She was right, there was definitely something going on.

'A few days, you say?' Jeremiah queried, ushering her towards a chair.

'Yes, I'm over here to collect a party of VADs from the hospital and take them to France. It's common practice for an experienced VAD to do that, and this time it's my turn. I'm able to answer a lot of the questions they invariably have, which makes them more prepared for what they're actually going to find when they get there.'

'I see,' Jeremiah murmured. That made sense. 'Pity it's not longer.'

Her father was different, Katherine thought. More relaxed in his manner. Yes, that was it. More at ease than she remembered in the past. Less stiff somehow.

'And how is it "over there"?' Jeremiah asked softly.

'Pretty awful, Papa. But if you don't mind I'd rather not talk about it.'

His expression became grim. 'That bad, eh?'

She nodded.

'Any regrets?'

'No. None whatsoever. I did the right thing. I know that.'

Jeremiah exhaled slowly, his gaze fixed intently on Katherine. 'It's so good to see you again. I can't tell you how good. Or how much I worry about you.'

She smiled at the love and caring in his voice. Dear old Papa. Different in some ways perhaps, but the same in others.

They were interrupted at that point by Henrietta returning with a steaming cup of chocolate. The housekeeper had pinned her hair up, Katherine observed. And changed into an old housecoat more in keeping with her position.

'Here you are, Mrs Crabthorne. This'll warm the cockles,' Henrietta declared cheerily.

'Thank you.'

For the briefest of moments there was a look in Jeremiah's eyes as Mrs Webb went past him that sent a chill through Katherine. She knew then with utter certainty where the smudge of lipstick had come from.

Her father and his housekeeper were having an affair.

Chapter 27

Tim banked his Camel and headed home, his observation mission complete. It was his fourth flight of the day and he was bone-weary.

Just north of Thiepval he noticed a long, creeping wraith of yellow mist winding its way along, and through, the trenches below. He went cold all over, knowing it to be poison gas.

Men, British Tommies, were desperately trying to put on their masks. Others, whom the gas had already caught, were twisting and turning in their death throes. One chap, clutching his throat, was running wildly out of control, only to collapse headlong into the mud at the bottom of the trench he was in.

Another man was dancing grotesquely on the spot while madly flailing his arms. Beside him yet another was clearly vomiting bright-crimson blood.

'Dear God in heaven,' Tim muttered as the gas and the trenches fell behind him. There were hundreds of Tommies down there, perhaps thousands, many of them already dead or dying. It had been a sickening sight.

Bile rose in his throat, which he swallowed back. What a terrible way to go. He'd heard it was an excruciating death

– sheer agony while the gas burnt and seared your throat. Nor was it a quick end, for it could take some while before welcoming oblivion came.

When would this insanity end? he asked himself for the umpteenth time. It seemed to be going on for ever, and in the meantime daily horrors like the one he'd just witnessed were being perpetrated by both sides.

He pulled the stick back and started to climb. Up and up he went until he reached the plane's ceiling of 19,000 feet, where he levelled out.

He sucked in breath after breath of clean, sweet air. Up here above the clouds he could have a short respite from what was happening below. Get away from it all. Experience sublime peace.

All too soon he had to drop down again, back to the ongoing nightmare.

'I wish I had time to visit Mama before I return to France,' Katherine said to Jeremiah during lunch. 'But of course that's impossible.'

He didn't reply to that but continued eating.

'It does worry me how ill she's been.'

Jeremiah's fork stopped halfway to his mouth. 'Ill?'

'For months and months now. She mentions it in every letter she writes.'

Jeremiah was frowning. 'Your mother hasn't been ill, I know that for fact. I was down at Oaklands a few weeks ago and the staff told me she's been right as rain. Quite chipper, one of them said.'

It was Katherine's turn to frown. 'So why would she write to the contrary?'

Jeremiah dropped his gaze, torn by indecision. Then, abruptly, he made up his mind. He couldn't have Katherine over in France worrying about her mother when she needn't.

'I can't say why your mother's been doing that in particular,' he stated slowly, staring Katherine straight in the eye. 'But I'm afraid her many illnesses over the years have been something of a sham.'

Katherine went white. 'Are you telling me she's been lying?'

'So it would appear,' Jeremiah replied reluctantly. 'I can assure you, the staff at Oaklands were insistent that she's been in fine fettle, apart from a summer cold last July, I understand.'

Katherine's mind flew back to the conversation she'd had with Ruth after Miles had proposed – the very reason she'd agreed to marry him. 'Are you absolutely certain about this, Papa?'

'Yes, I am.'

'But why?'

He cleared his throat. This was damned difficult. But Katherine was grown up, he reminded himself. A married woman, now a widow. 'It all began shortly after you were born,' he stated quietly.

Jeremiah laid down his knife and fork and sat back in his chair.

'After you were born,' he repeated, 'your mother . . .' He broke off and coughed. 'Well, just let me say that she wasn't particularly keen on the physical side of our relationship after that. I believe the illnesses were simply a long line of excuses.'

Katherine couldn't believe she was hearing this. She'd never even suspected. But now she came to think about it, it all made sense. 'So she's not dying, then?'

Jeremiah stared at her, aghast. 'What on earth makes you think that?'

'Because she told me so.'

'What!' he exploded.

Katherine related the conversation in question to a thoroughly appalled Jeremiah.

'Damned bloody woman,' he muttered in fury when Katherine had finished. 'That was unforgivable. Of all the conniving . . .'

He bit his lip, then turned away so that Katherine couldn't see his face. Ruth was her mother after all.

'Would you have married Miles otherwise?' he queried, his face still averted.

Katherine was boiling inside, absolutely furious with Ruth. 'I don't know, Papa,' she answered truthfully. 'Maybe, maybe not. What I can say is that I did agree to marry him because of that conversation. To please Mama.'

Jeremiah turned again to look at Katherine. 'I'm so sorry, darling. I'm so, so sorry.'

'It's not your fault, Papa, you didn't lie. And Miles and I were happy together, I can't deny that.'

'Which is hardly the point.'

'No,' she agreed. 'It isn't. I can only think Mama said what she did because of Tim Wilson. She certainly didn't want me to marry him, due to his being poor and his lack of prospects, as she put it.'

'Interfering bitch,' Jeremiah hissed, at that moment hating Ruth. He'd never hated her before, but he did now.

'Wait till I next speak to her. She'll get more than just a piece of my mind.'

'Don't, Papa. Leave it to me. It was my life that was affected, after all.'

Not interested in the physical side of marriage, Katherine reflected grimly, understanding perfectly what her father – a red-blooded man if ever there was – meant by that. How could Ruth have been so cruel and selfish? It was deplorable. Now she understood why her father was having an affair with Mrs Webb. Any resentment or disapproval she'd had regarding that now disappeared.

'Poor Tim Wilson,' Katherine said softly. 'I know he must have taken that blow very badly. He loved me a great deal, you see.'

'And you?'

Katherine sighed. 'At the time I believed I did. Then there was my coming-out and Miles. I just sort of got swept along with it all.'

Jeremiah pushed his plate away. 'I've lost my appetite.'

Katherine gave him a thin smile. 'And me.'

'Ruth has a lot to answer for,' Jeremiah muttered darkly, his features contorted into a scowl.

Katherine merely nodded, trying to come to terms with all that she'd just learnt.

One thing was certain: she'd never forgive her mother. Never.

What a racket, Major Brown thought as he came out of his office. The men were certainly boisterous tonight and no mistake. Lieutenant Collingwood was hammering away on the old piano, with everyone else grouped round him singing their heads off. There were bottles, mostly empty, everywhere.

Oh well, he reflected. Better this than sitting around moping about the day ahead. He didn't care how much they sang or drank as long as they were fit to fly in the morning.

Spotting Smallbone busily tidying up, Brown gestured him across. 'Do you know where Captain Wilson is? I can't see him anywhere,' he asked when Tim's batman reached him.

'He's in his room, sir.' Smallbone lowered his voice. 'Sitting in the dark, sir. Told me to bugger off when I went in earlier. Most unlike the captain, sir.'

'In the dark, you say?'

'That's right, sir. He has a candle, I know, because I put a new one there this afternoon, but he hasn't lit it.'

How odd, Brown thought. 'Thank you, Sergeant, that's all.'

'Thank you, sir.'

Brown glanced over at the door to Tim's room. If something was troubling Tim, then he should know about it. He picked up a half-full bottle of cognac *en route*.

He tapped. 'Wilson?'

There was no reply.

He tapped more loudly. 'Wilson, it's Brown. Can I come in?'

Still no reply.

This time it was a rap. 'Wilson, I know you're in there. Be a good chap and answer.'

Again no reply.

Brown grasped the handle and slowly opened the door.

Sure enough, as Smallbone had said, the room was in darkness. Tim was sitting at the table, his outline silhouetted against the window behind him, through which moonlight was shining.

'Are you all right, old boy?'

Tim grunted.

Brown closed the door and made his way over to the table, where he laid the bottle. Producing matches from his pocket, he lit the solitary candle.

'Jesus Christ!' he swore when he saw that Tim was shaking from head to toe with tears running down his face.

Tim stared up at Brown. 'I'll be all right in the morning, sir. I'll be able to fly. Honestly.'

Brown opened his mouth, then closed it again. He'd seen this sort of thing before.

'Can I have a drink, sir? I've run out.'

'Of course.' Brown poured him a large one, which Tim swallowed greedily, some spilling down his chin in the process.

Brown sat down facing him. 'What brought this on?' he asked softly, his concern evident.

'Don't know, sir. It just started a couple of hours ago and I can't get it to stop.'

Without being asked, Brown refilled Tim's glass and poured himself one. 'How long since you've had any leave?'

Tim laughed. 'Haven't, sir. Not since arriving in France over a year ago.'

Brown swore again. 'Then I'm going to give you some. A whole month should do the trick. God knows I can't spare you. You're the best and most experienced pilot I have. But clearly you need a break.'

'You can't give me leave, sir,' Tim protested. 'General HQ will never sanction it.'

'Sod General HQ!' Brown snarled. 'A bunch of fancy brass hats sitting in a swanky *château* twenty miles behind the lines, drinking the best wines France has to offer and eating *foie gras*. What do they know? Damned little, in my book. They won't even issue the men with parachutes in case they take fright and jump out. I ask you! What sort of callous idiots are they? It's easy to be brave sitting in a *château*, but it would be a different tune if they were the ones having to fly. They'd issue parachutes quickly enough then. It's the same with leave – they push the chaps too hard at times. A human being can only take so much after all. Especially in this slaughter house.'

He threw the cognac down his throat. 'I'll give you the necessary papers in the morning and they need never know. If anything is ever mentioned, which I doubt, I'll concoct some cock-and-bull story to satisfy them.'

A whole month, Tim thought. It was a miracle.

'Don't worry about this, Wilson,' Brown said sympathetically. 'It gets to us all sooner or later. Quite understandable in the circumstances. You have a lie-in tomorrow and by the time you get up and have breakfast I'll have transport arranged. Straight to Amiens and a train from there to Calais. You'll be home before you know it.'

'Thank you, sir,' a thoroughly grateful Tim croaked, wiping his tears away with the sleeve of his tunic.

'You'll be all right. I promise you. You just need to get away from this carnage for a while, that's all.' Brown came to his feet. 'Now, there's a helluva singsong going on out there. Get yourself sorted and come and join in. All right?'

Tim realised that his shaking had begun to subside. 'I'll try, sir.'

'Good chap.'

It took an hour. But when Tim came out of his room he was fully composed, dry-eyed and steady as a rock.

Brown nodded his approval.

Katherine sat looking out of the train window as the others in the party chattered excitedly about what lay ahead for them in France. She was thinking about her mother.

The only reason she could come up with for Ruth writing to say that she was ill was to make Katherine feel guilty at having agreed to go to France in the first place. This was Ruth's revenge, if you liked, having her daughter worry and feel guilty. Well, there would be no more of that now that she knew the truth.

Katherine had already decided what she was going to do. It might be years yet before she managed to return to Oaklands, so she'd write. Not straight away, but after her temper had cooled and she'd thought through exactly what she was going to say.

Then she'd write telling her mother precisely what she thought of her and her lies.

It would be a letter Ruth wouldn't forget in a hurry. She'd make damned sure of that.

Off in the distance she saw the outskirts of Southampton, where they'd be embarking for Dunkirk. She hoped the crossing, like the one coming over, wasn't going to be too rough.

Tim had managed to ring from Paddington to tell Minna

to expect him, having decided that this time he wouldn't spring a surprise on her. He could just imagine the welcome he was going to get. Minna would be ecstatic.

Minna had decided to wait for Tim in their private parlour. After he'd rung she'd tried to go on working, but had stopped after only a few minutes, too excited to concentrate on anything other than his return.

Every few seconds her eyes strayed to the clock on top of the mantelpiece. What was keeping him? she fretted. He should have been here by now. He must have had trouble getting a motor taxicab, she decided.

Now, she told herself, she wasn't going to cry. She wasn't. There would be no blubbering. Again her eyes sought the clock.

Finally she heard a key in the outside door. He was back. Her son was back! She came slowly to her feet. 'I'm in here, Tim!' she called out.

For a moment she didn't recognise the stranger who entered the parlour and smiled at her. He was so changed from the old Tim she remembered from the last time he was here.

'Hello, Ma. It's good to see you.'

She flew into his arms, each hugging the other tight. 'Oh, my darling, my angel,' she husked.

Tim closed his eyes, breathing in the scent of Minna's hair, which he knew so well from his childhood. A scent he'd never expected to smell again. The feeling he had was one of sheer euphoria.

Minna pulled herself away slightly and stared into his face. It was gaunt and heavily lined, the hair above his temples grey, with silvery flecks shot through the rest. He'd aged a dozen years and more.

'You're so thin,' she observed in a cracked voice.

'I missed your home cooking.'

'And . . . and . . .' She broke off and sobbed.

'Don't go on, Ma. I'm here and that's all that matters.'

'You look older, Tim.'

He gave her a tight, cynical smile. 'I know. I see it every morning in the mirror while shaving.'

A young man had gone off to war, she thought. A fully mature one had come back. Redvers would be so proud, as was she.

He glanced about him. 'Nothing's changed. Good. I was hoping it hadn't. I wanted everything to be exactly as I recalled.'

Minna blinked back tears. 'I'll soon feed you up again. Give me a week or two and you'll be just as you always were.'

No, he thought. That would never happen. A little weight put on, yes, but his outlook was changed for ever.

'Are you hungry?'

'I could use a drink first. It's been a long journey.'

Minna nodded her understanding. 'Let's go on through to the kitchen, where they're all waiting for you. They're as excited as I am.'

It was strange being home, Tim reflected. It was as if he'd stepped back in time into a world long gone. There was a surreal quality about everything, as if he were in a place of ghosts and shadows lacking substance.

'You're so tense, wound up.' Minna, still in his arms, frowned.

'I suppose I am,' he replied slowly. Nowadays that was

natural for him, having been living on the edge for so very long. It was going to be odd relaxing, not worrying about the next flight or mission, thinking it might be his last, seeing chaps arrive one minute only to be shot down and killed the next. Not to be dicing with death on a daily basis. 'Do you know what I want most?' he said to Minna.

'What, son?'

'To sleep. Just that. To sleep.'

The profound weariness in his voice made her insides ache.

'Hello, Elyse. How are you?'

Like Minna, she didn't recognise him right away. 'Dear God, it's you, Tim. How wonderful!'

He handed her the bunch of flowers he'd bought. 'For you.'

'Why, thank you. They're gorgeous!'

He grinned at her obvious pleasure. 'I hope I haven't called at a bad time?'

'Well, I'm not dressed yet, if that's what you mean. Always was a lazy slut in the morning. But come in, come in.'

There it was, her perfume, strong in his nostrils, as always when she was around. 'I wanted to see what you've done with your house.'

Elyse laughed. 'And so you shall. How long have you been home?'

'Three days now, most of which I've spent in bed trying to catch up on my sleep.'

She stared at him, seeing all manner of things reflected in his face and eyes, but predominantly pain. Her heart went out to him for he'd clearly suffered a great deal. It was a face that also shocked her, though she was trying not to show it, because of how much it had changed. The grey patches at his temples made him look rather distinguished, she decided. They were certainly attractive.

Elyse having temporarily disposed of the flowers, Tim exclaimed in amazement on entering her sitting room, as she called it. The walls were painted an ochre colour, with three largish Oriental rugs fastened to them. The various lampshades were unlike any he'd ever seen, again with obvious Oriental characteristics. The furniture was old, with more light rugs thrown over it. In one corner was a rocking horse, and in another a huge brass urn on which were depicted a series of sexual acts.

Elyse looked in amusement at his stunned expression, that being the reaction she usually got when a visitor entered the room for the first time.

The carpet was also Oriental in design with heavy tassels at either end. There was an Indian coffee table and all sorts of weird and bizarre knick-knacks. 'Well?' she queried.

'The honest truth?'

'The honest truth, Tim.'

'I'm speechless.'

'You don't like it then?'

He shook his head. 'I didn't say that. I'm sure it all grows on you, given time.'

Elyse pulled her négligé more tightly about her and sat down on a grey-and-blue velour comfy chair. 'I suppose you could describe it as Bohemian.'

'I can't argue with that.'

'Whatever, it suits me and that's all that matters. I find the overall effect rather womblike.'

Tim blushed. 'Well, that's one way of putting it.'

'Sit down and I'll put the kettle on in a minute. I want to hear everything.'

He felt himself tense. 'About what?' he queried innocently.

'The war, silly. What you've been up to "over there".'

Tim watched her light a cigarette. 'I see you haven't given those up.'

Elyse inhaled deeply, meanwhile regarding him through what he could only have described as cat's eyes. 'I've cut down quite a bit and feel the better for it. But I don't think I could give up entirely. I enjoy them far too much.'

She looked beautiful, he thought. Even more so than he remembered. There was a sort of ethereal quality about her that he didn't recall. 'So how are you getting on away from the theatre? Are you missing it?'

'Not really,' she lied smoothly. Of course she was, like billyo.

'That surprises me.'

Elyse shrugged. 'I had the chance to move on, and I did. Now I find myself thoroughly enjoying the sheer indolence I've fallen into. Laziness has become my middle name.'

He was curious. 'So how do you pass the time?'

She laughed. 'I sometimes ask myself that. I garden, for a start, though there's little to do at this time of year. To my utter amazement I've discovered I have green fingers.'

He arched an eyebrow. He was amazed as well.

'I tell you, darling, during the spring and summer I'm busy as a bee out there. Geraniums, gladioli, asters, japonica, mahonia, escallonia, I grow them all.'

'I'm impressed.' And he meant it.

'I also planted an apple tree and a damson, which are doing famously. But the *pièce de résistance*, as far as I'm concerned, is a palm tree. Of which, you know, there are quite a number in the area. Having my own palm tree rather appealed somehow.'

'You must show me this garden before I leave.'

'Oh, I will!' she enthused. 'After I get dressed I'll give you the tour.'

He nodded, then said, gesturing about him, 'Where did you get all this stuff? Not Torquay, I'm sure.'

'Quite right. London actually. I go up every so often to keep in touch with Molly and Seamus, plus other friends, and that's when I also go round shops – rather different ones, shall we say – that I know. I have everything sent down.'

An African carving caught his eye. It was of a woman with an incredibly large backside and long, pendulous, pointed breasts. He thought it hideous.

'Now enough about me,' Elyse declared. 'What about "over there"?'

He dropped his gaze to stare at the carpet. 'I'm afraid I'm going to have to ask to use your toilet.'

'It's upstairs facing you, you can't miss it,' she replied slowly with a frown.

'Thank you.'

Jumping up, he left the room.

'Do I take it that's a subject you don't wish to discuss?' Elyse asked him a few minutes later on his return.

'What subject?'

'The *war*, Tim.'

He sat down again, but wouldn't look at her. 'I prefer not to,' he replied so quietly that Elyse almost didn't hear him.

'That bad, eh?'

He closed his eyes and he was back there, over the German lines, with 'Archie' popping all around, his Camel bucking under him. He saw another Camel receive a direct hit and explode, burning and blazing debris spiralling earthwards. Sweat was clammy on his forehead, his knuckles white on the controls, fear a living thing in his belly trying to eat him alive.

'Tim?'

He snapped his eyes open again. 'Sorry, Elyse. Sorry.'

'You've gone quite pale,' she said anxiously.

'I'm all right. Honestly I am.'

'Are you sure?'

He nodded.

No more questions or probing about France, she decided. Not when it did that to him. 'I have an idea,' she declared suddenly. 'I was going to make some coffee, but as it's almost noon why don't we go out for lunch?'

'That would be nice,' he enthused.

She came to her feet. 'I'll have to get bathed and dressed, which will take about half an hour or so. Do you mind waiting?'

'Not in the least.'

'Then that's what we'll do. I'll be as quick as I can.'

'Don't rush on my account.'

She smiled at him, thinking what a lovely man he'd become. 'Right then,' she said and swept from the room as if she was making an exit in a play.

While running the bath Elyse chose her wardrobe for the occasion. A grey woollen suit that was quite severe in cut, but which showed off her figure admirably. Blue shoes and a matching cloche hat made up the ensemble. It was only lunch in Torquay, after all!

It took her just over an hour to get ready, a dash of perfume being the final touch. Then she went downstairs again to discover Tim fast asleep in his chair.

Wake him or not? she wondered. And decided not to. The poor chap was clearly still exhausted after all he'd been through. Hadn't he told her that he'd spent most of the three days he'd been back in bed? No, let him sleep.

It was three in the afternoon when a mortified Tim finally awoke, instantly full of apologies.

'Don't worry about it,' she assured him, sitting opposite him, having been reading a novel. 'I just didn't have the heart to wake you.' Elyse laid the book aside. 'Why don't I cook lunch myself? Cooking is something else I've become rather good at.'

'Only if I'm allowed to help.'

'Then you can start by opening the wine.'

Tim followed her through to the kitchen. He didn't want to be left on his own again. He wanted to be with Elyse.

Chapter 28

It had been a fantastic evening, one of the best Tim could ever remember. He'd been home a week and a half now, during which he'd spent a great deal of time with Elyse. She'd announced that it was her birthday and would Tim help her celebrate? He'd jumped at the chance.

First of all she'd cooked a wonderful meal, declaring that she'd rather do that than go to a restaurant, after which they'd gone out on a pub crawl – again Elyse's choice.

He'd protested that ladies didn't go to pubs, but she'd pooh-poohed that, reminding him that she was an actress by profession and they were used to breaking rules and conventions. By law, she'd informed him, actors were still thieves and vagabonds – he'd found that hard to believe, but apparently it was true – and where else did such people go but to pubs?

In The Bunch of Grapes, where they'd stopped off briefly, Tim had gone to the toilet to find on his return that Elyse had been propositioned by no fewer than three matelots, which she'd thought hilariously funny. He'd been less than amused, feeling terribly protective towards her.

In another pub, The Saracen's Head, Elyse had scandalised

those at surrounding tables by drinking several pints of rough scrumpy and smoking a small cigar that she'd produced.

Now the evening was finally drawing to a close and Tim was walking Elyse home, having failed to find a cab anywhere.

'Come in for coffee and a brandy,' she smiled when they reached her door.

'All right. I don't mind if I do.'

'I've really enjoyed tonight. Thank you,' Elyse declared when they were inside.

'I'm glad it was a good birthday for you.'

He went into the sitting room and sat down while she put the kettle on and fetched the brandy. He knew he was drunk – not rip-roaringly so, but drunk all the same. Leaning back in the chair he closed his eyes, telling himself he mustn't fall asleep.

'A penny for them?' Elyse asked when she rejoined him, having been in the kitchen for about five minutes.

His mood had changed during that time from one of elation to black despondency. 'Nothing,' he replied, shaking his head.

She handed him a brandy. 'Come on, what is it, Tim?'

'I was just thinking . . .' He broke off and scowled.

'Thinking what?' she prompted.

'That I'll be back in France again before I know it.' He sighed deeply. 'Christ, I wish I didn't have to go. I wish I could stay here in Torquay for ever.'

Seeing how disturbed Tim was, Elyse sat down with her own brandy and didn't bother returning for the coffee. She didn't say anything, but just listened.

'The people here don't have any idea what it's like in

France,' Tim said quietly, all manner of images flashing through his mind. 'They've absolutely no concept of the filth, disease, privation, hardship and sheer horror of it all. I'm speaking about the Tommies now. The PBI, poor bloody infantry. Those boys are truly at the sharp end.'

He had a gulp from his glass. 'We pilots fare better, but our losses are mind-boggling. Do you know what the average life expectancy of a pilot is when he reaches France?'

Elyse shook her head.

'Three weeks. That's all. Three weeks. They don't mention that in the newspapers. It's all jingoistic nonsense about us giving the Hun a good thrashing. That sort of claptrap. Well, if we're thrashing him, he's thrashing us back just as hard.'

Tim ran a hand over his face. 'I have nightmares, you know. Terrible, terrible nightmares in which I'm shot, burnt alive, trapped in an out-of-control plane or gassed. Death, Elyse, that's what I dream of. Death, death and more death, wondering when it's my turn and how I'm going to get it.'

He shuddered. 'And not only nightmares. I have daymares as well, if there is such a word. I walk down a street, sit in a chair, whatever, and I'm seeing it all, reliving it – the screams, the shouts, the rattle of machine-gun fire. And blood everywhere, always blood. Rivers of it, oceans.'

Elyse swallowed hard. She'd asked what it was like 'over there'. Well, now she was hearing. She too had had no proper idea.

Suddenly Tim barked out a laugh. 'I'd like to take one of those damned stupid women who hand out white feathers and . . .' He stopped, drew in a deep breath, then gave a quiet sob. 'Show her the reality of the situation. She might stop handing out white feathers then.'

He gulped down more brandy. 'They're all so young, you see. Boys, that's all. Boys. Many of them straight out of school. Four, five, six hours solo, which is nothing at all, then they're sent to us. Every morning, almost without fail, replacement pilots from the pool. Some of them never even live long enough to get unpacked.'

Elyse wanted a cigarette but felt if she lit up that might intrude on this somehow, break the spell, so she didn't.

'If I had my way,' Tim went on, 'I'd line up all of the General Staff, on both sides, and shoot the lot of them for the murderers they are.'

He looked Elyse straight in the eye, his expression one of utter anguish. 'I broke down one night, started crying, and the major found me like that. He's a good man, the major, the best. He said I was to come home on leave, take a break, which is why I'm here. To get my nerve back again, I suppose.'

She wanted to wrap him in her arms, comfort him. Try and take away some of his pain.

'Do you know what's been bothering me most of late?' he queried. 'For some while now, actually. I just can't get it out of my mind.'

Elyse shook her head.

'Silly in a way. That I'm going to die without ever having experienced a woman.' He hesitated. 'Please don't laugh at that.'

'I'm not laughing, Tim. Far from it,' she assured him earnestly.

'There are many chaps like me out there. Occasionally we go to Amiens for a night out, lots of booze and laughter, that sort of thing. Well, there are women there who'll accommodate you, for a price.'

'You mean prostitutes?' It seemed all right to talk now.

'Yes, a few of them are. Others are women whose men are away fighting and they want the extra money to get by. Or perhaps they're just lonely.'

'And you've never gone with one?'

He shook his head. 'I've thought about it, but it didn't seem right somehow. It wasn't exactly my conscience, but simply that I'd always imagined that when it did happen it would be different from that. It would at least be with someone I genuinely cared for and hopefully loved. They say it should be a very precious and special thing and I believe that.' He hesitated again. 'Am I being naïve?'

'No, Tim,' she replied softly. 'Romantic perhaps, but not naïve. I applaud your attitude.'

He drained the remains of his glass and gazed morosely into it.

Elyse stared hard at him, then, setting her own glass aside, rose and crossed over to kneel in front of him. Taking his hand, she squeezed it. 'Poor Tim,' she whispered.

'Yes,' he whispered back. 'Poor Tim indeed.'

'Would you like to go to bed with me?'

For a moment he thought he hadn't heard correctly. 'Say that again?'

'I said, would you like to go to bed with me?'

He was instantly thrown into confusion. 'I . . . I . . . wasn't telling you all that in the hope you might . . .' He trailed off.

'I know you weren't, Tim. And for what it's worth, I've come to care a great deal about you. That's one of your criteria, isn't it?'

'Oh, Elyse,' he croaked, lost for words.

'Well?'

He brought her hand to his mouth and lightly kissed it. 'I would love to. In fact there's nothing I'd like more.'

Elyse came to her feet and smiled down at him. 'Shall we go to the bedroom then?'

The first thing she did was put a match to the already laid fire. When that was ablaze she crossed over to a chest of drawers, on top of which lay a number of candles.

A fascinated Tim watched her light candle after candle, moving round to others as she did, until fourteen in all were flickering brightly. Like Christmas, he thought. That was what the candles reminded him of, Christmas.

Elyse then picked up what looked to Tim like a twig and applied a burning match to one end. When smoke was curling from the twig, Elyse placed it in what appeared to be a holder of some kind.

'What's that?' he queried.

'Incense. It comes from India and gives off a lovely aroma. You'll smell it in a moment.'

He already could. A curious, pungent odour that wasn't at all unpleasant.

Elyse came to him. 'Why don't you kiss me?'

He couldn't believe this was actually happening or what they were about to do. He prayed he didn't make a fool of himself in any way.

'Hmmh,' murmured Elyse, breaking mouth contact. 'You're nervous, aren't you?'

'A bit,' he confessed. 'It is my first time after all.'

'Well, there's nothing to be nervous about, I promise you.' She smiled beguilingly. 'Have you ever had a body massage?'

He shook his head.

'Then I'll give you one. It'll help you relax and get you in the mood.'

That jolted him, but he was game. 'All right.'

She pointed at the bed. 'Why don't you sit there while I get changed.'

He didn't reply to that, but simply did as she'd suggested. Never taking his eyes off her as she began to strip.

When she was naked she turned to him with a mischievous twinkle in her eyes. 'I'd forgotten that you've seen me like this before.'

'In the bath,' he acknowledged, thinking how gorgeous she was.

'I hadn't locked the door and then, suddenly, there you were.'

He nodded.

Elyse opened the wardrobe and took out the flimsiest of wraps, which she shrugged herself into. Tim thought it made her look like a fairy queen. The breath caught in his throat when she undid the clasps in her hair to let it tumble down round her shoulders.

'Do you approve?' she teased.

'Oh yes. Very much so.'

'Good. I want this to be a night to remember for you.'

As far as he was concerned, it already was.

'Now you, Tim.'

He stood up and, hands trembling, started with his tie. While he was undoing that Elyse opened a drawer, from which she produced a small bottle of oil.

She tried not to let her amusement show as Tim, clearly embarrassed, continued to undress.

'Lie face down on the bed,' she instructed when he too was finally naked.

Kneeling beside him, she poured oil along the length of his back, Tim wincing slightly at the coldness of it, and then set to work.

He sighed with pleasure as she expertly kneaded and smoothed, her hands surprisingly strong. How incredibly sensuous, he thought dreamily as, bit by bit, the tension melted from his body.

'Now roll over,' she said eventually.

When he was on his back Elyse trickled more oil down his front, then began to rub it in.

Tim gazed up at her through half-closed lids, marvelling at the voluptuousness of her beneath the wrap. Tentatively he touched the swell of the breast nearest him.

'That's right,' she crooned as she saw him twitch and harden. A little help, she thought, taking him in her hand.

When he was ready she straddled him and carefully guided him in, Tim continuing to watch her through half-closed lids.

Elyse undid her wrap and tossed it aside, a wisp of gossamer floating through the now heavily scented air.

Slowly, rhythmically, she began to move.

Tim came awake to find his face buried in Elyse's hair. She was fast asleep alongside him. How long had it gone on for last night? He couldn't remember – hours it had seemed. His mind sang in memory.

He stroked her side, feeling the fine hairs on her body beneath his fingertips. As he was doing that her eyes blinked open.

'Hello,' she whispered.

'Hello.'

'How are you this morning?'

She laughed when he told her.

'And you?' he queried hopefully.

'Thinking we should do something about that.'

He kissed her as he brought his body over hers.

Major Brown slammed down the telephone, incandescent with rage. What they were ordering was a suicide mission, plain and simple. He didn't have one pilot under his command anything like experienced enough to have a hope in hell of pulling that off.

Slumping into a chair, he put his head in his hands. Thirty miles inside enemy lines, intense ack-ack along most of the route, to bomb a chemical plant. And if the pilot did succeed in actually getting that far, then he had to come all the way back again past the very same ack-ack. And on the return leg there were bound to be enemy aircraft waiting in ambush.

Who could he send? For he had to send someone – orders were orders after all. He might as well select a pilot and blow the poor bugger's head off there and then, for at least that would save a plane.

The coward's way out was to ask for a volunteer. That way he wouldn't have to choose, wouldn't have to take the responsibility of selecting any one individual. Someone would volunteer, someone always did.

Coming to his feet again, he crossed to the table and studied the map laid out there, tracing the proposed route with his finger. Ack-ack, ack-ack. Suddenly he paused. Unless . . .

He studied the map with a fresh eye, mentally working out the fuel load and flying time. A deviation here, another there. Longer of course, but safer. Touch and go regarding fuel, mind you, but a distinct possibility. Perhaps this needn't be a suicide mission after all, he reflected. Particularly if you changed the deviations on the return journey.

And your luck held.

Tim was late coming down, even by his recent standards, Minna thought as she mounted the stairs, taking him a cup of tea. It was high time he was up and doing.

She tapped on his bedroom door. 'Tim?'

She smiled when there was no reply. Still out for the count, no doubt. She tapped again and opened the door.

Minna started in surprise to find the bedroom empty. Not only that, but it was obvious that the bed hadn't been slept in.

He must have been out all night, she realised, suddenly worried that something might have happened to him. Could he have met with some sort of accident? The only other alternative she could think of was that he'd stayed over at a friend's house.

Yes, that was far more likely. A friend's house, though she couldn't imagine who. As far as she was aware, most of his friends were in the Forces.

Then she had another thought. A woman? She frowned – that couldn't be right. It wasn't as if he'd come back to a girlfriend or anything like that.

Oh well, she sighed. She'd find out soon enough. She drank the tea herself, before taking the cup and saucer back to the kitchen.

* * *

It was early afternoon when Tim reappeared at The Berkeley, where he ran into Minna almost straight away.

'You missed your breakfast,' she said, giving him the chance to explain.

'Sorry, Ma. Just wasn't hungry. By the way, is my motor-bike still out at the rear? I think I'll have a tinker with it if it is.'

There seemed to be something different about him, but she couldn't put her finger on it. 'It's still there. I was hardly going to sell it after all.'

'You never know,' he beamed. 'You might have done.' And with that he left her, walking away humming jauntily to himself.

Curious, she thought. Not a word of explanation. Not a single word. One thing though, he was certainly happy enough. The happiest she'd seen him since coming home.

Whatever he'd been up to, she thoroughly approved of how it had changed his mood.

'Oh, my God! My God!' Elyse gasped. Then she convulsed beneath Tim, her hips grinding into his.

Tim, as sweat-slicked as Elyse, rolled off her a few moments later, smiling at the look of sheer ecstasy that lit up her face.

'That's very rare,' Elyse commented when she'd caught her breath.

'What is?'

'That – together, I mean. It doesn't happen very often.'

That was news to Tim. But then, he was still learning, with Elyse a most enthusiastic teacher. He noted that her eyes had become catlike again. He imagined he could almost hear her purr with contentment.

'I'm hungry,' Elyse announced.

Tim laughed. 'You usually are afterwards.'

'It never used to . . .' She hurriedly shut up when she realised what she'd been about to say. She tried never to mention past relationships.

'Never used to what?'

'Oh, nothing,' she replied dismissively and turned her face away from him. 'Are you hungry as well?'

'Only for you.'

The sincerity in his voice touched her. She was dreading the day that he had to leave. It was going to be so lonely without him, for in the short space of time he'd been home she'd become used to his company, to having him around, having him in her bed.

'I think I'll make one of my famous omelettes,' she proposed. 'Does that appeal?'

'Anything you make will be fine, Elyse. And certainly far better than what I get "over there". Sergeant Smallbone's cooking leaves a lot to be desired, believe me.'

She turned to face him again, remembering the young Tim she'd first met, so different from the man now alongside her. 'Why don't we have a bath together before we eat?' she suggested.

'We'll never get in. There isn't enough room,' he protested.

'I think there is. We can at least try.'

The idea of sharing a bath with Elyse excited him and he hoped she was right. If she wasn't, then he'd sit and watch her while she bathed. He'd enjoy that too.

Elyse sat up and reached for her cigarettes – her 'after-shag fag', as she referred to it. The first time she'd said that Tim had almost choked laughing, finding it hilariously funny, especially coming from a woman. He wasn't used to women saying rude things.

Elyse lit up. 'By the way, I've got something for you.'

'Oh?'

Reaching across, he traced a line down her wet back to the cleft of her buttocks, where he wiggled his finger.

'Stop that!' she smiled and moved fractionally away.

'Why?'

'Because I like it too much.'

That didn't make sense to Tim. Why ask him to stop if she liked it? As he was rapidly finding out, that was women for you. Completely illogical at times. At least so it seemed to him.

'In the wardrobe,' she said.

'What's in the wardrobe?'

'The present I bought you. It's hanging up.'

He couldn't imagine what it might be. 'Shall I go and get it then?'

'Of course.'

'How will I know what it is?'

She sighed. 'Don't be dense. Because it's the only male thing there, that's why.'

He made a grab for her. 'I am not dense.'

Squealing, she wriggled away. 'On you go. We've had enough of that for the moment. You don't want to spoil a good thing.'

'If you say so.'

'I do. Now hurry up. I want to hear what you think.'

He swung off the bed, now quite comfortable being naked

with her, and walked across the room to the wardrobe. When he opened it, it was obvious what his present was.

'Well?' Elyse demanded eagerly.

He slid the tartan dressing gown from its hanger. Hardly an expert on tartan, he thought this one was Black Watch. 'You shouldn't have, Elyse,' he chided her. 'This must have been very expensive.'

'Sod the expense. Does it fit?'

He put it on and tied it at the waist. 'Perfectly. Thank you.'

She nodded. 'I thought it would suit you, and it does. I'm glad I got the right size. I wasn't absolutely certain about that.'

'Well, you did.'

He went to her and kissed her lightly on the lips. 'Thanks again.'

'You're welcome.'

'Now shall we try the bath?'

Elyse was right: it was big enough for the pair of them.

Ruth came to the end of Katherine's letter, then dropped the hand holding it onto her lap. She was white with shock from what she'd just read.

How could Katherine? How could she! Of all the ungrateful, vindictive . . . Ruth closed her eyes. The trouble was that everything Katherine accused her of was true, including her lie about dying, in order to get Katherine to marry Miles.

Ruth looked about her, but everything had gone fuzzy at the edges, hazy. She had the beginnings of a terrible headache, and that wasn't made up for convenience's sake.

How could she face Katherine again? She simply didn't know. Or Jeremiah, come to that. It was going to be awful, so shaming.

She could deny everything of course, say that it was all absolute nonsense. Pretend she'd been misdiagnosed about dying. Would they believe that? In her heart of hearts she knew they wouldn't.

But Katherine and Miles had been a good match, she assured herself. She hadn't been to know that Miles would be killed in this ghastly war. Surely the end justified the means?

Only Katherine didn't see it like that, and, judging from her letter, was never likely to.

The pain that suddenly hit Ruth was like a thunderbolt, horrific in its intensity. Opening her mouth, she shrieked in agony, but no sound came out. Still silently shrieking, she tumbled from her chair to the floor.

Minna had just left the post office and was wondering what to do next when she spotted Tim and Elyse across the road, Elyse clinging to Tim's arm.

Minna stared in amazement. Tim and Elyse Davenport? They couldn't have met up by accident. Even considering that she'd been an actress, Elyse Davenport wouldn't be clinging to him like that. No, what Minna was seeing was a couple out together, relishing one another's company. There could be no doubt about it. Everything about the way they were behaving bore witness to the fact.

When they were further down the road Minna headed for the Café Addison. She needed to think about this.

* * *

It was wartime, Minna reminded herself, and in wartime, because of the special conditions that existed, normal rules, behaviour and morality sometimes went by the board.

She could hardly deny how happy Tim had been recently, clearly as a result of the relationship. And Tim was a grown man, quite capable of looking after himself.

Minna made up her mind. She wouldn't confront Tim with this. So far he'd said nothing about it and neither would she. It was probably only a passing thing after all – ships that pass in the night. And if Elyse Davenport, despite her age, brought Tim comfort and happiness, then that was good enough for Minna. At least she now knew where Tim had been spending his nights, which came as a relief in many ways.

She wondered what Redvers would have made of it all and decided he'd have taken the same attitude as herself. All too soon Tim would be back in France, risking his life on a daily basis, so let him have his moment without any comment or interference from her.

And she had to admit that Elyse was a good woman, one whom she personally liked a great deal.

They had her blessing. Even if it was a somewhat reserved, even bewildered one.

It had been an awkward evening so far, neither of them mentioning the fact that this was their last night together. Tim was due to catch a train in the morning.

'I've got something for you,' Elyse declared. 'Nothing really, but I would like you to have it.'

She glanced briefly at the clock. It would be bedtime shortly and then, after a few brief hours, time for Tim to go. Her heart was like lead at the prospect.

Tim sipped his wine. Elyse had been smoking and drinking fiendishly since his arrival, even more than usual. There was no need to ask the reason why.

She went to a drawer and took out what appeared to be a folded handkerchief. Going to Tim, she handed it to him.

He stared in surprise at what wasn't a handkerchief at all, but a small, cream-coloured envelope made out of linen, the flap of which was neatly stitched down. It made a rustling sound when touched.

'What's this?' he queried.

'From my garden, dried forget-me-nots. The gypsies swear they bring good luck.'

'Really?' He was amused.

'I want you to promise me you'll keep that about your person all the time you're away.'

Looking into her eyes, he could see how earnest she was. 'I promise.'

'Good.' She nodded in approval.

'Thank you. And you say the gypsies swear by this?'

'Oh yes. Very much so. And just remember, it was an old gypsy remedy that I used to cure your influenza all those years ago, so their charms and potions do work. You're living proof of that.'

He smiled at her. 'I shall treasure it, Elyse. If for no other reason than it's a reminder of you.'

She gently touched his face, wishing that time would stand still, that the dreaded morning would never arrive. 'You said a while back that you don't want me to go to the station to see you off. Won't you please change your mind?' she pleaded.

He shook his head. 'That's the way I want it, Elyse. No

emotional farewells, no tears, just a simple departure.'

'All right, Tim, if you insist,' she agreed reluctantly, her shoulders slumping.

'I do. I've even forbidden Ma to be there for exactly the same reason. It would only make things harder for me.'

He slipped the linen envelope of forget-me-nots into a pocket, thinking it the sweetest of gestures. He'd treasure it, as he'd said he would.

Elyse abruptly turned away. 'This is awful. I can't bear it. It's tearing me apart.'

'Shall I leave?'

'No!' she exclaimed in alarm. 'Don't you dare.'

'Then let's go upstairs and make the best of what time's left to us,' he suggested softly.

She hesitated, then took a deep breath. 'There's something I want you to know.'

Tim watched her closely, waiting for her to go on, wondering what was coming next.

Elyse's eyes misted over, and when she next spoke there was a choke in her voice. 'You're the best thing that's ever happened to me where men are concerned. I've had more love, cherishing and honesty from you during these past few weeks than I've ever had from a man before.'

'Oh, Elyse,' he whispered.

'I mean it, Tim. The best thing ever. And I thank God – no matter what the eventual outcome – that what happened did. It's something that can never be taken away from either of us. What we've had together.'

He laid his wine aside and came to his feet. 'Don't cry.'

'I'm not.'

'You're about to.'

She dashed away the beginnings of tears. 'You probably think me a sentimental old fool now.'

He shook his head. 'Not at all.'

'But I had to tell you, Tim. All my men in the past have been bastards, one way and another. All of them, in the end, have treated me shabbily. You're the exception, and it's breaking my heart that you're going away.'

He took her into his arms and held her tight. How good she felt against him, how wondrously female. He kissed her forehead, then slowly stroked her hair. 'I'd stay if I could. But that's impossible.'

'I know,' she husked.

'But believe me, I want to. Desperately so.'

She laid a cheek against his chest, feeling safe in his embrace, thinking how lucky she'd been, even if now it had to end.

Releasing her, he took hold of her hand. 'Shall we go upstairs?'

'Yes please,' she whispered.

He stared into her eyes, seeing the vulnerability reflected there, and much, much more. 'I'll never forget you, Elyse.'

'Nor I you. Forget-me-not, remember?'

He smiled, and so did she.

Tim slipped from bed and quietly began to dress. Their lovemaking had always been good, but what had gone on between them during the past few hours defied description, being unbelievable in its intensity, both mind- and body-shattering. To say he was exhausted, both mentally and physically, would have been a gross understatement.

How she'd clung to him, her hands seemingly always

moving, touching, caressing, urging the pair of them on to even greater heights. Again and again her cries of exultation rang around the room, her catlike eyes shining in the dark.

Now she was fast asleep with the hint of a smile on her face, her hair cascading over her shoulders.

When he was fully dressed Tim stared down at her, drinking her in, loving her, though that word had never been spoken between them.

'Goodbye, darling, sleep tight,' he whispered.

At the doorway he paused for a moment to gaze back at her. A final gesture of farewell, then he was gone.

It was a little later that a trickle of dark blood appeared from Elyse's nose, followed by more oozing between her lips.

Shortly after that her breathing stopped.

Chapter 29

T he squadron was airborne when Tim arrived back at the farmhouse, the only signs of activity being some mechanics repairing a couple of damaged planes. Tim went inside to report to Brown, knowing that the major would be in his office impatiently awaiting the squadron's return.

'Come in!' a strange voice called out when he knocked.

Tim frowned as he entered, expecting to find Brown with company. But Brown wasn't there. The man behind his desk was older and had only one arm, the empty sleeve being pinned to his uniform front. He too was a major.

Tim came to attention and saluted. 'I'm Captain Wilson, sir. Is Major Brown about?'

The one-armed man regarded him keenly. Briefly returning the salute he indicated a chair. 'Have a seat, Captain. I've been expecting you.'

Tim did as instructed, wondering what was going on. And where was Brown?

'I'm Major Courtney, Brown's replacement,' the man explained.

'Replacement, sir?'

'Yes. Brown's dead, I'm afraid.'

Tim's face froze in shock. 'Dead?' he repeated dully.

Courtney continued to regard Tim keenly. 'Sergeant Smallbone tells me you and Brown were close. Quite chummy was how he put it.'

Tim nodded.

'Well, your friend disobeyed orders and flew a mission himself. Foolhardy of course, but there we are. He left a note before taking off explaining his reasons for doing what he did.'

Tim shook his head. Brown gone west? It was hard to grasp, being so unexpected. 'Why on earth would be fly, directly contravening orders, sir?'

Courtney rose and crossed to the window to stare out. 'The squadron was given a rotten job to perform: a single plane was to bomb a chemical plant thirty miles into enemy-held territory. Ridiculous order, I suppose, but then so many of them are. Brown felt he didn't have anyone experienced enough to pull it off, and that sending one of the young-sters under his command at the time was tantamount to murder. So he elected to break orders and fly himself. Got the plant too, destroyed it utterly, but was killed legging it for home. He ran directly into Baron von Richthofen and that damed Flying Circus of his. The first intimation we'd had that Richthofen had been moved to our sector. Brown didn't have a hope against that lot.'

Courtney cleared his throat.

'Knew Brown myself, flew alongside him when we were both with Albert Ball's Number Five Squadron. Damned fine pilot, damned fine man.'

'Yes,' Tim agreed. 'About the man, I mean. I never saw him fly.'

'Then take my word for it. He was good.'

Tim's mouth suddenly went dry as it dawned on him that if he hadn't been on leave he, as the most experienced pilot apart from Brown, would have been the one flying that mission. Chances were that if he had, he'd now be dead and Brown alive. It was a sobering thought. He not only owed Brown a month's leave but also his life.

Courtney chuckled. 'He's to be decorated for what he did, whereas if he'd returned in one piece he might easily have been court-martialled. It's a funny old world, isn't it?'

Tim nodded. It was indeed.

Courtney went on. 'As a direct result of Richthofen appearing in our sector, the squadron's been strengthened, an additional six planes, plus a corresponding number of experienced pilots drafted in, in the hope that one of them might get Richthofen.'

Tim thought about what he knew of Manfred von Richthofen, a real baron and Germany's deadliest, most feared ace. He was called the Red Baron because the Fokker triplane he favoured was painted red on his instructions. His squadron was nicknamed the Flying Circus because it had followed Richthofen's lead and painted its planes, each a different colour, all the hues of the rainbow.

'I take it these new chaps haven't had any luck so far?' Tim queried.

'Sadly not,' Courtney replied, 'while our losses have been substantial.'

Tim felt a chill of fear at the prospect of going up against Richthofen. The last he'd heard, the German had over sixty kills to his credit. And now, sooner or later, he might well have to face him.

Courtney cocked his head. 'The squadron's returning. Shall we go out and count them in?'

'Of course, sir.'

'By the way, you'll be in charge of "A" flight, as before. Nothing's changed there. And the room you had is still yours. Smallbone's been as protective as a mother hen over it.'

Tim smiled. Good old Smallbone.

'Due to the increase in pilots some of them have had to be billeted in tents,' Courtney explained as they went outside. 'This place simply isn't big enough to accommodate all of them.'

En route Tim noted that the old piano was still there and wondered if there was a current member of the squadron able to play it. Curiously, there nearly always was.

Courtney swore. 'Two missing,' he said to Tim as, one after the other, the squadron taxied to a halt.

Tim could see they were now flying Spads as well as Camels. The Spad was an excellent aircraft, though his preference remained the Camel, as he found it more manoeuvrable.

A pilot came strolling towards them, Tim thinking there was something familiar about the man's rather distinctive walk. When he took off his helmet Tim recognised him instantly. Well, well, he thought. Now here was a surprise.

'What happened, Iveson?' Courtney demanded when the pilot reached them.

'Ran into some Gotha bombers heading for the French lines, about a dozen in all. We managed to shoot down three of them before their fighters arrived.'

'Richthofen?'

Iveson shook his head. 'No, sir. These were Pfalzes. We got two of them, but lost Brinkley in the process. I saw him go down in flames myself.'

Courtney sighed. Brinkley had only joined them the previous week and had showed great promise. 'Who's the second?'

'Cunningham. He crash-landed and might well have survived. I couldn't hang around to find out.'

'I see you've been promoted,' Tim smiled to Iveson, the very same Sergeant Iveson who'd been his flying instructor at Brooklands.

'And I've been hearing a lot about you. I'm told you're an ace with . . . how many kills is it?'

Tim shrugged. 'I don't count them.'

'You pair know each other then?' Courtney said, raising a bushy eyebrow.

Tim explained where and how they'd met, then extended a hand to Iveson. 'It's good to see you again.'

'And you, sir.'

Iveson ran a hand over his dirty, clearly strained face, deep lines of tiredness etched under his eyes. 'I think this calls for a drink, don't you?'

Tim laughed, for it was only nine-thirty in the morning. Now he knew he was back.

Depressingly there were only a few men left from before his leave, and after Tim had been introduced to the rest of the squadron he and Iveson, at Tim's request, took themselves off for a quiet chat.

'Tell me about Richthofen,' Tim asked.

Iveson's expression became grim. 'The most important

thing to know about him,' he replied slowly, 'is that he's a natural-born hunter. He did a lot of hunting before the war apparently, and actually enjoys killing his prey. And to him that's exactly what British and French pilots are: prey to be hunted down and shot.'

Iveson had a sip of Scotch before continuing. 'I've seen him in action several times, though I've never engaged him myself. He has incredible ability with that Fokker of his – uncanny almost. And his reactions are amazingly fast. I swear he could make that plane of his sit up and beg if he wanted to.'

'That good, eh?' Tim queried softly.

'Everything you've heard and better. There are those, and I'm not one of them, who say he can read the other pilot's mind when in a dogfight.'

An ice-cold lance of fear stabbed through Tim. 'I see.'

'Another thing is that he has nerves of steel – if he has any at all, that is. It's as if he considers himself inviolable, the idea that he might be killed never entering his head.'

'That could be a weakness,' Tim mused.

'If so no-one's taken advantage of it yet. The very sight of that red plane strikes holy terror into our chaps. Another reason why he's so successful. Half the time he's already won before he's fired a shot. But make no mistake, Tim, in my opinion he's probably the best pilot this war has produced so far.'

'Even better than Ball and Maddox?'

'In my opinion.'

Tim stared into his Scotch while he digested that. 'When did you get promoted to lieutenant?' he asked, changing the subject.

'A couple of months back. The powers that be decided I

was more useful over here than training young chaps at home. So I was given my commission and assigned to Number Fourteen Squadron. When Richthofen showed up I was one of those reassigned here.'

Tim nodded and indicated Iveson's now empty glass. 'Will you have another?'

'I won't, if you don't mind.'

Tim decided he wouldn't either. 'Courtney says I've got the rest of the day to settle back in. I'll be going out tomorrow with the dawn patrol leading "A" flight.'

'And I'll be leading "B".'

A natural-born hunter who enjoys killing his prey, Tim reflected. Richthofen sounded like a lunatic.

'Excuse me, sir, can I have a word?'

'Of course, Sergeant, what is it?'

Smallbone partially closed Tim's door behind him. 'Before he left Major Brown handed me this and said I was to give it to you if he didn't return. Told me you'd always admired it, sir.'

Tim stared at the ebony-handled cut-throat razor, a lump rising in his throat. 'That should have been sent home with the rest of his things,' he stated quietly.

'Begging your pardon, sir, but the major was quite specific.'

Tim took the razor which, as Brown had rightly said, he'd often admired. 'Thank you, Sergeant.'

'Only doing my duty, sir.'

'Thank you all the same.'

'Oh, and there'll be a fresh egg in the morning, sir. Cooked the way you like it.'

Tim smiled. 'I also have to thank you for holding on to this room for me while I was away. That was kind of you.'

'Not at all, sir. Not at all. It was my pleasure.'

And with that Smallbone left Tim, closing the door quietly behind him.

Tim stared again at the razor he was holding, remembering the man it had belonged to. He was going to miss Brown.

A lot.

'Henrietta?'

She came abruptly awake. 'Sorry, Jeremiah, I must have dozed off waiting for you. Are you all right?'

He thought how good it was to see her again, achingly so. 'I'm fine. The damned train was late, hours overdue. Don't ask me why, we weren't given an explanation. I just sat and stewed, like all the other passengers.'

'You poor thing,' she sympathised, rising from the chair she'd been in. 'Can I get you anything?'

'A cup of tea would be nice.'

'Then come to the kitchen while I make it. I want to hear everything.'

He followed her through and she immediately filled the kettle. 'Don't I get a kiss first?' he queried with a twinkle in his eyes.

She put the kettle on the range, then went straight into his arms. 'You can have whatever you want first,' she teased.

'A kiss will do for the moment.'

'Then, my darling, that's what you'll have.'

As they kissed he ran a hand down her back and over her backside, which made her wriggle slightly. 'That's better,' he breathed happily when the kiss was finally over.

'Now, why don't you tell me all about it.'

His expression changed and he released her. 'You got most of it over the telephone. Ruth has had a severe stroke, which has left her more or less paralysed. Her mind's gone – at least most of the time it is. Occasionally she'll be aware of what's going on, but mainly she just sits there staring blankly into space.'

'You mentioned that she can't speak?'

'So it seems. She certainly hasn't uttered since they found her. She either can't or won't.' He shook his head. 'You should see her, it's pitiful. Truly it is.'

Henrietta stared hard at him. 'What are you saying, Jeremiah?'

He realised what she was getting at. 'Don't worry, I have no intentions of moving back to Oaklands. I've found Ruth an excellent nursing home, where she'll be well looked after on a twenty-four-hour basis. And there she'll stay for the rest of her days. It wouldn't make the slightest bit of difference whether I was around or not.' He smiled. 'Don't think you're going to get rid of me that easily, for you're not.'

'I'm sorry,' she apologised. 'It was just the way you said how pitiful she was.'

'I'll never leave you, Henrietta,' he stated firmly. 'You can rest assured about that.'

'And I'll never leave you.' Relieved, she turned away to busy herself with the cups and saucers. 'So what are you going to do about Oaklands? You can't just let it stand empty.'

'Well, it wouldn't be that,' he replied. 'There's always the staff present. But you're right, and I've already decided that I shall speak to Katherine when I next see her. If she wants it, it's hers: if not, I'll put it on the market.'

Henrietta nodded her approval. 'Makes sense to me. Though won't it be a wrench parting with it?'

He considered that. 'Yes and no, I suppose. When I think of Oaklands now all I can remember are the unhappy years I spent there with Ruth. On the other hand, it has been in the family for three generations, so if Katherine wants to carry on there that's fine with me. The main thing is, this is now my home, here with you. This is where I want to be.'

A warm feeling spread through Henrietta to hear him say that. Those were her sentiments exactly.

'There is going to be a change, though,' Jeremiah declared.

'And what's that?'

'You and I are going to live openly together. Forget this housekeeper charade. We shall live as man and wife.'

'But what will Katherine say!' Henrietta protested.

'How she reacts is up to her and won't make the slightest bit of difference. My mind's made up on that. I do hope she understands of course. She is my only child, after all, and I love her dearly. But I also love you and, in this particular instance, that takes precedence.'

'There's the business side to this,' she pointed out. 'Won't it affect that, and the people you deal with?'

Jeremiah laughed. 'I don't care. I truly don't. I've made more than enough money to be able to cock a snook at the lot of them. Even if I never earned another penny, it wouldn't matter.'

'Openly as man and wife?' she repeated, this being the last thing she'd been expecting.

'That's what I said. You can change your name by deed poll to Henrietta Coates and who's to know the difference? That's how it's going to be.'

Henrietta stared at him, her eyes shining. 'I won't let you down, Jeremiah. I've told you that before.'

'I know you won't. It never entered my head that you might.'

'I do love you, Jeremiah. So very, very much.'

'Just as I love you.'

Henrietta took a deep breath, then sort of shook herself. 'Now what about something to eat? Surely you're hungry?'

'I was earlier, but not now. What I want most is to get into bed and snuggle up with you.'

Henrietta didn't reply to that. She was too overcome with emotion to speak.

Tim jumped down from his cockpit and went over to where Iveson was getting out of his plane.

'I wish they were all like that,' Tim declared breezily. 'Not a single Hun aircraft in sight during the entire patrol.'

'It certainly makes a change,' Iveson replied, removing his goggles and helmet. 'It was almost a pleasure-flight.'

Tim laughed. 'Hardly that.' It had surprised him how wound up he'd been, waiting for something to happen. A month was a long time to have been away.

Iveson stared eastwards, his brow furrowed in thought. 'He's out there somewhere, Richthofen and his Circus, just waiting. It's only a matter of time before we run into them again.'

'But not this morning,' Tim smiled.

'So it would appear,' Iveson agreed drily. 'But don't forget there's still this afternoon to come. We're bound to be sent up again. And then, who knows?'

Tim strolled back to his Camel to instruct the mechanics

who were already dealing with it about some adjustments he wanted carried out.

Minna laid down her pen and sighed. This was proving so difficult, as she'd known it would be.

She was about to write to Tim to tell him about Elyse Davenport's death. The trouble was, how did she put it? She wasn't supposed to know he'd been having a relationship with her, for it had simply never been mentioned. Neither that nor the fact that Tim slept at Elyse's house most nights. After the first time he'd had the good sense, and courtesy, to rumple his bed every evening before going out, so that it appeared to have been slept in, when of course it hadn't.

Perhaps she shouldn't mention Elyse's death at all, as it was bound to upset him dreadfully and possibly interfere with his concentration when flying. There again, for all she knew Elyse might have promised to write and he'd be just as upset when she didn't.

No, Minna finally decided. She'd tell him, but only referring to Elyse as an ex-guest, someone they'd both liked.

She picked up her pen again.

There they were, Tim thought, exactly where Courtney had said they'd be, hoisted high over Longueval. If there was one job they all hated it was shooting down and destroying barrage balloons. The damned things had a nasty habit of blowing up in your face.

The German spotters manning the baskets underneath had clearly seen them, for first one, then the other, quickly baled out. As they were floating to the ground the crew there hastily began winching in the balloons.

'A' flight were to attack, 'B' flight to provide cover. Tim waved to Iveson, who immediately started gaining height, with the rest of his flight following him.

Tim glanced round to ensure that his flight was in position. As leader he'd go in first, and if he failed they would all take it in turn until someone succeeded.

Here we go, he thought, lining up the nearest balloon in his sights. Moments later his machine-guns were chattering.

'Damn!' he muttered as he pulled away. He'd hit it, but it hadn't gone up. Behind him Burleigh was already making his approach.

Tim glanced up to where Iveson's planes were circling – no sign of the enemy yet. But they'd be along. The German ground crew had no doubt already been on the telephone.

Now Burleigh was pulling away, he too having failed, and McLeod was making his approach, his guns already spitting fire.

'Christ!' Tim exclaimed when the explosion took place, turning his eyes away from the blast that caused his Camel to sway and bump violently.

When he looked back there was no sign of either McLeod or his plane. Nothing at all.

Grimly Tim turned in the direction of the second balloon.

He was in bed with Elyse, lying with his back to her, she with her arms wrapped around him. He smiled when she kissed him on the shoulder.

'You're not to worry, Tim,' she whispered. 'When you need me I'll be there. That's a promise.'

'Hmmh,' he murmured contentedly.

'You must remember that.'

'I will,' he replied, whispering as she was.

'Think of me as your guardian angel.'

For some reason that didn't sound silly at all. In fact, he took great comfort from it.

'Now sleep,' she crooned, and he felt himself languidly drifting off.

'Sleep, my darling.'

Chapter 30

Another mission over, Tim thought wearily. This one a solo behind enemy lines, to take photographs, which had passed off uneventfully. He noted as he made his way towards the farmhouse that 'B' flight was up, with the rest of 'A' flight awaiting new orders.

He glanced back at his Camel, where the camera was already being unloaded, and hoped the photographs would be all right. He guessed they were to do with the big new push that was rumoured to be in the offing.

'There's post for you, sir,' Sergeant Smallbone informed him as he went inside. 'I've put it on your cot.'

'Thank you, Sergeant.'

Smallbone handed him a large glass of Scotch as he'd now been instructed to do after every flight. Tim took the glass and drained it.

'Another, sir?'

Tim shook his head. 'A cup of coffee would be nice, though.'

'Coming right up, sir.'

Tim had a bit of friendly banter with several members of his flight before going to his room. When he picked up the letter he recognised the writing as his mother's.

* * *

'Your coffee, sir.'

Tim, staring out of the window, didn't reply.

'Will there be anything else, sir?'

This time Tim heard Smallbone and turned a grief-stricken face to the sergeant. 'No, that's fine.'

Smallbone hesitated. 'Are you all right, sir?'

Tim stared at the sergeant, then slowly shook his head. 'Not really. I've just learnt of the death of a good friend.'

'Oh, I am sorry, sir. Killed in action?'

'No, she died at home. A long-standing illness apparently, which I knew nothing about. She was a rather wonderful lady, whom I was extremely fond of.' His hand automatically went to the tunic pocket containing the linen envelope of dried forget-me-nots.

Smallbone could see how distraught Tim was. 'Would you like your luncheon served in here later?' he asked quietly.

'Yes, that's a good idea.'

'Just leave it to me, sir.'

Smallbone closed the door behind him, having already guessed that the lady in question was a very 'special' friend of Tim's. The poor bugger.

God knows what time in the morning it was, Tim thought in despair, and so far he hadn't slept a wink, continually tossing and turning, thinking about Elyse, reliving the past month which they'd more or less spent together.

He'd had no idea she was ill: she'd certainly never mentioned it, not even a hint. There had been that persistent cough of hers, which he'd put down to far too many cigarettes. But apart from that, nothing.

Minna hadn't specified what the illness had been, only that Elyse had passed quietly away in her sleep, to be found several days later by her cleaner, who'd immediately summoned the police.

'Oh, Elyse,' he whispered, still not having fully taken in that she was gone. She'd seemed so full of life, so vibrant. It was hard to imagine that even then she must have been dying.

He uttered a silent prayer in her memory, not only for having known her, but for those glorious weeks when they'd been lovers. Weeks that he would never forget.

He pictured her face – Elyse laughing, now flushed with passion. Her warm body joined to his, hearing the words she sometimes spoke on such occasions.

He recalled the bath they'd had together and what fun that had been: she soaping him, he her, delighting in the sight of her naked body, as he always did.

Laughter – there had been a great deal of that. Tenderness too, not just in their lovemaking, but in a thousand other different ways. Lovers, and friends. Yes, that was decidedly so. He was going to miss her terribly.

Not that it would have lasted of course, for the difference in their ages was too great for that. But the brief period they'd spent together had been as right and rewarding as any relationship could ever be.

'Oh, Elyse,' he whispered again. 'Sweet, sweet lady.'

He was still wide awake, reminiscing, grieving, when Smallbone called him for the dawn patrol.

Tim's mouth suddenly went dry as he spotted the unmistakable, gaudily painted planes. Richthofen and his Circus had finally shown up.

He glanced over at Iveson, who gestured that he too had seen them. Tim gestured back that they were to engage, Iveson giving him the thumbs-up that he understood.

Tim pulled back on his stick, having decided to gain height, and the rest of 'A' flight followed suit. Iveson and 'B' flight meanwhile continued at the same altitude, Iveson having elected to do so.

Tim levelled out again, both sides now rapidly closing. Of all the enemy planes the Red Baron's was by far the most distinctive.

It soon became a macabre dance of death, as ferocious a dogfight as Tim had ever experienced. He managed to get on the tail of a purple Fokker with zigzag black stripes on it, and opened fire, his machine-guns chattering furiously.

The German looped, trying to reverse positions, but Tim followed him and kept them as they were. Out of the corner of his eye he saw a Camel explode in mid-air, but didn't know whose it was.

The German banked and dived, with Tim in hot pursuit behind him. The pilot was good, Tim thought. This wasn't his first encounter by a long chalk.

The German's manoeuvres became almost demented as he tried every trick he could think of, but he couldn't shake Tim, who stuck doggedly to his tail.

Tim fired yet again and a black ribbon of smoke billowed from the German's plane, which slowly flipped belly up and began arcing earthwards. Tim guessed that the pilot was already dead.

Moments later bullets began ripping into his own machine, neatly stitching their way along the fuselage. He immediately took evasive action from the green Fokker that had fired them.

On and on it went, with planes from both sides occasionally blowing up or being knocked out. Now it was Tim's turn to fire at the green triplane which he'd shaken free of minutes before. The German swivelled in his cockpit to stare back at Tim as he closed and started firing.

Suddenly the German slumped, his head dropping forwards onto the controls, and his plane went into a spin from which it never recovered. Tim had the grim satisfaction of watching it plough into the ground.

Then he saw it happen. The Red Baron himself riddled Iveson's Camel, the entire upper wing breaking off and fluttering away like some huge butterfly.

Richthofen followed Iveson all the way down, making absolutely certain of his kill.

'After that it broke up,' Tim said to an appalled Courtney, when making his report. 'I found myself in cloud with my fuel running low, so I headed for home.'

'Seven men in all, including Iveson,' Courtney croaked. 'Dear God in heaven.'

'It was certainly a mauling. Though, to our credit, we did get three of them,' Tim reminded him. That was a sop at least.

Courtney closed his eyes. The first thing he'd have to do was ring General HQ and tell them what had happened, then the pool to ask for replacement pilots and machines. They might not be able to bring him back to full squadron strength on either score.

He opened his eyes again and sighed. 'I'd give anything, *anything*, to have my arm back,' he stated.

'You still wouldn't be allowed to fly, sir. You're officer in command and those are the standing orders.'

Suddenly Courtney smashed a clenched fist onto the table in front of him. 'Damn that Richthofen and his Circus. Damn every last one of them!'

'Amen,' Tim quietly agreed.

Tim left Courtney's office to find Smallbone hovering. 'What is it, Sergeant?'

'I'm sorry to hear about Mr Iveson, sir. He was a proper gentleman.'

Tim smiled wryly. 'He was that, Smallbone.'

'I just wanted to say, sir. You understand?'

'Of course, Sergeant. I feel exactly the same way.'

'A proper gentleman,' Smallbone repeated with a catch in his voice and hurried off.

There was no fear, only resignation, Tim thought. He'd tried everything he knew about aerial combat, but to no avail. Perhaps they were right when they said Richthofen could read an intended victim's mind, for he certainly seemed to be reading Tim's.

The two squadrons had clashed over Thiepval and immediately the Red Baron had chosen to engage Tim. Short of trying to ram Richthofen, which the German would almost certainly manage to avoid, the end was now a foregone conclusion. Richthofen had outflown and out-thought him, and now Tim was a dead man.

Suddenly the strangest of feelings took hold of Tim, a sort of etherealness that lifted his spirits. And then he smelt it – the unmistakable aroma of Elyse's perfume.

'Guardian angel,' her voice whispered in his mind. 'Remember that.'

Tim could hear the clattering of Richthofen's guns above the roar of his engine. Abruptly they fell silent.

He twisted round in his cockpit to stare back at the German, who was busy wrestling with his guns. They've jammed, Tim thought jubilantly. The bloody things have jammed!

He banked, and moments later was able to lose himself in cloud that he could have sworn had somehow appeared from nowhere.

He was safe – he wasn't going to be killed after all. The relief almost made him wet himself.

The smell of her perfume had gone now, as had the strange feeling that had taken hold of him. All was back to normal.

He hadn't imagined it, he told himself. There was no doubt about it, he actually had smelt her perfume.

As he headed for home, Tim was in a daze.

'Come in and sit down, I could use some company,' Courtney smiled, laying aside the book on Plato he'd been reading. 'Care for a drink?'

'Thank you, sir.'

Courtney poured Tim some Scotch and topped up his own glass. That done, he settled himself again in a comfy chair by the fire.

'Nothing like a good fire on a cold night like this,' he commented affably.

'No, sir. There isn't.'

'So, Wilson, what can I do for you?'

Tim took a deep breath. 'Something happened today, sir, and I just have to talk to someone about it.'

Courtney nodded that he was listening.

'This has to be off the record, sir. If General HQ got to hear of it, they'd probably lock me away.'

Courtney frowned. 'Sounds interesting, go on. You have my word that what you tell me won't go any further.'

'Thank you, sir. Do you . . . eh . . .' Tim cleared his throat. 'I'm being serious now. Do you believe in ghosts?'

Courtney glanced away for the space of a few seconds, then brought his attention back to Tim. 'As a matter of fact I do.'

Tim had a sip of his whisky. 'Any particular reason for that, sir?'

'Yes, there is. But before I say what it is you must explain why you asked.'

Tim took another deep breath, then began recounting what had occurred that afternoon. The one thing he omitted was that he and Elyse had been lovers, instead describing their relationship as that of particularly good and close friends.

'Hmmh,' Courtney murmured when Tim had finished.

'I didn't imagine that smell, sir. I swear I didn't.'

'I'm quite prepared to accept that you didn't,' Courtney answered. 'How does that saying go? "There are more things in heaven and earth . . ."' He broke off. 'I can't remember the rest. People have believed in life after death and in guardian angels for a long, long time now, so why shouldn't both be true? I, for one, acknowledge that they might be.'

'I just had to talk to someone, sir – confide in them. Part of me, despite knowing that it happened, was thinking that I might be going round the bend.'

'I doubt that very much, Wilson. Though many good men have in this damned war.'

'Thank you, sir.' Tim nodded in relief. 'I find that very reassuring.'

Courtney smiled slowly. 'As for why I believe in ghosts, the answer's quite simple. We have one in the cottage I own. Haven't seen her myself, mind you, though I've heard her often enough. The only one who's actually seen her is my son, Rupert, when he was around three or four. Kept on mentioning the lady in a funny hat. We had no idea who he was talking about until it dawned on us that he was referring to the ghost.'

'And you've heard her, sir?'

'Quite distinctly on a number of occasions. I've been downstairs, knowing I was the only person in the cottage, and heard her moving about upstairs. Was a bit frightening to begin with, I admit, but we soon got used to her. A friendly spirit, I'm pleased to say, never causes any harm. She's just there from time to time.'

Both men fell silent and stared into the fire. 'Count yourself lucky, Wilson,' Courtney said after a while. 'I know I would in your position.' He held up his glass. 'A toast to your friend, eh?'

Tim also raised his glass. 'To Elyse!' Guardian angel, he added to himself.

April 22nd 1918 was a typical spring day, one that had dawned bright and sunny even if there was still a slight nip in the air. Tim was engrossed in a week-old copy of *The Times* when Courtney emerged from his office.

'Gentlemen, can you please gather round,' he requested.

More orders, Tim thought, rousing himself from his chair. He couldn't have been more wrong.

Courtney waited till he had everyone's attention, every eye focused on him. 'I have some news,' he announced, then paused dramatically. 'I've just heard from General HQ that yesterday Richthofen, the Red Baron, was shot down and killed.'

That was greeted by a stunned silence. 'Thank Christ,' someone finally muttered.

A rousing cheer suddenly erupted, several fists punching the air while others hugged one another. This was stupendous news. The German pilot they feared above all others was finally dead.

'Who got him?' Tim asked when the hubbub had quietened a little.

'A Canadian soldier apparently,' Courtney smiled. 'Richthofen's plane was flying low and the Canadian took a pot shot at him. Although badly wounded, Richthofen managed to bring his machine down and then died at the controls before our chaps reached him. A perfect landing too, I'm informed.'

Tim laughed. A soldier on the ground taking a pot shot! It was unbelievable.

Courtney held up a hand. 'I have one more thing to say, gentlemen.'

Everyone stopped talking to listen.

'The drinks are on me!'

For the second time a rousing cheer rang around the room.

Tim cursed impotently as he fought to keep his Camel – what was left of it anyway – aloft. 'A' flight had tangled with a superior number of Pfalzes, during which Tim's plane had been badly shot up. On top of that, while limping home he'd been further hit by 'Archie'. The stuttering engine told him it could conk out at any time.

He was going to have to land, he thought. And that meant capture, as he was still a fair way behind enemy lines. Breaking out of cloud, he glanced down at the ground to see exactly what was what.

His blood ran cold at the sight of yellow wraiths of mustard gas swirling everywhere, and German soldiers already dead or in the terrible throes of dying.

The engine was missing badly now. Surely it would be only seconds before it stopped altogether. If that happened he hadn't a chance of leaving the gas behind, but would land right in the midst of it.

'Come on, come on,' he urged. There was nothing left for him to do – everything that could be done from the cockpit had been. He stared down in horror as the Camel continued to lose height quickly.

He was now at about 100 feet and still dropping. Within moments his wheels would be skimming the top of the gas. 'Elyse,' he whispered. 'Where are you?'

'I'm here, Tim,' came the reply in his head. 'I'm here.'

As those words were spoken two things occurred at once. The strange, ethereal feeling took hold of him again, as if he was part of this world and yet not, and his engine stopped misfiring.

He pulled on the stick and miraculously – and it was a miracle – the Camel began to regain altitude. When he reached 3,000 feet he levelled out.

And then both the feeling and Elyse were gone. He was

himself again, with the engine running as smoothly as he could have wished and continuing to do so until the farmhouse and landing field came into sight, when it began misfiring once more. He was actually bumping along the ground when it conked out altogether.

Coming to a halt, Tim slumped over the controls, thanking Elyse over and over in his mind, although she was no longer there to hear him.

A number of mechanics had already surrounded his machine by the time he climbed out, all of them looking at the Camel in amazement. One opened up the engine and peered inside.

'Are you hurt, sir?' a mechanic called Harrington asked.

Tim shook his head.

'Then you're lucky, sir. Very lucky indeed.'

'The engine's totally buggered, smashed to bits by bullets and "Archie",' declared the mechanic who'd looked at it. 'How far did you fly it in this condition, sir?'

Tim gave him a rough estimate.

'That's impossible, sir!' the man exclaimed. Then, hastily apologising on remembering that he was addressing an officer, 'Beg pardon, sir. At least in my book it is. I don't see how you could possibly have kept going.'

'Everything's shot away,' another mechanic declared. 'The entire fuselage is ripped to shreds and the rudder's gone. This machine should have fallen right out of the sky.'

Tim managed a rueful grin. 'It very nearly did. And would have done, if I hadn't had a little help.'

'Help, sir?' the man queried, his expression puzzled.

'Oh yes,' Tim replied softly. 'I do believe somebody up there was watching over me.'

And with that he left the gawping mechanics and walked away on legs that were none too steady.

Tim and the rest of the squadron, including Major Courtney, sat watching the clock, each counting the seconds as they ticked by. When the clock struck 11 a.m. a collective sigh went up. Off in the distance the guns that had been booming fell silent. At 11 a.m., on the eleventh day of the eleventh month, after four and a quarter years of the bloodiest carnage that the world had ever known, peace had again come to the battlefields of Europe. Germany had at long last admitted defeat and signed an armistice.

It was over, Tim thought dully. And, against all the odds, he'd survived.

There was no cheering in the room like that which had greeted the news of Richthofen's death, no punching the air, just a group of men trying to take on board that the war was over.

Tim quietly excused himself and went outside, wanting to be alone while he savoured the moment. Savoured it, and offered up thanks that he'd come through it all unscathed.

He closed his eyes, remembering all the men, friends and colleagues, who hadn't. Harry Nutbeam, Paul Greville with whom he'd trained, Major Brown and Iveson, his instructor. Those and a host of others, all cut off in their prime. And what for? He was damned if he really knew.

'What a waste,' he said aloud. 'What a stupid bloody waste.'

Overhead a bird began to sing.

Tim had been expecting to find Paddington Station bustling

and was surprised that it wasn't. On a sudden whim he decided to travel first-class. It was a long journey, after all, and he wanted to be comfortable during it. He owed himself that at least.

Walking up the length of the train, he selected an empty carriage and went inside. A quick heave and the small case he'd brought with him was secured on the overhead rack. He settled himself into a corner and waited for the train's departure, which was due to take place in about five minutes.

It was almost time to go when the door was thrown open and a porter appeared carrying a case. That too went on the overhead rack and the porter disappeared outside again, where a short conversation ensued between him and a woman.

It seemed he was to have company, Tim thought, which was only to be expected. He glanced idly as a single woman entered the carriage, the position of her body temporarily obscuring her face. He turned to look out of the window, not wishing to appear either curious or rude. He was aware of her sitting on the same side as him.

With a jolt and a judder the train began moving, the driver tooting his whistle as they left the station and started the long journey to Devon. Tim flicked open one of several newspapers he'd bought and started reading as the train chugged merrily along.

The woman was fiddling with her handbag, muttering to herself, when she accidentally dropped a handkerchief on the floor.

Noticing this out of the corner of his eye, Tim was immediately on his feet. 'Allow me,' he offered gallantly and picked up the handkerchief. He got the shock of his life, when handing it back, to discover himself looking at Katherine Coates.

'Tim?'

He nodded.

'I . . .' She hesitated. 'You've changed.'

'The war does that to you, I'm afraid,' he replied ruefully.

They both gazed at one another in astonishment.

'This is a turn-up for the books,' he said eventually.

'Yes. Quite a coincidence.'

She too had changed, he thought. She was more mature, a woman as opposed to the girl he remembered. He sat back down again. 'I ran into your friend Louise Youthed in France, who told me that you'd lost your husband at Mons. I'm terribly sorry.'

Her eyes took on a distant look. 'That seems so long ago now. A lifetime ago.' She brought her attention back to Tim. 'I see from your uniform you were in the RAF.' The Royal Flying Corps and the Royal Naval Air Service had merged the previous May to form what was now known as the Royal Air Force.

He nodded. 'That's right.'

'I was a VAD.'

'I know, Louise told me.'

'And now?'

'Home to Torquay, which I have absolutely no intention of ever leaving again.'

She laughed lightly. 'My sentiments exactly. I shall be taking over Oaklands, as Papa lives in London now.' She'd stayed for several days with Jeremiah and Henrietta, during which time they'd had a number of very frank discussions.

She now understood their situation and, if not entirely approving, didn't disapprove either. Her father was happy and it seemed to her that was what mattered most.

'With your mother?'

Katherine briefly told him about Ruth.

'That's dreadful,' Tim commiserated.

Katherine didn't reply to that. 'I owe you an apology,' she said instead.

'For what?'

'I should have got in touch with you before I married, explained everything.'

Tim shrugged. 'You met someone else and fell in love. What's there to explain?'

Her smile was a cynical one. 'It wasn't quite as simple as that.'

'No?'

'No,' she stated firmly. 'I must have hurt you dreadfully. I'm so sorry.'

He glanced away. 'So was I,' he replied softly.

It was as if her heart turned over, and all the old feelings she'd had for Tim came flooding back. 'I was under a lot of pressure at the time, Tim.'

Now he didn't reply.

'And very impressionable. I also thought I was doing the right thing, believing my mother to be dying and wanting to please her.'

'Dying?' Tim frowned.

'Only one of many lies, as I've since discovered. I wouldn't tell that to anyone else, Tim, but I want to at least try and make amends.'

He listened carefully as she continued to speak.

* * *

Tim turned to Katherine as the motor taxicab drew up outside The Berkeley, Katherine having offered to drop him off *en route* to Oaklands. 'Trust Ma,' he smiled.

The front of The Berkeley was festooned with bunting and there were flags in several of the windows. A large hand-painted banner had been slung above the front door proclaiming: WELCOME HOME, TIM.

'I can just imagine what's going to happen when I get inside,' he said.

'And she doesn't know when you're arriving?'

'No. I wrote before leaving France saying that I was on my way and to expect me when I got here. I couldn't be more explicit than that.'

'I've no doubt the fatted calf awaits,' Katherine smiled.

'And buckets of tears.'

Katherine stopped smiling and placed a hand over Tim's. 'I'd like to see you again. Soon.'

It was her emphasis on the last word that told him how serious she was. 'You will. Give me a couple of days to try and settle in and then I'll be in touch.'

She nodded. 'I'll be waiting to hear.'

It was unspoken between them, but they both knew this was a fresh beginning. A new start.

Tim kissed her tenderly on the lips before getting out of the taxicab and waving it on its way.

Then he went indoors to the emotional homecoming he knew awaited him.

Minna had told him the precise location of the grave, so he had no trouble in finding it. He stood for a while in silence, then bent and placed the bouquet of flowers he'd bought on the rich, brown earth.

'Thank you, Elyse,' he whispered. 'God bless and keep you.'

He touched the pocket containing the linen envelope with the dried forget-me-nots, tears welling into his eyes. For the briefest of moments he could smell her perfume and then it was gone. He knew he'd never smell that scent again, that this time she'd left for ever.

He took a deep breath and turned away. He was meeting Katherine for lunch and afterwards intended paying Ricketts a visit to ask for his job back.

As he headed out of the cemetery his mind was filled with thoughts of Katherine and the life they'd have together.

Postscript

There were a number of claims concerning who fired the shot that killed Baron von Richthofen – a mystery that has never been solved. I have recounted a version that could well have been the one given to Tim's squadron the day after the Red Baron's death.

Other bestselling titles available by mail:

The prices shown above are correct at time of going to press. However, the publishers reserve the right to increase prices on covers from those previously advertised without prior notice.

——————————— sphere ———————————

SPHERE
PO Box 121, Kettering, Northants NN14 4ZQ
Tel: 01832 737525, Fax: 01832 733076
Email: aspenhouse@FSBDial.co.uk

POST AND PACKING:
Payments can be made as follows: cheque, postal order (payable to Sphere), credit card or Maestro. Do not send cash or currency.

All UK Orders	**FREE OF CHARGE**
EU & Overseas	25% of order value

Name (BLOCK LETTERS) . . . .

Address . . . .

. . . .

Post/zip code: . . . .

☐ Please keep me in touch with future Sphere publications

☐ I enclose my remittance £ . . . .

☐ I wish to pay by Visa/Mastercard/Eurocard/Maestro

Card Expiry Date ☐☐☐☐   Maestro Issue No. ☐☐